Praise for
A Most Agreeable Murder

Named a Most Anticipated Book by:

Entertainment Weekly · Book Riot · CrimeReads · Publishers Weekly · Blogorama · Modern Mrs. Darcy

A June 2023 *Library Reads* pick!

A *Publishers Weekly* "Book of the Week" pick!

"Despite its title, [*A Most Agreeable Murder*] is as much a parody of Regency conventions as it is a jaunty sendup of the locked-room mystery. Julia Seales is an American screenwriter, but she's clearly a devout Anglophile. It's with a loving hand and a gimlet eye that she guides us through one fateful evening among the ever-so-proper elite of the aptly named township of Swampshire."

—*The New York Times Book Review*

"A delightful cocktail that mixes elements of the Bridgerton series, Jane Austen's *Pride & Prejudice* and Agatha Christie's Miss Marple mysteries . . . the payoff is a wealth of wit, hilarity and suspense."

—*People* (Book of the Week)

"Wish *Bridgerton* had a bit more Agatha Christie flair? That's what Julia Seales offers up with her debut, which finds the only slightly respectable Beatrice Steele at a ball surrounded by potential murder suspects. Beatrice has long been obsessed with true crime (a nod to our own modern true crime podcast phenomena), but when an eligible bachelor drops dead in the middle of a ball, Beatrice must cast aside her lady-like duties to indulge her inner sleuth."

—*Entertainment Weekly*

"An utterly delightful murder mystery, *A Most Agreeable Murder* reads as if a giggly Jane Austen dipped her pen in blood. (Not too much blood, mind you; it's all quite decorous.) I loved every page of this very silly romp."

—*The Seattle Times*

"*A Most Agreeable Murder* begins as social satire and ascends into deadly knockabout farce. . . . There are dotty eccentrics, secret passageways, false identities, a rumored ghost, three acts' worth of delicious banter—and an irrepressible heroine born from the ashes of her own trial by fire."

—*The Wall Street Journal*

"Without exaggerating, it's one of the funniest cozy mysteries I've ever read."

—*Book Riot*

"The book is an entertaining and witty tale that combines elements of Jane Austen's world with the intrigue of an Agatha Christie mystery. Readers can expect a delightful blend of comedy, suspense, and the pursuit of justice. [Seales] leads readers on a thrilling adventure filled with twists and turns that will keep them guessing until the very end."

—*Blogarama*

"This hilarious debut cozy mystery-comedy set in the English countryside has it all: games of whist, dashing gentlemen, a disgusting swamp, needlepoint, bioluminescent frogs, footnotes, a guest list of quirky characters, and scones. Imagine *What We Do in the Shadows* meets Jane Austen, with a dash of *The Addams Family*. Full of laugh-out-loud moments and fun twisty turns, I didn't want to put it down."

—BRIGID MISSELHORN,
Modern Mrs. Darcy 2023 Summer Reading Guide

"[An] exceptional debut . . . The intricate plot races along at a sprightly pace, and Seales delights with her sharp humor and accomplished sense of narrative control. Jane Austen fans will be enthralled."

—*Publishers Weekly* (starred review)

"In Seales' tongue-in-cheek Regency murder mystery . . . the character types are endearingly familiar to anyone who has ever read a Jane Austen novel, and the dialogue crackles with wit, outrage, subtext, and pluck. Beatrice, a true Sherlock Holmes within her restrictive social world, is a delight, and while the characters may be familiar, Seales' over-the-top caricatures succeed in being humorous rather than cliché. . . . The result is a deliciously dark delve into a world that seems genteel on the surface and teems with sex and violence and greed just underneath— not so unlike Austen's but with a morbid, rather than domestic, bent. Irreverent, satirical, and oh so much fun!"

—*Kirkus Reviews* (starred review)

"Seales's outstanding debut marries Jane Austen pastiche and locked-room mystery for a sharp, wildly entertaining whodunit."

—*Publishers Weekly*

"Absurdly entertaining, with twist upon twist upon twist, *A Most Agreeable Murder* is a most agreeable read! Jane Austen fans will appreciate the insightful observations as well as the wry humor that pokes fun at certain well-known characters and tropes. I look forward to more of Beatrice Steele's adventures—as well as that of the mysterious (and delightfully dashing and grumpy) Inspector Drake!"

—MIA P. MANANSALA, author of *Arsenic and Adobo*

"I adored this: a comedy of manners meets murder mystery, just as thrilling as it is gorgeous."

—SOPHIE IRWIN,
author of *A Lady's Guide to Fortune Hunting*

"*A Most Agreeable Murder* is an utter delight. A fast-paced mix of marriage plot and manor house murder mystery with something for everyone: a scintillating romance, an intricate puzzle to solve, and layers of snarky, pointed wit that would make Austen proud. I snorted and swooned my way through this book in record speed—it's some of the most fun I've had reading all year. Cozy mystery fans, this is a must."

—ASHLEY WINSTEAD, author of *The Last Housewife*

"*A Most Agreeable Murder* is a delightfully entertaining debut that kept me engrossed from the beginning right through to the satisfying end. Witty and clever, it's like something Agatha Christie and Jane Austen might have created were they able to collaborate, only with its own wonderfully unique spark. Be prepared to laugh out loud at the comedy, gasp at the murder mystery, and altogether have a thoroughly great time!"

—INDIA HOLTON,
author of *The Wisteria Society of Lady Scoundrels*

"If you grew up reading Jane Austen and Agatha Christie (or are a more recent fan of *Bridgerton* and *Knives Out*), you will adore *A Most Agreeable Murder*. An effortless blend of witty delight and sexy suspense, this book is everything I want in a summer read."

—KATE STAYMAN-LONDON,
nationally bestselling author of *One to Watch*

A MOST AGREEABLE MURDER

A NOVEL

JULIA SEALES

A Most
AGREEABLE
MURDER

RANDOM HOUSE NEW YORK

2024 Random House Trade Paperback Edition

Published in the United States by Random House, an imprint and division of Penguin Random House LLC, New York.

RANDOM HOUSE and the HOUSE colophon are registered trademarks of Penguin Random House LLC.

Originally published in hardcover in the United States by Random House, an imprint and division of Penguin Random House LLC, in 2023.

This book contains an excerpt from the forthcoming book *A Terribly Nasty Business* by Julia Seales. This excerpt has been set for this edition only and may not reflect the final content of the forthcoming edition.

LIBRARY OF CONGRESS CATALOGING-IN-PUBLICATION DATA
Names: Seales, Julia, author.
Title: A most agreeable murder: a novel / Julia Seales.
Description: First edition. | New York: Random House, [2023]
Identifiers: LCCN 2022037648 (print) | LCCN 2022037649 (ebook) |
ISBN 9780593450000 (trade paperback) | ISBN 9780593449998 (ebook)
Subjects: LCGFT: Detective and mystery fiction. | Novels.
Classification: LCC PS3619.E25514 M67 2023 (print) |
LCC PS3619.E25514 (ebook) | DDC 813/.6—dc23/eng/20220816
LC record available at https://lccn.loc.gov/2022037648
LC ebook record available at https://lccn.loc.gov/2022037649

Printed in the United States of America on acid-free paper

randomhousebooks.com

2 4 6 8 9 7 5 3 1

Book design by Diane Hobbing

To my mom, Pam
Thank you for raising this morbid creep.
You're the best.

A MOST AGREEABLE MURDER

Miss Arabella Ashbrook presents

THE ANNUAL AUTUMNAL BALL

Mr. and Mrs. Stephen Steele and their daughters,
Beatrice, Louisa, and Mary, are requested
to attend the ball at Stabmort Park
on Tuesday next at six P.M.
And not a second before!
We await your confirmation of attendance,
and any song requests.

GUEST LIST

Mr. Hugh Ashbrook, 66, patriarch of Stabmort Park
Mr. Daniel Ashbrook, 32, son, heir to Stabmort Park
Miss Arabella Ashbrook, 22, daughter

Mr. Stephen Steele, 50, patriarch of Marsh House
Mrs. Susan Steele, 48, his wife
Miss Beatrice Steele, 25, eldest daughter
Miss Louisa Steele, 21, middle daughter
Miss Mary Steele, 18, youngest daughter

Mr. Martin Grub, age unknown, cousin to Mr. Stephen Steele
and heir to Marsh House

Captain Philip Peña, 33, naval captain

Mr. Frank Fàn, 26, gentleman

Miss Helen Bolton, 53, matriarch of Fauna Manor

Miss Caroline Wynn, 24, orphan and socialite

Mr. Edmund Croaksworth, 32, wealthy gentleman

Guest of Mr. Croaksworth, 29, information on situation
unknown

CHAPTER 1

Introductions

In the English countryside there was a small township called Swampshire, comprised of several lovely mansions and one disgusting swamp. This was the home—one of the mansions, not the swamp—of Beatrice Steele. The swamp was inhabited by an overpopulation of luminescent frogs. The visual effect at night was arresting, though the incessant croaking deterred some who might have otherwise chosen to settle the charming village.

Beatrice Steele was plump, with a cheerful gap in her front teeth and a white streak in her black curls, gained during a particularly competitive round of whist. She had a passionate disposition and a lively wit, which endeared her to friends and family—most of the time. For Beatrice was curious by nature, and therefore noticed too much, felt too much, and wondered too much about life outside her village. Others considered this behavior an unnecessary to-do, as Beatrice would surely settle down with one of the young men of Swampshire in a mansion that hadn't been overtaken by frogs, start a family, and live happily from then on.

This was the expected path of a lady, for there were strict rules of decorum in Swampshire. Years ago, the town's founding father, Baron Fitzwilliam Ashbrook, had fled the raucous city of London for the countryside in search of a place he could shape on principles of perfect etiquette. In a matter of mere months, he penned a pamphlet professing these principles: *The Guide to Swampshire*. Believing that women were particularly prone to temptation, he wrote the accompanying books *The Lady's Guide to Swampshire, Volumes I and II*. He also wrote *The Lady's Guide to Swampshire (Travel Edition)*, lest a woman find herself in an indecorous situation while on the go. These books became the foundation of the Swampshire social scene.

Failure to adhere to these rules could tarnish a woman's reputation beyond repair. According to *The Lady's Guide*, a disgraced woman was forbidden to call upon friends, entertain suitors, or even remain close to her family, lest she corrupt them by association. No self-respecting lady would speak to her, and no gentleman of honor would make her an offer of marriage. She could not even patronize local dress shops or ribbon stores.

Friendless, single, and dressed in last season's garb, a fallen woman would therefore be forced to leave the village. Only a morally corrupt city would accept her, and once she made it to Paris, she would surely be robbed by a mime and left for dead. But she might not even get that far. Bedtime stories in Swampshire told of women who, while attempting to flee, were swallowed up by one of the region's infamous "squelch holes," never to be seen again. Therefore, women were reassured that commitment to etiquette was for their own good. Rule-breakers could not be permitted to corrupt this safe, orderly, idyllic world.

But despite growing up with these values, despite these rules having been ingrained in her mind since childhood, Beatrice

Steele harbored a dark secret: She was obsessed with murder. Not the act of *committing* it, but the act of *solving* it. She loved nothing more than to consider the intricacies of a suspect's motivations, determine the killer, and then watch this killer be brought to justice.

Her particular fascination with crime began with a plan to peruse her father's imported London paper. She intended to read the social column, "Who Is More Respectable Than Who," but could not get past the grammatically incorrect title and instead turned her attention to a different article: "Gentleman Detective Sir Huxley (and Assistant) Takes the Case." It did not befit a young lady to look at such things, but before she could stop herself, she had devoured it.

The article detailed the circumstances of the grisly murder of a man named Viscount Dudley DeBurbie. It told of his young beloved, Verity Swan; his immense collection of jewels, which had gone missing; his suspicious butler; and the dashing detective who accepted the case—Sir Huxley. Huxley's motto was *Super omnia decorum:* "Decorum above all." He believed that solving cases would reinstate the social order, which was the most respectable thing one could do. Nothing was more important than propriety.

Beatrice was transfixed. She had never considered that a genteel person might solve crimes as a hobby. She herself found no satisfaction in the approved hobbies for young women outlined in *The Lady's Guide to Swampshire*. She was terrible at needlework, had no musical ability, and was banned from drawing because her artwork was so bad that it frightened people. Conversely, she found the hunt for murderers captivating. It granted her a sense of fulfillment, a sense that she was making the world a better place by (vicariously) pursuing justice.

And perhaps deep down she reasoned that if she knew what evil lurked in the world, she might be prepared to face it.

Before long Beatrice was obsessively collecting papers, desperate for news on the hunt for the killer. Her family thought it strange that Beatrice, once so social, began to forgo their evening card game to lock herself upstairs. Beatrice, enthused by her newfound passion, dropped hints that she was in love. She knew this was the only way to pacify her mother and guarantee hours left alone for her to "swoon and fantasize"—or whatever it was women did in these situations. Her mother happily accepted this excuse.

In a way, Beatrice *was* in love. She was gripped by the potential motive for the murder, the clues indicating that the killer may have known the victim, the way every detail surrounding the case had potential significance. It also didn't hurt that Sir Huxley was devastatingly handsome. In his newspaper etching he was strong-jawed, with an asp-topped cane and a pristine top hat. His assistant was a man named Inspector Vivek Drake, a man with a scarred face and eye patch. Drake's newspaper etching was far less flattering; he was always pictured with a scowl. Therefore, Beatrice was not surprised when the unseemly Drake pointed the finger at the young lady, Verity Swan. Sir Huxley admirably defended her honor and innocence, ever the true gentleman.

Ultimately in the DeBurbie case, the butler was charged and Huxley hailed a hero. He fired his scowling assistant, Drake, and opened a luxurious office near the West End. Thereafter, the crime column transitioned into an account of Huxley's day-to-day as a private investigator. Beatrice followed it with relish, imagining herself next to Huxley, peeking into alleys or discussing theories in his mahogany study. She underlined intriguing details with flowing lines and doodled "Huxley and Steele" in each article's margins. She even attempted to stitch a cameo of the gentleman. Her lack of skill at needlework ensured her interest would remain undetected, as everyone thought she had embroidered a potato.

Unfortunately in Swampshire all of this made her—one shudders to even say—a morbid creep. There are many types of creeps, of course: the peeping Toms, the lurkers, those who dare to show up at a party twelve minutes earlier than an invitation states—but in Swampshire, creeps of the morbid variety were considered the most unsavory. If anyone found out about Beatrice's secret obsession, she would be publicly disgraced and shunned. Politely, but completely.

Therefore she knew her hobby could not last. A gentleman might have been able to live in both worlds, but not a lady. Certainly not a lady in *Swampshire*. Eventually, Beatrice would have to grow up and become a respectable woman for the sake of herself and her family. This would likely occur next week, she always assured herself. Or, possibly, the week after.

But today, she found herself in the turret of Marsh House, the Steeles' cramped but charming home, trying to fit in an examination of one more article before the evening's ball. She was so absorbed that she barely noticed the muffled sounds of her father tying a bucket of water above a door frame somewhere downstairs.

Mr. Stephen Steele was lanky and bald, with a curled mustache and a penchant for pranks. His collection of fake blood capsules, array of rubber knives, and tendency to hide in dark corners and jump out at his daughters had likely contributed to Beatrice's spirited disposition. She always brought a sharp wit to the table, and he always brought a pooting pillow. (The pooting pillow was Mr. Steele's invention and his most prized possession. It was an inflatable rubber cushion that, when placed on an unsuspecting victim's seat, would create the loud sound of broken wind.) Nothing thrilled Mr. Steele more than pretending to die into his soup. His commitment to this bit would have been applauded if the joke did not instill such fear in his wife and daughters. The Steele women were not permitted to inherit their estate, as its deed dictated that it could be granted only to a man. The Steeles had no fortune to fall back on; the house was their only asset. Therefore, should Mr. Steele ever fall into his soup and *not* pop up cackling, the mansion would pass to their closest male relative, cousin Martin Grub. If one of the girls could simply marry Mr. Grub, everything would be fine, but he was completely disgusting, so this was unlikely.

Which is why Beatrice's mother had to be the practical one in the marriage. Mrs. Susan Steele was a formidable (albeit short) woman. What she lacked in height she made up for in loudness of voice, confidence of demeanor, and a seven-inch updo. It was from Mrs. Steele that Beatrice inherited her keen understanding of human nature, though Mrs. Steele used this to gain friends and exert influence instead of to analyze criminals. Organized and outgoing, Mrs. Steele knew how to put a plot into action. Her daughters' future marriages were Mrs. Steele's main scheme. If she spoke of anything apart from wedding bells, her family had yet to hear it.

"Beatrice!" As if on cue, Mrs. Steele interrupted Beatrice's concentration with a screech from the base of the turret's staircase. "You should not be hiding out up there! You must use any extra hours in the day to take a turn about the garden in case any gentlemen are watching! A lady is *always* one step ahead."

Beatrice glanced outside. Shadowy swampland surrounded Marsh House, and the deep green of the land blurred with the darkening sky. *A storm is coming,* she thought with a delicious chill. It was hardly time for a walk. But as the eldest daughter who couldn't seem to get her nose out of a book and a ring on her finger, she was used to her mother's persistent pestering.

"What could you possibly be doing that's more important than finding a husband?" Mrs. Steele pressed.

The victims' entrails were ripped from their corpses and arranged in a heart.

"Thinking about my beloved," Beatrice said cheerfully, and stuffed a moth-eaten shawl under the door to stifle the sound of her mother's continued protests.

It was risky to read during the day, Beatrice knew; she used to wait until everyone was asleep to analyze the papers. But lately she had become more and more engrossed in seeking clues, scribbling down notes, and developing theories. How could one be content with an afternoon spent playing the pianoforte when a killer was on the loose?

She turned to the paper once more, taking in the words on the page.

LONDON MENACE STILL AT LARGE

Sir Huxley vows to apprehend the so-called London Menace, even as the killer's body count rises. On Friday, just steps from Huxley's London office, three bodies were found slashed at the neck, a bloody knife left nearby. There was a message left on Huxley's window, written in blood: "Ha-ha-ha. You cannot catch me."

Beatrice set down the newspaper, deep in thought. "A message specific to Huxley . . . this suggests that the killer knows him," she murmured. "Usage of the word 'cannot' as opposed to 'could not' suggests the killer will murder again. Adding a dash between the 'ha's tells me that the killer is not educated on proper punctuation." She examined the sketch, trying to get a proper look at the wounds on the drawing of the bodies. "The question is: Why do the wounds not match the blade of the knife?" Mulling this over, she took a piece of letter-writing paper from the windowsill next to her ink pot, picked up her quill, and began to scribble.

Dear Sir Huxley,
   Greetings again from your most devoted reader.

Beatrice knew that an unmarried lady writing to an unmarried gentleman was wildly lewd, but she allowed herself to maintain the correspondence for two reasons: One, Sir Huxley did not *know* she was a lady, as she signed the letters with only her initials, "BS." Two, it could not technically be considered a full correspondence, as he had never replied.

She was just finishing her letter when she was interrupted again, this time by an ear-shattering scream. Startled, Beatrice looked out the turret window for the source of the noise.

In the distance she could just make out her sister Louisa, sprinting across the swampy field. With relief Beatrice realized that Louisa was screaming in excitement, not fear; her run was joyful. Louisa's hair looked like a streak of fire as she moved, dress rippling and arms pumping powerfully. She expertly launched herself over a cluster of glowing frogs, landed softly on a tuft of moss, performed a somersault, and continued running without missing a beat.

Stunningly beautiful and sweet, the Steeles' middle daughter, Louisa, was the golden child who was sure to save them all with an advantageous marriage. Though Beatrice's mother wanted *all* her daughters to marry well, the entire family agreed that Louisa was the most attractive, the most accomplished, and therefore the most likely to make a moneyed match. She had thick red curls, a pleasing smatter of freckles across her delicate nose, and well-defined muscles thanks to a passion for sport. She liked to jump headfirst into life, literally: Louisa was active and graceful, good at everything from dancing to skeet shooting. Though fiercely competitive, Louisa had a talent for making all feel welcome. She could convince even the stuffiest old man to join a game of ninepins, and then would happily trounce him. She was the complete package, and the Steeles were proud (and protective) of their family gem.

Though Beatrice had spent her youth being bested by Louisa in everything from cricket to curtsying, she was never jealous. She tried to teach Louisa everything she knew and to guide her life in the right direction, and was truly proud of how accomplished her sister had become.

As she watched Louisa cross the moor alone, Beatrice felt a pang of guilt. Normally, the sisters walked to town together on the morning before a ball. They would purchase new ribbons, gossip, and imagine which gentlemen might ask for a spot on their dance cards that evening. But Beatrice had forgone that morning's stroll in order to spend more time with her current case.

The front door banged as Louisa rushed inside.

"News from town!" Louisa cried. "Everyone come to the parlor at once!"

Beatrice felt certain that the news could not be *so* earth-shattering. Nothing exciting ever happened in Swampshire. Still, she accepted the summons and began to hide the evidence of her unseemly hobby. She pried open the turret's window seat, inside of which was a thick stack of yellowing papers, letters, and notes. She placed the latest paper on the top of the stack and then pushed the seat closed. She replaced a small pillow atop the window seat— a gift from her dear friend Daniel Ashbrook, embroidered with a quote he said had reminded him of Beatrice: *A lady's nook is incomplete without a book.*

With another pang of guilt, Beatrice averted her eyes from the quote as she scrawled her initials at the bottom of the letter to Huxley. Other than Louisa, Daniel was Beatrice's closest friend, but he knew nothing of her secret hobby. True, he encouraged Beatrice to borrow any books she wanted from his personal library, though he believed that she was perusing classics and not crime, due to some stealthy book cover swapping. Still, he *was* the one person in Swampshire who shared her sense of curiosity about the world. Since childhood, they had eagerly passed books back and forth and exchanged fascinating revelations about their findings. Mrs. Steele naturally assumed that Daniel was the man over whom

Beatrice was lovesick. Beatrice did not deny this assumption, as it allowed her to read for hours uninterrupted. And in any case, she found Daniel perfectly agreeable—though their friendship had never progressed beyond an amiable rapport.

But what would Daniel, her trusted confidant, think of her if he knew what she was hiding? If he found out the object of her true passion? Despite all they shared, she knew he would never approve.

She folded the pages and tucked the letter into her bodice. The post-boy would come by soon to collect their letters, and she could send it off with him while her family was distracted with ball preparations. She then pulled on gloves to conceal her fingers, which were ink-stained from the newspaper, and made her way to the parlor downstairs, where the rest of her family was gathered.

Mrs. Steele and Louisa stood inside by the fireplace, both practically jumping up and down in excitement.

Beatrice's other sister, Mary, sat at the pianoforte, making little notes on a sheet of music titled "Ode to the Moon." The youngest of the Steele family, Mary was very private. Though sound traveled easily through the thin walls of Marsh House, Mary somehow roamed undetected, often appearing abruptly when no one had heard her approach.* Indeed, Mr. Steele did not seem to realize she was in the room. He sat in an armchair engrossed in a book of picto-funnies, then dropped it, startled, when Mary plinked out a jarring chord.

"Finally," Mrs. Steele exclaimed as Beatrice entered the room, "you've emerged from pining for your beau!"

Beatrice tried to affect a lovesick expression, moving past her

---

* Mary was withdrawn, reticent, and overall mysterious. What most knew about Mary was that she had mousy hair and appreciated walks in nature. What most did not know could fill several tomes.

mother to avoid any follow-up questions. She dodged a splash of water from the bucket her father had fixed above the parlor door, and moved to take a seat next to him. She paused by a rumpled cushion and then lifted it to find Mr. Steele's rubber pooting pillow.

"However did that get there?" her father asked innocently as Beatrice handed it to him. Mrs. Steele intercepted it and threw it out an open window.

"Now that no one is *distracted*," she said pointedly, "Louisa may tell us her news."

She took Louisa's hands and the two sank to a seat on a tufted settee.

"I heard it from Arabella Ashbrook just now," Louisa said, "during our trip into town."

"You went with Arabella?" Beatrice asked in surprise.

"She was available," Louisa said, shifting uncomfortably on the settee. "I did call up to you before I left, in case you wanted to come, but you didn't answer. I'm sorry," she added, her wide eyes now shining with remorse.

"Oh . . . no. It's fine," Beatrice said quickly, trying to reassure her. "Not to worry."

Arabella Ashbrook, Daniel's younger sister, was the hostess of the evening's festivities. Arabella and Louisa had been spending an increasing amount of time together, much to Beatrice's chagrin. She found Arabella self-important and snobbish. But Beatrice had been so engrossed with her reading—could she really blame Louisa for finding a friend who was far more *available*?

Louisa continued, glossing over the awkward moment. "It is about the ball this evening—"

"Is it canceled?" Mr. Steele interrupted. "That would be happy news indeed."

"That would be *terrible*," Mrs. Steele cried.

Beatrice thought fleetingly that if something terrible *did* happen, at least it would be something new. Immediately, her throat tightened with guilt. She did not *want* something bad to occur. Boredom was preferable to distress.

Wasn't it?

"Anyhow," Louisa said loudly, "my news."

Everyone looked at her, finally quiet.

"The guest of honor tonight," Louisa said in a passionate whisper, "will be *Mr. Edmund Croaksworth.*"

Mrs. Steele shrieked and fell back on the settee in a faint. Louisa grabbed Beatrice's hands and pulled her into a happy jig. Though Beatrice wasn't quite sure what was happening, she felt a rush of excitement as she twirled, gazing at her sister's shining, eager face. Even Mr. Steele lowered his book of picto-funnies, intrigued, and didn't notice as the frog in his pocket made a break for it.

Mary, however, stared at them all in confusion. "Who is Mr. Edmund Croaksworth?"

As usual, they ignored her.

RESTORING ORDER WITH HUXLEY

[Excerpt]

A cold wind is blowing through London, and it is not the chill of autumn approaching. There is a killer in our midst.

I know this city. I have lived here all my life; you readers know my passion for order and justice stems from my desire to keep our home safe. To ensure it is the London we have always known it to be. To keep the shadows down dark alleys at bay.

But these shadows are seeping into the streets. Those of you who keep up with my column have heard of the dangers of the London Menace. Last night he killed again. Even as his body count rises, I feel more certain than ever that I will be the one to bring this fiend to justice. Those who know any information which might be of use in the case are advised to contact me at once.

Readers of last week's column will also be happy to know that Mrs. Barker's kitten was under her settee all along, and thus is safe and sound.

CHAPTER 2

Preparations

It is a fact known throughout Swampshire that a rich gentleman is prey hunted by every young woman. From her sister's and mother's excitement, Beatrice gathered that Edmund Croaksworth must be such a quarry.

She knew he was not a Swampshire resident, though she found the name oddly familiar. She sifted through her memory, trying to place it.

"I was helping Arabella Ashbrook pick out new garden shears when she let the news slip," Louisa told Mrs. Steele, who had recovered from her faint and was now fully energized, as one could only be at the prospect of a fine hunk of flesh attending the evening's ball. All four Steele women made their way into the chamber Beatrice shared with Louisa. To his relief, Mr. Steele was left alone in the parlor with his picto-funnies.

The bedroom was divided into halves. Beatrice's corner was an explosion of books, abandoned embroidery projects, and half-drunk cups of tea. Beatrice tried to keep it neat, as a lady should, but it seemed to have a mind of its own.

Louisa's side, on the other hand, was always tidy. This is because Mrs. Steele had taken it upon herself to straighten up each morning, knowing how easily Louisa could get distracted. Racquets for battledore and shuttlecock, skittles pins, and old metal balls for bumble-puppy all had a designated location, thanks to Mrs. Steele.

As Mary followed them inside, she tripped over a pile of Beatrice's books but recovered with doglike agility and landed on her sister's bed.* Beatrice joined her, taking an absentminded sip of tea from a cup on her bedside table and then spitting it out upon realizing that it had fermented.

"You'll have to look perfect," Mrs. Steele said, rifling through Louisa's scant wardrobe. The family could not afford a luxurious selection, especially since the clothes seemed to always get destroyed: Beatrice's with ink stains, Louisa's from various athletic activities, and Mary's from goodness knew, whatever caused a dress to rip completely in half. But truly, the clothes didn't matter. They were just a gilded frame around the true masterpiece: Louisa Pamela Steele.

"Perhaps the pink frock?" Louisa suggested.

"You wore that at last month's ball," Beatrice reminded her. "And I've always thought you look best in green."

"I prefer pink—" Louisa began, but Mrs. Steele interrupted.

"We should be thinking about what Mr. Croaksworth prefers, dear. Do you think he likes lace? Ribbon? A plunging bodice?"

---

* Mary had her own bedroom, which she forbade anyone else from entering. They gladly followed this rule, as there was always a smell of raw meat emanating from within, and everything inside was covered by an unexplained layer of fur.

"Surely he shall be most attracted to her mind and personality," Beatrice said lightly.

"Don't be ridiculous," Mrs. Steele said as she rifled through the closet.

"What more *do* you know of Croaksworth, Louisa?" Beatrice asked, turning to her sister. "I know I've heard his name before, but I cannot place him. I assume he is wealthy, attractive, and eligible, so you may skip over *those* specifics."

"Those are hardly facts to skip," Mrs. Steele said. "The man has eight thousand a year!"

"Eight thousand what?" Mary asked.*

"He was Daniel Ashbrook's best friend in school, though Arabella said the two men have not spoken since then," Louisa explained. "Has Daniel mentioned him to you before, Beatrice?"

"No," Beatrice murmured. "Why haven't they spoken? Did something happen?"

"I'm not sure," Louisa began, but Mrs. Steele interrupted.

"Perhaps you would know, Beatrice, if you and Daniel didn't discuss just characters from books instead of your lives, or any *plans* for the *future*." She shot Beatrice a meaningful look.

"Mr. Croaksworth's parents recently perished, leaving him a great sum of money," Louisa said hastily, blessedly directing Mrs. Steele away from another lecture.

"Oh! How did they die?" Beatrice asked, her interest piqued.

"Beatrice!" her mother said warningly.

"I just want to know so I don't accidentally say anything to Mr. Croaksworth that could bring up bad memories," Beatrice said quickly.

---

* Like all genteel families, the Croaksworths kept their fortune in the bank and lived off the interest (in pounds) of the principal balance. Mary did not understand this—she had developed a heightened sense of smell but a dampened sense of finance.

"It's very tragic," Louisa said. "They had just moved to a new mansion in Bath with fifty-nine bedrooms. Unfortunately, the two of them got lost on their way to breakfast. Their servants didn't find them until it was too late—they had wasted away."

"How awful," Beatrice said, leaning forward. "Do the inspectors suspect foul play?"

"No birds were involved. The Croaksworths were simply terrible with directions," Louisa replied.

"Croaksworth," Beatrice repeated. Suddenly it fell into place: "I recall now—his sister went missing!"

It had not been Louisa, Mrs. Steele, or Daniel who had mentioned Mr. Croaksworth; Beatrice recognized the name from one of the yellowing newspaper articles hidden in her turret.

"How would you know anything about that?" Mrs. Steele snatched a lace shawl and snapped it at Beatrice's ankles. "Page sixty-eight of *The Lady's Guide* clearly states that women must not speak of missing persons cases."

"Perhaps that is why few missing people are recovered," Beatrice pointed out, lifting up her feet to avoid a lace thrashing.

"Actually, Mother, it was reported in the society columns," Louisa explained. "Alice went on an extended holiday."

"For two years?" Beatrice asked, raising an eyebrow.

"If they said so, it must be true," Mrs. Steele said with a note of finality. "Rich individuals have their own ways of doing things. We must focus on the good: Mr. Croaksworth has no sister, no parents, and is looking for a shoulder to cry on."

"That's hardly good for *him*," Beatrice said.

"It certainly is. Edmund has inherited a great deal, and money heals all wounds," Mrs. Steele said sagely.

"Don't you mean *time* heals all wounds?" Beatrice asked.

"No . . . that doesn't sound right. It's definitely money," her mother replied. She held a dress up to Louisa's brawny form. "Now, we must ensure that Mr. Croaksworth falls madly in love with you—"

"He could fall in love with any one of us," Louisa interrupted, catching Beatrice's eye. "Beatrice's wit is unparalleled, and men adore funny women."

"Do not joke, Louisa. It is unbecoming," Mrs. Steele said tartly.

Beatrice took Louisa's hand. "You are gracious, Lou. But it is unnecessary! I hope you don't think that I am jealous that my younger sister might secure an attachment before me; I would never allow such a thing to come between us."

"That is reassuring, as it is likely to occur," Mary said somberly.

Louisa pulled her hand away from Beatrice, looking uncomfortable. Beatrice's empty palm felt suddenly clammy. Did her sister not believe her?

"Sometimes a younger sister turns out more desirable than the eldest," Mrs. Steele said matter-of-factly. "No one faults you for being born so handsome and so good-natured, Louisa. Beatrice shall find someone eventually, someone who can tolerate her, or perhaps be tricked into—"

"But Mr. Croaksworth shall only have eyes for you," Beatrice interrupted. "And I am perfectly pleased by that. Though I admit, his past is unusual—"

"Do not dwell on it, I beg you," Mrs. Steele said. "If you find yourself starting to ask untoward questions, stick something in your mouth." Beatrice raised her eyebrows at the suggestion. "For example, some soup," Mrs. Steele added.

"I'll be sure to have a bowl of it at the ready all evening, though it will make dancing difficult," Beatrice replied.

"This isn't a joking matter!" Mrs. Steele snapped. "Mr. Croaksworth is an unfortunate young man. You're about to be in the same boat if you're not careful. You *must* marry, or you will essentially kill me. Is that what you want? To starve your own mother? To watch my body decay out on the street, until I'm just a pile of bones for wild dogs to pick at?" Mary perked up.

"There is no need to fear," Beatrice said firmly. "Louisa shall make an excellent match."

"And so will you," Mrs. Steele added.

"Yes, yes, of course," Beatrice assured her. "We know the roles we must play. You have nothing to worry about, Mother."

Looking a bit pale, Louisa put two different shoes on and stepped toward her full-length mirror, standing on one leg and then the other as if to decide which slipper made her seem more desirable. Beatrice rose from the bed and stood next to her sister. She lowered her voice so only Louisa could hear.

"You can't let Mother get to you," she whispered. "I know she puts so much pressure on you to find a husband, when maybe that's not what you want. . . ."

"Of course it's what I want," Louisa said sharply. Beatrice drew back in surprise at her sudden harsh tone, and Louisa looked instantly regretful. "I mean, it is my duty, and I cannot shirk my duty," she said.

The letter to Sir Huxley, hidden in Beatrice's bodice, suddenly felt heavy.

Mrs. Steele shoved her way in between the sisters to hand Louisa a green gown. Louisa stepped into it and struggled with the buttons, trying to fasten them, but the fabric tore in two.

"It doesn't fit," Mrs. Steele said impatiently. "I hope all that cake you've been eating was worth sacrificing your entire married future and sending us all to our deaths."

"One must always consider the moral cost of a meal," Mary said darkly.

"I'll mend it." Beatrice tried to grab the dress, hoping to be helpful, but Mrs. Steele pulled it from her reach.

"Absolutely not. Your stitching would ruin the gown. She can wear the white muslin instead. We have no time to waste," Mrs. Steele continued. "We have only three hours and fifty minutes until the ball!"

Mary, Mrs. Steele, and Beatrice set upon Louisa and got to work. They plucked each individual unwanted hair off her body, leaving her sun-kissed skin reddened but smooth. Then they covered her with a beauty paste made from swamp mud (a popular beauty treatment in the region; the mud contained the same luminescent properties as the frogs and thus gave the complexion a beautiful glow). Once this had dried, Mrs. Steele scrubbed it off, and Beatrice doused Louisa in sweet-smelling rose oil. As Mary had the strongest hands in the family, she was the designated stay-lacer; she cinched Louisa into the perfect, compact shape. Over the top of the stays went layers of underclothes, petticoats, and then the chosen white muslin dress. Beatrice pressed Louisa's curls and gently twisted her sister's hair into a complicated updo, and Mary tucked a white lily amidst the braids. While the two sisters perfected Louisa's fiery locks, Mrs. Steele painted her face to match, applying just the right amount of rouge.

Downstairs, Mr. Steele put on his jacket and thus was ready to go.

Finally Louisa stood in front of the women in her family and gave them the full force of her looks. Thanks to the mud treatment—or, Beatrice thought, her sister's own natural beauty—she was glowing.

"You are a vision!" Mrs. Steele gasped. "Our home shall remain intact!"

"And now, for the finishing touches," Louisa said, and picked up a vial from her vanity. It was filled with inky black liquid. She unscrewed the vial and tipped her head back, then released one drop of the liquid into each eye. "Arabella gave me this belladonna to use for the ball. She grew it herself; it makes the pupils pop," she explained as she placed the vial into her dress pocket and blinked.

"You are the most beautiful woman in town," Mrs. Steele said, tears running down her cheeks. "And, Beatrice, you look acceptable— you shall surely be considered the fourth prettiest."

"What number prettiest am I?" Mary asked.

"I've never thought about it." Mrs. Steele turned to scrutinize her youngest daughter. "But you have a wonderful heart."

Suddenly, there was a knock downstairs.

"The post-boy," Beatrice said eagerly. "I have a letter for him."

Before her mother could protest, she rushed down the stairs and wrenched open the front door. The post-boy stood there with his satchel, hand already outstretched in anticipation.

"To London," Beatrice told the post-boy, and he nodded. She drew the letter from her bodice and pressed it into his hand.

"I've something for you as well," the boy said, and passed her a thick parcel. Before she could inquire as to what it was, he had turned away and mounted his horse. He took off, mailbags bouncing on either side of the saddle.

Beatrice looked down at the parcel. It was addressed to the entire Steele family. She flipped it over and stared at the seal. It was a red, waxen roach encircled by a "G."

"What is it?" Mrs. Steele asked, stepping into the entryway. "Is it from Daniel?" But her excited face fell when she saw the seal. "That is cousin Grub's seal," she said, and snatched the parcel from Beatrice's hands. She tore it open and skimmed the first of a thick stack of papers, and then gasped.

"What is it?" Beatrice asked. She wrenched the parcel back from her mother and read the beginning of a letter. It was written in scarlet ink.

To Whom It May Concern:

This notice is to inform you that MR. MARTIN GRUB (hereinafter referred to as "PLAINTIFF") has submitted

a petition to declare MR. STEPHEN STEELE (hereinafter referred to as "DEFENDANT") mentally unfit and
therefore unable to manage Marsh House.

A trial to evaluate this allegation shall be set for
Wednesday next. Should Mr. Steele be determined unfit,
he shall be removed from the property at once, and the
living passed to Mr. Grub.

"I don't understand," Beatrice said. "What does it mean?"

"I have always feared this," Mrs. Steele breathed. "Mr. Grub is
making a play for Marsh House. He isn't content to wait until your
father's death; he means to have it *now*. And for this to arrive tonight, of all evenings!"

"Do you think he orchestrated the delivery on purpose, to
upset us before the ball?" Beatrice asked, and her mother nodded
grimly.

"No doubt he did. Disgusting man."

As their closest male relative, Mr. Martin Grub was set to inherit
their estate, should the Steele sisters fail to marry and produce an
heir. This was particularly unfair because he had already inherited
four other estates from various relatives, by somehow outliving
them all. No one knew exactly how old he was, just that he hoarded
money yet always wore the same old-fashioned, tatty suit. When he
had them over for dinner, he requested that *they* bring the food. And
once, when Beatrice borrowed a handkerchief, he sent her an in-
voice for its cleaning.

"Thank goodness you and I found it first," Mrs. Steele whispered to Beatrice. "We mustn't let Louisa know; she cannot be
distracted from her purpose."

"But Father isn't unfit," Beatrice said, a lump forming in her
throat. "No one would believe such a claim."

They both looked toward the parlor, where Mr. Steele was collapsed in his armchair, tongue lolling to one side. His eyes were closed, and there was a machete lodged in his head.

His eyes suddenly snapped open, and he began to laugh. He whipped off the machete, which was connected to a headpiece.

"Had you fooled, didn't I?" he yelled to Beatrice and Mrs. Steele. "You should have seen your faces! You were almost as scared as the vicar last Sunday!"

"We're doomed." Mrs. Steele turned to Beatrice, her voice growing urgent. "There is no more time to dillydally when it comes to your relationship with Daniel. If your father is found unfit, and you girls are still unmarried—"

"We will lose everything," Beatrice finished, stunned.

Mrs. Steele swallowed hard, her fingers clutching the papers. Then she marched into the parlor, toward the fireplace, and flung them into the flames.

"We have not been bested yet," she said firmly. "Grub may think he has us, but nothing can stand between Louisa and Mr. Croaksworth's fortune."

Except one thing, Beatrice thought.

If anyone knew that she was writing to Sir Huxley, that she was reading crime articles, Beatrice would be declared unmarriageable, be socially exiled, be sent away to some unknown land, tarnish Louisa's reputation by association, and cause her family to waste away in despair.

Thunder rumbled somewhere in the distance.

Her mother was right, Beatrice thought. They had not been bested yet. No one knew Beatrice's secret—and it would stay that way. As she glanced out the window and saw the post-boy galloping away from Marsh House, she made herself a promise: She would think not at all of murder or crime. She would be the perfect sister, the perfect lady, and their family would be saved.

THE LONDON BABBLER

This Detective Was Famous. . . .
You Shan't Believe What He Looks Like Now!

Everyone in London knows the name Sir Huxley. This gentleman detective has captivated the hearts and minds of newspaper readers everywhere, intrigued by his efforts to keep our streets safe. But what happened to his former assistant, Inspector Vivek Drake?

Readers will recall Sir Huxley's trusted, grizzled, eye-patch-wearing right-hand man. He was always alongside Sir Huxley doing something or other. That is, until the murder of Viscount Dudley DeBurbie, whose butler discovered him at the foot of his staircase, fatally stabbed in the back. DeBurbie, who was active in the social scene of London, was well-known for his collection of precious jewels, which mysteriously went missing on the day of his death. Sir Huxley and Drake disagreed about the culprit. Drake inexplicably suspected DeBurbie's beautiful lady companion, Verity Swan, but Sir Huxley revealed that the lowly butler was the true killer. After their public dispute, they severed their partnership, and Drake disappeared.

So where is he now? You shall be shocked to learn that, despite his fall from grace, he is still in London. Dressed in threadbare clothes and last season's shoes, Drake roams the streets, desperate to take on a case—any case. But who would hire this man, whom Huxley has deemed "rigid" and "unfeeling"?

We caught up with Inspector Drake at King's Tavern and Tea. Shivering, hands wrapped around a mug for warmth, he claimed it is *Sir Huxley* who is the inferior detective.

When asked how he was faring since his public embarrassment, while his previous employer's star continued to rise, Drake slammed down his tea (causing *quite* a scene).

"First off, he was my partner," he said in a voice far too loud for the tranquil tavern. "Secondly, Sir Huxley is a duplicitous swindler who has fooled you all. He has no more brains than a brick wall, spends more time combing his mustache than solving cases, and would rather flatter ladies than obtain witness statements. That's what he did with his Verity Swan. In a complete breach of appropriate behavior for an investigator, he claimed he was in *love* with her. Has he ever discussed *this* sordid detail? You may also remember that Miss Swan disappeared as soon as the butler was wrongfully put behind bars. Is this not suspicious? Furthermore, what of the missing jewels? Huxley never uncovered their location. He is clearly useless as an investigator. The man is vain, arrogant, and does not even know how to fence."

Harsh words from the disgraced former partner. Perhaps, we might venture to say, a little petty? Unlike Sir Huxley, who, when asked to comment, remained a perfect gentleman.

"I wish him the best with all of his future endeavors," he said over sherry at Brovender's Social Club. Ever taking the moral high ground, even when insulted, he continued: "I maintain the hope that Vivek Drake shall overcome his shortcomings and perhaps even one day solve a case. But I fear he may remain heartless, brainless, and gumptionless. As a side note, I *can* fence. An inspector *must* know how to fence."

CHAPTER 3

Transport

The Steeles owned no personal carriage, a great source of shame to Mrs. Steele, as she felt it pointed to their limited income. The lack of a carriage was a relief for Mr. Steele, as he found horses "too large to make sense." For her part, Beatrice would have appreciated the freedom a carriage of her own could afford—but of course, she wouldn't have been permitted to go as far as her imagination traveled.

It was a very cold evening. As all the women wore thin muslin, they were grateful to pack into the hired carriage, though it smelled of stale cigars and previous occupants' perspiration. Mrs. Steele sat in the middle. Her towering hair tickled the ceiling of the pink-velvet-lined compartment. Mr. Steele insisted on the window seat; he preferred to keep an eye on the horses "in case they try any funny business." Louisa, Mary, and Beatrice crowded in around their parents, filling the small space with a haze of perfume and anticipation.

Beatrice glanced out the window at her home, dark and silent upon their departure. It faded into the distance as the carriage began to putter down a worn dirt path. The trees lining the way were like shadowy figures with arms reaching toward her, their twisted limbs silver and strange in the haze of dusk, as if they were trying to pull her back. She almost wished the branches *would* stop the carriage and that she could race back to her turret—but she knew she must go forward. After all, if an advantageous match did not occur this evening, there might be nothing to which she *could* go back.

The carriage ambled along, and Beatrice half listened to her family's chatterings as she watched the sun sink into the horizon, obscured by dark clouds. Rain fell in a steady drizzle, and Beatrice saw lightning flicker in the distance. A bolt illuminated the hill, and she caught a glimpse of a man walking along the side of the road, his cape billowing in the wind.

"There's someone there," Beatrice whispered, leaning forward in a sudden movement. Mary and Louisa immediately crowded next to her, straining to see.

"Probably just a farmer, out for an evening stroll," Mrs. Steele said, but also pushed forward to look.

"He can't be Swampshirian," Beatrice reasoned. "No one here would risk a walk in impending hail."

"Is it Mr. Croaksworth?" Mrs. Steele asked immediately.

"He will arrive by carriage—won't he?" Louisa asked nervously.

"Perhaps he understands the danger of horses," Mr. Steele said.

Beatrice pounded on the front of the compartment. "Please, stop the carriage."

The Steele family all had to grab hold of their seats as the carriage ground to a halt, settling unevenly on the muddy path. Without out the noise of the horses and carriage wheels, all they could hear now was the howl of the wind outside. Mary's ears twitched.

"We must see if he needs assistance," Beatrice told her family.

"After all, a storm is coming." Without waiting for their response, she pushed open the carriage door. Brisk air rushed into the compartment, and Beatrice shivered with excitement. *There was a stranger in Swampshire.* She couldn't help herself; she was intrigued.

"Wait," Mrs. Steele said, grabbing Beatrice's arm to stop her. "He could be a murderer, or worse, a Frenchman!"

"But, Mother, aren't we supposed to offer charity to someone in need, even if they are found outside the proper gathering places?" Louisa asked, eyes wide.

"I must check." Mrs. Steele pulled *The Lady's Guide to Swampshire (Travel Edition)* from her reticule and began to flip through the pages. "I know a lady cannot approach a man without introduction. . . ."

"Then Father will do it," Beatrice said.

They all turned to Mr. Steele, who shrank slightly behind his mustache. He loved all his children—Louisa was strong and good-natured, and Mary was also his daughter—but Beatrice made him laugh. He could not say no to her. Therefore he poked his bald head out of the carriage and yelled toward the shadowy figure in the distance.

"Pardon me! Might I offer you some assistance?"

The man turned toward the carriage. As he did, a bolt of lightning flashed across the sky, illuminating his face.

Beatrice gasped. He had a long scar down one cheek, and an eye patch concealed his left eye. His right was a piercing emerald green. She recognized him instantly as Inspector Vivek Drake. The sketches of him in the newspaper, alongside his noble employer, Sir Huxley, had been very accurate—Drake looked just the same as his portrait, right down to his scowl.

She felt a sudden anger rise inside her as she recalled the terrible things Drake had said about Sir Huxley, denouncing his skills, daring to accuse Huxley of inappropriate behavior—Huxley, of all people!—when Drake was clearly just jealous of his former employer's success. The man was a fraud and a cad.

So what was he doing *here*?

Drake began to walk toward the carriage.

"On second thought, we should continue on," Beatrice said quickly. "I'm sure he's fine. Just out for a stroll, as you said, Mother."

But it was too late. Inspector Drake approached their carriage and stopped just outside of the compartment door, his shoes squelching in the mud.

"Good evening," he said, his voice soft, with the faintest hint of an Indian accent.

The Steele family stared at him, all speechless. The scant moonlight cast his scarred, handsome face in an odd glow.

"Good evening, sir. I . . . like your eye patch," Mr. Steele said finally.

"Thank you," Inspector Drake replied. "I presume you all are off to the Ashbrooks' ball?"

"Yes," Mr. Steele affirmed. "How did you know?"

"You are headed east, and this town has no other destinations beyond this point. You are also dressed in ball attire," Drake observed.

"Jolly good. You are most intelligent, sir!" Mr. Steele said. He never could dislike anyone for long, and certainly not someone so quick on his feet.

"If he is *so intelligent*, why is he on foot in such terrible weather?" Beatrice muttered, unable to hold her tongue.

"I don't like carriages," Drake said, turning to scrutinize her with his piercing eye.

"You aren't by any chance . . . Mr. Edmund Croaksworth?" Louisa asked, taking in Drake's jagged scar and his silk eye patch.

"No, I am *not*," Drake scoffed.

"But you know him," Beatrice surmised, leaning forward.

Drake held her gaze for a moment and then nodded slightly.

"Yes," he said, "I am a guest of Mr. Croaksworth at this evening's ball. We are traveling together."

Surely Mr. Croaksworth would not simply be *friends* with a disgraced assistant detective, Beatrice thought. Surely he would have some reason for inviting him along—but *what*?

However, she had no time to protest; her mother's apprehension had vanished.

"Good sir! Any gentleman who knows Mr. Croaksworth is a friend of ours indeed!" She pushed her family aside to make room in the cramped cabin. "You should not be out there in the harsh weather. I insist that you ride with us the rest of the way to the ball."

Drake hesitated, looking apprehensively at the carriage.

"He said he does not like carriages, Mother," Beatrice muttered.

"Yes, but I insisted, so to decline my offer would be very rude," Mrs. Steele said, her voice suddenly icy.

Her face, frozen in a frosty smile, was illuminated in another flash of lightning, and Drake moved toward the carriage. Few could resist Mrs. Steele when she used this tone; such was the gift of a mother.

Drake had to hunch over to fit his tall frame into the tiny compartment. He took a seat next to Beatrice, and she tensed, acutely aware of his body heat.

Mr. Steele pulled the carriage door shut, cutting off the cold breeze. He banged twice on the coach's ceiling, and the horses went back to a trot. Everyone stared at the stranger in their midst, who shrank uncomfortably, as if he could make himself smaller by sheer force of will. This was useless, as he was quite tall.

"Now," Mrs. Steele said, "you must tell us about your friend Mr. Croaksworth. We're overjoyed that he's attending our gathering this evening. I'm sure he will like what he sees." She winked at Louisa, who flushed.

Drake turned to Louisa and took in her appearance. "That is a large lily you have in your hair," he remarked.

"Yes," she said, touching it gently. "My favorite flower."

"The white lily symbolizes virtue," Drake continued matter-of-factly, "and devotion. But it is also, in Greek myth, representative of rebirth and motherhood. Not to mention that it is presented at funerals. Making it, most prominently, a symbol of death."

The carriage filled with awkward silence. Had someone died? Beatrice thought with a shiver. Was this why Drake was here? But news traveled fast in such a small town. If something *had* occurred, the Steeles would have known. Furthermore, if a crime *had* transpired, who would hire a substandard detective like Drake?

"Lilies are also toxic to cats," Mary said, breaking the awkward pause. "A perfect flower."

"Louisa means it in the virtuous way," Beatrice cut in. "In a *bridal* way." She gave Louisa an encouraging smile. "After all, the one question we don't have to ask is whether Mr. Croaksworth is seeking a wife." She would not let Drake's sudden, unexplained presence get in the way of her true purpose that evening: to ensure Louisa secured the man of her dreams.

"I assure you," Drake said, his tone matter-of-fact, "he is not."

"Excuse me?" Beatrice said, snorting in indignation. "You can't possibly know that."

"And yet I do," Drake said, turning toward her.

"How do we know that you speak the truth?" Beatrice shot back. "You might be a *liar,* for all we know."

"Beatrice!" Louisa said, eyes widening. "What has gotten into you? Perhaps he's right, and Mr. Croaksworth only means to visit with Daniel this evening."

"Aha!" Mrs. Steele cut in, jabbing a finger at Drake. "I know exactly who you are!" Beatrice was momentarily stunned that her mother had also recognized Inspector Drake, until Mrs. Steele continued: "You are some friend of Mr. Croaksworth's from the city, who means to stop him from falling for a country girl. Perhaps you consider Mr. Croaksworth too highborn for us, so you followed him and invited yourself to the evening's festivities." She tilted her chin up with pride. "I assure you that your efforts shall be in vain. We may live in the countryside, but we follow a strict code of conduct. We are just as well-bred—nay, *more* so—than the society in London. Mr. Croaksworth shall find that my daughters are all proper ladies."

"I see you have me all figured out," Drake said to Mrs. Steele. "Since my efforts will fail, I shall abandon them at once." Beatrice expected him to say something further, but instead he leaned back against the compartment cushion and fell silent.

She stared at him, perplexed. It was a bizarre experience to see someone from the newspapers stroll off the page and into her small town. But he clearly did not want to discuss his reasons for doing so, and she could not ask without coming under suspicion. His presence was trouble—Sir Huxley knew that, and Beatrice was now sure of it too. But the importance of the evening for her family's future was too great for her to get wrapped up in Vivek Drake. She squared her shoulders and mentally resolved that she would stay far away from this man over the course of the evening. *He was not worth it.*

She forced herself to look outside the carriage window into the darkness of the night, lit with the occasional glow of a wild frog darting through the swamp. As she regarded the countryside, the carriage crested a hill, and another sudden flash of lightning illuminated an imposing mansion in the distance.

They had arrived at Stabmort Park.

THE HISTORY OF STABMORT PARK

[Excerpt]

Drawn by the rolling hills and natural hot springs, nobles attempted to settle Swampshire many times throughout the years. However, most fled the region once they encountered the strange frogs, constant hailstorms, and dangerous squelch holes peppering the terrain.

Baron Fitzwilliam Ashbrook was undeterred, determined to create a livable society out of the quagmire. In the seventeenth century he constructed Stabmort Park, a sprawling mansion, to serve as the new village's country seat.

A four-story residence, Stabmort Park boasts imported columns in the front, stables, and a fashionable greenhouse, which was added in the late eighteenth century. It has a turret—every respectable mansion does—whose often-flickering light in the window is a source of jovial rumors in the neighborhood regarding "the ghost of Stabmort Park, who reads by candle above."

Inside, the underground level is home to a bathing room with a natural spring. Above it rests the kitchens and servants' quarters. The ground floor houses the parlor, the lavatory, the hallway to the greenhouse, and the ballroom. The floors above this contain a series of bedrooms, each more ornate than the last.

Built to accommodate a large family and an ample staff, and outfitted with rooms for any potential event, Stabmort Park represents the power of the nobility and its dominance in the region. Of course, there have been less jovial rumors that Baron Ashbrook built such a large home because he was "compensating," but this particular gossip has been disputed.

CHAPTER 4

Arrival

Just as the Steeles' carriage pulled up to the imposing mansion, the light rain hardened into hail. Hail in Swampshire meant eyeball-sized pellets of ice dropping haphazardly from the sky. As a result, the Steeles—and Inspector Drake—ran across the bridge to the porch, rushing to avoid the downpour. All feeling slightly dented, they pushed their way through the large front doors and into the mansion entryway.

The entryway was mercifully inviting, with plush carpet and flickering sconces that gave off welcome heat. The Steeles took a moment to compose themselves in this antechamber. They shed their cloaks and did a routine check for ice bruising. Thankfully, there was none, except on Mary, but no one noticed.

"I've been here a thousand times, but Stabmort Park always seems bigger at each visit," Louisa said, staring wide-eyed at a portrait of the town's founder, Baron Fitzwilliam Ashbrook. He gazed down his aquiline nose at her, his expression stern.

"You must get used to opulence," Mrs. Steele said as she rearranged Louisa's ringlets. "Before long you'll be the mistress of a mansion twice this size."

Beatrice gave her cloak to the Ashbrooks' footman, who placed it in the coat closet. The man turned toward Drake with his arms outstretched, but Drake shook his head.

"Thank you, but I shall keep it on."

The footman continued to hold his arms outstretched, his eyes wide in confusion. "But . . . sir, traditionally we collect—"

"And I am rejecting this tradition."

"Please, sir," the footman said, and began to tug at Drake's cloak.

As the footman and Drake struggled over the garment, hissing arguments at each other, Louisa came up next to Beatrice.

"Why do you think Mr. Croaksworth invited this ill-mannered man?" she asked in a low voice.

"It is confounding," Beatrice said, "but I suppose we must not pry." The words sounded sarcastic on her lips, but Louisa did not seem to catch this; she nodded earnestly.

"You are right, of course. My apologies."

The footman finally succeeded in tearing off Drake's cloak. As he ripped it away, something silver fell to the floor and rolled toward Beatrice's foot. She stooped to pick it up.

It was a spoon, old but well polished. Its handle was formed in the shape of a dog.

"I'll take that," Drake snapped, and snatched the spoon from Beatrice's hand. Without his cloak, she could see that his suit was old and out of fashion. Still, he stood tall, his proud air overshadowing his shabby clothing.

"There shall be silverware provided at dinner later, sir," Beatrice said. "No need to bring your own."

"That is for the best, as mine is now covered in mud," Drake said irritably. Beatrice looked down to see a patch of mud on the carpet, in the shape of a shoe print.

"Odd," she murmured.

"What's odd?" Drake asked, tucking the spoon into his pocket.

"Nothing," she replied, but then, unable to stop herself, said, "It's just that the mud has wild honeysuckle in it." She pointed at a sprig of the flowers, ground into the scarlet rug. "That only grows at Adler's End, by the stream."

"What is Adler's End?" Drake asked.

"It's a wooded area by a creek, at the boundary of the Ashbrooks' property," she explained. "When it rains too much, the creek overflows, and it can be dangerous. And it always rains too much in Swampshire."

"I've noticed," Drake said.

"What's odd," Beatrice continued, "is that someone would be down there. Hugh Ashbrook has forbidden anyone from stepping foot at Adler's End. It's far too dangerous."

"It seems someone in Swampshire has broken the rules," Drake said, raising an eyebrow.

"How dare you, sir," Mrs. Steele gasped. "They would never!"

"Perhaps the mud is fake," Mr. Steele suggested, "and part of a clever little joke. Do you think Hugh Ashbrook has lifted his ban on trick dung?" He reached into his pocket.

"I doubt it, though one can always hope," Beatrice said, gently stopping her father's arm.

After the strange appearance of Drake and the rush to get inside Stabmort Park without getting caught in the storm, she had forgotten all about Grub's claims against her father. But now, as she looked at Mr. Steele's crestfallen expression, it all came rushing back.

She could not allow herself to get distracted again.

"If everyone is properly freshened up, I suggest we enter the festivities," she said brightly, turning away from Drake and striding toward the ballroom doors.

The footman opened the doors for the Steele family, revealing a brightly lit ballroom. Mrs. Steele pushed Louisa in first and then coughed loudly, perfectly orchestrating a dramatic scene so that all the guests would turn and see her most beautiful daughter enter. Beatrice and Mary trailed behind.

The ballroom was large and illuminated with hundreds of white candles. There were bouquets of pink roses arranged on side tables. Arabella Ashbrook, who adored gardening, created floral arrangements using plants from her greenhouse. She had outdone herself this evening; the sprays were lush and filled the air with a pleasant aroma. A quartet of musicians sat on the landing, tuning their instruments. The room was a far cry from the perilous weather outside. One could almost forget the brewing storm, except for occasional flickers of lightning illuminating the moors outside the ballroom's tall windows.

Beatrice and Louisa methodically linked arms and began to take a turn about the room. This was always the first order of business upon arriving at a ball; it allowed them to both see and be seen.

Ordinarily, they would also remark to each other about the evening ahead, but tonight Louisa was uncharacteristically quiet.

They passed scattered chairs and drink tables, lined up against the gold-papered walls in anticipation of guests who would require respite between numbers.

"Don't forget to count out your steps in the minuet," Beatrice instructed Louisa.

"I never forget," Louisa said.

"And spot your turns so you don't get dizzy," Beatrice continued. "It can be tricky when Arabella picks music with such a quick tempo. I'm certain she does it to try to trip us up."

"I'm sure she merely enjoys brisk numbers," Louisa replied, ever generous.

"You assume the best of people, Louisa," Beatrice said as she patted her sister's hand. "I shall toast to that tonight."

She stopped in front of a long table laden with punch. It was the sisters' tradition to toast to something before the beginning of every ball; Louisa normally chose a kind concept such as "romance" or "everyone's happiness." Beatrice usually toasted to "seeing a new face for once," which almost always was in vain.

But Louisa shook her head. "Thank you, but I think I shall skip our toast tonight."

Confused and crestfallen, Beatrice tried to mask her hurt as Arabella Ashbrook sauntered up to greet them.

She was a fair-haired beauty with stunning yet severe features. Lively and shrewd, Arabella was known for her impeccable taste in both gardening and clothing. She dressed in the latest fashions, threw frequent balls to show off these outfits, and was responsible for announcing the highly anticipated Color of the Year. The entire town of Swampshire looked to Arabella to tell them what they should like, and she welcomed this responsibility. She was as strict with people as she was with her garden; she seemed to be able to bully any plant into beauty.

Arabella also had a jealous streak and had on multiple occasions given Louisa a lousy tip on what the latest look would entail. This had led to Louisa's showing up in a gaudy quilted dress, something called "hand socks," and once, very shockingly, pants. Beatrice was infuriated on her sister's part, seeing right through Arabella's tricks, though Louisa never seemed to mind. She had actually enjoyed the pants. Therefore the two had somehow become good friends.

"Darling," Arabella said as she embraced Louisa. "You wore white. How *bold*."

"Louisa *is* bold. And beautiful. And, unlike you," Beatrice said under her breath, "*polite*."

"Did you say something, Beatrice?" Arabella said, raising her voice. "You should speak up if you have anything fruitful to add to the conversation. Or were you merely talking to yourself, as you are wont to do?"

"When battles of wits are scarce, sometimes one's best opponent is oneself," Beatrice said with a pained smile.

"I should like to witness *that* battle. It would be interesting to see a fight in which no one is armed," Arabella replied. "Though perhaps you *are* armed. . . . Your earrings look positively . . . dangerous." She screwed her face into an expression of barely disguised distaste.

Of course Arabella had immediately recognized Beatrice's dangling earrings as paste and not real gems. Embarrassed, Beatrice toyed with the jewelry in discomfort. She had thought they caught the light in a fetching manner but they now felt garish.

"Not everyone can afford precious stones, Arabella," she said, trying to sound lighthearted.

"True," Arabella said, "but you can't buy taste."

"I wish you two wouldn't bicker," Louisa said quietly, casting her eyes to the floor.

"It's all in good fun, even if your sister doesn't know how to have any." Arabella patted Louisa's shoulder, then tugged at her arm. "Now come, I must show you the dance list. I've created the perfect evening for the guest of honor. Can you believe Mr. Croaksworth has ten *thousand* a year?"

Before Beatrice could protest, Louisa and Arabella made their way across the ballroom arm in arm, heads bent together as they whispered and giggled. Louisa was instantly more relaxed, more talkative. A knot of confusion and frustration formed in Beatrice's stomach and tightened as she watched the two. She forced herself to look away and caught the eyes of Mr. Daniel Ashbrook. Beatrice was pleased to see him break into a smile at the sight of her. Tonight was the night to secure an engagement, and Daniel was her top suspect.

No, not suspect! Prospect, she chided herself.

Daniel was intelligent, kind, and by-the-book in his politeness. In fact, he had created his own literal book of advice tidbits, the contents of which he doled out when he deemed it necessary. The neighbors tolerated this because Daniel was so earnest, and because he was a descendant of Swampshire's forefather. Just like his great-great-great-great-great-grandfather Baron Fitzwilliam Ashbrook, Daniel seemed to truly want to help his community. He was also incredibly handsome. Advice sounded better when it came from the mouth of an Adonis: Daniel had pure blue eyes, golden hair, and a jawline to die for.

Daniel's and Beatrice's mothers had been close friends, so their children had grown up together. After Mrs. Ashbrook passed, the families continued their acquaintance, spending every Christmas together at Stabmort Park. Mrs. Steele was not the only one who thought the two might form an attachment; many others in Swampshire noted the kinship between them. But Beatrice had never swooned over Daniel, the way her mother insisted a lady would when in love. This might happen eventually, Beatrice thought, but she no longer had time to wait.

She smiled in a way she hoped looked enticing as Daniel strode across the room toward where Beatrice stood near her parents, who were making their own turn about the room. Mary trailed so closely behind Mr. and Mrs. Steele that she was nearly hidden.

"Are you well, Miss Steele?" Daniel said when he approached, looking concerned. "You have the most peculiar expression."

"I'm fine," Beatrice said, her smile falling.

"I am glad to hear it, for we have a lovely evening ahead of us," Daniel said. He gave a small bow to Mr. and Mrs. Steele. "Thank goodness you all arrived unscathed," Daniel continued, not noticing the huge bruise blooming on Mary's temple. He turned to Mr. Steele. "How is everything at Marsh Hall? I trust the chrysanthemums are in bloom?"

"Yes, you and Arabella must come and see them," Mr. Steele said excitedly.

"Your eagerness concerns me, sir," Daniel told him. "I hope I shall not find any false snakes in your garden."

"Of course not," Mr. Steele said, eyes flashing mischievously.

"We shall have your family for dinner Friday next," Mrs. Steele suggested. "It has been far too long since we hosted you."

"Preparations for this evening have kept us engaged, I'm afraid," Daniel said.

"I am glad you chose tonight for the ball, instead of the full moon," Mary said solemnly, using a stray piece of hail to ice her bruise.

"The music selections we have made are a bit difficult. You all must take care with the dance steps," Daniel said, not hearing Mary, as she now stood directly behind him. "*A misstep in a dance is a turned-ankle chance.*"

"When do you expect the guest of honor?" Mrs. Steele interrupted.

"I am not certain of his approximate arrival time—" Daniel began, but then Mr. Steele cut in.

"I hope he has a good sense of humor," he said. "I have been very disappointed by the lack of merriment displayed by most of the gentlemen in this town lately."

"The gentlemen here are perfectly merry," Mrs. Steele said, irritated.

"I don't know why they should be," Mary said. "Life is pain."

"Daniel. Could you escort me to the refreshments table?" Beatrice cut in, pulling Daniel aside. Her family, though she loved them, were wont to dominate a conversation—and she preferred to plant the seeds for an offer of marriage without their butting in.

"I have something for you," Daniel said once they were out of earshot of her family. He withdrew a small book from his jacket pocket and held it out to her.

"*Doors of the English Countryside,*" Beatrice said, reading the title.

"You mentioned last week at tea that Marsh House could use some redecorating," Daniel explained. "I recalled that this book has an informative section on paneling. It might prove useful."

"Thank you," Beatrice said, touched that he had remembered such a small detail. He did not know that she had been thinking of her turret at the time; she had amassed so many newspaper clippings that she needed to expand her storage space. Still, she was pleased. She flipped through the book, passing sections on windows, paint colors, and locks. Perhaps it *would* prove useful in learning how to add additional secret compartments, she thought. She looked up and smiled, and drew a small tome from her own pocket. "I brought a book for you as well."

Daniel took a pair of spectacles from his pocket, placed them on his nose, and read the title. "*The Tragedy of Mistress Lamarre.*"

"It's a gothic," Beatrice explained, "and I know you normally don't find them palatable, but this one is set in Italy. And since you have always wanted to visit there . . ."

Daniel closed the book and smiled at Beatrice over his spectacles. "I shall read it the moment the ball has ended," he said. "I am sure it will educate me on Italian society—and provide ample amusement as well."

Beatrice smiled back at him. She then swallowed, trying to determine how to ask the questions to which she wanted answers.

"You and Mr. Croaksworth . . . have not seen each other in a while," she said, attempting a tactful tone that would not seem too prying. "I was surprised that he imposed upon your hospitality by bringing a guest. What are your thoughts on this slight in etiquette?"

"I will admit that I was surprised when Edmund wrote to me after so many years," Daniel confessed, gaze flicking over to Drake, who stood in a corner observing everyone with an inscrutable expression. "I didn't expect to hear from him again after the way we ended things. But after his parents' death, he seems to have experienced an awakening. He told me he wished to reconnect with old friends and live a better life, which of course I commend. One should always try to improve oneself, both intellectually and emotionally; I was pleased to invite him to the ball this evening."

He looked off into the distance, his expression faraway. Beatrice wanted to press further about their seemingly complicated history but sensed it would be fruitless. After his mother's passing, Daniel had been prone to melancholy moments; he was liable to retreat deep into his own thoughts, and once there, he was unreachable. She was not likely to get further information from him—at least not now.

"Could I have some soup?" she said finally, after an awkward moment of silence. "My gullet is parched."

Daniel's distant expression cleared, and his gaze returned to Beatrice. "Of course," he said, and promptly doled out some soup and handed it to Beatrice. She gulped it so quickly that it scalded her throat.

"Planning to keep sustenance on your person so you can dance all night, are you?" Daniel said, raising an eyebrow. "I hope you'll save me a spin."

Before she could say, *Of course, you must have the first dance,* there was a crack of thunder. Everyone in the ballroom seemed to startle simultaneously.

"The storm is getting worse," Daniel observed. "We've done up the guest rooms, just in case. Most likely everyone will be able to get home—but *a man prepared*—"

"—*is a man who cares,*" Beatrice finished. "Your favorite adage, I daresay."

"Am I so predictable?" Daniel asked with a smile.

"Only because I know you." Beatrice grinned back.

"You do know me better than anyone, don't you, Beatrice?"

Daniel suddenly clasped Beatrice's hand. "With all the business of my reconnection with Edmund, I have not seen you much as of late. Perhaps . . . I might call on you this week? Once you read *Doors of the English Countryside* and I peruse this gothic, we shall have much to discuss."

Beatrice was momentarily speechless in surprise. Daniel had called on her family before, but he had just said he would call on *her*. He was a precise man, she knew—was his word choice an indication that he was ready to move their relationship forward?

"Of course," she said finally, and he gave her hand a squeeze.

True, she felt no flush in her face and no flutter of the heart. As a girl, that was always how she'd imagined romance. But Daniel was a proper match. He had a fortune, his home was close to her family's estate, and they got along perfectly well. Comfort and security were much more important, and more realistic, than flights of fancy.

And if she was honest with herself, she only felt flushed in that way when reading a particularly gripping murder case.

Daniel suddenly looked over Beatrice's shoulder, and she spun, thinking that the guest of honor had arrived.

Instead, she saw Martin Grub: the man who would inherit everything once her father passed. Or, indeed, the man who might inherit everything immediately should he win his petition to declare Mr. Steele unfit to manage his estate.

Grub seemed to have grown even more hair since she last saw him. It was sprouting from both his ears and his nostrils. He wore his usual drab suit, festooned with a bejeweled brooch that bore a family crest Beatrice was certain was not his own. He immediately set upon the far end of the refreshments table. She saw him slip several pieces of cheese into his pockets, as well as copius amounts of trifle. It was ridiculous that he should scavenge in this way, and that he should try to make a move on the Steele home; he had just come into yet another inheritance only a month ago. And everyone knew the Steele dwelling was respectable but modest—it was hardly an estate anyone would go to such lengths to secure. No doubt Grub would sell Marsh House and then keep the earnings from it locked away with the rest of his wealth. But no, she told herself firmly, Grub would not see another penny—at least not from them.

"Cousin," Mr. Martin Grub said as he approached Beatrice. Even from a distance, she could smell his wet, stale breath—its scent oddly similar to that of coins.

"Mr. Grub," she said, quickly taking a step backward.

"Good evening, Mr. Grub," Daniel said politely. He was ever the gentleman, even when faced with a disgusting specimen.

"Lovely to see you both." Mr. Grub grasped Beatrice's hand and planted a sticky kiss on her glove. His palms were thickly callused, scratching at the fabric, and his kiss left a wet print. She was grateful it wasn't on her skin. Beatrice averted her eyes from Grub but then caught sight of her mother watching from across the ballroom.

Mrs. Steele shot Beatrice a look that said clearly, *Be polite, Beatrice. He* is *an eligible bachelor.*

Beatrice shot back a look that said, *If I had to marry this man, it would be a short marriage, for I would die of disgust.*

Mrs. Steele raised her eyebrows as if to say, *Your life* will *be short if you don't get married.*

"And you, cousin," Beatrice finally said to Mr. Grub, swallowing her simmering agitation. "I trust you are well?"

"I am wonderful," Grub said in his monotone voice, snot going in and out of his nostril as he panted for breath. He suddenly sneezed, and spittle sprayed Beatrice in the face.

"My goodness," Daniel said, and immediately pressed a handkerchief into Beatrice's hand.

"I had thought to ask for the first dance," Grub continued as Beatrice, horrified, dabbed at her face.

"You want to dance with *me*?" she asked, incredulous.

"Not in this state. You should go clean yourself up," he sneered, indicating her dripping face.

For a moment, Beatrice imagined what it would feel like to slap him. Satisfying in the moment, she was sure, but with steep repercussions, which stayed her hand.

"You are right," Beatrice said through gritted teeth. "I must excuse myself."

She dropped a quick curtsy and then left Daniel and Mr. Grub by the tureen of white soup. As she was leaving, she passed by Inspector Drake.

He stood against the back wall of the ballroom, vivid next to faded gold wallpaper. He looked quite out of place amidst the dripping crystal and well-dressed guests, she thought; he clearly was uncomfortable with such forced formality. Even his rumpled suit seemed to resist it.

She could not think why no one else seemed interested in him; he was so tall and commanding that she herself could not seem to look away.

The tension within her boiled over, spilling onto Drake. "Why are you here?" she snapped.

"I was invited," he replied.

"And why are you staring at me?" Beatrice pressed.

"How would you know that I have been staring, unless *you* have also been staring?" he pointed out, the corners of his mouth curling into a smirk.

"I regret to inform you that your attempts to engage me shall not work," she said firmly. "I only care for dancing."

"Of course," Drake said with a small bow of his head. "That must be why you are glancing at everyone's shoes, because of *dancing*. Certainly not because you are wondering who tracked in the honeysuckle and mud."

"Precisely," Beatrice said. "Though the bloom *was* fresh, so one of the men here must have tracked it in this evening. Not that I noticed."

"A woman may have tracked it in," Drake pointed out.

"The footprint was in the shape of a man's boot," Beatrice replied.

"Ah," Drake said, raising an eyebrow, "but isn't that conjecture? A lady could, hypothetically, wear boots."

"In Swampshire, the acceptable footwear for ladies at a ball is a silk slipper," Beatrice said.

"Rather impractical," Drake said, glancing down at her feet. They were already slightly stained from her excursion into the muddy road; though she had attempted to wipe them off in the entryway, they were now brown instead of blue. "Think of how far you could go with a sturdy pair of boots."

"I don't need to go anywhere," Beatrice insisted, as much to herself as to Drake. "I belong right here."

As she pushed past him, she accidentally brushed her arm against his.

She was unnerved to find that the touch set her entire body aflame.

DOORS OF THE ENGLISH COUNTRYSIDE

Inscription

To Beatrice,

I hope this shall provide helpful inspiration in your re-decorating journey. What a thoughtful idea to breathe fresh life into Marsh House. I have always thought you have excellent taste.

There is no need to return it to me; the tome is yours to keep.

Fondly,

Daniel

PS: Do you recall when we played hide-and-seek that one rainy day at Stabmort? You tried to crawl into a cupboard and found yourself locked inside. Perhaps this book would have come in handy at that time, since there is a section on bolts and latches!

I still laugh today when I think of you back then, seven years old and triumphant, kicking straight through the cupboard to free yourself.

CHAPTER 5

Omens

The Ashbrooks' powder room was a thing of beauty, if marred by ugly family portraits. A painting of Great-Aunt Agnes Ashbrook hung on the back wall, her face so annoyed that it was almost as if she knew she was hanging in the privy.

In the room, there were also three large mirrors with pouf chairs, and a back room for the commode. Beatrice ducked inside to find one of the poufs occupied by Miss Helen Bolton.

"Good evening, Miss Bolton," she said, dropping into a curtsy.

Miss Bolton screamed in fright but broke off when she saw that it was only Beatrice.

"Thank heavens," she said breathlessly, "I thought you were a ghost."

"Not yet," Beatrice replied with a smile, taking a seat at a pouf next to the jumpy woman. "But if I fail to secure an engagement soon, my mother will likely send me to an early grave."

Miss Bolton had a nervous disposition, a high-pitched voice, and an upturned nose, making her strikingly similar to a little dog. She would not have minded the comparison; Miss Bolton adored animals and had filled her mansion with strays. She took in anything with a broken wing or paw, mended their injuries, and let them run free throughout her halls. Miss Bolton adored Beatrice, and Beatrice suspected this was because Miss Bolton viewed her as yet another stray. In a way, Beatrice thought, she was right.

Tonight, Miss Bolton wore a purple velvet dress, with a matching hat. The hat had a tall ostrich feather sprouting out of the top, which Beatrice suspected had been shed by one of Miss Bolton's four pet ostriches.

"What an interesting headpiece," Beatrice remarked, and Miss Bolton beamed.

"I assure you, this hat is necessary to survive a ball."

"I suppose it is an excellent conversation starter. Still, it's not as intriguing as your fish," Beatrice replied, recalling the woman's outfit at last month's ball. It had featured a fishbowl, which contained live specimens, balanced atop her head, and Miss Bolton was forced to walk at a snail's pace so as not to spill water onto the dance floor.

"So true, but I simply couldn't wear the fishbowl hat a second time. It would be gauche to attend a ball in an outfit I have already debuted," Miss Bolton said, offended.

In spite of this insistence, Beatrice knew that Miss Bolton was far from fashionable—but etiquette dictated that she must be invited to every ball. She was, after all, very wealthy. As the last living Bolton, she had inherited a fortune. Miss Bolton had enough in the bank to buy any house she wanted.

Miss Bolton smiled at Beatrice, but the expression did not reach her eyes. She still seemed uneasy, her small shoulders rigid.

"Are you about to jump out a window and make a run for it?" Beatrice teased. "I might join you."

"I shall do nothing of the sort," Miss Bolton said.

"And yet you sit at the very edge of your seat," Beatrice observed.

Miss Bolton blew out a breath, accidentally snuffing out several candles. "Must you notice *everything*, my dear?" she sighed.

"Yes," Beatrice replied with a smile. "Therefore you should simply tell me what is the matter and save me the trouble of discerning it myself."

She tried not to look at the portrait of Great-Aunt Agnes. In the now scant light, the woman's expression had gone from annoyed to malicious. It made Beatrice uneasy.

"Oh, very well. I arrived early this evening at precisely five forty-eight," Miss Bolton began, her voice halting.

"You arrived early to a party?" Beatrice asked, raising an eyebrow. Arriving early was not expressly forbidden but still considered tasteless.

"I wanted to ensure that I was here when Croaksworth came in, to get a good look at him before he was whisked away by all the young ladies," Miss Bolton explained.

"Don't tell me you stumbled upon something scandalous, or I shall be devastated that I did not also arrive early," Beatrice said with a smile.

"I'm sure it was nothing." Miss Bolton shook her head as if to chide herself for speaking at all. "Just a misunderstanding."

"Of course." Beatrice nodded. "If you don't want to tell me, you don't have to."

The phrase was the most ladylike way Beatrice could pry information from a person, and thankfully it worked.

"When I arrived at Stabmort Park, I thought I saw Arabella in a window—her hands covered in blood," Miss Bolton blurted. "I came inside at once, in a panic—but by the time she greeted me, the blood was gone."

"That is very strange," Beatrice whispered, heart pounding. "Naturally, you couldn't confront her about it, because you had only seen it due to the impropriety of arriving early."

"Exactly!" Miss Bolton cried. "But I just don't understand. Why would Arabella have blood on her hands?" She blinked up at Beatrice pleadingly.

Beatrice hesitated.

This was not the first time Miss Bolton had recounted a dramatic story. She frequently spoke of strange occurrences such as misplaced meat, phantom scratches at the door, chewed-up slippers, and a doglike creature that slept on her porch during certain moon phases. Beatrice was certain that all of these instances were due to the hordes of animals living in Miss Bolton's home. She loved the woman but also saw her as an example of what she might be if she could not let her darker habits go: all alone, knitting shawls for cats, prone to fanciful fits of imagination.

"It was likely just a cut from a thorn," Beatrice answered soothingly. "The ballroom is filled with rose bouquets; no doubt she pierced herself by accident." She knew the words must be true as she spoke them but could not help feeling disappointed. She would have liked to believe Arabella was up to something strange. "We should forget it and talk of happier things," Beatrice went on, as much to herself as to Miss Bolton. "Are you working on any new plays?"

Miss Bolton lit up. She adored theater and considered herself an amateur playwright—though Beatrice was the only person who would attend her performances, as the rest of Swampshire misplaced their invitations in the fireplace. Beatrice knew too well the loneliness of forbidden passion and therefore could not abide the thought of Miss Bolton's acting out scenes with only cats as her audience. The woman must have at least one patron.

"I have been writing an important piece on the decline of bourdaloues," Miss Bolton said. "No one ever speaks of it."

"An oversight we must remedy," Beatrice said, not particularly looking forward to this performance but pleased to see that Miss Bolton was relaxing.

"Today's toiletries are far too advanced," Miss Bolton continued. "For example, take in this scent." She picked up a bottle of perfume from a cluster of glass bottles lining a shelf and spritzed it in the air. Beatrice wrinkled her nose.

"There is such a thing as too much gardenia," Miss Bolton said, "though Arabella would disagree."

As Miss Bolton set the perfume bottle back on the shelf, Beatrice caught a flicker of movement in the mirror. She turned to face the dominating portrait of Agnes Ashbrook.

"Her eyes," she whispered. "I thought they moved."

She stared into Great-Aunt Agnes's squinting gaze, like glinting sapphires encased in folds of sagging skin. She had no wrinkles from smiling; the careful strokes of paint captured only hard frown lines etched into her stern face.

"Don't tell me you're seeing things now, too," Miss Bolton said nervously. "Hysteria normally does not set in until one's fortieth year—"

But she left her thought unfinished, for the portrait had moved again. This time, Beatrice could see that it was not just Agnes's eyes moving—the entire portrait was coming untethered from the wall.

"It's going to fall," Beatrice gasped, and moved forward to catch the heavy gold frame. She was too late: The huge portrait slipped from its mountings and fell to the floor with a crash. The frame cracked, sending a slash through the canvas and distorting Agnes's stern face.

Beatrice pushed Miss Bolton back just in time, saving her from shards of gilded wood.

"Are you all right?" Beatrice said, examining Miss Bolton for any injuries. The tiny woman was unscathed, though shaken.

"She must have been poorly affixed to the wall," Miss Bolton said breathlessly, staring up at where the portrait had fallen from its mountings. The floral paper was now peeled back to reveal a mottled brown stain.

Beatrice stepped forward to examine it, running her hands along the decaying wall.

"Perhaps the damage is from the moisture in this room . . . or improper installation of wallpaper," she theorized.

"People say this house is haunted," Miss Bolton whispered.

Beatrice could not deny that there was something about a foreboding house on a stormy night that made one inclined to consider the supernatural. But she could not get caught up in another one of Miss Bolton's tall tales. No one in town took her fears seriously; Beatrice would do well to ignore them, too.

A crack of thunder sounded somewhere far off, and they both jumped, then laughed.

"The only thing we should fear is the weather," Beatrice said lightly.

"I am afraid we might be stuck here if the hail worsens," Miss Bolton said, wide-eyed. "Thank goodness my kittens have one another for comfort. And the shawls I knitted for them."

The powder room door suddenly swung open. In the reflection of the many mirrors, Beatrice cringed as she watched Miss Caroline Wynn step into the room.

"Miss Wynn! What a pleasure!" Miss Bolton said, rushing over to embrace the young lady in excitement. "Beatrice, it is your best friend, Caroline Wynn!"

Beatrice tried to smile, but she could tell without even glancing at her reflection that it looked more like a grimace. Everyone in Swampshire believed women of the same age were destined to be soul companions (as Daniel always said, "*Two ladies of the same age shall surely be on the same page*"). Though Louisa and Arabella had followed that convention, Beatrice had never found much common ground with Caroline Wynn.

Caroline had arrived in Swampshire just two years ago, after her great-grandfather Jonathan Wynn's tragic death. No one knew Mr. Wynn *had* a great-granddaughter, so everyone was surprised and overjoyed to find that she was an orphan of great talent and beauty. Before long she was widely known as the most attractive woman in Swampshire—superseding both Louisa and Arabella—and was the guest of honor at any ball, dinner, or squelch hole rescue mission. Everyone sent her gifts and helped her fix up Mr. Wynn's old mansion until it shone—free of charge, of course. One must always help out a beautiful, well-bred orphan.

Many men in Swampshire vied for her hand. Initially, it seemed Philip Peña was her favorite. Some even speculated that he was about to almost think about considering making her an offer of marriage. But of course, this ended in heartbreak—he was poor and of no social standing, and Caroline was a fine lady. Everyone agreed that they were simply not suited for each other. Everyone except Philip Peña, who left town, inconsolable, and enlisted in the navy.

Caroline was not only the most beautiful lady in Swampshire, she was also the most accomplished. She was excellent at drawing, played the harp and pianoforte, took regular walks to maintain a rosy complexion, spoke French and Italian, read sermons daily, wrote poetic letters, cultivated an understanding of basic botany, danced gracefully, nursed injured baby birds back to health, made scones that were never dry, visited the poor and brought them said moist scones, did excellent needlework, and could juggle without ever dropping a ball. Accordingly, Caroline was considered a pinnacle of feminine beauty and grace. Beatrice, however, simply could not see what all the fuss was about. She thought scones tasted better dry.

"Miss Bolton and Miss Steele!" Caroline beamed, flashing rows of sparkling white teeth. She returned Miss Bolton's embrace and then dropped into an elegant curtsy to Beatrice. "I thought I heard your melodious voices."

"They could never be as gorgeous as yours!" Miss Bolton said with delight. Beatrice struggled to control her expression. Caroline never showed up to any of Miss Bolton's plays, but that never upset Miss Bolton because "the young woman was probably busy with so many other wonderful and more interesting things." Apparently Beatrice was not thought to have the same eventful social calendar.

Caroline turned to embrace Beatrice—who patted Caroline's back awkwardly—and then the young lady took a seat on a pouf. She looked annoyingly beautiful this evening; she had not a hair out of place and wore an ornate emerald choker that caught the light and glittered. The gems sparked a pang of jealousy in the pit of Beatrice's stomach; she herself could only afford a ribbon around her neck as jewelry. And, of course, her hideous fake earrings. It seemed unjust that Caroline should have both riches *and* everyone's goodwill.

"Pardon me if I interrupted," Caroline said to Beatrice and Miss Bolton, "but I needed a moment of respite. Captain Peña is here."

Miss Bolton gasped. "No! But you two were once nearly almost talking about potentially . . ."

"Becoming engaged," Caroline whispered. "Yes. It is a pain to see him now, after we parted on such bitter terms one year ago, when he left for the navy."

"You poor thing," Miss Bolton said, shaking her head in sympathy. "But you were only doing what was right. An heiress like yourself needs a man from a similar station."

"And what a challenge it must be to find a man who can live up to your perfection," Beatrice said, raising an eyebrow.

"Indeed," Caroline said earnestly.

"You two will want to catch up, I know," Miss Bolton said, moving toward the door. "You don't want the likes of me, such an old and decrepit woman, infringing on time between close bosom friends." She shuffled out of the room.

"We're not actually . . ." Beatrice began, but her words trailed off. Awkward silence mixed with the overpowering gardenia perfume still hanging in the air.

"I am so glad to have you here tonight," Caroline said suddenly, grasping Beatrice's hand. "As a woman who is the same age as me—well, a bit older, actually—I'm sure you understand the complicated feelings I harbor regarding the captain."

"Not *exactly*," Beatrice said, her hand feeling limp in Caroline's. "You recall that I have no beau."

"But surely there is *some special man* you wish to discuss," Caroline said, eyes wide. "This is what close lady friends talk about in confidence."

"I'm sorry to disappoint you, but there is no one. I so *wish* I could be a better close friend to you." Beatrice tried to muster her most apologetic-looking face. The last thing she wanted to do was discuss her love life—or lack thereof—with Caroline Wynn.

"*I* could never disappoint anyone," Caroline said earnestly. "Though of course it is challenging. From the moment I walked in tonight, I felt that everyone expected me to perform."

Beatrice was surprised at this sudden honesty. "That *is* a burden I can understand," she said. Had she misjudged Caroline? She felt a stab of guilt; it seemed that they *did* have something over which to connect. "It is difficult to live up to expectations—to pretend to be someone you are not," she continued, leaning forward slightly.

"What?" Caroline asked, scrunching up her nose. "I meant that everyone was disappointed to see hired musicians. I know they all prefer when *I* perform on the harp and pianoforte."

"Ah, yes," Beatrice said, face burning in disappointment and embarrassment. She leaned back once more. "What sorrow that we have been deprived of your beautiful compositions."

"You must not be too upset," Caroline said, and, to Beatrice's horror, pulled her into another hug. Caroline smelled sweet, her perfume so subtle that Beatrice was sure it must be more expensive than anything the Steeles owned. Beatrice sniffed, and Caroline gave her a squeeze.

"Do you like my signature scent? It is called Evening Rose," she whispered into Beatrice's ear. "It was made especially for me by our local *parfumier;* he said he was inspired by my elegance. He would not even permit me to pay for it. Can you believe such kindness?"

Beatrice pulled away before Caroline could inhale her own scent of dust and ink.

"I cannot believe it, truly," Beatrice said. "Now . . . we should get back, before anyone becomes too distraught by your absence."

"Good thinking," Caroline said with a nod. She looped her arm through the crook of Beatrice's elbow, and Beatrice begrudgingly allowed herself to be led into the hallway. She felt a welcome rush of cool air upon exiting the stuffy powder room.

As she followed Caroline back toward the ballroom, Beatrice could still feel the gaze of Great-Aunt Agnes boring into her. It seemed like a strange omen—of what, she did not yet know.

JOURNAL OF MARY STEELE

[Excerpt]

Beatrice has withdrawn yet again to the turret. Mother claims she shows all the signs of lovesickness. I hope it is this, and not a sickness much worse. Love can be cured by either marriage or rejection. But some illnesses can never be shaken.

In any case, it is inconvenient that she has disappeared so much of late, as it puts far too much attention on me. This morning Mother noticed that my hair has grown several inches since last week. She never used to notice such things— and I prefer it that way.

Louisa is not herself lately, either. I thought I heard her open her bedroom door late last night. This morning I asked her where she went, but she said nothing.

Then again, perhaps she did not hear me. No one ever does.

CHAPTER 6

Gossip

Beatrice and Caroline entered the ballroom to see a quartet of musicians in a corner. They looked spirited and lively as they tuned their instruments. The dancing had not yet begun; the guests were clustered at the edges of the empty dance floor, whispering to one another.* The echo of strings being tuned mingled with anxious conversation. It seemed everyone was suspended in time as they waited for the guest of honor. Miss Bolton passed by Beatrice and Caroline, hurrying toward the musicians.

"They got the Bartholomew Babies," she said breathlessly. "I wonder if the cellist remembers when I threw my shawl to him back in 1768."

"I hope they'll be properly tuned. I adore music, but my ear is so sensitive to pitch," Caroline told Beatrice. "Even one note off-key causes me great distress."

---

* Except for Mary, who had snuck down to the kitchens for a snack of meat.

"You suffer so much," Beatrice said dryly. "Life must be a constant trial."

"It is," Caroline replied, "but friends like you help me soldier on."

Beatrice felt a small stab of guilt. Caroline was tiresome, yes, but she had been nothing but kind to her. Was Beatrice being unnecessarily uncharitable?

She caught sight of Louisa and Arabella huddled on the landing of a staircase overlooking the ballroom, anxiously watching the door. Beatrice had to admit to herself that another companion might not be the worst thing.

"Caroline," she began awkwardly, feeling suddenly vulnerable, "perhaps you might join me for a drink before the first dance begins? We could toast to . . . our friendship."

"How sweet," Caroline said, smiling, "but I never drink. It's too much for my delicate constitution. But you are so sturdy; you should enjoy some punch! If you'll excuse me, I have not yet given my regards to everyone in this room. We can reconvene later."

"Or not," Beatrice muttered as Caroline glided away to make her rounds. She watched as Caroline greeted several guests, until the young woman froze in front of a tall, uniformed man.

"Captain Philip Peña," Beatrice murmured to herself. "He *is* back."

Philip Peña had left Swampshire a year ago to join the navy, inspired by his older brother, a Venezuelan soldier who was raising funds for the revolution. Peña had always been a tall man, but he now had broad shoulders, a full beard, and a more serious glint in his dark eyes. At the hip of his uniform was a gleaming scabbard for his cutlass. No wonder Caroline was so on edge this evening, Beatrice thought. Captain Peña looked undeniably impressive. Perhaps Caroline regretted her prior rejection.

"Evidently, he made quite a fortune in the navy," a smooth voice said, which Beatrice instantly knew belonged to Mr. François Fàn—known around town as Frank.

"You'd be overboard at the first vision of a siren," Beatrice said, whipping around so fast that she nearly tripped, and Frank put a gloved hand on the small of her back to steady her.

"Miss Steele, I seem to have made you weak at the knees." He gave her a little bow and a grin. He was dashing and good-looking, with dark eyes, unkempt hair, and a dimpled chin, but Beatrice knew better than to become bamboozled by his charms. Too many young women were taken in only to have their hearts broken; Frank was a notorious rake.

"Hardly," she replied, rolling her eyes. "Rather, I was surprised to see you here—rumor had it that you'd been in Paris so long you'd sprouted gills."

As was customary in Swampshire, Beatrice did not approve of France, which was where Frank's parents resided. His mother, Élodie, was descended from French nobility, and his father, Cheng Fàn, was a painter from China who had emigrated to France as a young man. Cheng had taken an assignment to paint Élodie and fell in love. The two of them had married and moved to Swampshire to raise a family.

The Fàns remained in Swampshire until Frank was of age, and then the homesick Élodie insisted that they return to her true homeland. Frank chose to remain and oversee their estate. However, he often visited their French château, always returning tan and smelling of cheese.

"I wouldn't miss this ball for anything." Frank leaned scandalously close to Beatrice, and she caught a whiff of his cologne. He always used a bit too much, though she had to admit that it had a pleasant, spicy smell that overpowered the Camembert. "Did you miss me?" he whispered with a wink. "*I* was perfectly sick without *you*."

"I'm sure there's a tonic for that," Beatrice told him.

"You must have at least longed for my visits to Marsh House," Frank said, raking a hand through his thick hair. A lock fell in front of one of his dark eyes, and he tilted his head. Beatrice had the impression that he knew exactly how roguish it made him appear. She might have been seeking a beau this evening, but she knew not to look to Frank for anything real. Men like him used words like "forever" when they actually meant "until sunrise."

"I regret to inform you that gentlemen are lining up to read their poems and songs to us," Beatrice said, crossing her arms. "We had no time to miss you."

"But do they recite their declarations of love with as amorous a voice as mine?" Frank put a hand to his throat. Beatrice's eyes fell on his gloved fingers.

Frank normally eschewed the formality of gloves—most likely so he could caress ladies' palms with his bare fingers. But she spotted a small bulge on his covered pinkie finger. *A ring?* she wondered. Judging from the size, it was small, with an orblike shape. Perfect for a lady.

"Mr. Fàn," Beatrice said, meeting his sparkling, dark eyes, "do I see a *ring* on your finger?" She stepped forward, and Frank took a sudden step back. His flirtatious demeanor faltered; he seemed taken aback by her observation.

"Of course not," he said, forcing a crooked grin.

"Did you travel to France to obtain a family heirloom?" Beatrice pressed. "And if so . . . does this mean Swampshire's most infamous bachelor means to settle down?"

"Only if you are willing," Frank said. He grabbed Beatrice's hand and twirled her in a circle, and then dipped her low.

"That shall be difficult," Beatrice said, staring up at him upside-down, "for I have heard you are already promised to a dozen others."

Frank righted her. "I would give them all up for you, Miss Steele."

"I'm sure," Beatrice said, raising an eyebrow, "but what are *you* in comparison to the mysterious Mr. Croaksworth?"

"Louisa must be excited. Your mother, no doubt, hopes for an attachment," Frank said, looking irritated. Perhaps Swampshire's most notorious ladies' man did not like the idea of someone usurping his title, Beatrice thought.

"I'm sure my mother would *never* speak of marriage," she said dryly. "She hardly thinks of it, except on days ending with 'y.'"

Frank chuckled, but Beatrice saw that the laughter did not reach his eyes.

"I understand why you wouldn't be eager for the competition," she began, "but what's *really* wrong, Frank?"

Though she disapproved of his debauched attitude, she knew the man had a good heart. Indeed, whenever he went foxhunting with the rest of the gentlemen in town, he would secretly smuggle the fox to Miss Bolton's house for her to keep as a pet.

"Nothing," Frank said, "except that your neckline is far too high. Why keep such a bosom hidden?" But he did not gaze down at her décolletage, his eyes wandered off into the distance across the ballroom.

"You don't have to tell me if you don't want to," Beatrice tried again, and Frank sighed.

"Fine. I cannot help but remember how the Croaksworths thought the Ashbrooks beneath them. It's why Edmund and Daniel haven't seen each other for so long. I was not far behind the two of them at school; I remember their schism."

Beatrice made a noise of irritation. Why must the stupid intricacies of the social hierarchy get in the way of everything?

"I know, it's ridiculous. The Ashbrooks are very well-bred," Frank said, misinterpreting Beatrice's disdain.

"True," she allowed, "they are this town's Coventrys."

"Who?"

Beatrice felt her cheeks burn. The wealthy and connected Coventry family had been axed to death in one of Sir Huxley's cases.

"Just . . . people I read about in the social column," she said, covering. "Very well-bred. Like the Ashbrooks."

"Or me," Frank said, snaking his hand around Beatrice's waist.

"Don't be ridiculous, Frank. You are incredibly disreputable," Beatrice shot back.

Frank smiled, and Beatrice could see the tension in his shoulders easing. Beatrice was not one to fall for flattery, therefore he could relax around her.

"In any case," Frank continued, unable to stop the momentum of gossip, "the Croaksworths thought very well of their 'good breeding.' But now they're dead, and Edmund can do what he wishes."

"This all explains why Daniel did not ever mention Mr. Croaksworth to me," Beatrice surmised. "No doubt he was embarrassed to be deemed socially inferior. Though I admit, I don't see why that should carry so much weight in matters of true friendship."

"Most do not share this indulgent opinion, Beatrice," Frank said, looking at her with a strange expression.

"Mr. Croaksworth is different from his parents," Beatrice said firmly. "If he has chosen to resume his friendship with Daniel, he must not agree with their views. And I'm sure one look at Louisa will make him care nothing for wealth and rank." She saw Daniel making the rounds, shaking his guests' hands, and felt a sudden rush of kinship. "Daniel is kind to invite Mr. Croaksworth to Swampshire, despite the Croaksworths' previous indiscretions."

"I heard the Ashbrooks didn't actually extend the invitation," Frank said, his hand still on Beatrice's back. She caught another whiff of his spicy cologne. "Edmund invited himself. But Daniel accommodated Edmund and even made him the guest of honor."

Beatrice's appreciation deepened. Daniel always knew the right thing to do. He hadn't even mentioned the slight to her, and instead had protected his guest from any judgment. But alongside her appreciation, she felt a strange pang of jealousy. If *she* had invited herself to a ball, she would have sparked outrage, yet Mr. Croaksworth was welcomed with open arms.

She broke from her reverie as she saw Mr. Hugh Ashbrook approaching them. Frank must have noticed as well, for he took a step away from Beatrice and said in a falsely jovial voice, "The Ashbrooks do throw such wonderful celebrations. And Mr. Ashbrook himself is such a pinnacle of manliness. Oh, Mr. Ashbrook! I did not even see you there."

"I am delighted to hear you are enjoying yourself, Mr. Fàn," Hugh Ashbrook cut in, extending a hand and pumping Frank's up and down. He then took a handkerchief from his pocket and wiped off his palm. No one took offense, however; it was the older man's habit.

Mr. Hugh Ashbrook considered his health to be of the utmost importance, rising early each morning to administer a variety of concoctions and lotions thought to fortify his figure. He also abstained from smoking cigars, mixed seltzer with his wine to give it a "healthy pep," ate nine small meals a day, refrained from travel, and took long walks each morning to visit his fortune-teller, Madam Jessica. Other than a few flecks of gray in his thick, golden hair—which he concealed with yet another tonic—he looked almost just as he had in his youth. This was felicitous, as Mr. Ashbrook was vain: He was the reason so many ancestral portraits obscured Stabmort Park's floral wallpaper. They were meant to remind everyone of his good breeding. He also commissioned a portrait of himself every six months, to show he was maintaining a good constitution. These adorned the walls of the mansion's ballroom, so dozens of Hughs in various poses stared down at the guests.

"Always glad to see you, Mr. Ashbrook, sir," Frank said. "You look even younger than usual." Beatrice tried not to roll her eyes at the young man's obvious flattery. But it worked: Mr. Ashbrook beamed.

"I agree!" Mr. Ashbrook said, and then turned to Beatrice. "Good evening, Miss Steele. You are the ninth-loveliest woman at this ball."

"Thank you," Beatrice said with a curtsy, "though I think there are fewer than nine women in attendance."

"Is that right?" Mr. Ashbrook said, but did not correct his assessment. He had harbored a grudge toward Beatrice ever since she'd informed him that his Afternoon Tea Potion was just hot water. She knew she shouldn't have mentioned it, but sometimes these things simply slipped out.

"I hadn't even *noticed* other women in attendance apart from you, Beatrice," Frank said smoothly. He turned to Mr. Ashbrook and tipped his head gallantly. "Except, of course, your beautiful daughter. Arabella is stunning; no doubt she inherited her looks from you."

"She did," Mr. Ashbrook said haughtily.

"We are so happy you chose to throw this get-together," Beatrice said, hoping she sounded gracious. It would not do to stay on Hugh Ashbrook's bad side. After all, he might one day be her father-in-law. "My sister is thrilled," she added.

"Ah, dear Louisa was such a help with planning," Mr. Ashbrook said, brightening. He had always, at least, shown a fondness for the middle Steele daughter. "Such a lovely girl. Her assistance was appreciated; I'm afraid I was incapacitated in the lead-up to tonight." He dabbed at his forehead with his handkerchief. "I had a touch of the fainties."

"The fainties?" Frank repeated, confused.

"A terrible illness," Mr. Ashbrook explained mournfully. "You always feel as if you're going to faint."

"And *do* you faint?" Beatrice asked.

"No. But it's awful to think that one might." Mr. Ashbrook

sighed. He suddenly swayed, his eyes rolling backward, and Frank put out a hand to steady him. Beatrice fanned him with one of her gloves, and his eyes fluttered open. "I'm fine, truly," he said, his voice hoarse. "I just shouldn't be exerting myself so much. My mystic, Madam Jessica, warned me that any strain could be detrimental. Thankfully, she was able to sell me a daily miracle tonic that won't *cure* me but will at least help. Cost a fortune and has to be taken at a very precise time each day, but it's worth it—one's health must come first." He glared at Beatrice as if daring her to inquire about the composition of the tonic.

"It must," she said after an awkward pause. Mr. Ashbrook still looked irritated, and she felt a pang of anxiety. Daniel would never make an offer of marriage to someone his father disliked. She must make more of an effort. "Your home looks so elegant this evening," she said sincerely, gesturing to the illustrious ballroom. "Daniel lent me a book on decoration; if Marsh House can resemble Stabmort Park even marginally, I shall be pleased."

"What book was this?" Mr. Ashbrook asked, brow furrowing.

"*Doors of the English Countryside,*" Beatrice replied, and withdrew the book from her pocket to show Mr. Ashbrook. She was pleased that he seemed diverted by this topic; if she could discuss books with him, perhaps they might have at least one overlapping interest.

"Architecture does not seem like something that would be fascinating to a lady, Miss Steele," Mr. Ashbrook said. "The inner workings of construction and composition are not topics for a tender mind." Before she could protest, he lifted the book from her hands. "I shall return this to its proper place." He nodded at Beatrice and then Frank. "If you'll excuse me, I must oversee the final touches of the dining room," he continued. "The air seemed musty, and I shudder to think what that would do to my lungs."

"I hate to add a task," Beatrice cut in, trying to move past her frustration at having a book plucked from her grasp so abruptly. "But I must report that the portrait of Great-Aunt Agnes has fallen from the wall in the powder room."

"Oh dear," Mr. Ashbrook said. "I shall inform Daniel. He's always trying to fix that."

He darted away, and Frank turned back to Beatrice.

"I see you and Mr. Ashbrook are as close as ever," he said, stifling a smirk.

Beatrice sipped her punch through pursed lips. She missed those years before her coming out into society, when Stabmort Park was a world of curiosities to be explored. A world before her every move was scrutinized. Now she felt as if it were a prison— and the ballroom her cell.

"I'd be careful if I were you," Frank said lightly. "There is something strange in the air tonight."

"The mustiness," Beatrice teased, but privately she agreed with Frank: Tonight *did* feel different.

An engagement had always seemed a strange hypothetical that would occur . . . eventually. But now, with Edmund Croaksworth on his way, not to mention Grub's advancement on their estate, everything felt so much more *real*. Though, she thought, the appearance of Inspector Vivek Drake seemed like a vestige of her secret taunting her. Why, on the evening she meant to finally take on the role expected of her, had he appeared?

Suddenly, the string musicians broke off playing. The candles seemed to flicker, and the din of distant conversation dimmed. Everyone's heads snapped to the front of the room as two footmen rushed to open the heavy ballroom doors. They pried them open and in came . . .

A flurry of hail pellets.

But after the hail strode . . .

Mr. Edmund Croaksworth.

My darling,

I know writing directly is inappropriate, as we are not officially attached, but we both know our true feelings so I trust you shall forgive me. I had to send you this note, for each time I catch a glimpse of your face, I am astounded yet again by your unparalleled beauty.

To what could I even compare your looks? The roses are jealous of your lips, the songbirds of your dulcet voice, flowers (you know which ones) of your particular eye color. Please say you shall save me a dance when we are reunited at the ball.

You are the only woman who can truly captivate me. I specifically love everything that makes you, you.

Yours,

Frank

—Note from Frank Fàn, copies of which were sent to: Beatrice Steele, Louisa Steele, Arabella Ashbrook, Helen Bolton, Caroline Wynn, and several French women (exact number unknown)

CHAPTER 7

Dancing

"What weather you have here in Swampshire," Mr. Croaksworth said as he shook ice from the ends of his glossy hair. "I nearly didn't make it because of the hail. And also because I made fifteen wrong turns. Terrible sense of direction—a family trait—but I pressed on. I wouldn't miss this for the world."

He wore a silk top hat, well-made and clearly expensive, which he swept off to reveal a carefully combed swoop of chestnut hair. His eyes were green, his teeth white, and his haunches firm. Even his shoes were still polished, despite the now outrageous weather outside, and each step he took was self-assured and comfortable. From the whispers around the ballroom and the admiring looks, Beatrice could tell that everyone felt he was just the sort of thing a gentleman should be: agreeable.

Mr. Edmund Croaksworth was handsome, there was no arguing with that—yet Beatrice could not help fixating on his shoes. How had they maintained such a shine after enduring a trek from his carriage through the mud? He must have stopped to polish them, more concerned about appearing pristine than arriving on time. This vanity made her wary.

"Glad you could make it despite the unfavorable weather," Daniel said. "I have an excellent book about how cloud patterns predict potential storms. I could lend it to you, should you take interest in this for future travels."

"I'm not much of a reader, as you may remember," Mr. Croaksworth said with another laugh, "but not even hail the size of plums could have kept me away. It's been far too long." He put out his hand and grasped Daniel's, pumping it up and down with vigor.

As she pushed her way to the front of the crowd clustered before Mr. Croaksworth and the Ashbrooks, Beatrice noticed a shadow cross Daniel's face—no doubt as he considered the reason for the long separation. But all was well now, she surmised as the men fell into amiable chatter. If Mr. Croaksworth's parents had once disapproved of the Ashbrooks and thought them socially inferior, Mr. Croaksworth clearly did not share this feeling. He appeared perfectly pleasant.

"I prefer sunshine to hail," Mr. Croaksworth said, "though when one is inside, it does not matter so much."

Beatrice leaned closer, hoping to hear Mr. Croaksworth mention his preferred pastimes or some other snippet that might reveal his character.

"I like rain *sometimes*," he continued, "but only if the plants have become too dry."

The guests seemed to hang on Mr. Croaksworth's every word, enraptured.

"He's right," Miss Bolton said, nodding. "Sun *is* the best weather."

"So aptly put," Mrs. Steele agreed.

"Snow is better than hail, though I only like to see it at Christmas," Mr. Croaksworth continued, and Beatrice glanced across the ballroom, watching as the heads bobbed in agreement.

She raised her eyebrows, incredulous. Did the man speak of anything besides the weather?

"He is a sparkling conversationalist," a voice said quietly.

Beatrice turned to see Inspector Drake just behind her, an amused look on his face.

"That's not very kind. He has just arrived," she said, trying to keep her expression neutral.

"Wait until you hear his take on types of grass."

"I do hope he considers green the best kind," Beatrice replied, the corners of her mouth twitching. "If not, he might incite a riot."

Drake broke into a grin, and Beatrice felt a strange pang of— something. She was not quite sure. But before she could say anything more, a sudden *bang* reverberated through the ballroom. A hush fell over the guests.

"What was that?" Miss Bolton whispered in fear.

"Everything is fine," Daniel said, but he glanced out the tall windows nervously. "Just a bit of thunder."

"Thunder! My fourth-favorite form of weather," Mr. Croaksworth said jovially.

The sky was pitch-black now, and bolts of lightning flashed in the distance, like white cracks in dark porcelain. Swampshire was no stranger to storms, but this one was shaping up to be the worst Beatrice had seen in ages. They were fortunate they had made it to Stabmort Park safely, she thought—leaving would be quite another story.

"Beatrice, come here," Mrs. Steele hissed. She utilized the moment of distraction to her advantage and positioned Louisa and Beatrice directly in front of Mr. Croaksworth. "Daniel, aren't you going to introduce us?" she asked pointedly.

"Of course," Daniel said with a polite bow. "Mr. Edmund

Croaksworth, please meet our dear friends Mr. Steele, Mrs. Steele, and their two daughters, Beatrice and Louisa."*

Mr. Croaksworth nodded politely at Beatrice and then turned to Louisa.

He froze, transfixed, as she dropped into a curtsy and fluttered her eyelashes. "It's a pleasure," she said sweetly. "In case you were wondering, I also love a warm day. My sister Beatrice and I often picnic in our garden when the sun is shining, to enjoy a perfect afternoon breeze. Beatrice makes wonderful scones for the occasion; just dry enough to pair perfectly with a cup of tea. One feels as if the possibilities of one's life are endless in moments like these—don't you agree?"

She looked over at Beatrice, but Mr. Croaksworth did not trace her gaze; he merely nodded, clearly already enchanted with Louisa. Beatrice had seen it happen many a time: A man met her sister, and it was as if everyone else in the room disappeared. Who could blame them? Louisa was so gracious, so kind—anyone she met was sure to be charmed.

Louisa, on the other hand, seemed overly aware that everyone was watching her. She self-consciously pulled her shoulders back, though her posture had already been perfect, and folded her palms in front of her. Beatrice noticed her sister's hands shaking, ever so slightly.

"I prefer hail," Beatrice said in a loud voice, and everyone turned to look at her instead. From the corner of her eye, Beatrice could see Louisa relax as the focus shifted.

"I suppose it's good that you live here, then," Mr. Croaksworth said earnestly. "It seems this kind of weather occurs often."

"It does. But that shouldn't deter you from enjoying our town,

---

* Mary had returned from the kitchens, but she remained unnoticed; she was wearing a gown in the exact same shade as the marble pillars of the ballroom, and thus blended in completely.

as we have much more to offer than hail," Beatrice assured him. "London could not hold a candle to Swampshire. Or so I'm told. I have never been."

"The Steeles are Swampshire natives as well," Daniel told Mr. Croaksworth.

"Of course," Mr. Croaksworth said with dawning recognition. "Beatrice Steele. How could I forget? Daniel spoke of you often at school—the girl who once read a thousand-page novel in one sitting!"

Beatrice flushed, pleased. "An exaggeration."

"She is being modest," Daniel said with a smile.

"Indeed. It was two sittings," Beatrice replied. She could practically feel her mother tensing up beside her, so she rushed to add, "Of course, when selecting my reading material, I stick to the stories suitable for ladies."

"How lovely. What are your favorites?" Mr. Croaksworth asked, and Beatrice cleared her throat.

"Oh, I adore . . . anything about women moving from one drawing room to another," she began. "And, er, friendships between . . . ponies and horses . . ." She trailed off, but Mr. Croaksworth nodded vigorously.

"That's good to hear," he said. "I was worried you might be one of those women that passes around all sorts of frightful reading material. Gothics, ghost stories, titillating tales . . . One must be careful, lest one's mind become corrupted."

"Beatrice's mind is completely uncorrupted," Louisa said earnestly. "She has just the sort of intelligence men adore."

"Louisa is right," Beatrice said, matching Louisa's earnest tone. "I have received many love notes about my wit. Though they are often disguised as strongly worded letters which request I hold my tongue."

"That is terrible someone would write such a letter to you," Mr. Croaksworth said, suddenly gravely serious.

"I jest, sir," Beatrice assured him. "The Steele sister who inspires love notes is not me but Louisa. She would never tease you so."

"I hope not," Mr. Croaksworth said, looking back at Louisa with a smile. "I fear I could not bear to be teased by *you*, Louisa."

Louisa seemed at a loss for words, looking from Mr. Croaksworth to Beatrice, and Beatrice jumped in again to assist her demure sister.

"Louisa is an excellent sportswoman, Mr. Croaksworth. Do you enjoy games?"

"Oh yes, all sorts." Mr. Croaksworth smiled.

"Any one sport in particular?" Beatrice pressed, raising her voice above the appreciative murmurs of the other guests rippling around the room.

"Whichever one everyone else enjoys," Mr. Croaksworth said with a shrug.

"Such a pleasant man," Mrs. Steele said appreciatively.

Was "pleasant" the word for him, Beatrice wondered, or was "dull" a better fit? She looked to Louisa, but her sister had a blithe expression across her youthful face.

"Ah, where are my manners?" Mr. Croaksworth said suddenly, and beckoned to Inspector Drake. "Please, allow me to introduce you all to my travel companion, Mr. Vivek Drake."

Beatrice held her breath, waiting to see a flash of recognition from anyone else in the room, but they all simply turned and watched as Inspector Drake—or *Mr.* Drake, as Croaksworth had called him—approached the circle. It took an awkwardly long time for him to arrive. He seemed in no hurry to socialize.

"Mr. Drake and I have business in Bath. I suggested that we stop by Swampshire on our way," Mr. Croaksworth said, still speaking mostly to Louisa. "Might as well take in some pleasures before getting to business."

"I have yet to feel the pleasures of Swampshire," Drake said dryly, "but I am here nonetheless." He caught Beatrice's eye but then quickly looked away.

"What *is* your business?" Mrs. Steele asked, and Beatrice leaned forward, eagerly awaiting his response. He paused before finally giving a reply.

"Carriages," he said. "I am considering investing in them."

"Didn't you tell us quite specifically that you dislike carriages?" Beatrice pointed out, unable to stop herself.

"They are unsafe," Drake said. "But I could perhaps invest in . . . safe ones."

"You should develop a horseless carriage," Mr. Steele suggested. "*That* would be safe."

"Wait a moment," Mr. Croaksworth said, looking around in confusion. "Have you already met?"

"Not formally. The Steeles forced me to ride with them when they saw the storm approaching," Drake explained.

Beatrice cleared her throat. "We extended you the *charity* of a ride once my father introduced our family, yet you declined to give us your name at the time," she clarified. It was becoming increasingly clear why Sir Huxley had parted ways with Inspector Drake: The man had no manners.

"Forgive me for such a lapse in precious etiquette," Drake replied. "I shall try harder not to offend from here on out. Perhaps we might discuss our favorite type of music—a topic suitable for genteel ladies. My favorite is all kinds."

"So is mine!" Mr. Croaksworth exclaimed.

"What a coincidence," Drake said, maintaining eye contact with Beatrice.

Another crackle of thunder echoed above.

"I hope the storm will clear up soon," Mr. Croaksworth said brightly. "This would be terrible to travel through."

"Do you mean to stay long here?" Louisa asked Mr. Croaksworth. "Despite the weather? And the frogs?"

"Frogs?" Mr. Croaksworth asked, confused.

"Never mind the frogs," Mrs. Steele cut in quickly, "you should stay! It's beautiful here—and it has been fifty-three days since the last squelch hole–related incident."

"London is a wonderful city, but I *have* been desiring a respite in the country," Mr. Croaksworth told her. "Perhaps Swampshire is exactly what I need. With the warm welcome we have received at Stabmort Park, I could see myself spending the rest of my days here." He spoke the last words directly to Louisa, who looked down at her slippered feet, bashful.

"Speak for yourself," Inspector Drake said tartly. But still his glance lingered on Beatrice.

"My dear Mr. Croaksworth!" Arabella Ashbrook said loudly, her words—and her angular body—finally cutting into the circle of guests. "Now that you have been properly introduced to everyone, we must start the dancing!"

Beatrice could not help noting Arabella's hands. She expected to see bandages upon her fingers, which might reinforce the notion that the blood Miss Bolton had seen was merely from thorn pricks. But her hands were bare and unblemished.

Had Miss Bolton truly imagined the whole thing?

"Normally my dance card is completely full before a ball even begins," Arabella went on, "but I took the liberty of leaving a few slots open. . . ." She flashed a dance card in front of Mr. Croaksworth, and he dutifully scribbled his name next to one of the minuets.

"Might I ask," he said, turning back to Louisa, "whether your card is free for the first dance?"

Louisa turned as red as her curls. "Well—Mr. Fàn wrote his name in the slot—"

"Frank writes his name under the first dance on all the ladies' cards," Beatrice interrupted, rolling her eyes at Frank. He stood near Caroline now, leaning against one wall. He caught Beatrice's

eye and flashed her a roguish grin. Beatrice took Louisa's card and
scratched out Frank's name. "There," she said, offering Mr. Croaksworth the card. "All free."

"I am very glad to hear it," Mr. Croaksworth said, writing his
name neatly on Louisa's card. She smiled up at him, basking in the
glow of his attentions.

"Don't forget to count—" Beatrice began as Louisa took Mr.
Croaksworth's arm.

"—the steps. I know," Louisa said, giving Beatrice an exasperated glance.

"Mr. Drake," Mrs. Steele said brightly, "perhaps you might
dance with my other daughter for the opening number." To Beatrice's horror, her mother continued: "When she isn't making so
many unbecoming jokes, Beatrice is an adequate conversationalist."

As Drake turned to look at her, Beatrice felt as if her heart had
stopped beating.

"Thank you, but I will not be dancing this evening," he said,
and stalked away.

"What a rude man," Mrs. Steele sniffed.

"You don't know the half of it," Beatrice breathed, her entire
body feeling hot with mortification. How dare Drake reject her
before she even had the chance to reject *him*? It was incomprehen-
sible.

"He is clearly not a viable option; you must therefore focus
on your beau," Mrs. Steele replied. She gave Beatrice a soft shove
toward Daniel Ashbrook.

Beatrice did not protest; she smiled in relief as she approached
Daniel, who immediately extended a hand.

"Miss Steele," he said graciously, and expertly pulled her into a
minuet. As he drew her close, she could smell the subtle scent of
begonia. *He must have a new shaving powder,* she thought. It suited
him.

Beatrice and the rest of the women on the dance floor did a synchronized round of choreography. It involved footwork and twirling around stationary male partners, and Beatrice always had to concentrate lest she miss a step. She was irritated to see from the corner of her eye that Caroline Wynn was keeping the beat perfectly, and even added an extra twirl.

Daniel and the other gentlemen watched in appreciation as they continued stepping and snapping.

Beatrice was not excellent at dancing; she knew the steps well but could never quite get her body to match the positions. Unlike Louisa, who always seemed to know exactly where her limbs were at all times, Beatrice flailed around a bit too much and bungled every few moves. But Daniel did not seem to mind. He was a skilled enough dancer for the both of them, and before long Beatrice was laughing along with the crowd, her cheeks warm and heart happy. She was finally enjoying herself.

The musicians played the last note of the opening number, and everyone clapped, their spirits high. Beatrice beamed at Daniel, whose eyes sparkled merrily.

"Shall we dance another?" he suggested as the quartet struck up another minuet, but Beatrice shook her head.

"It would be improper to dance two in a row," she said, feeling bashful as she added, "unless we were attached." She stared into his pure blue eyes, hoping he might say something that would indicate his thoughts on the matter. A simple *Of course we are attached, and by the way, will you marry me?* would have sufficed.

"Well . . ." he began, and her heart thumped. Was Daniel about to make an *offer?*

But before he could continue, Beatrice caught a whiff of an earthy, metallic scent. She turned in horror to see that Mr. Grub had crossed the dance floor and was now practically clinging to her side.

"I was promised a dance," he whined, and Beatrice's stomach dropped. She shot a pleading look at Daniel. But, polite as ever, he bowed and allowed Mr. Grub to sweep Beatrice up in his bony arms. Grub's callused hands snagged her gloves as he dragged her away from Daniel's soft, warm palms.

"I am glad I could rescue you," he wheezed, and immediately stepped on her foot.

"I did not need to be rescued," she said sharply, prying her foot out from under his. "I am perfectly capable—"

"Your sister danced the first number with Mr. Croaksworth, and he has not been able to keep his eyes off her," he interrupted, as if she had not spoken. "I expect that tonight, we will join them in starting rumors of affection." Mr. Grub seemed to be attempting to sound romantic, but the effect was dampened by the spittle he sprayed into her hair as he spoke.

"I think not," Beatrice said.

"If you and I were to form an attachment, any petitions against your father might . . . go away," Mr. Grub replied.

"How dare you bring up your ridiculous suit, your extortion, here, at a civilized affair?" Beatrice interrupted, appalled. "And don't you know that bribery is hardly a suitable path to matrimony?"

"Litigation is my love language. And you must realize, it is a practical path," Grub said, seemingly unaware of Beatrice's distress. "Our attachment is mutually advantageous. It would behoove you to secure your fortune, and it would behoove *me* to marry and produce heirs, so I could ensure my family line will receive my other inheritances."

"How do you have *more* inheritances?" Beatrice asked in disbelief.

Mr. Grub shrugged. "I have outlived many," he said simply. "But some of my upcoming bequests are contingent upon my producing an heir, so I have decided that I need a sturdy wife who could produce children."

"A romantic proposal," Beatrice scoffed, "but once again, I must refuse." She would do anything for her family, she thought, except this. Even the threat of poverty could not persuade her into accepting a proposal from this horrid man. Surely no judge would grant his suit. And it would not matter, she felt sure; Mr. Croaksworth was already enraptured with Louisa.

Beatrice and Grub danced awkwardly, past Arabella, who had weaseled her way into a dance with Mr. Croaksworth. Beatrice was intrigued to see Arabella whisper something to Croaksworth. The young woman looked perturbed.

Was she chiding him for favoring Louisa? Did she consider his obvious interest a slight? Beatrice leaned forward, straining to catch a snippet of the conversation.

"You are considering my proposal?" Mr. Grub also leaned forward, mistaking Beatrice's sudden silence as an opening.

"Absolutely not," Beatrice said, instinctively taking a much larger step backward.

She collided with her father, who squatted by the soup tureen, taking something from a bag and placing it in the soup. The effect was swift: The tureen fell over, drenching Captain Peña's uniform. Mr. Steele dropped the bag, and dozens of frogs leapt free. Several ladies screamed, Louisa tripped as she tried to avoid a frog, Daniel politely caught her, and Captain Peña yelled, "Amphibians adrift! Abandon ship!"

"Aha! Very good assist, Beatrice," Mr. Steele said, chortling. "You have thoroughly elevated my prank."

"It was unintentional," Beatrice said, her cheeks burning in embarrassment.

Mrs. Steele shrewdly slid open a window and ushered the distressed frogs outside. A rush of air blew through the ballroom, rustling the ladies' skirts and rumpling the gentlemen's cravats.

Beatrice shivered as she felt the sting of the cold air pass through her.

"What is going on?" Mr. Ashbrook asked sharply. He had fainted on a chaise at the edge of the ballroom, but now he roused himself and stared, agape, at the mayhem.

"It was Mr. Steele, causing trouble as always," Grub said, pointing a knobby finger at Mr. Steele. "I fear he is losing his mind," Grub added in a dramatic whisper. There were several gasps, and Beatrice felt a pang of panic.

"It was not my father's fault," she said quickly. Everyone turned to stare at her. "It was a slip of the slipper."

"Who would have thought such a shoe might betray you?" Drake said, and she glared at him, her cheeks burning.

"You must get out of those clothes," Mr. Ashbrook said to Captain Peña. "You'll catch your death of cold."

"It's perfectly warm in here," Captain Peña protested.

Mr. Ashbrook ignored his objections. He crossed the room and took Captain Peña's arm, pulling him across the ballroom. "I'm sure Daniel will have something upstairs that will fit you."

"Perhaps we should all take a break," Mr. Croaksworth suggested.

"I am happy to welcome the men into our study, and the ladies may join Arabella in the parlor," Daniel offered. "We planned to retire to these rooms after dinner, but I think it shall be acceptable to enjoy a card game a little earlier than expected, under the circumstances."

"What a splendid idea," Arabella said, but she shot an irritated glance at Beatrice. Clearly, Arabella was not happy to have her dance with Mr. Croaksworth cut short. She reluctantly led the guests out of the ballroom, but Beatrice lingered to help her mother check for any remaining frogs.

Normally Mrs. Steele cut an imposing figure, but she seemed small then, standing there with her now-drooping hairdo and a little frog in her palm. Beatrice felt a pang of sympathy. Yes, her mother was single-minded, but she wished only to provide for her daughters. Beatrice could not hold it against her.

"This was just a minor setback, I'm sure," Beatrice assured her mother as she helped scoop frogs outside. "Tonight is going well."

Mrs. Steele's eye twitched. "I just hope we can secure an engagement," she said, "*before it's too late.*" She withdrew something from her reticule and passed it to Beatrice—*The Lady's Guide to Swampshire (Travel Edition).* "Keep this with you," she said firmly. "We can't afford any more slip-ups."

Beatrice begrudgingly took the book—which was just as thick as it was tall—and placed it into her reticule. She wished she still had *Doors of the English Countryside.* It did not seem gripping either, but at least it hadn't been so heavy.

She looked up to see the final frog they had released. It bolted across the moor, navigating through the pelting rain and hail and fading into a little glowing spot. Beatrice thought that it looked as if the frog were escaping Stabmort Park—while anyone still could.

JOURNAL OF
MR. EDMUND CROAKSWORTH

[Excerpt]

Today was so eventful and interesting that I must record it all, lest I forget a thing.

When I arose this morning there was a chill, and I dressed in my brown wool jacket. I ate one egg for breakfast, along with some tea. By the afternoon the sun came out and it grew very warm. I put on my lighter brown jacket and took a turn about the garden. After this I came inside and had cold pheasant with bread, and more tea. In the evening it became cool once more, so I put my brown wool jacket on again. I put it over the top of my lighter brown jacket without remembering to remove the inner layer! This inspired such hilarity that I had to summon my valet back from his day off. He was most unhappy, as he had some sort of obligation at the church with his lady friend (he kept muttering about "being in the middle of saying our vows"), but when I showed him what had happened he understood the necessity for the summons. "You see, I am useless without you!" I told him as he helped me fix the terrible blunder.

Once my outfit was restored, I sat down to a dinner of more cold pheasant. This time I had wine instead of tea for my beverage. All in all, it was a very eventful day; you can understand why I thought to record it at once. I am almost too tired to write this now after such excitement.

Tomorrow I leave for Swampshire. I do hope they don't serve cold pheasant at the Ashbrooks' ball. I could not possibly eat it a third time!

CHAPTER 8

Whist

The parlor was a pastel confection, cluttered with love seats in blues and pinks, a cheerful fire lit in the white marble fireplace. A delicate chandelier hovered above the card table, which was surrounded by four brocade armchairs. Though the decoration looked sweet, the gameplay would be anything but. Brutal, bloodthirsty, unyielding—this was the card game whist for the women of Swampshire, and Beatrice adored every second. It was the one socially acceptable way she could unleash her darker instincts. She took a seat in an armchair by the fire and began to shuffle a deck of cards in excited anticipation.

The other ladies ambled into the parlor. Arabella and Louisa were arm in arm, conversing in low voices. Mrs. Steele and Miss Bolton trailed behind, and Beatrice watched as Miss Bolton snaked a hand into her hat and withdrew a biscuit. Mary crept inside and immediately went to the shadowy window seat; it was her usual haunt.

To Beatrice's unhappy surprise, Inspector Drake stepped in after Mary.

"The men are retiring to the study, sir," Beatrice called out. She had hoped she might be able to speak with Louisa during the card game, to surmise her sister's opinion of Mr. Croaksworth, and did not want Drake sticking his nose in her business.

"I was not asked to join them," he said. A muscle in his jaw tensed. "I take it from your frosty reception that I am not welcome here, either." He turned to go. Beatrice felt a pang of compassion. In spite of her feelings toward him, she knew what it was like to feel as if one did not belong anywhere.

"On the contrary," she said, dealing a hand with a businesslike air. "One must never be too friendly before a game of whist; it signals weakness."

Inspector Drake looked back at her in surprise.

"Is that an invitation?" he asked.

In reply, Beatrice indicated the chair across from her. Drake took it. Perhaps she'd be less irritated with him once she thoroughly trounced him, she thought.

Louisa and Arabella finally ceased their whispering, having noticed Drake's presence.

"What do we have here—a fox in the henhouse?" Arabella said tauntingly, regarding Drake. "I warn you, sir, that even though whist is considered a lady's game, we are far better at cards than the gentlemen. If you are looking for an easy win, you won't find it here."

"Though we only gamble ribbons and pocket money," Louisa added. She and Arabella took the empty seats at the card table. Louisa placed a coin on the tabletop, but Arabella stopped her hand.

"I'm tired of playing for pocket change or ribbons or 'pride,'" she said. "I already have those things. I'd like to raise the stakes."

"We couldn't possibly pledge any real sum," Beatrice said begrudgingly. Arabella knew they had none; it was gauche of her to even suggest gambling.

"Beatrice, you make it sound as if we are impoverished," Louisa chided her. She turned over her glove so no one could see the hole at the wrist, from years of wear, as she glanced at Drake. Beatrice knew it was not Arabella her sister worried about, but Croaksworth; her sister must be concerned that Drake would report back any findings to his friend. But Arabella continued.

"I wasn't thinking of money," she said, her sly smile widening. "When I visited Edmund and Daniel at school years ago, I was introduced to a much more exciting form of gameplay. It had become popular among the students. Perhaps tonight, we should adopt this method."

Beatrice scanned the players at the table and caught Drake's intense eye staring back at her. She immediately turned away from him, determined not to give him any reaction to observe.

"Instead of pledging pounds, we pledge . . ."—Arabella paused for effect—"secrets."

"I don't have any secrets," Louisa said. She shifted in her armchair and then looked up at the crystal chandelier. Its reflection in her wide eyes made them sparkle strangely.

"I'm sure you do," Beatrice said with a little smile. "Think of our childhood friend Penelope Burt. The three of us had plenty of secrets."

Penelope Burt was a lady made up by Louisa and Beatrice, years ago. If ever something went wrong—a vase broke, a dress was torn, Mary wandered off into the woods while Louisa and Beatrice were meant to be minding her—they blamed it on Penelope. Of course Mrs. Steele knew there was no such person, but Louisa and Beatrice had never broken in their insistence that she existed. They had even gone so far as to hire an actress from a traveling play to pay a call to Marsh Hall, in character as Penelope. Beatrice had spent all her pocket money on the endeavor, but for the look on Mrs. Steele's face, it had been worth it.

"Penelope who?" Louisa said, knitting her brows together. "I don't know what you're talking about, Beatrice." She turned her gaze to Arabella and widened her eyes as if trying to communicate something telepathically to her friend.

"I'm sure you'll think of something," Arabella insisted, ignoring Louisa. Without waiting for approval from the others, she tore four pages from Louisa's score book. One always had to bring one's own paper to the Ashbrooks' house; Daniel did not like loose leaves floating around ("*A paper with no book is a very messy look*," he always said). Arabella passed one each to Louisa, Beatrice, and Drake. She saved the last for herself.

"We shall all write down our secrets. Whichever team wins can read the others' pages and throw their own into the fire."

"I don't know . . ." Louisa said. "Mother wouldn't like it." She scratched at a stain on the brocade cushion of her chair, as if she could make it disappear by some magic of her glove. Beatrice noted her sister's nails digging into the fabric, leaving indents.

Arabella looked over at Mrs. Steele, who was deep in conversation with Miss Bolton, both ladies sipping from glasses of sherry. Miss Bolton pulled a tube from within her enormous hat and refilled Mrs. Steele's glass with more of the scarlet liquid.

"Your mother is quite preoccupied," Arabella noted. "Don't be so dull. Unless," she added tauntingly, "you want Edmund to hear that you don't enjoy his little game."

"Yes, Mr. Croaksworth dislikes anything dull," Drake said. "Which must make his opinion of himself sadly low."

"I'm sure nothing would change Mr. Croaksworth's good opinion of *Louisa*," Beatrice cut in, trying not to let slip a smirk, "though he might be interested to hear that you were pressuring all of us to gamble, Arabella." She put a hand over Louisa's to stop her sister from scraping at the chair cushion. Louisa loosened under Beatrice's grip, looking abashed, and Beatrice withdrew her hand.

"It would be just like you to tattle, wouldn't it, Beatrice?" Arabella said snidely. "You are *so* well-mannered. As well-mannered as a stick in the mud."

"I am not," Beatrice replied hotly. "I mean, I *am*. . . ." She looked at Drake, who raised an eyebrow at her. She quickly turned away, cheeks burning.

"This isn't breaking any etiquette!" Arabella maintained. "It's just a bit of fun."

Beatrice opened her mouth to protest again on Louisa's behalf, but Louisa squeezed Beatrice's forearm to stop her from speaking again.

"Ouch." Beatrice drew back in pain.

"I'm sorry," Louisa said quickly. "But really. It's fine. Like Arabella said . . . it's just a bit of fun. For once, won't you just play along?"

Chastised, Beatrice took a piece of paper.

Louisa turned to her own paper and scribbled on it, then folded it in half before Beatrice could see what she had written.

Beatrice glanced at Drake, who was already folding his paper, as well.

"Having trouble thinking of a secret, Miss Steele?" he asked.

"As it so happens, I am. *My* reputation is pristine," she said pointedly.

"I believe you have much more going on below the surface than anyone realizes," he said quietly.

"You must, as well," she replied. "I would hate to think that you truly are as impertinent as you seem." With that, she turned to her own paper.

Surely her interest in murder would have once been a secret to astonish them all, but she had left that behind so long ago. Now it was completely in the past. Ancient history. Therefore, after a moment of deliberation, she scribbled, *I stole a ribbon at the market.*

It was a lie, but Beatrice reasoned that it was scandalous enough to serve as her secret—but not salacious enough to tarnish her reputation.

She folded her paper and then looked up, avoiding Drake's gaze. Had it been a mistake to invite him into the game?

The only other guests in the parlor were Mary, Miss Bolton, Mrs. Steele, and Mr. Grub, who were all otherwise engaged at the far end of the room: Mary plunked away at a pastel pianoforte, playing a foreboding piece that sounded akin to animalistic howls. Mrs. Steele had moved toward the door, her ear pressed against it as she clearly listened for any noise to indicate that the men were returning. Miss Bolton had withdrawn a pair of knitting needles and yarn from her hat and was working on something that looked suspiciously like a scarf for a dog. Mr. Grub, who must have snuck in after Drake, was perched on a pink settee. He watched Beatrice intensely, hand clutched around a punch glass. She refocused her attention on the game, trying to ignore her cousin—but feeling quite disconcerted by his expression.

Once all four players had scribbled secrets onto the papers and folded them in half, they placed them in a pile.

"If I may?" Drake said, and Beatrice reluctantly handed him the stack of cards.

"You'd best not try to pull one over on us," Arabella warned as he began to shuffle. "And no table talk either."

Even a wink or a yawn would be called out as cheating. After Maddie Bennet and Andrea Creel's streak of dropped handkerchiefs and false-sneeze signals back in '77, they would take no chances. (Maddie and Andrea had been exiled after their bout of cheating and now lived in France as penance.)

"I assure you, I am honest," Drake replied. Beatrice let out a cough of disbelief, but it was drowned out by his snap of the cards on the table, which Drake followed with such a flashy show of shuffling that Arabella gasped.

"Well then," she said, "let the game *begin*."

The first few tricks went to Beatrice and Drake, but Louisa and Arabella forged ahead for the next five.

As the game went on, pressure began to mount. Beads of sweat formed on foreheads, and blood pounded in the ears. By round thirteen, the intensity was palpable and the game was tied.

Beatrice felt Drake's eyes on her hands, and she felt as if he could see through her gloves to her ink-stained fingers. With a chill, she wondered—what did he know? She preferred to be the observer, not the observed, and Drake watched her with too much scrutiny. She could not understand the reason behind this, and it made her uneasy.

"You play well, Miss Steele," Drake said, his final card in his hands.

"That makes one of us," she quipped, though it was untrue—she would not admit it, but Drake was an astute player.

"I have never been so nervous to turn my card," Louisa said, her last card clutched against her chest.

"For the secrets," Arabella said dramatically.

Louisa played a ten of hearts, Arabella a jack of spades, and Beatrice a ten of clubs. They all turned to Drake, holding their respective breaths—and, with a flourish, he brandished an ace of hearts.

"Take your prizes," Arabella said in disgust, shoving the stack toward Drake.

He immediately unfolded one of the papers, and Beatrice leaned in to read the cramped handwriting. She had to hand it to Arabella—the game was more of a thrill when there were actual stakes involved. And of course, Beatrice didn't mind finding out information about her neighbors. But before she could read what was scrawled on the page, there was a sudden flurry of movement. Mrs. Steele wrenched open the parlor door, Mary broke off playing the pianoforte, and the women at the card table all looked up.

"The men are returning from the study!" Mrs. Steele yelled over the din of rain and hail pounding at the windows.

Immediately, she rushed from the room, Arabella following close behind. Drake stood and offered a hand to Beatrice to help her to her feet.

"I am perfectly capable of standing on my own," she said tartly.

"I do not doubt that, Miss Steele," he said, and withdrew his hand just as she relented and reached out to take it. He strode away. She stumbled to her feet, thrown off. She took a step after him, confused and embarrassed. But then she remembered that the coveted secrets lay on the card table, unread.

She turned to see Louisa still at the table. Her sister quickly picked up the papers and threw them into the fire, where they curled into ash. Louisa's face was twisted into a strange, serious expression as she watched the papers burn.

"We never got to read the secrets," Beatrice said, and Louisa jumped. She turned, and for a moment they just looked at each other.

"If anyone asks," Louisa said, her face easing into a bright expression, "that terrible Penelope Burt made them disappear."

"How awful that she showed up here without an invitation," Beatrice said with a smile as she linked arms with her sister. "She shall be exiled from Swampshire yet again. Perhaps this time it will take."

The two sisters exited the parlor arm in arm, leaving it empty, alight with the smoldering embers of the secrets. But still, Beatrice burned with curiosity.

What was her sister hiding?

CHAPTER 9

Collapse

Beatrice followed Louisa back into the ballroom, where the men had already reentered. The air was filled with the scent of cigars and port, the guests' voices now louder, their movements loose.

Beatrice stepped close to Louisa and lowered her voice, trying to capitalize on the moment alone.

"What are your thoughts on Mr. Croaksworth?" she asked.

"He is a pleasant man. One can find nothing about which to complain," Louisa said vaguely.

"I would suggest that you—" Beatrice began.

"I should get him some more punch. Mother always says that punch encourages dancing." She gave Beatrice a little nod, excusing herself, and hurried over to the punch table. Beatrice watched Louisa take up the ladle. She began to dole out portions, passing crystal glasses filled with sticky pink liquid around the crowd of chatting guests. Everyone's movements seemed to loosen as they sipped.

Except Mr. Croaksworth, Beatrice noticed as she shifted her gaze. He wore a serious expression as he accepted a punch glass from Louisa and drained it in one gulp. He looked ill at ease, eyes darting around the room, posture much more rigid than when he'd first arrived.

He seemed to recover after the punch; he approached Louisa and gave a small bow. He was asking for another dance, Beatrice thought with a prickle of excitement.

Whatever was bothering him had nothing to do with Louisa, clearly: Two dances signified an attachment. Louisa and Mr. Croaksworth would be as good as engaged before the night was over—Beatrice was certain now.

Arabella suddenly cleared her throat and clapped her hands. The ball guests turned to look at her.

"You all know," Arabella said, "that I normally save the more *nontraditional* dances for the end of the evening. But tonight, as we are already very *off schedule* due to a *soup incident* caused by *Beatrice Steele*"—she glared at Beatrice—"I thought we might jump ahead to learning a dance that is all the rage in Italy." She motioned for the musicians to begin playing, and they obediently struck up a dramatic tune. Arabella flung her hands to the ceiling and called out, "I present to you . . . the *danza della morte!*"

Beatrice felt a sting of annoyance. Of course Arabella would choose the most complicated dance to try to thwart Louisa's budding romance with Mr. Croaksworth.

She suddenly felt hot breath on her neck. She turned to see Mr. Grub, waiting expectantly.

"Beatrice," he wheezed, "shall we attempt to survive this one together?"

"I already promised to dance with someone else," Beatrice said quickly, looking around in desperation.

Louisa and Mr. Croaksworth had paired off; Daniel was kindly bowing to Mary, who looked surprised but pleased; and Frank was whispering something in Arabella's ear that made her giggle. Captain Peña bowed to Caroline, Mr. Steele twirled Miss Bolton, and Mr. Ashbrook was lecturing Mrs. Steele about "the dangers of moving too vigorously."

"I see no other available partners," Grub said, confirming what Beatrice could see for herself. She felt a flood of irritation pass through her as she realized.

There *was* one available man.

"Mr. Drake has asked me," she said loudly.

At his name, he looked up from where he had been standing against the wall, and she immediately pulled him into the intricate dance.

"I do not wish—" he began, but Beatrice immediately grabbed his hands.

"Please," she hissed. He opened his mouth as if to protest again but caught sight of Mr. Grub watching them. At that moment, Mr. Grub slurped up a string of spittle that dribbled from his lips.

"Just this one, then," Drake said, relenting.

He was a stiff dancer but managed to somewhat replicate the position Arabella and her partner, Frank, were demonstrating in the center of the floor.

The *danza della morte* was a scandalous dance, as the couples were required to be a foot apart and nearly brush elbows, and Beatrice got a strange thrill as she felt the warmth emanating from Drake's elbow.

"I know you did not wish to dance with me, but I found myself in a difficult situation," Beatrice said as they moved to the music. "Once this song is over, you may go back to glowering in the corner."

"I never said I did not wish to dance with *you*," Drake said, withdrawing his arm as if burned from where she had nearly touched him. "I did not want to dance at all. I am only here because Mr. Croaksworth wished to stop in Swampshire on our way to Bath. I don't attend many balls, though you may have already ascertained that."

"And how would I have done so?" Beatrice asked, turning a shaky pirouette.

"I have noticed that you make a study of everyone you encounter, though you seem deeply uncomfortable with my attempts to do the same to you," Drake replied. "In fact, you have been determined to dislike me from the moment you set eyes upon me."

Beatrice's cheeks burned. He may have crossed Sir Huxley, but Drake had done nothing to *her*. He had even saved her from Grub. Perhaps he was a faulty detective, but he was not *her* enemy. She opened her mouth to apologize, but Drake continued before she could speak.

"I think I can surmise the reason for your dislike."

Beatrice swallowed, nerves tightening her throat.

Had he guessed her secret? Had he realized she disliked him because she was a loyal follower of Sir Huxley?

"I have heard of the strict code of etiquette in Swampshire," Drake went on. "It was precisely why I did not wish to stay here long. You are exactly the type of woman I expected to encounter."

"And what type of woman is that?" Beatrice asked, perplexed.

"A snob," Drake replied.

Beatrice drew in a breath as he suddenly pulled her toward him. They were nearly a foot apart—the most sensual portion of the dance. The flickering candlelight illuminated Drake's scarred face.

"You don't know me at all," she said.

"You don't know me either," he replied.

"Don't I, *Inspector Drake*?" Beatrice shot back.

A startled, confused expression rippled across his face. "But how did you . . ." he began, clearly recalculating his opinion of her.

Regret rushed in immediately. She had spoken rashly, stupidly— she had been so concerned that he would guess her secret that she had revealed it herself.

But before Beatrice could formulate an excuse, change the subject, take back the words she had just uttered, a scream rang out. She turned to see her sister clapping a hand over her mouth.

Louisa was with Mr. Croaksworth in the center of the room, but something was wrong.

"These lights are too bright," he yelled, and there were a few confused titters.

"We could blow out some candles," Louisa said, confused, but Mr. Croaksworth did not seem to hear her. His face had turned pale, and he staggered out of rhythm with the lively *danza della morte*.

"The angel isn't an angel at all—can't you fools see it?" he yelled, and then coughed, sending a sudden spatter of blood across Louisa's white gown.

"Mr. Croaksworth!" Louisa cried.

He gave no reply but convulsed violently, knocking into the punch table. The punch bowl fell to the floor and shattered into a thousand sparkling shards. Mr. Croaksworth stumbled around, shoes crunching on the glass, and then collapsed.

The dancers all screamed and dispersed, leaving him sprawled on the floor in a pool of pink punch, eyes glassy.

He was dead.

Dear Arabella,

It has been so long since I gazed upon your beautiful
face, but still I remember every detail. So much keeps us
apart—but I feel certain our love can overcome anything.
I have enclosed seeds for you in this envelope. By the
time they bloom, I hope that we can be together again. If
not, I shall see you in every rose I pass.

Yours,

SB

CHAPTER 10

Hysteria

For a moment everyone was silent, and then Mr. Steele started a slow clap.

"Bravo, good sir," he said, "what a prank! Truly the most convincing false death I've ever seen!"

Several guests let out bursts of confused laughter, but Beatrice took in Louisa's ashen face and the spatter of blood across her dress, and knew: This was no jest.

She launched into action as if she had been waiting all evening— and perhaps all her life—for something of this nature to occur. She ran to where Mr. Croaksworth was collapsed on the ground and knelt beside him, pink punch seeping onto the edge of her thin muslin gown.

"Arabella, give me your pocket mirror," Beatrice demanded.

"What? Why?" Arabella sputtered. "And why are you on the floor? You are behaving in a most shocking manner!"

"Your pocket mirror," Beatrice insisted. It was too late now to change her course; everyone was staring at her in confused silence.

Finally, Arabella reached into her bodice and withdrew a small mirror with a miniature of herself painted on the exterior. Beatrice took it and held it up to Mr. Croaksworth's nostrils.

It was a trick of Sir Huxley's, on which he often relied. Fog on the mirror meant breath—life. No fog meant no breath.

She pulled back the mirror to see her clear, unclouded reflection.

"I regret to inform you that Mr. Edmund Croaksworth," Beatrice said, standing to face the guests, "is dead."

The crowd broke out into fearful whispers and gasps.

"But are you sure? He was about to propose to Louisa, I know it!" Mrs. Steele cried.

"Unfortunately, I am sure. There's no breath, no heartbeat, no potential for an engagement," Beatrice told her.

"It is the worst tragedy imaginable!" Mrs. Steele cried.

Caroline swooned, and Captain Peña rushed to her side. Mr. Ashbrook crumpled into a full faint before anyone could come to *his* aid. Mrs. Steele knelt to fan his face, and his eyes fluttered open.

"My fainties," he whispered. "They are upon me."

Amidst the chaos, Beatrice went immediately to her sister and pulled her into an embrace. Louisa stood still as a statue, and Beatrice drew back.

"Are you all right?" she asked, grasping her sister's hands. Louisa's palms were clammy, her face the color of pale marble.

"I—I don't understand," Louisa said. Her eyes brimmed with confused tears. "He can't be—" But her voice was too ragged to finish the sentence.

"What happened to him?" Arabella demanded. "He was fine a moment ago!"

"Until he started dancing with Louisa," Grub said.

"She had nothing to do with it!" Beatrice stepped in front of her sister, arm raised protectively.

"He must have been ill," Mr. Ashbrook said shakily. "He never should have been dancing so much. I've always said that it's horrible for one's health."

"*Too many minuets can the body upset,*" Daniel added, his eyes wide. "I feel terrible. I should have noticed that he was ailing."

"We can't just leave him there," Miss Bolton said. "Should we bury him?"

"I call dibs on his bones," Mary whispered.

"He's not one of your pet birds, Miss Bolton," Arabella snapped. "We can't just *bury* him. Especially not in our yard—my garden is very carefully cultivated! A grave would *completely* throw off the balance."

Beatrice tuned out the guests' arguing voices as she turned back toward the body. She felt strangely calm. For once she knew exactly what to do.

She noted the way Mr. Croaksworth's arms and legs had fallen at odd angles: Clearly he had not been in control of his body while falling or else he would have thrown out his arms to catch himself. His chestnut hair was damp against his sweaty forehead, his face strangely animated by the flicker of candlelight, his eyes open but unseeing.

"What if he died from a contagious illness?" Mr. Ashbrook clutched his throat. "We need to fetch a doctor, before our home is filled with diseased corpses!"

"It's already haunted," Miss Bolton cried. "I knew it. This is so much more dramatic than my production *Changing Commodes Throughout the Years*—"

"This isn't some sort of *theater* piece, is it?" Mr. Ashbrook interrupted.

"If it is, it's not a very funny one," Mr. Steele said.

Beatrice's eyes met Daniel's, the understanding of what she had already determined dawning on him.

"This man didn't die naturally," Beatrice confirmed. Daniel let out a shaky breath.

"You're sure?" he asked in a low voice.

"Mr. Croaksworth said he found it bright in this room, but there is only a glow of candlelight. It's rather dark," Beatrice began, her gaze drawing back to the body. It was horrifying, but she found she could not look away. "Strange," she murmured.

"Strange indeed, Miss Steele," Drake said, and everyone whipped their heads around to stare at the previously silent guest.

He had been watching Beatrice, arms crossed, but clearly could stay silent no longer. He approached the body and examined one of Mr. Croaksworth's eyes. "His pupils are dilated."

Beatrice stared at the man's glassy gaze and shuddered. This, she had never seen in the papers.

"He complained of a headache, and kept drinking punch," she added, looking up at Drake. He nodded.

"This indicates a dry mouth and throat," he said.

"His speech was slurred, his face flushed," Beatrice continued.

"Perhaps he had too much to drink. We've all engaged in too much revelry before," Frank suggested. "A bit too much punch, a stolen kiss . . ."

"An upstanding man knows when to take his grog and when to leave it," Captain Peña said sternly.

"Perhaps Edmund wasn't such an upstanding man," Frank shot back.

"Of course he was," Arabella snapped. "My family doesn't keep company with gentlemen who aren't upstanding."

Beatrice looked from guest to guest, taking in their reactions. Was Frank just a bit too cavalier? His face did not look as pale, as terrified, as those of the other guests. She had noticed a tinge of dislike before—and he and Mr. Croaksworth *had* known each other at school—but nothing in their conversation suggested he would rejoice at the man's expiration.

And Captain Peña—he still stood tall, though Beatrice noted that his hands shook. Wouldn't a navy man be stoic in the face of death? Mr. Ashbrook and Arabella, for their parts, were only focused on themselves—were they truly not disturbed by the scene?

"Please, don't fight," Caroline said, pressing a fluttering hand to her heart.

To Beatrice's irritation, this protest cut the guests' reactions short, and they all masked any feeling with a sudden veil of decorum. As Drake began to speak again. Beatrice turned back to him—and the body—once more.

"He was confused, saying something about an angel," Drake recalled. "Hallucinations, delirium . . . This looks to me like he was exhibiting the symptoms of—"

"Poison," Beatrice finished.

Drake gave her a nod of confirmation and summed up his thought: "Edmund Croaksworth was murdered."

Beatrice felt a shudder pass over her. It was terrifying and thrilling, all at once.

"No!" Mrs. Steele cried, clapping a hand to her mouth. "Not . . . not . . ."

"Murder," Beatrice finished for her in an exhilarated whisper. "Murder, at Stabmort Park."

"Right. Then we shall be on our way," Mrs. Steele said, and began to round up her family in a panic. She grabbed Louisa's arm, and Louisa let herself be pulled along like a rag doll, her face still ashen. Mrs. Steele wrenched open one of the ballroom's enormous windows, but she was immediately blown back by a huge gust of wind and fell to the floor in a tumble.

The sky glowed purple from lightning, and rain poured from the heavens. Icy shards of hail blew into the ballroom, snuffing out half the candles. The storm raged, no longer in the distance, but upon them.

"Close the window!" Mr. Ashbrook yelled. Daniel rushed over and slammed it shut. The ballroom was silent once more. The ladies' updos were now deflated and the men's jackets rumpled from the harsh wind.

"This storm is far too treacherous," Daniel said, turning to help Mrs. Steele to her feet. "You must all stay until it passes."

"Why in the world would I *stay*?" Mrs. Steele cried. "A man has just been killed!" She stared down at the body in terror and then looked up at the other guests. "And one of you is a murderer."

Miss Bolton gasped. "Surely no one here would ever do such a thing!"

"Who else could have done it? A *ghost*?" Arabella cut in, her voice sharp.

"Let us all not forget that *she* was dancing with him as he fell," Grub repeated, and everyone turned to see him pointing a bony, shaking finger at Louisa. "If anyone is responsible, it is Louisa Steele."

Beatrice's exhilaration was replaced with pure anger.

"How dare you," she hissed, taking a step toward Grub.

He curled his hand into a fist. "Just look at who she has for a father," he continued. "The man is insane. Perhaps he drove her to it—or even did the deed himself."

"Don't listen to a word my cousin says," Mrs. Steele growled. "He only means to further his own interests."

"Precisely. I am completely sane," Mr. Steele said. A bit of blood suddenly dribbled down his chin. Miss Bolton gasped. "Pardon me," Mr. Steele said, dabbing at it with his handkerchief, "I popped a capsule when I thought Mr. Croaksworth had devised a clever caper. I wanted to join in . . ." He ducked a swatting from a teary-eyed Mrs. Steele.

"We must solicit the authorities at once," Arabella said.

"But they won't be able to reach us in this storm," Captain Peña said, looking out the large ballroom windows, which revealed dark swampland. "Their carriage would capsize." He was right: The rain pooled in sinkholes, and the ground was covered in a layer of hail. No one could come to Stabmort Park in such conditions—and no one could leave.

"Then that means," Miss Bolton began, voice shaking with terror, "that we are trapped alone with a killer!"

The guests began to yell over one another, panic rising to a frenzy. The ball was descending into chaos.

Beatrice inhaled and exhaled, trying to stay calm. What would Huxley do in this situation?

That was it. "We need Sir Huxley!" she cried. Her voice rang bright and clear above the cacophony.

Suddenly, the room fell silent.

"Who is Sir Huxley?" Arabella asked slowly, her eyes narrowing at Beatrice.

"He's . . . an inspector. A real inspector." Beatrice felt as if she were shrinking, acutely aware of the stunned faces staring back at her.

"And how would you know a real inspector, Beatrice?" Arabella replied, her tone edging toward accusatory.

"Surely a lady would not be abreast of . . . *criminal matters*," Caroline whispered. "It's too unseemly to imagine!"

"This is a ghastly offense," Mr. Ashbrook said, staring at Beatrice with a stern expression.

"I raised her better than this," Mrs. Steele said, swaying. Mr. Steele gripped her, staring at Beatrice with a pleading expression, as if willing her to say it was just a joke.

"I'm sure this is a misunderstanding," Daniel said, and Beatrice turned toward him. He looked at her with the same hopeful, pleading look her father had. "Beatrice has a simple explanation," he continued. "Don't you?"

Beatrice's mouth felt dry, and she opened it, willing herself to say something—*anything*—to excuse this slight. But she was paralyzed with panic.

"I told Miss Steele about Sir Huxley. He is famous in London." Drake's deep voice suddenly echoed throughout the ballroom. "And I worked with him, as a detective." He seemed almost surprised at himself as he spoke, his eye resting on Beatrice. She could only stare at him, still frozen.

"I don't understand," Mrs. Steele said. "I thought you were a gentleman seeking a wife!"

"And in Swampshire, gentlemen do not discuss such inappropriate topics in mixed company, *sir*," Arabella said, her voice acidic.

"This is what Beatrice told me," Drake assured her. "It was my error, not hers. And I am sorry to have misguided you."

"Oh, thank goodness. *You* may commit such an error without *complete* ruin," Mrs. Steele said in relief. "But a *lady* . . ." She shook her head at Beatrice, who merely stared back in bewilderment.

"Yes, well," Inspector Drake continued, "*I* am a workingman, an inspector, and I can solve this murder."

"Why would we want *him* to help us, if this Sir Huxley is the best?" Arabella interrupted. "We are the Ashbrooks. We must have *the best*."

"I can send word for him," Daniel suggested. "One of the servants can travel to London; their skin is thicker, so they are more likely to survive. He could most likely reach us after sunrise. *When hail comes without warning, it clears up by morning,* as I say."

"We're meant to wait until the *morning,* trapped with a homicidal *madman*?" Mrs. Steele cried.

"That would constitute great danger," Mr. Steele said, his teeth still bloody red, "and I have expressly promised my wife to avoid great danger when possible."

"I am too young to die!" Frank cried out. "I have only just begun to sow my wild oats!"

Louisa, turning paler by the second, looked from one guest to another in fright.

"It is settled," Mr. Ashbrook said firmly. "We must take what we can get, until this Sir Huxley is able to reach us. And the best for now seems to be you, Inspector Drake." He nodded toward Drake.

"Thank you for your vote of confidence," Drake said dryly.

"But if you are to investigate this murder, you must not commit any more egregious indiscretions." Mr. Ashbrook pointed at him sternly. "I won't allow it here in Stabmort Park, the homestead of my ancestor, the great Baron Fitzwilliam Ashbrook."

"Might I make a suggestion then, Father?" Daniel asked. Mr. Ashbrook nodded, and Daniel continued. "If Drake takes the case, Beatrice should assist him. *A corpse on the floor is no excuse for manners out the door.*"

"What?" Beatrice felt as if she were trapped in some bizarre dream, sure she would wake up at any moment. She pinched her arm—but still, she found herself in the ballroom, Mr. Croaksworth's body collapsed in the center, and her neighbors all looking from Daniel to Beatrice in confusion.

"She is a model Swampshirian," Daniel continued, "and can advise him accordingly. I would do it myself, but *in matters of etiquette, women are trusted never to forget.*"

"I don't know if it is appropriate," Mrs. Steele began. "Beatrice, check *The Lady's Guide*—"

"I work best without a partner," Drake said.

"Everyone, silence," Mr. Ashbrook yelled. "I have had *enough* of this chaos!"

They all broke off, chastened by his authoritative tone. Mr. Ashbrook stood tall underneath a portrait of himself in a power pose.

He put a hand on his hip, emulating the same pose. It was not as effective as it could have been; Mr. Ashbrook swayed slightly, as if he might faint again. Daniel took a step forward, holding out a helpful hand, but his father waved him away.

"I am all right, thank you, son." He cleared his throat. "This is what we shall do, and I will hear no more objections: Inspector Drake will determine what has occurred here. Miss Steele will assist him, to ensure he follows proper etiquette. Miss Bolton will chaperone."

"Do I have to?" Miss Bolton said weakly, but Mr. Ashbrook spoke over her.

"The rest of you will be escorted to separate chambers, to rest and recover proper bearing. Just because something horrible has occurred, it does not mean we must become hysterical."

"Doesn't it?" Miss Bolton whimpered.

"No," Mr. Ashbrook said firmly. "After all—we are English."

MR. McCROCKETT'S SHOP-O-TRICKS

Receipt of Purchase

One rat figurine
One bag of false fleas
Six miniature firecrackers
Wallpaper, custom
Note: "Purchaser has requested sheath of wallpaper, painted to look like a door where there is none, for purpose of humorous deceit."
Fifteen capsules of false blood
And
One pistol

Bill of fare to Mr. Stephen Steele
Swampshire

CHAPTER 11

Observation

As Daniel began to lead the guests from the ballroom, Inspector Drake made his way toward the corpse. He knelt in front of it, and Beatrice followed suit.

Miss Bolton hovered by the ballroom doors. She watched the other guests exit with a look of yearning on her face.

"I'll just chaperone from over here," she called to Beatrice and Drake, adding quietly, "out of the way of any specters."

"Judging by the severity of his symptoms, I'd say he was given a high dose of the poison," Drake said to himself, inspecting Mr. Croaksworth's body.

"He looks awful," Beatrice said, feeling unsettled as the reality of the scene began to sink in.

She had seen sketches of corpses in the crime columns, but she had never known any of those people before reading of their death. It was sobering to see a man lifeless when he had been so exuberant just a short time ago.

Well, not *so* exuberant, she thought. She felt guilty admitting it, even to herself, but she found Mr. Edmund Croaksworth much more interesting in death.

"Someone wanted him to suffer," Beatrice said as she regarded Mr. Croaksworth's ashen face and bloodstained lips.

"We don't know that," Drake replied, shaking his head dismissively.

"It is a hunch—" Beatrice began, but Drake interrupted.

"Hunches are unhelpful, Miss Steele. We must consider the facts: The signs of poisoning set in after the break. The suddenness and severity of them make me believe that Mr. Croaksworth received the dosage sometime during—or after—the men were in the study."

"Poison is generally a woman's weapon of choice, is it not?" Beatrice began. "And Caroline Wynn was the only woman not in the parlor during the break—"

"Your sister Louisa served Mr. Croaksworth a glass of punch shortly before he died," Drake cut in.

Beatrice felt horror trickle down her spine. "How dare you," she whispered. "Louisa would never—"

"I merely meant to demonstrate the danger of assumptions," Drake said, matter-of-fact. "*Never* rely on a hunch."

He put his hand into Mr. Croaksworth's jacket and gently withdrew a handful of items. He examined the first item in the flickering candlelight. "Pocket watch. Looks normal—engraved with an 'EC.'"

"'EC,' for 'Edmund Croaksworth,'" Beatrice said immediately, but Inspector Drake shrugged.

"Perhaps. We cannot be sure."

She resisted the urge to roll her eyes. Surely there were *some* assumptions that were safe to make. The watch was in Mr. Croaksworth's pocket, with his initials on it—the idea that it belonged to him was hardly farfetched.

Drake held up the second item. It was a tarnished gold frame encircling a miniature in beautiful detail of a lady with flame-red hair.

Louisa.

"Louisa was so attached that she had already gifted Mr. Croaksworth her miniature," Beatrice said, grabbing for the object. She gazed at her sister's sweet expression in the drawing. "It must have been meant as a token of love. What a tragedy that it ended up in the pocket of a corpse."

She looked up to see Inspector Drake moving to tuck the last item from Mr. Croaksworth's pocket away.

"What is that?" she asked, and tore it from his hand before he could protest.

It was a letter, the paper worn as if read over and over again. The edges were rough, seemingly torn from a book. Though the ink was faded, Beatrice could still make out the words upon the page:

> *Dear brother,*
> *By the time you read this, I will be gone. I cannot tell you where I am going, for fear that you shall try to stop me. My mind is made up. I hope that, in time, I can explain every-thing and that you will understand. Until then, all my love—*
>
> *Alice*

Beatrice looked up.

"This is from Alice Croaksworth!" Beatrice exclaimed. "Does this mean she *is* alive? I wonder when Mr. Croaksworth received this?" She looked up at Drake excitedly, but his face held no reaction. "This is a letter from Mr. Croaksworth's sister, who has been missing for *two years*," Beatrice clarified. "An extraordinary discovery."

Still, silence from Drake. Beatrice could have heard a pin

drop—or a luminescent frog croak, were they not burrowing into the muddy ground for safety from the raging storm outside.

"You aren't surprised," Beatrice said as she realized—"You knew about this letter already."

"Perhaps Edmund mentioned it to me in passing," Drake muttered. "After droning on about . . . how breezy it has been in London." He would not meet her gaze, instead looking determinedly at the parquet floor.

"I see. . . ." Beatrice spoke slowly as she began to piece it together. "Of course you knew about this letter already. Because you were *hired* to find her, weren't you? *That's* why you were traveling with Mr. Croaksworth." She lowered her voice so Miss Bolton could not hear—though the woman was out of earshot, she lingered in the doorway, clearly wishing to be anywhere else but Stabmort Park.

Drake pursed his lips, but he nodded. With a thrill, Beatrice turned the letter over to examine the postmark. "This was sent from Bath. I take it this is the last place Alice was seen?"

Drake gave an almost imperceptible nod. "Swampshire is halfway between London and Bath," he explained. "Mr. Croaksworth and I meant to spend the night here and then continue our journey in the morning."

Beatrice looked at the letter once more. A shiver rippled down her spine. "The letter was written in scarlet ink," she noted. "My cousin Grub uses the same shade."

Inspector Drake pulled the letter from Beatrice's hands, folded it, and tucked it into his jacket pocket. "So do many people. That is a mere coincidence."

"Your methods are strange," she said with a flash of annoyance. Must he really dismiss *everything* she said? "From Sir Huxley's description I always thought of you as an assistant who spoke little. I never knew why," she went on.

"I was never his *assistant*, I was his *partner*—" Drake began.

"Now I see that you are quiet because you look only at facts. You do not consider what these facts might mean," Beatrice interrupted. "Therefore you have little to add."

"I have my own methods," Drake said stiffly. "And I would appreciate your compliance with them. I covered for you before, but do not forget that I know about your indiscretion, your immense breach of your community's precious etiquette. . . ."

"I beg your *pardon*—" Beatrice began hotly, but Drake went on, lowering his voice to a hiss so Miss Bolton would not hear.

"What would your friends and family say, if they knew you *were* a fan of the criminal detective Sir Huxley? Obviously you read his column. That explains why you disliked me from the moment we met. He does not hold me in high regard, and neither do his *fans*." He looked at her, mouth pursed in distaste, and Beatrice felt a pang of embarrassment.

"And what would they say if they knew Sir Huxley had deemed you 'gumptionless' and then *fired* you?" she shot back, her embarrassment giving way to anger. Who was he to judge her? She was satisfied to see his eye narrow; she had clearly touched upon a sensitive subject. "I know that no one in London will hire you, except apparently Mr. Croaksworth," she said, pressing on. "Now that he is dead, you have no work. You need to solve this murder in order to redeem yourself."

"And you need *me* to stay quiet so you are not disgraced," Drake snapped.

"Then we have a deal," Beatrice said. She leaned forward and held out her hand. Drake looked at it, confused.

"What deal?"

"You keep my secret, and I keep yours," Beatrice said firmly.

Reluctant but resigned, Drake clasped Beatrice's hand.

His palm was warm and his shake firm. She felt as if her own hand were on fire from his touch, and she quickly withdrew as if burned.

"To the study, then," she said, pushing herself to her feet. "The *alleged* scene of the crime. Miss Bolton can accompany us," she added, nodding toward the door, where Miss Bolton still stood. Her hat seemed to wilt at Beatrice's words.

"Believe me, Miss Steele, I would not do anything indecorous," Inspector Drake said, striding from the ballroom. "Except perhaps throttle you out of annoyance."

"I was just thinking the same thing about you," Beatrice said, exiting the ballroom and leading the way into the study.

Perhaps they were not off to the *best* start—but they had only just begun, she assured herself. They would find the killer, and bring that killer to justice.

CHAPTER 12

Evidence

The Ashbrooks' study was on the ground floor of the house, in the westernmost corner. It was lined on all four sides with neatly organized bookshelves, containing mostly encyclopedias and classic literature, except for one handmade book poking out in the middle marked "*Advantageous Advice,* by Daniel Ashbrook."

Beatrice moved to follow Inspector Drake into the study, but he held up his arm to stop her from going any farther than the doorway.

"Wait here," he instructed.

She hung back while Drake entered. He stared around at the room, observing the towering bookshelves, a settee, and an armchair.

"Looking for the card table, Inspector?" Beatrice asked sweetly.

The muscle in his jaw tensed. Though this was where the men had retired to play cards, there were none in sight. Apart from the bookshelves, the settee, and the armchairs, the room was empty.

"Is this the wrong room?" Miss Bolton peeked inside, confused.

"No," Beatrice said, finally stepping inside with purpose. She pulled back a rug to reveal a trapdoor on the worn wooden floor. "Not everything can be seen on the surface, Inspector," she said, triumphant. "Some things *are* found through conjecture."

"Or from prior knowledge of an unusual house," Inspector Drake shot back.

Beatrice scoffed. "Yes, I did use this spot for games of hide-and-seek as a child," she allowed, "but no one told me about it; I found the trapdoor on my own." She pointed to the carpet. "This rug is often turned up at the corner. Mr. Ashbrook would normally not allow such a tripping hazard, which is what made me notice it years ago."

"What an ingenious child you were," Drake said dryly. "Do tell me more of your precocious exploits."

"I'm sure they will come up over the course of this investigation, since you clearly need assistance," Beatrice shot back.

Drake shook his head in annoyance and turned away. He wrenched the trapdoor open to reveal a winding staircase, leading into darkness.

Beatrice plucked a candlestick from a wall sconce, and took a step toward the trapdoor. The flickering flame from the candle sent shadows dancing along the narrow stairs, revealing jagged stone walls.

"You cannot go down there," Miss Bolton said, staring into the depths. "Do you feel that coldness? It is a spirit; I am sure of it."

"Nonsense," Drake said. "The chamber is merely cool due to its position under the floorboards."

"There is something vile in that room, I can feel it," Miss Bolton insisted. "I shall not cross the threshold. However . . ." She pulled a pair of opera glasses from within her hat. "I will not forgo my duties as your chaperone. I can use these to watch from a safe distance, and then there is no need for me to go down into some hellish secret room."

"Very well," Beatrice said, and descended eagerly into the hellish secret room.

When she reached the bottom of the chamber, she used the flame of the candle to light several more in sconces along the walls. Their warm glow illuminated a small card room: Four leather chairs were pulled up around a card table, the air thick with the scent of rich tobacco. Whereas the parlor was soft and pastel, the card room was harsh and dark, with stone walls and spare furnishings. It was bitterly cold and had a small fireplace containing only ash. The only décor in the room was a faded tapestry hanging on one wall.

It was as if the men had just been there; there was still an indentation in each of the leather chairs where they had sat. An abandoned game of cards was scattered on the table, and four cigars rested in the ashtray, still smoldering. The now-lit candles cast flickering shadows along the walls, like ghosts of the men who had just been here.

"The scene of the poisoning," Beatrice whispered, inhaling the scent of the rich tobacco.

"Allegedly," Drake said, correcting her, but he could not put a damper on Beatrice's enthusiasm. She took a lap around the card table, brushing her hand along it, breathless.

She wasn't merely reading an article with a list of clues. *She was here,* finding them herself. Now that the shock had worn off, she found . . . it was exhilarating.

"Four empty glasses of port. Four hands left on the table . . . clearly, there was a card game," Inspector Drake said, scribbling in his yellow book as he paced, taking in the room. He was so tall that he had to stoop slightly to walk around. Beatrice felt oddly aware of his presence.

She picked up one of the cigars and examined it. Drake grabbed it from her and set it back on the ashtray.

"Can you please not touch everything? You are compromising my investigation," he said.

"Three cigars. Someone did not partake," Beatrice replied.

"I see that," Drake snapped. He looked down at his hands. "They certainly used enough oil."

He turned to examine the cards, and then a small score sheet. "Vingt-et-un," he observed. "A betting game in which players attempt to have their cards add up to twenty-one—"

"I know how to play vingt-et-un," Beatrice interrupted.

"I beg your pardon," Drake replied. "I was unsure if ladies were only permitted to play whist. Your customs are unknown to me."

"London cannot be *so* different from Swampshire," Beatrice said.

"There is a code of etiquette, to be sure," Drake allowed. "But as a member of the working class, I am not expected to adhere to it. I never would have interacted with any members of high society, had it not been for my former partnership with Sir Huxley." He cleared his throat and looked up at Miss Bolton, who watched through opera glasses from her perch at the top of the stairs.

"Naturally I know nothing about him," Beatrice said, also glancing at Miss Bolton.

"Naturally," Drake echoed. He turned back to the score sheet. "They played the best of thirteen rounds." He examined the paper, which listed the initials of the players—C, C, A, F.

"Mr. Croaksworth, Captain Peña, Ashbrook, and Frank," Beatrice surmised. "It seems Mr. Croaksworth won the game overall— though Frank took several rounds." She fanned out the cards, then held up an ace of hearts and bent it. The card was stiff.

Drake made a noise of irritation, but she ignored it. "The deck must be new," she said. "The card is not yet soft." She paused, examining the fanned deck.

Another ace of hearts was partially concealed. She pulled it out.

"It's a trick deck," she told Inspector Drake excitedly. "Two aces."

"The evidence could suggest that someone was cheating," he said, moving closer to her to look at it. "Very astute, Miss Steele."

She felt a rush of satisfaction at his words and eagerly flipped the card so he could see a design on the back: It gleamed in gold, emblazoned with a purple iris in the center. "Purple irises are the symbol of France," she said.

"I thought that was the fleur-de-lis."

"They are one and the same." She examined the card, looking at the tiny purple petals peppered with gold. "And there is one guest at this ball who was recently in Paris. Frank."

Inspector Drake scribbled something in his notebook.

"Not to mention that he behaved unusually after the killing," Beatrice added. She leaned over to look at Drake's notes, but he pulled them from her sight line. As he did so, his hand brushed Beatrice's arm. Both drew back immediately.

"I beg your pardon," Inspector Drake said.

"It is not a problem," Beatrice said, strangely out of breath. Something about his touch made her insides twist as if she had swallowed poison herself. It was a sensation she had never experienced, though it was not unpleasant.

Drake turned from her, moving stiffly, and crossed to the fireplace. Beatrice did not think he meant to observe the embers; it seemed he simply wanted to get as far away from her as possible. Difficult, in such a small room. But suddenly he knelt in front of the fireplace and plucked something from the ashes.

It was a scrap of paper with words scrawled on it. The edges were singed, as if someone had lit a flame, but the small room was drafty. It had clearly been blown out before the page had been destroyed. He withdrew it from the cold ashes, unfolding it.

"What is it?" Beatrice asked, crossing to examine the paper.

Inspector Drake read aloud. "'I, Edmund Croaksworth, shall owe the bearer of this slip twenty thousand pounds.'"

"Twenty thousand?" Beatrice gasped, snatching the paper. "But he won, so he didn't have to pay. Still—such a sum would entice *anyone* into a card game, I'm sure."

"Would the other gentlemen in attendance have been able to match this bet?" Drake said, clearly aghast at the amount. "I do not wish to speculate on anyone's wealth, of course, but . . ."

"No, that is a fair point," Beatrice said, nodding. "The Ashbrooks are the only family who could afford this ante, but I do not think Daniel or his father would gamble with such high stakes." She looked up suddenly. "Daniel, Frank, and Mr. Croaksworth all went to school together, years ago. Arabella told us that it was the fashion among the schoolboys to bet for secrets instead of money. What if the other players pledged private confidences in place of pounds?"

"It's possible," Drake allowed. He picked up a fire poker and dragged it through the ashes. Beatrice's exuberance dimmed to disappointment.

"I suppose that whatever they shared, it is gone now."

"Yes. . . . If there were secrets, they died with Croaksworth," Inspector Drake said pensively. "But if someone revealed something they didn't want getting out . . ."

". . . That could be a motive," Beatrice finished, her excitement sparking once more. She tried to stand but tripped slightly. Drake put out an arm to steady her.

"Are you all right, Miss Steele?" he asked, knitting his brows together in concern.

"What's going on down there?" Miss Bolton called out.

"I'm fine," Beatrice said, exasperated. "My slipper caught on something." She pointed to the floor, where her silk shoe was caught in a patch of something sticky. She tore it away and stared at the floor.

"What is that?" Drake said, and traced a trail of tacky sludge into a corner of the card room.

It led to the faded tapestry hanging on the wall, which Beatrice now saw was a weaving of the Ashbrook family tree. The branches were thick with names and portraits of their noble Swampshire ancestry, as well as small stitches denoting particularly advantageous marriages.

"The trail ends here," Inspector Drake observed.

He drew back the tapestry.

Behind it was a large mirror, framed in gold—a beautiful piece, if it had not been broken clean in half. A seam of glue, still tacky, kept it together—and a plank of wood was nailed across it. The glue had dripped down the mirror, the adhesive staining the floor.

"Someone broke the mirror," Drake said, eyebrows knitted together in confusion.

"Perhaps in anger?" Beatrice suggested. "Though they seem to have tried to fix it."

"Beatrice," Miss Bolton gasped from upstairs, clutching her opera glasses in fright, "Arabella's bloody hands! You don't think . . . if she broke the mirror, and was injured, perhaps—"

"Bloody hands?" Drake interrupted.

"Miss Bolton thought she saw something earlier this evening," Beatrice said. She raised her eyebrows at him and cocked her head toward Miss Bolton, hoping he would understand her meaning: Given her history, Miss Bolton likely had imagined Arabella with blood on her hands, waving in the window.

Though now, she reasoned, that the evening was unfolding in such a way—perhaps Miss Bolton *had* seen something.

"I will need to speak with Arabella," Drake said, looking from Beatrice to Miss Bolton. "And the rest of the guests. Clearly someone knows more than they are letting on."

He climbed the stairs out of the study, and Beatrice followed him as his words echoed in her mind: *Someone knows more than they are letting on.* The realization was finally, fully setting in that one of her neighbors—one of her friends, even—was a murderer.

Beatrice and Drake climbed from the trapdoor, and Beatrice draped the rug over it once more.

"Daniel is the one Mr. Croaksworth came to see; I wish to question him first," Drake said. He turned and extended his notebook to Miss Bolton. "I will need my full attention on each suspect during questioning. Therefore, may I entreat you to take notes, madam?"

"Me?" she said, clearly pleased. She eagerly took the notebook. "Why, yes—I would love nothing more than to create a script for this tragedy."

"Thank you," Drake said, "just the facts, if you please."

"Of course," Miss Bolton said, and withdrew a plumed quill and pot of ink from her hat. "I know exactly what to do."

EXCERPT FROM A PLAY
BY MISS HELEN BOLTON

SCENE I

Daniel Ashbrook's personal chambers. Bookshelves filled with well-worn tomes, heavy velvet drapes, one fraying armchair, and one settee. A desk pushed next to the window is cluttered with colorful bottles of ink and feathered quills. Clearly Daniel is a man of great intelligence, though he might expand his creative horizons by attending one of Miss Bolton's plays, instead of always sending notes that he must "politely decline."

Inspector Drake, Beatrice Steele, and Miss Bolton sit on the settee, Miss Bolton in the middle, as befits such an exemplary chaperone.

Across from them sits Mr. Daniel Ashbrook.

INSPECTOR DRAKE: I understand you and Croaksworth met years ago, at school?

MR. DANIEL ASHBROOK: Yes, I always think back on those times fondly, even if they ended with a rift. When Edmund reached out to mend that rift, I thought we would return to how things used to be. Now . . . I'm sorry. It's just a shock.

MISS BEATRICE STEELE: Take your time, Daniel. You are in mourning.

MR. DANIEL ASHBROOK: Technically, there is no specific mourning period dictated for losing a once-estranged friend, but perhaps I could adopt the period appropriate for losing a cousin, or even a brother. There was a time when we were that close.

CHAPTER 13

Heartache

Beatrice watched as Inspector Drake leaned back, taking in Daniel with a scrutinizing stare.

She had never been in Daniel's chambers. Even when they were young and they had run around Stabmort Park like it was their own personal playground, his room had felt, somehow, off-limits. She looked around as Drake questioned Daniel, their voices a soft rumble.

The furniture was old but clean, the room crowded with towering bookshelves and well-worn armchairs. The walls were covered in star charts, diagrams of the human body, and maps showing the development of Swampshire throughout the years. It was like peering into Daniel's well-organized, erudite mind.

Her gaze lingered on the four-poster bed in one corner. If she became Mrs. Daniel Ashbrook, this was where she would sleep, she could not help thinking. Could she see herself here, reading the books from the shelves? Sleeping in the enormous bed, Ash-brooks from the past glaring down at her? She stared at the plain white coverlet draped across the mattress, then quickly looked away. She could not imagine it now, but she supposed that this could eventually feel like home.

"You used the phrase 'once-estranged' to describe your relation-ship with Croaksworth," Inspector Drake was saying to Daniel. "What was the reason for the separation?"

"Edmund's parents thought my family beneath them," Daniel said, his voice slightly hoarse. "They insisted he cut off all contact." He shook his head sadly. "*When a family stands so tall, they have a long way to fall.*" He suddenly shivered. "I beg your pardon, but might I light a fire?"

Beatrice stood to oblige, but Drake held up a hand.

"I would prefer not to disturb anything in this room."

"This room is not a crime scene, Inspector," Beatrice said in ir-ritation.

"And Beatrice's lips are turning blue," Daniel pointed out.

Truthfully, she had not even noticed the cold; she had been too distracted with sneaking glances around Daniel's private quarters. But her friend had her best interests at heart, ever the gentleman even in the face of tragedy, she thought gratefully.

"Very well," Drake grumbled, and shed his jacket. "Take this." He shoved it gruffly toward Beatrice.

She caught a whiff of his orange scent as she pulled it on. She had never worn a man's jacket before. Drake's was shabby but warm, and it felt strange and audacious to be suddenly enveloped in his body heat. She slipped her hands into the pockets and felt the crackle of paper.

She knew it was Alice Croaksworth's letter, which Edmund had been carrying with him when he died. How horrible, Beatrice thought, that the Croaksworth family had been struck with so many tragedies. A sister missing, parents dead, and now Mr. Croaksworth, murdered. No doubt Miss Bolton would think them cursed—and Beatrice would agree.

There was something cold in the other pocket. Beatrice withdrew it and held it to the side, so neither Drake nor Daniel could see.

It was Inspector Drake's spoon. Delicate and small, yet heavy—clearly solid silver. As she looked at it closer, she took in the ornate dog on its handle: It was a Scottish terrier with a boxy frame and playful beard. Again, she thought how strange it was that he walked around with a spoon in his pocket, and such an odd one at that. She tucked it back into his pocket, her fingers curled around its handle.

"Tell me about the card game that occurred in the study," Drake continued, and Beatrice looked up in interest.

"I declined to play cards," Daniel replied.

"That explains why there were only three cigars but four glasses of port," Beatrice said. "'A' must be Mr. Hugh Ashbrook. Your father enjoys drinking but does not smoke, isn't that right, Daniel?"

"Yes," Daniel said with a nod at Beatrice. "He calls it 'the devil's breath.' But he *does* enjoy cards; my father always says that gambling gets the blood pumping."

"It did the opposite tonight," Drake said. "Where were you during the break, then?"

"At my father's insistence, I retired to my personal chambers to give Captain Peña a change of clothes, after his garments were submerged in soup. I then remained here," Daniel said. He took his hands off the arms of the chair and placed them in his lap.

Beatrice noted that there was dampness on his chair from where his palms had been. Nervous sweat, she thought.

Was Daniel hiding something?

"Why did you remain?" Drake pressed.

"I had much on my mind," Daniel said finally. "Reuniting with an old friend forces one to take stock of one's life. I could tell that Mr. Croaksworth was looking to settle down, to secure an engagement, and I began to think . . . perhaps I am ready for that, too."

Beatrice felt her breath catch in her throat as Daniel met her gaze and then quickly looked away.

Did he mean . . . her?

"*When you open your heart, a great love can start,*" Daniel went on. He suddenly stood up and crossed to his desk. "Forgive me. I do not wish to forget that adage; I must write it down." He rifled through his desk but began to grow exasperated. He murmured to himself, "Yet another quill gone. And my best ink, as well. That *thief . . .*"

Inspector Drake stood. "Thief?"

Daniel's cheeks reddened. "Forgive me. I should not gossip—"

"Sir, a man has been murdered," Drake interrupted brusquely, clearly annoyed. "I believe it may be permitted this once."

"It is just that every time Mr. Martin Grub visits Stabmort Park, items go missing," Daniel explained.

"Aha!" Beatrice said, also rising to her feet. Both Daniel and Drake stared at her. "I knew there had to be an explanation for the quilt," she went on.

"What quilt?" Daniel asked, confused.

"The quilt I sewed for you," Beatrice explained. "When I gave it to you last Christmas, you said you would sleep with it every night, but I noticed only a plain coverlet on your bed." Her cheeks felt hot at the admission that she had been snooping, and she avoided his eyes.

"Grub must have absconded with that as well." Daniel shook his head angrily. "He ought to be ashamed of himself. *Stealing is never an idea that is clever.*"

"I think that's enough rhyming for now," Drake said firmly, moving for the door. "We shall talk to Grub at once and determine what else he may have stolen."

"Thank you for your help, sir," Daniel said to Drake, rushing to open the door for him. "I am sure that Sir Huxley will appreciate your excellent groundwork on the investigation."

"And *I* am sure that when he arrives, he shall find the murderer apprehended and restrained," Drake replied, and stomped out of the room.

Miss Bolton and Beatrice followed. Beatrice lingered, looking back at Daniel.

"Thank *you* for your help as well, Beatrice," Daniel said quietly. "I do not know what we would all do without you. What *I* would do without you."

She nodded, trying to think of some reply. But she was too overwhelmed by his words, and the evening's events. So she merely turned to follow Drake down the dark hallway of Stabmort.

EXCERPT FROM A PLAY
BY MISS HELEN BOLTON

SCENE II

The cloakroom of Stabmort Park. A velvet-lined antechamber just off the front entrance, this closet is filled with guests' cloaks and outer clothing.

When the door opens, Inspector Drake, Miss Steele, and Miss Bolton find Mr. Martin Grub squatting on the floor, sifting through the garments. He jumps as they enter, surreptitiously pocketing a coin he pulled from one of the cloaks.

MR. GRUB: I was just ensuring that our outerwear was safe. One can never trust servants to arrange garments properly.

Inspector Drake holds out a hand, and Mr. Grub begrudgingly hands him the coin.

MR. GRUB: You are wasting your time questioning me, sir. I was too busy watching Miss Beatrice Steele to notice anything this evening. We have decided to enter into an engagement.

INSPECTOR DRAKE: I didn't realize you two were attached.

MISS BEATRICE STEELE: We are not. And we never shall be.

The air in the small room is suddenly fraught. Clearly, Miss Steele is uncomfortable, especially since she has just come from her true love's chambers.

MR. GRUB: Miss Steele likes to tease, but she will give in to my whims eventually. What many don't know is how persuasive, how attractive, how charming I—

INSPECTOR DRAKE: I'm sorry to interrupt, but you have a bit of snot coming out of your nose. Would you like a handkerchief?

MR. GRUB: There's no need.

INSPECTOR DRAKE: Ah. I've never seen a gentleman suck in like that.

CHAPTER 14

Impertinence

Beatrice backed away from Mr. Grub. She could not fathom how she was related to this man—and she certainly could not stomach the idea that he could inherit her family's estate. The thought alone made bile rise in her throat.

"That is a baseless accusation," Grub was saying to Drake in outrage. "I did not *steal* anything; Daniel told me I may visit Stabmort Park whenever I like—"

"Because he is generous," Beatrice cut in.

"—and if I took anything, it was never without permission," Grub finished. His pants and jacket clinked as he moved to cross his arms defensively.

"What about our estate?" Beatrice asked, before she could stop herself.

Grub scoffed. "What of it?"

"You are already set to inherit it upon my father's death," she said, "but you filed a petition to declare my father insane, so that you could take it even sooner. However. If Louisa had married Mr. Croaksworth, you would have lost out on this inheritance. Therefore you could have killed Mr. Croaksworth to prevent losing the estate you think is yours."

For a moment it was quiet in the little cloakroom, and Beatrice felt a flicker of satisfaction. But then Mr. Grub snorted with laughter. "That is ridiculous," he said. "You should not lob such accusations, Beatrice, if you want to be *my* wife."

Beatrice glanced over at Drake, now expecting him to dismiss her words as well. But instead, he stared thoughtfully at Mr. Grub.

"Mr. Croaksworth was a threat to you," he said, "and now you have been accused of stealing. These facts do not suggest innocence—"

"I shall stop you there, Inspector," Grub interrupted. "I hardly spoke with Mr. Croaksworth, and I did not consider him any *threat*. He was a young, arrogant upstart."

"Mr. Croaksworth was young, yes, but could hardly be considered an upstart," Drake replied. "His family is part of the social elite."

"Wealth and good breeding are not the only important factors in determining a man's gentility," Grub insisted. "One must consider hardiness. Fortitude. *Stamina.*"

"You thought Mr. Croaksworth weak?" Drake asked, raising an eyebrow.

"His parents have passed, his sister disappeared, and he is now dead," Grub told him. "Gentlemen protect their fortunes so they may pass them to their descendants and secure their lasting social position. But the Croaksworth family line has died out because of weakness."

"I would argue it died out because someone murdered him," Drake replied. "And as Miss Steele has just pointed out, you have a very clear motive."

"Me?" Grub asked, eyes widening. "Why would I kill someone, when I can just wait for them to die on their own?"

"That is a horrible thing to say about a man who has been killed," Beatrice said in disgust.

"Compassion makes a man vulnerable," Grub said. His posture showed a lack of concern at such scrutiny; he seemed to almost enjoy the conversation.

"Lack of compassion makes him suspicious," Beatrice shot back.

Grub sighed.

"The most suspicious person here is not me. It is Hugh Ashbrook." He withdrew a scrap of paper from his pocket and handed it to Inspector Drake. "I found *this* in his cloak. Not that I was rifling through it. I merely stumbled upon it."

Drake unfolded the paper and scanned it.

"It is a note of cancellation for three cases of champagne," he told Beatrice, handing it over to her.

"The Ashbrooks always serve champagne the morning after a ball, at sunrise," Beatrice explained.

"Exactly," Grub said triumphantly. "Why cancel this order, unless Ashbrook knew there would be no toast—only *death*?"

He smiled smugly, and Beatrice felt a trickle of horror pass over her. Mr. Grub was awful, but why else *would* Mr. Ashbrook have canceled the champagne?

"I will ask Mr. Ashbrook for his explanation," Drake said, and pushed his way from the cloakroom. "But I am not finished with you, sir."

"I wish we were," Miss Bolton muttered, pinching her nose.

Drake exited. Beatrice and Miss Bolton followed, leaving Grub alone in the closet, oozing the scent of dung.

EXCERPT FROM A PLAY
BY MISS HELEN BOLTON

SCENE III

A cramped closet filled with glass vials.

Beatrice, Inspector Drake, and Miss Bolton stand inside; they watch as Mr. Hugh Ashbrook sorts through his collection of tonics and creams.

MR. HUGH ASHBROOK: Canceled champagne? I don't recall. . . . But memory loss *is* a symptom of the fainties.

He fans himself weakly, trying to act as if he is innocent, but there is guilt lurking under the surface. Everyone can clearly see it. They all think of how he once gave Miss Bolton an eye cream because she was "really looking her age, and even though she doesn't have a husband doesn't mean she must let herself go." No good can come from a man like Mr. Ashbrook.

CHAPTER 15

Disrespect

"You played cards with Captain Peña, Frank, and Edmund during the break," Inspector Drake said, examining a shelf filled with a cluster of glass bottles.

Mr. Ashbrook, Inspector Drake, Beatrice, and Miss Bolton had all crowded into the tiny tonic cabinet. All four walls were lined with glass shelves, on which various bottles and pots were neatly arranged. Mr. Ashbrook had organized the tonics alphabetically and placed a small label beneath each one, describing its contents.

"I played cards?" Hugh Ashbrook asked in confusion, rubbing his hands with a peppermint-scented lotion.

"Do you not remember this either?" Inspector Drake asked. He shot Beatrice a skeptical glance. He reached into his pants pocket for the scorecard. Beatrice noticed him pause, a confused expression flitting across his face, but it passed quickly. He withdrew the score sheet and held it up for Mr. Ashbrook to examine. "Your initial is listed there," Drake went on. "'A' for 'Ashbrook.'"

"Ah. Yes. It must have slipped my mind," Mr. Ashbrook said, shaking his head as if that would jog his memory. "As I said—Madam Jessica, my healer and clairvoyant, told me that memory loss can be a symptom of the fainties. She gave me a daily mixture that is meant to help. It must be taken promptly at half past seven each evening, but I missed my dose; that must be why I can't recall the game. Or the canceled champagne. Perhaps I should cut down on the sherry," he added, giving a weak laugh.

"Port," Beatrice said, correcting him, and both men in the room turned to look at her. "The glasses at the card game had dregs of port, not sherry," she said.

"That must be it," Mr. Ashbrook said, nodding at her. "I never drink port normally. I suppose tonight I was caught up in the revelry."

Drake turned back to the neat shelves. "You have quite a collection of medicines here."

"Do look around," Mr. Ashbrook said excitedly. "I am always happy to introduce people to my health regimen. I often get inquiries about it, as I maintain such a youthful countenance."

Beatrice examined a bottle at eye level, trying to ignore how her arm brushed against Inspector Drake in the tight quarters.

"'Andy's Gargle,'" she read from the plaque below it. "'Use at night to aid with digestion.'"

"And it certainly does aid in that," Mr. Ashbrook said, nodding.

"'Marquess Jesse's Spirit of Begonia,'" Miss Bolton read from another, looking at a crystal bottle filled with violet liquid. "'Soothes the soul.'"

"Hm. I don't recall from where I purchased that particular tonic," Mr. Ashbrook said thoughtfully. "Generally I find my soul is very soothed. It's my physical body that needs aid."

"'Gray powder,'" Inspector Drake read, picking up a small pot.

"Oh, that is quite good," Mr. Ashbrook said with a serious nod. "Mercury with chalk. It's an excellent purgative."

"Suffice it to say you have certain tonics in this collection which, if administered incorrectly, could be toxic," Drake said to Mr. Ashbrook, who looked confused.

"The aim of my collection is healing, not harming," he replied.

"A killer would not share that aim. Are you missing any items?" Drake asked.

"Oh, no," Mr. Ashbrook said, shaking his head. "I would have noticed. Though . . ." He trailed off.

"Yes?" Beatrice prompted, and Mr. Ashbrook sighed.

"When I came in here earlier this evening, the door was open. I'm sure I left it closed and locked. However, nothing was missing." He sighed. "Of course I suspect Mr. Grub. That man can't seem to keep his sticky fingers off of anything. But he usually leaves a terrible scent in his wake, and I detect no offensive odor."

Beatrice inhaled, expecting to detect Grub's lingering metallic, earthy stench. Instead, she smelled only a light fragrance. Sweet, like roses.

"I have noted Mr. Grub's tendencies," Drake said with a nod. "Does he hold on to the items?"

"As far as I know," Mr. Ashbrook said, confused. "Why do you ask?"

Drake reached into his pants pocket and withdrew an empty vial. "I found this, slipped into my pocket," Drake explained. That must have been what he felt earlier, Beatrice realized.

"That is definitely one of mine," Mr. Ashbrook said at once, reaching for it.

"Do you know what it would have contained?" Drake asked.

"I . . . can't remember," Mr. Ashbrook said. "It should be labeled. You think Mr. Grub took it and . . . put it in your pants pocket?"

"I do not know," Drake said, shaking his head.

"Unusual," Beatrice said, looking from Drake to Mr. Ashbrook. "Why would he have done this?"

"I do not know," Drake repeated. "But, Mr. Ashbrook, if you notice anything else missing, please alert me at once." Mr. Ashbrook tried to take the vial, but Drake shook his head. "I must keep this. If you remember what the contents were, and they prove to be poisonous, I am sorry to say that this could have been the murder weapon."

"This is all so terrible," Mr. Ashbrook said, swaying slightly. "I expected this evening to end in an engagement between my daughter and Edmund." His knees buckled, and Drake held out an arm to steady him. "Thank you," Mr. Ashbrook said. "I fear my fainties have grown rather severe."

"From my understanding," Drake said, clearly confused, "Mr. Croaksworth showed interest only in Louisa."

Mr. Ashbrook shook his head. "I am certain that Mr. Croaksworth was only being polite," he said firmly. "Arabella and Edmund became engaged years ago."

"Arabella and Mr. Croaksworth were *engaged*?" Beatrice repeated, stunned by this sudden revelation. "I never heard about this."

"They broke it off," Mr. Ashbrook explained. "This was disappointing, but it was decided just after my wife passed. Arabella was in mourning, and we all agreed it was best to postpone. However, I am sure Edmund's flame for Arabella never went out."

Confusion rippled through Beatrice. Mr. Croaksworth had said nothing of any attachment to Arabella, and neither had Daniel. Louisa had never mentioned it, and surely *she* would have known; she and Arabella had grown so close. Had Arabella tried to keep it a secret? Or was Mr. Ashbrook mistaken?

"Interesting," Drake said thoughtfully. "And are you certain they separated because of your wife's death, or could it have anything to do with the Croaksworths' belief that your family was too low in status to associate with theirs?"

Beatrice grabbed his arm to stop him, but it was too late. Mr. Ashbrook turned bright red, his handsome face twisted in anger. He stood, tipping his chin up and staring down his nose at Drake.

"My family is of noble blood, sir. How dare you suggest that anyone would consider us *not good enough*?"

He protested passionately, but Beatrice could not help noting that though Mr. Ashbrook looked angry, he did not look surprised.

"I wouldn't expect you to understand anything about my family," Mr. Ashbrook continued, glaring at Drake. "You are no one of importance."

Beatrice stepped in front of Drake. "Sir. There is no need to be discourteous," she said. Mr. Ashbrook turned to appraise her. She felt as if she were shrinking as he eyed her worn gown, her cheap jewelry, and finally, her stained slippers.

"I did not ask *your* opinion, Miss Steele," Mr. Ashbrook said finally. He did not have to say anything more; she knew exactly what he thought of her by that searing gaze. It was a look meant to put her in her place.

She squared her shoulders, a sudden determination welling within her. "Your *son* asked my opinion," she said. "Daniel wished me to maintain decorum, and I consider your words impolite." She tilted her own chin up to match his.

"It's fine, Miss Steele," Drake said, "it's nothing I have not heard before."

"Inspector Drake is helping us; we should not disrespect him," she pressed.

"Perhaps Daniel's trust in you was misplaced," Mr. Ashbrook shot back. "He thinks you respectable. But I am not so sure. I have never seen such impertinence."

His words made Beatrice's body flood with panic. Mr. Ashbrook could easily destroy her reputation—and any chance she had at securing an engagement with Daniel. His threat was clear.

"Now I must ask you to leave," Mr. Ashbrook continued, "lest you cause my forehead to wrinkle."

He pushed Miss Bolton, Inspector Drake, and Beatrice out of the cramped tonic closet. As she exited, flushed with embarrassment and indignation, Beatrice saw a book wedged on one of Mr. Ashbrook's shelves.

Doors of the English Countryside. The book he had confiscated from her earlier that evening.

She snatched it and shoved it back into her pocket, just before Mr. Ashbrook slammed the door to the closet behind them.

"Considering the facts, Mr. Ashbrook looks very suspicious," Drake said thoughtfully, glancing at the closed door to the tonic room. "His claim that he does not remember anything is unlikely. After all, he played cards during the break, so he had an opportunity. Additionally, he considers himself frail; poison would therefore be an appropriate choice of weapon. His closet, furthermore, provides access to such poison."

"And he may have motive," Beatrice replied. "Mr. Ashbrook insists that Croaksworth and Arabella were separated because his wife had just died, but perhaps this is simply what he used as an explanation."

"I thought the same thing," Drake said with a nod.

"Perhaps what *truly* happened was that the Croaksworth parents intervened to separate Edmund and Arabella," Beatrice finished.

"So you are saying that Mr. Ashbrook held a grudge all these years," Drake said, "and then murdered Croaksworth for revenge?"

"If he knew about all of this, it's possible," Beatrice said with a nod. "He is a prideful man. And he would do anything for his family. If he thought that Mr. Croaksworth had rejected Arabella . . ."

Drake nodded thoughtfully, then leaned closer to Beatrice. "You have known Mr. Ashbrook for many years, have you not?"

"Our families are friends," Beatrice told him, "but that is because his late wife and my mother were so close."

"Mrs. Steele and Mrs. Ashbrook were the same age," Miss Bolton offered, as if this explained it.

"And they shared many common interests," Beatrice said firmly.

"But Mr. Ashbrook has never been the same since her death," Miss Bolton continued in a frightened whisper. "He used to be— well, not quite *jolly,* but at least respectful. You must not judge all Swampshirians by his behavior just now; as he has grown older, he has placed an increasing importance on good breeding."

"And no doubt his wife's untimely fall to consumption caused him great distress over his physical health," Beatrice added. Mr. Ashbrook had never been a second father to her, by any means, but she had watched him open gifts on Christmas. She had seen him dance minuets with his wife and celebrate birthdays with his children. He had changed after his wife's death, becoming more judgmental, more prideful. He had withdrawn and spent more time with his tonics than his neighbors. But now she wondered: Just how much had he changed?

She followed Inspector Drake and Miss Bolton into the shadowy hallway of Stabmort Park and took in a breath. The tonic room had been claustrophobic, its sweet-scented air stifling.

"We should speak with Arabella next," Drake was saying, when Beatrice suddenly froze in her tracks. Drake turned back.

"Are you all right, Miss Steele?"

"The scent in the closet," Beatrice whispered. "It smelled like rose. *Evening rose,* to be exact." She looked up at Inspector Drake. "Evening Rose is the signature scent of Miss Caroline Wynn."

EXCERPT FROM A PLAY
BY MISS HELEN BOLTON

SCENE IV

A golden harp sits in the center of the Stabmort Park music room. To the left of the harp is a pianoforte.

Seated in between the two instruments is Caroline Wynn, who plays a beautiful tune on the harp with her right hand and accompanies herself on the pianoforte with her left. She begins to sing. She is incredibly talented, and her voice soars like an angel's.

ENTER Beatrice, Miss Bolton, and Inspector Drake. Beatrice slams the door behind them, and Caroline Wynn breaks off the music.

MISS CAROLINE WYNN: You poor dears, you must be exhausted. Come here and I shall give you some scones; I always keep them in my reticule in case I see someone in need.

CHAPTER 16

Lies

Beatrice sat across from Caroline Wynn, a scone in her hand and a scowl across her face. Of course Caroline thought of nothing but *their* comfort, when *she* was the one being questioned; she acted as if she were hosting afternoon tea instead of being interviewed in the course of a murder investigation.

"Beatrice, might I offer you a handkerchief?" Caroline said quietly. "You have a few scone crumbs on your lip." She held out a handkerchief, and Beatrice snatched it irritably.

"Shall I play a bit more while you eat?" Caroline suggested, gesturing to the harp and pianoforte. "I know music can be very comforting in trying times. If only I had been playing earlier, perhaps Mr. Croaksworth would still be alive."

"Are you suggesting that your music could have *healed* him?" Beatrice asked, crumbling her scone in one fist and Caroline's handkerchief in the other.

"Of course not, I'm not *that* good," Caroline said with a tinkling laugh. "I simply mean that music can often soothe anger. Whoever did this may not have been moved to such awful violence if I had only been more diligent."

"Unfortunately those who decide to commit such crimes are rarely stopped by a kind word or pretty tune," Drake said, pursing his lips. Beatrice was glad to see that he didn't seem taken in by Caroline's fluttering behavior. He took a seat on a chair across from the harp, back straight and face set.

"You're right," Caroline said softly, her eyes pricking with tears.

Beatrice took in her appearance with suspicion. Caroline was well-dressed as usual, in a pristine muslin gown. Her hair was pulled back in an elegant chignon, her face open and sweet. The only jewelry she wore was a single pearl on a ribbon around her neck.

Odd, Beatrice thought, her eyes lingering on the pearl. She was sure Caroline had been wearing an emerald choker earlier that evening. She had noticed it especially because the piece was so irritatingly becoming on Caroline's pale, swanlike neck. Why would Caroline have switched her jewelry halfway through the evening?

"What a fetching piece," Beatrice said, nodding at the choker. "The pearl looks so natural, as if it were plucked from the ocean by Captain Peña himself."

Caroline's expression fell, and Beatrice felt a flicker of triumph. It seemed Captain Peña *had* given Caroline the necklace. Were they still in love?

But Caroline quickly rearranged her features back into a bland smile.

"The captain did gift me this necklace, as a token of affection. However, our attachment was so long ago that it seems like another lifetime. I told him as much."

"Your attachment was only a year ago," Beatrice pointed out.

She leaned forward, growing impatient. "What we truly want to know is: What were you doing in Mr. Ashbrook's tonic closet?"

"The tonic closet?" Caroline said, blinking innocently. "I don't know—"

"You left behind your scent, the one designed just for you," Beatrice interrupted, "so there is no use lying. Did you go there during the break? You were not in the parlor; everyone assumed you had retired to the ladies' room to rest."

"She does have such a gentle disposition," Miss Bolton allowed.

"I *did* retire to the ladies' room," Caroline insisted.

Inspector Drake leaned forward and sniffed the air. Caroline looked to him, confused.

"Does my scent offend you?"

"It is a bit strong," Drake said, "but that was not what caught my attention." He turned to Beatrice. "Her perfume is gardenia, not rose."

"What?" Beatrice leaned forward and inhaled.

He was right. She did not smell Caroline's signature scent—the subtle rose she had noted earlier in the evening, and in the tonic room. Now Caroline smelled strongly of gardenias.

"You changed your perfume," Beatrice said. "Why?"

"I have been wearing this scent all night," Caroline replied. "But if it is displeasing, I would be happy to wash it off—"

"You are lying," Beatrice interrupted. She stared at Caroline, but her wide eyes betrayed nothing. "You were not wearing that scent earlier; I remember. We discussed it!" Beatrice went on. "But there *is* gardenia-scented perfume in the powder room of Stabmort Park," she remembered. "Miss Bolton and I smelled it."

"That's true!" Miss Bolton agreed quietly, her hand fluttering toward her chest.

"Perhaps you went into Mr. Ashbrook's tonic room and stole poison. But you realized that your perfume left a lingering smell, so you went to the powder room and doused yourself in a different scent, to avoid suspicion." Beatrice suddenly leaned forward, alight with another revelation: "Before Mr. Croaksworth died, his last words were: 'The angel isn't an angel at all—can't you fools see it?' The killer is someone who seems innocent. Angelic. Who else could that be . . . but you?"

Miss Bolton gasped. For a moment Caroline blinked up at Beatrice, swaying slightly. And then she keeled over into a faint.

Miss Bolton rushed to her, drawing a small bottle of smelling salts from within her hat. She knelt next to Caroline and waved the salts under her nose.

"She's faking it," Beatrice said in frustration. "I had her!" She whirled around to look at Inspector Drake for confirmation but he had not moved from his place on a settee.

"It does not add up, Miss Steele," he said. "Even if Caroline had stolen the poison, she was never close enough to Mr. Croaksworth this evening to administer it."

"What if," Beatrice said, thinking aloud, "she had a partner. Someone who has always been in love with her. Someone who would do anything for her."

"You mean Captain Peña?" Drake asked, considering. "That is an interesting theory."

"Don't you mean an unreasonable hunch?" Beatrice could not help shooting back.

"Yes," Drake said, his mouth twitching. "That is precisely what it is."

"I don't think I can go on," Caroline said weakly from the ground. She sat up in Miss Bolton's arms, revived but shivering. "I am so sorry, but my heart can't take such needling from my dearest friend."

"No matter," Beatrice said. "We shall get the answers we desire elsewhere."

Caroline hobbled out, and Beatrice turned to Miss Bolton.

"I hope you have it in writing that Miss Wynn broke wind as she exited," she said, and Miss Bolton looked up, confused.

"I didn't hear it."

"I assure you," Beatrice said, "it occurred." She stuffed Caroline's handkerchief into the pocket of Drake's jacket unceremoniously, thinking that it was quite all right to not be friends with everyone who was one's same age.

EXCERPT FROM A PLAY
BY MISS HELEN BOLTON

SCENE V

In the belly of Stabmort Park, the bath room is dark, lit only by the luminescent glow of a natural spring in the center of the stone chamber.

Captain Peña stands straight-backed at the edge of the ledge surrounding the spring, staring into the green-tinged waters. It is not surprising he would find himself here, as he seems almost pulled toward the water, his body listing toward it, his face rugged and serious.

ENTER Beatrice, Drake, and Miss Bolton. Everyone cannot help but stare at his rippling muscles; he is far different from the boy who left for the navy a year prior.

INSPECTOR DRAKE: Captain, good evening. It's refreshing to finally speak to someone who actually holds employment.

CAPTAIN PEÑA: My appointment in the navy was a *duty*, sir. Not a job.

CHAPTER 17

Oaths

Though most prominent members of society preferred to take the waters in Bath, there were several natural springs in Swampshire that locals enjoyed. Stabmort Park was built upon one of those springs. This was the oldest room in the mansion, the spring surrounded by ancient stone, and one of Hugh Ashbrook's prized sources of bragging rights about his home. But Beatrice had not been here since childhood; the healing waters were reserved for the gentlemen, lest any lady show more skin than the designated six inches of décolletage. Though Captain Peña, with his weathered face from his year at sea, would now fit in well with the distinguished gentlemen who would gather here, Beatrice noticed he still had a youthful, earnest look in his eyes.

However, he also had one hand curled around his cutlass scabbard. It glinted in the glow from the spring, its silver appearing oddly green.

"Please describe the nature of your current attachment with Miss Caroline Wynn," Drake said, his voice echoing in the stone room. "Did you return to Swampshire to see her?"

Captain Peña leaned even closer to the water, as if straining to escape the question.

"Last year, Caroline cut our tether and set me adrift," he said tersely.

"Did you think to . . . reel her back?" Drake asked awkwardly.

"I don't wish to discuss Caroline," Captain Peña began, "for I don't wish to prematurely scuttle what might sail. Caroline and I may still find our way back to each other—"

"She rejected you because you were not a man of means," Drake cut in. "Mr. Edmund Croaksworth, on the other hand, was wealthy. Did this inspire jealousy?"

"I did not see Edmund as competition," Captain Peña said sternly. "I, along with the other guests, thought he had capsized in Louisa's ocean."

"Did Mr. Croaksworth confide this during your card game, at the break?" Inspector Drake asked.

"I did not play cards," Captain Peña replied. "Miss Beatrice Steele spilled soup all over me, so I spent the break swabbing my deck."

Inspector Drake held up the score sheet they had found in the study. "This score sheet lists C, C, A, and F. Are you saying that you were not present at the game? That you are not the other 'C'?"

"I was fathoms away," Captain Peña insisted, squinting at the sheet.

"'C' must stand for someone else then," Beatrice said to Drake, frustrated. *Who* had been at that fateful card game?

It was warm in the room, a natural heat emanating from the glowing waters of the bath, and Beatrice withdrew the handkerchief Caroline had given her. She dabbed at her forehead with it, feeling as if she were being boiled alive. She suddenly paused and looked down at the handkerchief, which was embroidered with an "EC."

"Why would Caroline have had Mr. Croaksworth's handkerchief?" she murmured. "As Inspector Drake observed, she was never close to him . . . that we saw. Unless the fourth person at the card game . . . was *her*."

Miss Bolton gasped.

"A lady would not play cards, alone, with men," she said in dismay.

"Caroline lied about her scent. What if she used gardenia scent . . . to cover the smell of cigar smoke from the card room?" Beatrice said excitedly. "Or the smell of copious port. I *knew* she drank!"

"'Twas I," Captain Peña interrupted, and they all stared at him. His voice echoed in the small, dark room, as if he were confessing again and again. *'Twas I. 'Twas I.*

He cleared his throat and went on: "I played cards. I joined late, once I was shipshape. Caroline was not present. As Miss Bolton has said, it would not be appropriate for a woman to play cards with gentlemen, unchaperoned."

"You just told us you weren't there," Drake said, irritated.

"I misspoke," Captain Peña said. "I meant that I didn't play the *first* round of cards. I arrived on deck late."

"And you played with Mr. Croaksworth, Frank, and Hugh Ashbrook?" Drake asked.

"Aye." Captain Peña placed a hand on his chest as if taking an oath.

Beatrice thought she saw a shadow of something pass over his stern face, but it was hard to decipher behind his thick beard. He was lying, she was certain—but she had no way to prove it. It was infuriating.

"I *did* notice someone who seemed irritated that Mr. Croaksworth was so fixated on Louisa," Captain Peña said quietly. "Arabella Ashbrook. A captain must note these relationships between shipmates; I saw that she was unhappy. On edge. Cheeks red, and not from scurvy."

"We shall talk to her next," Drake assured him.

Captain Peña shook his head with a sigh. "I never expected such peril ashore. There was never any poison on the high seas." He regarded Beatrice and Inspector Drake as if sizing them up. "We are all counting on you both to find whoever is responsible for this terrible occurrence," he said sternly. "The guests are filled with fear. Please know that you have me at your disposal, when it comes time to restrain whoever committed this crime. We must be ready to take down the killer." He indicated his cutlass. "*Si vis pacem, para bellum*—if you wish for peace, prepare for war."

Drake raised an eyebrow. "Let us hope it does not come to *that*," he said.

EXCERPT FROM A PLAY
BY MISS HELEN BOLTON

SCENE VI

Arabella Ashbrook's chambers. A room filled with Parisian furniture, fashion sketches, and a brocade chaise over which Miss Ashbrook is draped, heaving with melodramatic sobs.

MISS ARABELLA ASHBROOK: Pardon my tears. I've just lost my future husband.

MISS BEATRICE STEELE: There aren't any tears coming out of your eyes.

Now that Miss Steele mentions this, everyone notices that Arabella's face is dry. She immediately sits up and fluffs her hair, flustered.

MISS ARABELLA ASHBROOK: How dare you. I'm not crying *yet;* I'm just thinking about how awful it will be when I *do.*

CHAPTER 18

Rumors

Arabella's suite was well decorated in the finest fashion, with a lace-draped four-poster bed in one corner and a vanity in the other. She had a cedar wardrobe stuffed with gowns, all custom-made, and a wall filled with sketches of her wearing these gowns. Beatrice was overwhelmed by the excess of colors, scents, and textures. In the center of the room was a billowing gown draped on a dress figure, its red fabric almost reflective. It was clearly made in the Color of the Year, and Arabella must have planned to don it at the traditional Color Announcement portion of the ball. It was the first time Beatrice could remember that they had skipped this important event.

Beatrice reached out to touch the gown. The fabric was silky smooth and lush, and the design avant-garde. She would never have been able to accomplish something so complex. Whoever had designed the garment had painstakingly created it for Arabella. It fell in delicious waves to the ground, evoking a beautiful—

though admittedly gory—image, considering the events of the night.

"Someone thought they saw you earlier tonight with blood on your hands," Drake said measuredly, glancing askew at Miss Bolton. "Can you offer an explanation for this?"

"Blood on my hands?" Arabella said in confusion. "I am certain that wasn't me."

"Perhaps this person saw you wearing this gown and mistook it for a wound," Drake said, indicating the red garment. Miss Bolton shook her head slightly but stayed quiet.

"Perhaps," Arabella said, still looking confused.

"It is beautiful," Beatrice said. "Is it from Paris?" She exchanged a look with Drake, who leaned forward slightly to gauge Arabella's reply.

"Yes," Arabella said, adding proudly, "It was designed especially for me." Her brow was set, and her movements careful and controlled.

She did not seem like a woman in mourning.

"Have you recently purchased anything else from Paris?" Drake asked. Beatrice knew he was thinking of the fleur-de-lis playing cards in the study, with their gold-and-violet design. Now she leaned forward in interest, excitement building at the prospect of a lead—until Arabella shook her head.

"I have not been to Paris in years. We used to go every year. I was a muse to . . . some seamstresses there. But my father never approved. When my mother passed, he stopped the trips altogether. Many designers still have my measurements, and they send me gowns. But I have not set foot on French soil in a long time. The gowns are all I have." Her voice caught, and for one moment, Beatrice could see what *real* emotion looked like on Arabella.

"Tell me about your relationship with the deceased," Drake said, watching Arabella closely.

Arabella shook her head as if to wake herself from a trance. "Edmund and I knew each other from years ago," she said, composed once more. She seemed strangely comfortable for someone being questioned after a murder. Beatrice noted how Arabella melted into her chaise, relaxed, whereas Daniel and Caroline had perched on the edges of their seats.

Arabella continued: "We met when I visited Daniel at school. The moment I laid eyes upon Edmund, I knew we were destined to be together. I simply adored the man."

"We have heard that the two of you formed an attachment in your youth," Drake replied. "Were you ever engaged to Mr. Croaksworth?"

"Who told you that?" Arabella asked, and Beatrice noted that she looked caught off guard by the question.

"Your father. He said he expected you to rekindle your affection this evening," Drake said.

"We did have an attachment, years ago," Arabella said. She swallowed.

"So why didn't you marry him?" Beatrice prompted. "It would be an advantageous match. You said yourself that you were 'destined to be together.'"

"My mother died, and so we decided to end the engagement," Arabella snapped. "One can hardly expect a girl to get married in a black wedding gown." She shuddered. "You'll have to excuse me. I am still so upset from this entire ordeal. I will probably not be able to court any men for a very long time, since I'm essentially a widow."

"Mr. Croaksworth hardly spoke to you this evening," Beatrice pressed. "He spoke only to my sister. He did not seem to be in love with you—he seemed to be in love with *Louisa*."

For a moment Arabella glared at Beatrice, and Beatrice clamped her mouth shut. Anxiety flooded her limbs.

Had she gone too far? Arabella was of a higher station than

Beatrice, not to mention Daniel's sister. It could be ruinous to offend her.

"Say what you want to say, Beatrice," Arabella said, her voice dangerously sharp. "Do you think I killed Mr. Croaksworth because I was jealous of Louisa?"

"No one is making any accusations," Drake said evenly. "We are merely gathering information—"

"Edmund and I have history," Arabella interrupted, still addressing Beatrice. "You couldn't possibly comprehend. Besides, Louisa's not some helpless child," Arabella said, shaking her head. "She *likes* the competition. We spoke about it before Edmund even arrived. We had an understanding."

An understanding, Beatrice thought. *What could this mean?* Something caught in her memory. A paper, curling into ash. Arabella's and Louisa's secrets, lost to the embers. What had they each written?

"Louisa can make her own decisions," Arabella went on. "What she does is not up to *you*." She smoothed her skirt. "If Mr. Croaksworth wanted to be with Louisa, I would have supported it. I would not have *murdered* him."

"Did your engagement truly end because of your mother's death, or was there another reason?" Beatrice said, her gaze fixed on Arabella.

"What other reason would there be?" Arabella replied, stonefaced.

"The Croaksworths were proud," Beatrice replied. "Perhaps the truth is that they ended the engagement because they thought you were not good enough for their son. Your family passed it off as a mutual decision, to save face."

"That's ridiculous! The Croaksworths are hardly the epitome of perfection. They could never be, with that unfortunate scandal marring their reputation," Arabella scoffed.

"You mean the recent death of Mr. Croaksworth's parents?" Drake asked.

"No . . . Edmund's sister," Arabella said. "Alice Croaksworth."

Beatrice felt a tingle at the name.

"Do you know something about Alice's disappearance?" Drake asked slowly.

"Oh, Alice didn't disappear," Arabella said with a smirk. "She was sent away."

Drake and Beatrice exchanged a look and then turned back to Arabella.

"You mean—"Drake began, and Arabella shot him a significant look as she indicated her stomach.

"She was in trouble," she said, miming a rounded stomach. "I could not say anything more, without being indelicate. You understand."

"I never heard of this from Mr. Croaksworth," Drake said, shaking his head.

"You wouldn't have," Arabella replied. "If he knew, he would never have spoken of it. Think of the shame on their family! These things must be kept secret, for everyone's sake."

Beatrice inhaled sharply. If Alice Croaksworth had birthed a child out of wedlock, this would have been quite the controversy. "But it has been two years," she whispered, almost to herself. "If she *had* been . . . in a family way . . . would she not have returned by now?"

"Alice and Edmund's parents were extremely strict," Arabella said. "I can't imagine she would be permitted to return. One slip, and you are sent away forever." She laughed, but Beatrice noted that it sounded hollow. Forced.

Her eyes drifted over to her wall, and Beatrice traced her gaze. Arabella stared at a row of fashion sketches, her own face staring back, swathed in charcoal dress designs. She said she had been a muse to seamstresses, plural, Beatrice noted—but all the sketches seemed to be drawn in the same hand.

"These designs," Beatrice began, gesturing to one of the sketches. "Who made them?"

"Sophie Beaumont," Arabella said immediately. "She is the most respected dressmaker in Paris. Once again, I wouldn't expect *you* to know such things."

"I think we're done here," Drake said, rising to his feet.

"Did Sophie draw all of these?" Beatrice asked, ignoring Drake. She felt as if she were on the verge of something—and as Arabella met her gaze, Beatrice's heart beat faster.

"Yes," she said. "She is very inspired by me."

Beatrice felt as if pieces of a puzzle were sliding into place, but before she could ask more questions, Arabella rose to her feet.

"If you wish to speak of France so much, go talk to Frank. He was just there. *I* have told you everything I know," she said, her words pure ice.

She pointed at the door in an invitation for them to exit. Her pink gown swished as she slammed the door after them.

As Beatrice backed away from Arabella's chamber, she heard a creak somewhere in the distance. Like footsteps.

"Is someone there?" she called out. Miss Bolton drew in a breath, and Drake looked at Beatrice sharply.

"Did you hear something?" he asked, on edge. But Beatrice shook her head.

"I suppose it was nothing," she murmured.

But as they made their way down a dark staircase, she thought she could hear—ever so faintly—the creaking once more.

EXCERPT FROM A PLAY
BY MISS HELEN BOLTON

SCENE VII

The billiard room of Stabmort Park features a green baize-topped billiard table, gray wallpaper, and several marble busts of Ashbrook ancestors. Mr. Frank Fàn holds a long pole and leans over the table, tapping a ball with a clack. As always, he looks dashingly handsome.

ENTER Inspector Drake, Beatrice, and Miss Bolton. Frank greets them all with his trademark roguish wink.

MR. FRANK FÀN: Miss Steele, Miss Bolton—how do you both maintain such ravishing complexions, even in the face of such a trying evening?

MISS BEATRICE STEELE: Perspiration.

MR. FRANK FÀN: Ah, yes. It is the dew upon the bloom of your womanhood—

INSPECTOR DRAKE: Sir, please do not force me to arrest you.

MR. FRANK FÀN: I am not the murderer!

INSPECTOR DRAKE: That sentence was a crime.

CHAPTER 19

Implications

"Alice was not in a family way. That is a vicious rumor," Frank said as he did a lap around the billiard table, inspecting the ball as if deciding where to strike it. "Gossip can be so brutal." He leaned down and got into position to make a hit.

"Did this gossip come up during your card game with Mr. Croaksworth?" Drake asked. He stepped out of the way of the long cue just in time; Frank swung it around with a flourish to line up his shot.

"No, the whispers permeated the social scene in London, where I have several . . . female companions. They keep me abreast of hearsay; women like to confide in me," Frank explained. "And you are mistaken about the card game being *mine*—I did not partake."

"Your initial 'F' is on the scorecard," Drake said. Frank slipped and hit the ball at an awkward angle. It ricocheted into a corner of the table. He cleared his throat and straightened to stand.

"Must have been a mistake," he said. "Perhaps someone has a

nickname which begins with 'F.'" He looked from Drake, to Beatrice, to Miss Bolton. "Anyone fancy a game?"

Beatrice picked up a cue.

"I would like us to stay focused on the investigation at hand,"
Drake said, cocking the eyebrow above his eye patch. "And are billiards even considered an appropriate game for ladies in Swampshire?"

"Page three hundred and four of *The Lady's Guide*," Beatrice replied. "Ladies are permitted to handle balls while playing billiards."

Drake snorted, and Frank gave Beatrice an appreciative nod.

"We must keep our spirits up somehow, and Miss Steele is a
worthy opponent. We shall see if her aim is as sharp as her wit,"
Frank added with a wink, and Beatrice cleared her throat.

As she leaned over to line up her own shot, she observed Frank
out of the corner of her eye.

Could this man she had known for years be a killer? Yes, he was
a shameless flirt, but nothing about him felt sinister. She could not
imagine him murdering anything other than a lady's hopes for marriage.

She leaned down and struck her ball. It careened forward and
knocked into Frank's, sinking his into a pocket.

"A hazard for me," she said, straightening. "I wonder it *wasn't*
you playing cards, Frank, as the 'F' who played the game was badly
beaten—as you are about to be again, just now."

As Frank moved past Beatrice to line up his next shot, he placed
his hand at the small of her back. This was one of his signature
moves, but now it felt as if it carried a warning.

"If 'F' lost, that's proof it wasn't me," Frank said lightly. "I never
lose a game, Miss Steele. Whether it is cards, billiards . . . or the
battle for a woman's heart. It is all about strategy." He pulled his
ball from the pocket and positioned it to make another hit, but he
moved too forcefully and missed his ball altogether.

"I see. Is your strategy to cheat?" Inspector Drake asked calmly.

"Gentlemen never cheat," Frank replied. "Their words are honest—in the moment."

"We located a trick deck in the study," Drake replied. "Would this be considered honest?"

Frank's fingers turned white as he gripped his cue. "I don't know why you're asking me," he said with a laugh. "I have no use for silly tricks."

"I have a question," Beatrice said. "To whom were you planning to propose this evening?"

"Why, are you hoping to secure an attachment?" Frank took a step toward her, and she could smell the strong scent of his cologne mingled with sweat.

He was nervous, she thought. Why?

"Remove your gloves," she told him. The ring he had would be revealed, she knew, and then Frank would be forced to divulge his secrets.

"I was unaware we were playing *this* type of billiards. Shall my cravat be stripped off next?" Frank teased as he slowly pulled off his gloves, one finger at a time.

"Aha!" Beatrice said, but her smugness was premature.

Both of Frank's hands were bare. The ring—whose outline she had seen, just hours before—was gone.

"Where is it?" she demanded. Frank shrugged, but the gesture seemed overly casual. He trembled slightly as he pulled his gloves back on, moving a bit too quickly.

"I don't know what you're talking about." Frank crossed his arms. "You know how much I adore you, Beatrice, but I simply cannot be tied down to one woman. You understand."

"Of course we do," Miss Bolton said with a kindly nod of her head.

"I am young," Frank continued, flashing a roguish grin at Miss Bolton. "I must be free to come and go as I please. But I never forget you, Miss Bolton. Or you, Miss Steele—"

"Are the two of you involved?" Drake interrupted, looking from Frank to Beatrice.

"Yes," Frank said, at the same time Beatrice said, "Absolutely not."

"Frank thinks himself 'involved' with every woman in town," Beatrice said, irritated. "He is accustomed to having his pick of us at each ball." She leaned forward. "Were you frustrated that Mr. Croaksworth caused such a stir? Normally it is *you* the ladies make eyes at."

"I had no problem with Croaksworth," Frank said, but his voice sounded taut. "All the fuss over him was, of course, ridiculous. Everyone thought him a perfect gentleman, yet he was very forward. Did you not see him with Louisa?"

"Excuse me," Beatrice said, irked by this sudden turn of the conversation. "Mr. Croaksworth treated my sister with the utmost respect. She is a *lady*."

"They were dancing very close. Scandalously close," Frank said. "Though of course, I have heard that they were previously . . . acquainted."

"*What?*" Beatrice slammed down her cue stick. "Louisa met Mr. Croaksworth for the first time this evening."

"That you know of," Frank replied. "Ladies often have rendezvous which they keep quiet. Everyone was talking about it tonight."

"I haven't heard anything of the sort," Beatrice insisted. "And I'm sure I don't know what you are implying with such talk!"

"Good, because it is unsavory," Frank said. His eyes, which usually sparkled flirtatiously, were now flat. He continued: "Croaksworth was a charming, handsome man. He could have easily swayed Louisa to do something . . . unseemly. Then again, gossip can be so brutal."

He winked. It was not the coy wink he usually gave; this gesture held nothing but malice.

Without stopping to consider her actions, Beatrice lunged across the billiard table, reaching for Frank. Before she could even decide what she was going to do, an arm encircled her waist, yanking her back. She was suddenly breathless to find herself in Inspector Drake's arms. Miss Bolton looked on, quill held in midair and mouth agape. Beatrice stilled and moved to pull away, but Drake held her in his steady grasp for a beat longer. His heavy breath matched her own.

"I beg your pardon," Drake said, clearing his throat, as he finally released her. "I thought it would be better to stop you, before you did something you would regret."

"A delicate lady could only bruise my heart, not my body," said Frank in a weak voice. He was behind the billiard table, his arms and his cue raised in a pitiful defense against Beatrice's near pummeling.

"I would not call Miss Steele delicate," said Inspector Drake, turning back to Frank. "I think she is quite capable of bruising you."

"It is simply a lovers' spat," Frank insisted. "As the Steele women know, all is fair in love and war."

Beatrice clenched her hands into fists so tightly that her nails bit into her palms. They itched to throttle Frank. She was so angry that she hardly registered the embarrassment of Drake's physically stopping her from attacking a man.

Though, if she was being honest with herself, her body tingled where Drake's hands had brushed her waist.

"If anyone behaved inappropriately toward ladies tonight, it was *you*, Frank," she said, looking up at him in disgust. "You are lying about being involved in the card game, you clearly hated that Mr. Croaksworth was so popular with the women, and you would probably choose poison as a weapon so as not to soil your perfect suit—the evidence is mounting." She stared into his eyes. "You should tread carefully."

Frank stood, shaky on his feet. "Miss Steele," he said, regaining his composure as he squared his shoulders, "I think it is *you* who should tread carefully."

He began to walk toward the door, his threat lingering in the air like smoke.

Drake reached into his pocket and withdrew the cards emblazoned with the fleur-de-lis. "Don't forget your trick deck!" he called out to Frank.

"Thank you," Frank said sharply, turning back and extending one hand to take the cards. He froze, realizing his mistake. "I . . . mean . . . I . . ." He had no rebuttal and instead rushed out of the billiard room empty-handed.

Beatrice finally released her nails from her hands, slowly uncurling her fists.

"Thank goodness you maintained propriety," Drake said. She whirled around to face him, but he did not look angry; in fact, he seemed almost amused.

"I had to defend my sister's honor," Beatrice said. She straightened her gown, flustered. "Just don't tell my mother."

"We shall see if it comes up," Drake said. "I wish to speak to Mrs. Steele next."

As she followed him back into the hall and down a dark passageway, heart still beating fast, Beatrice had the sudden, chilling feeling that someone was watching her. She whirled around, ready for another confrontation. But when she turned, there was no one there.

EXCERPT FROM A PLAY
BY MISS HELEN BOLTON

SCENE VIII

A guest room of Stabmort Park. The drapes are drawn open to reveal a storm of hail outside. Louisa sits by the remains of a fire. Her face is ashen, and Mr. Croaksworth's blood stains her gown.

Poor little Louisa seems to shrink on her small chair. She has not looked this devastated since she lost a round of shuttlecock at her seventh birthday party. Mrs. Steele dabs at the bloodstain with a handkerchief. Mr. Steele paces. Mary's feet are visible where she hides behind a velvet curtain. Beatrice, Drake, and Miss Bolton sit by the fire on a settee.

MRS. SUSAN STEELE: Of course Mr. Croaksworth fell for Louisa instantly. He had eyes.

She looks at Drake's eye patch.

MRS. SUSAN STEELE: No offense.

CHAPTER 20

Explanations

Beatrice regarded her parents as they sat across from Inspector Drake, behaving exactly as she could have expected: Her father was in complete denial that any tragedy had occurred, his expression puckish, and her mother was a bundle of nerves. Mrs. Steele drew a fan from her bosom and flicked it open, waving it at herself vigorously in distress, as if the cool air could alleviate the situation at hand.

But Louisa was frozen. She stared into the fire, her gaze vacant. She had bags under her eyes, and her curls—once neatly arranged— were now a mess. The bloodstain across her gown made it look as if Louisa had been stabbed in the heart. And in a way, Beatrice thought, she *had* been.

"How are you? Do you need any water, anything to eat? Some sherry for your nerves?" Beatrice asked quietly as Drake began to question Mr. and Mrs. Steele. She reached out to take Louisa's hand. But Louisa snatched her hand away before Beatrice could grasp it.

"This is all simply devastating," Mrs. Steele was telling Drake. "To think, Mr. Croaksworth was about to marry my daughter, and then he just dropped dead. No one has worse luck than me."

"Apart from Mr. Croaksworth," Drake replied.

"Are we *sure* this isn't an elaborate comedic performance?" Mr. Steele said, regarding everyone in the room one by one as if expecting someone to crack a smile and finally admit that he was right. "These balls can be so boring. Hugh Ashbrook agrees—he's been falling asleep all night."

"From the fainties," Beatrice said, turning from Louisa to her parents.

"Where were you during the break, Mr. Steele? Only four played the card game, and I have not heard of your whereabouts," Inspector Drake continued.

"I suppose you'll find out," Mr. Steele said with a mischievous grin. Mrs. Steele tossed her hands in the air, exasperated.

"Tell him the truth; this is hardly time for tricks, Stephen. A man is dead!"

"Exactly. We need a laugh now, more than ever," Mr. Steele insisted. But he relented, turning back to Inspector Drake. "When I arrived in the study, the card room was closed up and I assumed the card game already in play. I seized the opportunity to find the perfect hiding spot for my false rat. Since my wife insists I spoil everything, you shall find it under the little rug in the study."

Drake nodded. "I shall confirm that. Now, I understand you approved of the potential match, Mrs. Steele. But what were your thoughts, sir?"

Mr. Steele seemed surprised and confused by the question. "I don't have an opinion on these matters," he said, eyes widening.

"I don't permit it," Mrs. Steele explained.

"Surely a father has at least a *thought* about the man who might marry his daughter," Drake said, pressing him.

"I liked him?" It sounded more as if Mr. Steele was posing a question rather than replying.

"And you thought him appropriate for your daughter?" Drake asked. "Fathers can be very protective. Well." He paused, knitting his eyebrows together. "*Some* fathers."

"He seemed inoffensive to me. If I believed otherwise, I would have spoken up. . . . I certainly wouldn't want anyone to hurt Louisa," Mr. Steele allowed. "She is a precious angel."

"Interesting word choice. An angel . . ." Inspector Drake said thoughtfully. "Mr. Croaksworth's final words were 'The angel isn't an angel at all.'" He turned to Louisa, who was still staring silently into the fire. "Louisa. I can see you are upset, but I will need you to answer some questions to clarify what exactly occurred this evening. First, there was an implication that you and Edmund spent time alone. That you . . . *knew each other* before tonight."

Mrs. Steele gasped, and Mr. Steele flinched as if he had been slapped.

"Forget Frank's ridiculous accusation!" Beatrice said firmly, irritated that he had even brought this up. She turned to Louisa. "Rest assured I put a stop to it right away."

"Thank you," Louisa whispered, but she still avoided her sister's eyes. Beatrice watched as she dug her fingers into the soft fabric of her armchair, leaving little half-moon indentations from her nails.

"Could you please recount your night?" Drake pressed. "As you spent much of your time with Mr. Croaksworth, anything you saw—any detail or observation—could prove helpful."

"It's all a bit of a blur," Louisa said, "but I shall try. As you know I arrived on time, and Arabella and I eagerly anticipated Croaksworth's entrance. When he finally made it, we were introduced, and I danced with him."

"What did you discuss during the dance?" Drake asked. "Did he say anything that might signify an enemy, or any unease? Did he mention drinking anything unusual?"

"No, he mostly discussed his favorite color, which was all colors," Louisa said miserably. "He was very polite."

Her voice caught, and Mr. Steele withdrew a small silver flask from his jacket pocket and offered it to her.

"Lemonade, my dear?" he asked gently.

Louisa took the flask but did not drink. "How terrible to think that the entire Croaksworth family is now lost forever," she murmured. She turned her wide eyes up to Drake. "What will happen to his body?"

"Don't worry about all of these particulars, Louisa," Beatrice said, leaning forward. "You mustn't concern yourself with such dark thoughts."

"I expect he shall be sent back to London and buried in a family plot," Drake told Louisa, his voice unexpectedly gentle. "But we can arrange for you to get your miniature back before that happens."

"My miniature?" Louisa asked, confused.

"It was in Mr. Croaksworth's pocket when he passed," Drake said, now looking at her more intensely. "Did you not give it to him?"

"Oh," Louisa said slowly. She licked her lips and then nodded. "Yes, I did. We were growing close. I thought . . ." Her voice broke.

"You are too good, Louisa," Beatrice said with a rush of sadness for her sister. "Perhaps you should lie down. Do you need a blanket? I shall fetch you one—"

"I can do some things on my own, Beatrice," Louisa said, her voice suddenly strained.

"That's not what I meant," Beatrice said, distressed. Why was Louisa shutting her out, even now?

"It is clear that Mr. Croaksworth's attentions were focused on Louisa this evening," Drake said, "and I have to consider: Would this have put him in danger? Would someone have wanted him dead . . . because of her?"

Louisa inhaled sharply.

"That's ridiculous," Mrs. Steele snapped. She pulled Louisa to her feet and placed a protective arm over her daughter. "We have told you everything we know. Now, my daughter needs to rest."

"Yes," Beatrice said, "Arabella can loan you a different dress, Lou. And you can freshen up with some belladonna for your pupils, like you like."

Louisa's shoulders stiffened. She still did not look at Beatrice, her eyes now trained on the floor.

"Isn't belladonna a plant?" Drake asked.

"The juice from its berries is used as a beauty product for young ladies," Beatrice answered, glancing over at him. He was staring at Louisa with a sudden interest. "It's for the eyes," Beatrice continued. "It makes the pupils larger."

"Edmund's pupils were enlarged at the time of his death," Drake said slowly. "Belladonna may be used for beauty, but if the juice from the berries is ingested—"

"It is a fatal poison," Beatrice finished in a whisper. A prickle of unease ran down her spine.

"Excuse me," Louisa said faintly, and Beatrice was alarmed to see that her sister's face had turned from a pale white to a sickly shade of green. "I feel ill."

"I have a few more questions—" Drake began, but Louisa suddenly clapped a hand to her mouth.

"I'm going to be sick!" She rushed out of the parlor.

"How dare you," Mrs. Steele said, jabbing a finger at Inspector Drake. Then she turned on Beatrice. "Aren't you supposed to be ensuring he behaves properly?"

She stomped away after Louisa. Inspector Drake shifted in his seat, and there was a sudden noise of breaking wind. He looked around, confused, and withdrew a rubber cushion from his seat.

"Pardon me," Mr. Steele said, gently taking the pooting pillow from Inspector Drake's hands. "My timing is usually better, but tonight proves . . . challenging." He tucked the cushion into his jacket and ambled off after his wife and daughter.

"Louisa has a gentle disposition," Beatrice said. She stared after her family as her father closed the door behind him. "She has not experienced such hardships before; she cannot be expected to—"

"Did she bring belladonna with her to the ball tonight?" Drake interrupted.

"Most ladies do. A vial of belladonna is a normal item to keep in one's reticule," Beatrice sputtered.

"But perhaps there is only one vial that is empty," Drake said softly. "Only one vial that was used for murder. Louisa was surprised when I mentioned the miniature on Edmund's person, as if she was not aware he had it," he continued. "This suggests that she gifted it to someone else, and then it somehow ended up in Edmund's possession."

Beatrice stood up, filled with indignation, but Drake held up a hand.

"I am merely considering the facts, Miss Steele."

"Then you should consider these. Hugh Ashbrook claims he does not remember the card game, or the canceled champagne, both of which could be tied to the murder," Beatrice shot back. "Mr. Grub has a suspicious number of inheritances and desires another—there's motive. Not to mention that Caroline Wynn was caught red-handed in multiple lies. Why are *these* suspects not at the top of your list?"

"I never said they weren't," Drake replied.

"Oh my." Miss Bolton, who had been scribbling silently up to now, paused her pen to look from Beatrice to Drake. "This is all very bad, isn't it?" she said weakly. "The killer could be anyone."

"I'm afraid so," Drake said, turning to her. "And now, Miss Bolton, if I could ask you a few questions."

EXCERPT FROM A PLAY
BY MISS HELEN BOLTON

SCENE IX

Miss Bolton dutifully takes a seat in the armchair next to the dwindling fire, now facing Beatrice and Drake, who sit across from her as if they are her opponents in a card game. She leans her elbows upon the card table and continues taking notes as Drake begins his questioning.

Outside, the storm rages on, hail pelting the window like a constant reminder that they are all trapped with no escape.

INSPECTOR DRAKE: Miss Bolton, what are your thoughts on Mr. Edmund Croaksworth? You are a single woman. Did *you* have any hopes of securing his attention this evening?

MISS HELEN BOLTON: Hardly! I am happily single. I have enough pets to keep me company; a husband would simply not fit in my house.

INSPECTOR DRAKE: Were you ever resentful of the fact that people mocked you? Perhaps resentful enough . . . to commit murder?

Miss Bolton has a brief recollection: her gentle mother, who died young; her austere father, who resented little Helen for living when his beloved wife was dead. She remembered how the feral kittens at the edge of their estate were her sole company, how she would perform skits for them, imagining that she were anywhere else. She also remembered how her father complained of the kittens' incessant mewling, and how one day he grew so annoyed with it that he lifted his pistol off the wall, his gaze resolute. And she recalled how she took his second pistol from

the wall and followed him, determined that no one would take away
her only friends in the world.

INSPECTOR DRAKE: Miss Bolton, did you hear what I said? You can
    stop taking notes now.

END PLAY.

CHAPTER 21

Analysis

Miss Bolton looked small, sitting by the fire, practically swallowed up by her enormous hat. Inspector Drake stood and paced the room, while Beatrice remained seated.

"There is one thing which might be of interest," Miss Bolton said in a soft voice. Drake stopped pacing and waited for her to continue.

"I don't know if it's any help," she said, sounding almost apologetic, "but after the break, I lingered in this room to adjust my hat." She nodded at a mirror above the fireplace, framed in gold. "It was the only looking glass not covered in too much dust. The Ashbrooks should find a new maid; their current help does not keep this place nearly clean enough—though of course, my own estate is filled with hairballs, it is difficult to manage such large houses—"

"Miss Bolton," Drake interrupted, "the item of interest?"

"Oh, yes," Miss Bolton said as two patches of red appeared on her cheeks. "While I was adjusting my hat, I heard Mr. Croaks-worth in the hallway. He was arguing with someone."

"With whom was he arguing?" Drake said, leaning forward.

"The other person did not say anything," Miss Bolton said, biting her lip. "But Mr. Croaksworth sounded angry. He said something like, 'I cannot prove anything yet, but I will,' and 'I like good people, and I am sorry to say that you are bad.' I was too scared to go look, so I hid until they had gone."

"And nobody saw you?" Drake asked.

"No, a woman my age tends to go unnoticed," Miss Bolton answered matter-of-factly.

"I see," Drake said. "And you are sure of what you heard?"

"Well . . . I *thought* I was," Miss Bolton said uncertainly.

"I ask because you also saw Arabella Ashbrook with blood on her hands. But she had no recollection of this occurrence," Drake said. "Is there anything else we should know that you have observed tonight, madam?"

"Yes," Miss Bolton said seriously. "I think there are supernatural forces at play here, Inspector. Perhaps they are responsible for the evil that has occurred this evening. Do you know the poems written of apparitions coming out of squelch holes? And the night wolves?" She leaned forward and whispered to him, hands cupped around her mouth. "I have seen one before, on my front porch."

"Hold on," Inspector Drake said, shaking his head. "Slow down. Supernatural forces?"

Miss Bolton's eyes widened. "Ghosts," she whispered.

"I see," Drake said. "And . . . what is a squelch hole?"

"A regional anomaly," Miss Bolton explained.

"Deep mud chasms," Beatrice added.

"I don't have any further questions about . . . night wolves," Drake said, "but I do want to know why you did not bring up any of this earlier. In particular, the argument you overheard in the hallway."

"I forgot," Miss Bolton said, shrinking under his severe gaze.

"You forgot about an argument between someone unknown and a man who was murdered. This seems like something one would remember," Drake said, shaking his head. "I must follow up by asking . . . do you have a history of hysteria?"

"You think . . . I'm crazy?" Miss Bolton dropped her hands and wilted. Even the feather on her hat seemed to droop.

Beatrice glared at Inspector Drake. "Miss Bolton is not hysterical. You wanted evidence—she has given you a lead."

"The night wolves?" Drake asked sarcastically.

"The argument between Mr. Croaksworth and an unseen person," Beatrice shot back. "Perhaps he knew something and was murdered for it."

"That may be—but I must consider *all* the evidence," Drake said. "Miss Bolton, you have described multiple instances of seeing or hearing things that no one else has mentioned. The evidence suggests that your 'visions' are fiction."

"If Miss Bolton says this occurred, then I believe her," Beatrice insisted, but Miss Bolton held up her small hand.

"Don't, Beatrice. It's nothing I haven't heard before. After all, I'm just a silly old maid. We can't argue with facts. If you'll excuse me," Miss Bolton uttered quietly, casting her eyes toward the floor as they filled with tears. "It seems my services are no longer needed . . . or helpful in any way."

She suddenly stood, and hurried toward the door.

"Miss Bolton, wait!" Beatrice said, rushing after her. She caught Miss Bolton's arm, but Miss Bolton broke away.

"He's right, Beatrice," she said, her voice hoarse. "Why trust a lady no one wants?" She backed out of the room, pulling the door shut behind her.

"Are you happy now?" Beatrice turned the full force of her anger on Drake. "You've upset a poor woman who has never shown any hint of a violent nature. She wouldn't hurt a fly— in fact, she catches them in jars and sets them free outdoors!"

"I have no doubt the Miss Bolton you know is an upstanding person," Drake said. "But the fact is that each person here cannot possibly be so, for one of them is a murderer."

"So who is it then?" Beatrice asked, and Drake blinked.

"I beg your pardon?"

"We have interviewed each guest," Beatrice said, "so now is the time for you to tell me . . . who do you think did it?"

Drake pursed his lips. He crossed and uncrossed his arms, and then cleared his throat twice.

"What is wrong with you?" Beatrice demanded.

"I have never been asked that question before," Drake said finally.

"But you worked with Sir Huxley for years." Beatrice was incredulous.

"He did not ask my opinion," Drake replied.

"I suppose as an assistant—" Beatrice began.

"I was not his assistant!" Drake interrupted. "I was his partner. At least, I *thought* I was." He shook his head in frustration. "But this is irrelevant. I cannot make a prediction, for there is one person I have not yet questioned." He paused and picked up the notebook Miss Bolton had left behind. "Miss Beatrice Steele."

"Me?" Beatrice laughed, but Drake's face remained calm. "Fine, then," she said defiantly. "Ask me whatever you wish. I have nothing to hide; *I* did not murder Edmund Croaksworth."

She suddenly felt acutely aware that she and Inspector Drake were, for the first time that evening, completely alone.

"Did you dislike Croaksworth, because he might take Louisa away if their relationship progressed?" Drake asked, pacing in a circle around her.

"Of course not. I just wanted someone who could take care of my sister and treat her well," Beatrice said, crossing her arms.

"Your observations regarding Croaksworth's beverages this evening lead me to believe that you know how to administer poison," Drake continued.

"Who doesn't?" Beatrice said. "You pour it into something. It's hardly an interesting method of murder."

"I find it strange you would use the word 'interesting' to describe murder," Inspector Drake said, raising one eyebrow.

"I misspoke," Beatrice said tensely.

"You were less than enthusiastic about the ball until Croaksworth died, at which point your eyes appeared much brighter and your countenance much more passionate," Drake said.

"It was the shock of it!" Beatrice protested.

"You rushed to insert yourself into the situation—"

"Daniel *suggested* I assist."

"He insisted. I could have rejected a suggestion," Drake snorted. "You have only interfered thus far."

"That's it," Beatrice said, "I've had enough. You refuse to follow etiquette, you are shamelessly offensive, and you ignore the contributions I have offered regarding the case at hand. Now you dare accuse both me and my sister. I do not have to stand for this."

Beatrice strode toward the door.

"Where are you going?" Drake sputtered.

"I'm going to find Miss Bolton. I want to catch the killer just as much as you do, but I'm not looking to insult every person who crosses my path as I do it."

"It was a question, not an insult—" Drake began.

"It was both, and you know it. You may have parted with Sir Huxley on bitter terms, but you might benefit from recalling his motto," Beatrice cut in. "'Decorum above all.' That is not just about behavior; it is about treating others with respect." She shook her head. "I'm sure you shall be fine without me." She strode out the door, slamming it shut behind her.

No one knows. We are safe, for the time being. Let us not talk of it at the ball, let us hardly even speak to each other so we shall not give anything away. We still have time to determine the best course of action.

But as I write this, I also know: We do not have unlimited time. The clock is ticking. We must make a decision.

Until I see you next—

Penelope Burt

CHAPTER 22

Threats

Beatrice rushed down the hallway, seething with frustration—and confusion.

She had always thought she could solve any crime if only given the chance. But she was realizing that Drake was right about one thing: Emotions did affect one's view of a case. Every suspect of Mr. Croaksworth's murder was someone Beatrice had known, and in some cases, someone she loved, like Miss Bolton. How could she put this aside?

And how could she put aside her dislikes, as well, she thought as she passed family portraits, flickering candles, and floor-length mirrors. Mr. Grub was a threat to her family; of course she thought him suspicious. Mr. Ashbrook had always judged Beatrice, and he might even stand in the way of her and Daniel. She found him suspicious, too. Not to mention Caroline. Were these individuals truly top suspects, or did Beatrice simply *hope* that they would be guilty?

"Miss Bolton?" she called out to the hallway in front of her. Stabmort Park was vast, and she had no idea where her eccentric companion might have gone. The maze in her mind made it no easier to think straight.

She needed to find clarity. She needed to talk it all through with someone who understood her.

Resolved, Beatrice turned down a hallway and began to walk in the direction of Daniel's chamber. It was wrong to visit him un-chaperoned. But she suddenly felt certain that he was the only person who might truly be able to help.

She paused, her eyes flicking to one of the mirrors in the hall-way.

She had seen something in its reflection. It looked, strangely, like the swish of a black cape. She took a step forward to get a closer look.

"Miss Bolton? Is that you?"

And then a hand clamped over her mouth. Beatrice flailed wildly, trying to get a look at her attacker, and could just catch sight of a dark figure draped in a cloak. The figure clasped gloved hands around her neck, and she fought as they began to squeeze.

There was a rustle of someone else in the hallway, and the dark figure loosened their grip, distracted by the noise. Beatrice felt a flood of relief as Inspector Drake rounded a corner. He was now approaching where she stood. If he would only look up, he would see Beatrice—but his eye was trained on the floor. She struggled against her captor, trying to shout for assistance—but the figure tightened their grip once more on her neck. Only a hoarse silence escaped her mouth. The figure pulled her roughly behind a suit of armor and pressed a hand over her lips, just as Drake passed them.

Black creeped into the edges of her vision, and she could feel her limbs going numb. Was this how she was about to die? Strangled in Stabmort, not even able to view the face of her killer?

No, she thought. This was not how it would end. She put up a hand. She could reach nothing but her own ears—but this would do. She tore one of her dangling earrings from her lobe and stabbed it as hard as she could through her assailant's gloves and into the soft flesh of their wrist. The figure hissed and dropped their grip from Beatrice's neck.

"Help!" Beatrice choked out, and she shoved the suit of armor over with a *clang*. At the noise, the figure tore away, disappearing in the shadows of the hallway.

Beatrice fell to the floor, gasping for breath. Her neck throbbed with pain, but her vision began to focus once more as she inhaled the musty scent of Stabmort. She had never smelled such sweet air.

"What is going on?" Inspector Drake appeared once more, out of breath. At the sight of Beatrice collapsed on the floor, he immediately fell to his knees.

"Miss Steele. What has happened?"

Beatrice pointed a shaking finger down the hallway. "Someone—attacked—me," she choked out.

Drake immediately jumped to his feet and took off in the direction in which she pointed. Beatrice stumbled to stand and clutched the wall to steady her.

She could hear a grandfather clock ticking somewhere in the hallway, the passage otherwise silent. And then soft footsteps echoed, growing closer.

Drake turned a corner and approached her, his face set in a strange expression. "There is no one there," he said.

Beatrice looked down the hall, bewildered. "How could they have gotten away so quickly?"

"I have no idea," Drake said, eye flashing. "But we should get out of the hallway in case they come back. . . ."

"In here," Beatrice said, and pulled him down the hallway. She pushed aside a large tapestry, revealing a door, and wrenched it open. Drake ducked inside, and she followed, pulling the door closed and bolting it behind them.

They were now in a small room, with only a window and writing desk. Beatrice lit a few nubby candles and then sat at the desk, still catching her breath.

"This was Mrs. Ashbrook's writing room," she explained. Cobwebs covered everything in the room; clearly, it had not been used since her death. No doubt it was too painful for any of the Ashbrooks to venture inside now.

Drake nodded, but he looked only at Beatrice, brows knitted together in concern. "You have finger marks on your neck." He reached out a hand. Beatrice flinched and he withdrew it awkwardly. He nodded to his jacket, which Beatrice still wore. "I would offer you my handkerchief, but it is in your pocket."

Beatrice reached into his pocket, and her hands found not his handkerchief, but his silver spoon. She withdrew it. "I wish I had been brandishing this during the attack," she said.

"And what would you have done, scooped out the killer's eyes?" Drake scoffed. He tore the spoon from her hands and shoved it into his pants pocket. Beatrice could not help glancing at his eye patch. "That isn't what happened to mine," Drake added, clearly tracing her line of sight.

"I didn't think it was!" she said hastily. "And in any case, I had my earring as a weapon." The garish jewelry no longer felt like the wrong choice, she thought with a shiver. She realized the sharp earring was still clutched in her palm, and she tried to stab it back into her lobe. Her hands shook, and Inspector Drake took it from her hands and gently put it through her earlobe, his rough hands brushing against her cheek as he did so.

"Do you need anything?" Drake asked, withdrawing, suddenly looking awkward. He cleared his throat. "Some . . . water?"

"I wouldn't say no to a stiff pour of whiskey," she said, "but unfortunately I do not think Mrs. Ashbrook kept any in here."

Drake's lips twitched. He reached into his pants pocket and withdrew a small flask.

"Unlike your father, I keep actual liquor in mine," he said, handing it to Beatrice. She took it and looked down at it. She had never actually drunk from a flask, and certainly not from a man's flask. It felt intimate to imagine his mouth brushing against it.

"You drink first," she said, and gave it back to him. "A man died tonight by poison, after all."

"Shrewd thinking," Drake said with a smile. He took a swig, the liquid making his lips sparkle in the dim candlelight. He handed it back to Beatrice, their hands brushing against each other. This time, neither pulled back, and their eyes locked. Beatrice lifted the flask, pressed her mouth to it, and took a sip. The bitter drink burned as it trickled down her throat, but her chest immediately grew warm.

"Thank you," she said as she handed the flask back.

"Keep it," he said. "You never know when you might need an unsullied beverage."

Beatrice looked down at the flask and ran her fingers over an image engraved into it. "A duck?" She raised an eyebrow.

"I have taken it as something of an emblem," Drake said, now looking embarrassed.

"Because a drake is a male duck?" Beatrice asked, and Drake nodded.

"It is an adopted surname. A nickname my mother gave me. As a child I followed her around like a duck. . . ." He cleared his throat self-consciously.

"What was her name?" Beatrice looked down at the duck engraved on the flask, pretending she could not see Drake's emotion. "Your mother, I mean."

"Nitara," he said quietly. "Nitara Varma." He suddenly shook his head, as if waking from a trance. "You should go to your parents' chamber. Whoever attacked you might come back. It is not safe."

"It is not safe for you either," Beatrice protested. "Or anyone."

"I shall instruct everyone to lock their doors," Drake said. "And then . . ." He let out a sigh of frustration. "And then, I don't know. We are no closer to determining the killer, and now they may kill again. What are we missing? What evidence have we overlooked?"

Beatrice knew he was frustrated, but she could not help feeling a slight thrill at the word "we." She was a part of his investigation— not just a spectator, but a true . . . something.

"I feel so foolish," she admitted as she rubbed the swollen skin of her neck. It burned, as if she could still feel her assailant's fingers on her flesh. "I never should have gone off alone. If I had read about someone doing that in the paper, I would have judged them, but here I was doing it myself—"

"It was not your fault—" Drake began. He leaned forward and touched her skin. "Your neck. It is inflamed." He brushed a finger across her neck, and she shivered involuntarily.

"It stings like nettles," she admitted, and then drew in a gasp. "*Stinging nettles. Belladonna.* They are both *plants*. And my assailant was wearing rough gloves—why did I not see it before!" She stood and rushed to the door, forgetting her injury, forgetting everything but the lead now in front of her.

"Where are you going?" Drake asked, confused.

"Both stinging nettles and belladonna can be found in Arabella's greenhouse. Rough gloves could be used for gardening," she explained. "Meaning that, in the greenhouse we may find the murder weapon—and the murderer thereafter."

Dear Arabella,

My studies are progressing well. I can speak Latin fluently now; I am certain this shall prove most useful. Have you managed to coax a blossom from the miniature rosebush yet?

Edmund informed me that he has spoken to Father about his interest in forming an attachment with you. Such wonderful news! However, he also mentioned that you have not given him a reply. I know you must want to marry him; he is an exemplary, well-bred man who could take care of you splendidly. His town house in London could fit a lovely greenhouse. If your reserve stems from not knowing him for long, I can vouch for his good character. Naturally, we can discuss this more when I am home. I plan to return to Swampshire in a week's time. I hope Mother is feeling better by then.

Fondly,

Daniel

PS: How is the Steele family? Has Beatrice been well? Perhaps you might tell her that I have a trunk of books for her. I shall bring it with me when I come.

CHAPTER 23

Discovery

As Arabella Ashbrook was a great lover of plants, Mr. Hugh Ashbrook had allowed her to build a glass-ceilinged greenhouse in Stabmort Park. It was attached to the rest of the manor via a long passageway, which opened into a room filled with vines, flowers, and several lemon trees. The roses were not unlike Arabella herself: prickly, in need of much attention, but beautiful nonetheless—as they were now, their fragrance perfuming the air of the greenhouse. Rain pattered against the glass ceiling, and the windows were foggy, creating a humid, stifling atmosphere as Beatrice slipped inside.

She was on edge, every sound making her jump, her hand flying to her throat. She inhaled deeply, trying to calm her beating heart. Though she normally appreciated the fresh scent of the plants, a cluster of gardenias was overtaking everything. She wrinkled her nose, overwhelmed by the aroma.

"*Atropa belladonna* is in the Solanaceae family," she said as she strode purposefully through a row of plants. Inspector Drake trailed close behind. The room hummed with the sound of insects mingled with the crackle of thunder outside.

"I beg your pardon?" he said, clearly overwhelmed by the floral maze surrounding them.

"Ladies should have extensive knowledge of botany. *The Lady's Guide to Swampshire*, chapter sixty-two," Beatrice replied.

"How many chapters are in this guide?" Drake asked.

"Two hundred fifteen," Beatrice told him. "In the first volume."

The garden was overgrown; Arabella clearly favored the wild English style as opposed to a tidy French garden.

"If there is belladonna here, it should be with tomatoes and potatoes. And aubergine, if Arabella grows any," Beatrice said as they wove through the green maze. "All members of the night-shade family."* Beatrice stopped at a cluster of tomatoes and ex-amined the surrounding plants. "Ah. No belladonna."

"Perhaps the murderer ripped it all up by the roots?" Inspector Drake suggested, coming up next to her and kneeling to look at the tomatoes.

"One would only need the berries to concoct a poison," Beatrice said, recalling Sir Huxley's "Poison Guidebook" (a helpful article that came out when he was in between cases). She peered closer at the soil. "In any case, this dirt is undisturbed. But I know it *must* be here. Louisa told me that Arabella grows belladonna in her greenhouse. She gifted Louisa some from her own garden." She looked up at Drake. "It is not *so* unusual that Arabella and Mr. Croaksworth might part after her mother's death, but I find it strange that they waited so long to rekindle an attachment, if they were truly in love."

---

* Solanaceae (nightshades) were quite popular in Swampshire, as opposed to the genus *Aconitum* (wolf's bane), which was strangely unable to grow in the re-gion.

"You think she was disingenuous in her interest?" Drake asked.

"Yes," Beatrice said firmly, "that much was clear by her false tears. And I can't help but theorize. . . . Perhaps Arabella never wanted to marry Mr. Croaksworth but felt pressured to do so by Mr. Ashbrook, who obviously desired the match."

"You think she could have killed him to avoid a forced attachment," Drake said, following her reasoning. "She did have means— her knowledge of belladonna and its poisonous property, as well as this garden, in which she could have grown the plant."

"It's just so extreme," Beatrice murmured.

"We should search the other plants," Drake said, rising to his feet. "There is no sense in speculation without tangible evidence."

He turned to make his way down another row of growth, but at that moment, the door to the greenhouse creaked open.

"Quick!" Beatrice hissed at Inspector Drake as she grabbed his arm. "Hide!"

Beatrice and Drake peered out from behind a tree to see who had entered, and Beatrice felt a thrill. Captain Peña and Caroline Wynn tiptoed inside, locked in a passionate debate. Caroline whirled around as Captain Peña carefully shut the door behind him.

"Philip," Caroline said, "it is most inappropriate for the two of us to be alone together, without a chaperone. What would everyone say?"

Beatrice had to strain to hear the conversation above the din of the rain hitting the glass ceiling; she cupped a hand to one ear. Inspector Drake, eyeing her, did the same.

He was closer than was proper, but she was unable to move away without risking detection. She was acutely aware of his body heat, the edge of his foot just touching her soft slipper.

"I know it has been long since we were almost maybe a bit considering perhaps starting to form an attachment, somewhat similar to what some people call 'love,'" Captain Peña began, "but even though I have been a-sea for many sunsets, I must tell you that my feelings have always remained ashore. I must bring them all on deck and confess that I have started to form an attachment some-what similar to thinking about perhaps—loving you."

"I told you!" Beatrice hissed at Drake, and he frowned at her.

"Be quiet," he mouthed. She could practically feel the tension radiating from his body, and he sat still as a statue.

"They could be in cahoots, driven to murder by some sort of love scheme—" Beatrice whispered.

Drake grabbed a lemon and shoved it in her mouth, the citrus stopping her outburst. She spat it out, glaring at him, but then turned back to Caroline and Captain Peña and fell silent.

"Philip," Caroline said, her voice fluttering, "this is all so sud-den. You must understand that seeing you, after all this time, was unexpected. Disquieting, even. Hearing you confess your potential *love* for me—this is almost too much to comprehend."

"Naturally," Captain Peña allowed. "Yet I can tell that you feel the same way. Even after this very long year, I know—we are each other's anchor."

"Please, Philip," Caroline said, mumbling something else indis-tinguishable over the pounding rain. Both Beatrice and Inspector Drake strained to hear, now each cupping both ears with their hands.

"Long ago you told me you could not marry me, and I under-stood that it was because I was no one of consequence and had no money," Captain Peña said. "Now I have earned a small sum in the navy—in a completely honest way, and not because of anything relating to piracy or discovering hidden treasure on a strange, for-gotten island. I believe I have established myself as a worthy gen-tleman."

"You have," Caroline said breathlessly. "Of course you have. But, Philip—I just—" Her voice cracked. "I can't be with you. I don't deserve you."

"More like she thinks *he* doesn't deserve *her*," Beatrice muttered.

"There are so many other eligible ladies in Swampshire who would be better matches for you," Caroline went on. "Four, in fact."

"They are all sea slugs in comparison to you," Captain Peña said in a rush.

"Rude," Beatrice said.

"I can't," Caroline said, pressing a hand to her forehead. Her bangs shifted oddly, and Beatrice leaned forward to try to get a better look but then pulled herself back. She could not get caught, even if she would have loved to catch a glimpse of Caroline's hairdo—and reputation—falling apart.

"Croaksworth is dead," Captain Peña said gruffly, "so it would be pointless to pine for him."

"I never pined for him," Caroline insisted.

"He pulled you aside," Captain Peña said, his voice growing low. "I saw it earlier this evening. He said that he wanted to talk with you. That he needed to ask you something. Do you mean to tell me that he was not making you an offer?"

"No," Caroline sputtered. "He was asking whether my gown would be considered eggshell or ivory. He said he was fascinated by the subtle distinctions in shades of beige."

"I have never loved any woman but you, and of course my mistress, the sea," Captain Peña interrupted, "but I must allow that I was away for a time. If you have been whisked into another man's current—"

"I tell you, I haven't—" Caroline began, but Captain Peña took her by the shoulders.

"I can prove my love to you, Caroline. I am not only rich and of consequence but unwaveringly loyal. I know it was you who played cards with Ashbrook, Fàn, and Croaksworth. No doubt Croaksworth won some secret off you."

Beatrice leaned forward, hanging on every word.

Caroline put a hand to her forehead, taken aback. "You are mistaken, Philip."

"I saw you exiting the study," Captain Peña continued. "I can still smell the cigar smoke on you, even through that lovely gardenia scent." He touched her cheek lightly, and she put a hand over his. "I assure you," he continued, "there is nothing to worry about. I have walked the plank for you and flung myself into the deep: I told the inspector that it was I who played cards. He believes I was the other 'C.'"

Beatrice gripped Inspector Drake's arm, as if to say, *I knew it! I knew she was hiding something.*

Inspector Drake inhaled sharply at her touch, and she quickly withdrew her hand. He glanced back at her as if to say, *Yes, I know you were right—but be quiet so we can get to the bottom of this. With facts and evidence.*

"Philip!" Caroline withdrew her hand from his and took a step back. "I didn't ask you to lie for me. You shouldn't have done it."

"I wanted to," he said. "Don't you understand? I care not what you've done! You could send a thousand men to Davy Jones's locker, and I would still love you."

"What else did Inspector Drake say about me?" Caroline asked. "I know he was traveling with Mr. Croaksworth. Did Croaksworth . . . confide in him?"

"Drake suspects nothing," Peña said, stepping toward Caroline. "I tell you, I am here for you. I will protect you."

"I know," Caroline said softly. She suddenly grasped Captain Peña's hands once more. "Would you really do *anything* for me? Even if I revealed to you something dark about myself?"

"There is nothing you could tell me that would diminish my feelings for you," he said, pressing his lips to her hands. "My love is no changing tide."

"I told you she was evil!" Beatrice whispered, wide-eyed.

"'Something dark' about herself? What is darker than murdering Edmund Croaksworth, in cold blood?"

Caroline suddenly looked over at the corner where Inspector Drake and Beatrice were concealed behind a cluster of plants.

"Did you hear something?" she asked Captain Peña, eyes narrowing. "Almost like a banshee trying to whisper?"

"Alas, my hearing is damaged from cannon fire," Peña said somberly. "All I hear is your beautiful voice, ringing in my ears, and the sound of the sea I left behind."

"Maybe Stabmort Park really is haunted." Caroline shivered. "We must go. We shouldn't be alone together, anyhow. If someone sees—"

"Please, Caroline, do not leave me."

"I shall rejoin you in the parlor, once I freshen up." She touched his face tenderly. "Oh, Philip. I do wish—but no. It cannot be. The seas of our love are simply too rough."

She turned and fled the greenhouse. Captain Peña lingered a moment, staring up at the rain pelting the glass ceiling.

"Poseidon, why have you cursed me so?" he howled, and then exited as well.

The moment he left, Beatrice jumped out from behind the lemon tree. "I told you!" she said, almost leaping into the air with excitement. "Didn't I say that there was something off about Caroline Wynn? This explains why there were only three cigars; she only partook in the port. And then she must have practically bathed in perfume to cover up the scent of the men's smoking. She never told us that Mr. Croaksworth confronted her about something; yet *another* lie! Not to mention this secret close encounter would have given her the opportunity to administer the poison."

It was everything she had hoped for. Caroline was proving more and more guilty as the inconsistencies surfaced. Beatrice was alive with adrenaline. Louisa was clearly innocent—the rat had to be Caroline.

"There is so much we do not know about her. So much that doesn't make sense," Beatrice continued. "She has only lived here for two years." She broke off with a gasp. "Drake. Alice Croaksworth disappeared two years ago, just before Caroline Wynn arrived in Swampshire. What if Caroline is connected to Alice's disappearance, too? What if she murdered her?"

"We mustn't get ahead of ourselves," Drake said. "There are holes in Caroline's story, yes—"

"She has charmed you like she charmed everyone else," Beatrice interrupted in frustration. "Even when she shows her true colors, you can't see it."

"I have never been charmed in my life," Drake replied, looking offended at the very notion.

"Then if it's not Caroline, what about Captain Peña?" Beatrice demanded. "He clearly thought Caroline was interested in Croaksworth. He could have murdered him out of jealousy."

"It is plausible," Drake allowed, "but we cannot know for sure until we find the murder weapon." He turned and began making his way through the winding maze of plants, examining each cluster of berries and blossoms.

Beatrice, still fuming, turned the other direction and began skimming the plants. She was about to give up, to run out of the room to confront Caroline herself, when she spotted something white in the dirt. She knelt to pick it up. It was a lily—the one Louisa had been wearing in her hair.

"Odd," she murmured, touching one of its crushed petals. Had her sister visited the greenhouse as well? Perhaps Arabella had brought her here to see the flowers at some point during the evening?

Something else in the dirt caught her eye, half-hidden in a

patch of stinging nettles. Beatrice stooped to retrieve a small glass vial, carefully avoiding the nettles. On the side of the vial, a label read: *Belladonna. Property of Louisa Steele. If lost, return to me, Louisa Steele.*

And it was empty.

Dread flooded her insides. She could already hear Inspector Drake's conclusion if he saw this. *The evidence points to Louisa.*

This was all wrong. Louisa was her sister and a gentle soul. She would not even know how to kill someone.

And yet. Louisa was twenty-one. A woman—and a woman, perhaps, with secrets. Did Beatrice herself not have one of her own, hidden under cushions and tapestries in her turret? If one Steele woman kept her true self concealed, perhaps a second did as well. Perhaps Beatrice did not know her sister as well as she thought.

"I have not found anything," Inspector Drake called over, frustrated. He began to walk toward Beatrice, and before she had time to second-guess her decision, she shoved the vial into her bodice, hiding it from him.

"I haven't found anything, either," she said breathlessly. "The poison must have come from another source, or in any case, all traces of it are gone now."

"Indeed. We could try looking elsewhere." Inspector Drake reached Beatrice and gave her an odd look. "Are you quite all right? You're perspiring profusely."

"It's warm in here," Beatrice said.

Before Drake could give a reply, a loud whinny sounded, followed by the echo of hooves and a carriage cutting through the pouring rain.

Someone was making an escape.

Dear Susan,

I came by to call, but your husband told me that you were out shopping for a new dress for little Mary. She is growing so fast! And is quite hairy, I must say. Perhaps you should ask Dr. Anderson if this is normal?

In any case, I assume that Stephen was not joking and that you are truly out shopping, so I thought to write you a brief note. What shall we do for Beatrice's birthday this year? I would be happy to host something at Stabmort Park.

Perhaps we might do a theme for the party. Arabella would enjoy helping me with this; she has an eye for planning. I shall send her over to Marsh House tomorrow and she can discuss everything further with Beatrice and Louisa.

Isn't it wonderful that our children all get along? I must confess that I harbor a hope Daniel and Beatrice might end up together. We could always wait to hold Beatrice's party until he returns from school for the holidays. Nothing feeds romance like a festive evening. . . .

There is something else I wish to discuss with you of a more serious nature. I shall stop by again, for it is a matter best spoken of in person. I think you are the only person who might understand and can advise me accordingly.

Unfortunately I cannot wait for you to return today; I am on the way to see Dr. Anderson myself about this dratted illness I cannot shake. While I am there I shall ask him about Mary's hair situation. Perhaps he might have a solution?

All my best—

Samantha Ashbrook

CHAPTER 24

Chase

Inspector Drake followed Beatrice as she sprinted to the stables of Stabmort Park. She knew them well, as the Ashbrooks often invited the Steeles for afternoon rides. Not wanting to waste time, she grabbed a cloak, jumped on the nearest horse, and took off into the hailstorm riding bareback. Whoever was making a getaway would never succeed—not on her watch.

"Beatrice!" Inspector Drake shouted.

She did not respond. She barreled along, hardly noticing icy pellets of hail slicing into her skin, for she was chasing a murderer. This was even more exciting than her previous rides, during which she would only *pretend* that she was chasing a murderer. The thrill of the reality was intoxicating.

Inspector Drake mounted the second-nearest horse and took off after Beatrice.

She was already a tiny speck, only visible by the cloak she had taken billowing in the wind like a flag. The ambling carriage was an even tinier speck in the distance. They were both barreling in the opposite direction of the dirt road, through mud and over-grown weeds. Inspector Drake leaned forward, urging his horse on, until he was nearly apace with Beatrice.

She pressed forward, gaining on the carriage, heart nearly pounding out of her chest in anticipation. The vehicle crossed into the forest at the edge of Stabmort Park.

Beatrice had never gone farther than Stabmort Park's east gate. No one went past this point, as the marshland beyond it was wild and contained many sinkholes.* This area was Adler's End. Judging from the trajectory of the runaway carriage, this was exactly where the unseen driver was heading. Beatrice was unperturbed by the route, following the carriage. She disappeared behind a copse of trees lining the edge of a rushing stream.

"Beatrice!" Inspector Drake shouted. "Wait!"

But she did not hear him, or if she did, she did not listen. He was forced to press on. He rounded the copse of trees, finally catching up to Beatrice.

Both of them watched in horror as the carriage barreled toward the rushing stream, showing no signs of slowing down. One wheel caught in a deep trench at the side of the stream and splintered in half. The ponies broke free from their reins and galloped away joy-fully, leaving the carriage dashed in the stream amidst a cluster of rocks.

There was nothing they could do: It was now a mess of snapped spokes and wood.

"Whoa, Nellie!" Inspector Drake called out as his horse sud-denly reared up on her hind legs, spooked by the loud crack of the

---

* There were also many animal carcasses that had been gnawed to the bone by something with inhumanly large fangs.

carriage. (Coincidentally, the horse *was* named Nellie.) It reared up again, and Inspector Drake flew off. Beatrice shouted as he fell onto the ground, and Nellie shot off into the field.

Beatrice quickly dismounted and rushed to Drake, but the moment she jumped from her own horse, it took off and followed Nellie.

"No!" Drake yelled after the horses, but it was in vain: They disappeared into the storm in a flurry of mud and neighs.

"Are you all right?" Beatrice asked, and reached out a hand.

Drake ignored it and pushed himself to his feet. "I'm fine." But as he turned, Beatrice could see that he walked gingerly on one ankle.

"You *are* hurt—" she began, but he interrupted her.

"There are more pressing matters at hand, Miss Steele."

Beatrice regarded him for a moment but thought better of making some retort. He was right, after all. She pointed to a deep trench on the side of the stream, next to a thick cluster of honeysuckle. "That caught the wheel."

Drake made his way toward the carriage, pounding rain obscuring his path.

"Wait, don't tread there—" Beatrice warned as he waded through mud toward the carriage, but it was too late: Inspector Drake stumbled on his injured ankle and fell right into one of Swampshire's infamous squelch holes.

The mud immediately swallowed him whole, leaving only his hand exposed.

For a moment Beatrice stared at the dark ground, her body frozen in terror. It was the fate she had always been warned about, the danger she had grown up fearing. But now it was no longer in the pages of a storybook or a parable told by a strict governess. It was happening. And in all the warnings she had been given about the dangers of squelch holes, no one had actually explained what to do when confronted with the reality of one. It was assumed that ladies would be helpless against them. Why fight fate?

Because, she thought, she was determined to win that fight. Feeling returned to Beatrice's limbs and she sprang forward. She lunged for Drake and grabbed his fingers, hardly able to keep ahold of him due to the still-raging storm.

She hurriedly looked around for something with which to drag Drake from the depths. A silver and sturdy object caught her eye: A shovel was lying next to the huge trench. She grasped it and shoved it into the mud, pushing Inspector Drake's hand onto it.

"Grab on," she yelled, and to her relief, his fingers curled around the shovel. With all her strength, she wrenched it upward, falling back into the mud with the effort.

As she pulled, she felt a ripple of fear at the thought that he might be lost forever. For some reason, the mere thought of losing him filled her with a pain she had never experienced.

She had always been alone, she realized, until she met Drake. Only he knew the real Beatrice. Only he saw the truth. She needed him—and he needed her. Neither of them could catch this killer alone. (Well, perhaps she *could,* she thought fleetingly, but two minds were certainly better than one.) They had embarked on this strange journey together, and she knew instinctively that they must complete it together, too.

With this thought she gave a final wrench, and her efforts worked: Inspector Drake emerged from the squelch hole, caked in earth and gasping, but alive.

He crawled onto solid ground and coughed up mud, as well as a small frog, which hopped away nonchalantly.

"Who in their right mind would ever live in this quagmire?" he yelled when he had finally caught his breath.

"It's very lovely in the summer," Beatrice said, and laughed with relief.

"I think you mad, Miss Steele," Drake said, shaking his head.

"Beatrice," she said, correcting him.

"I think you mad . . . Beatrice." His lips twitched, and he quickly looked down. He was still holding the shovel, and he examined it. "Where did you get this?"

"It was here," Beatrice said, pointing next to the trench.

"Someone dug this hole." Inspector Drake pulled himself to his feet. "Why?" He gripped the shovel and used it to point to the trench. "It is the size—"

"Of a grave," Beatrice finished. She swallowed. "You don't think—"

"The killer planned to bury Mr. Croaksworth there? It would be a foolish plan if so. The rain would disturb the corpse," Drake mused.

"Only one person has the answers to our questions," Beatrice said, turning toward the wreckage.

"Perhaps you shouldn't look," Drake warned as they both approached. "Let me."

"I am not some fainthearted lady who cannot maintain her composure," Beatrice began.

"Trust me, I would never mistake you for one," Drake shot back. "Just please, let me."

She relented, and he approached the carriage. Beatrice felt terror rise at the thought of the passenger's potential state. Could they possibly have survived such a crash?

Drake wrenched open the carriage door. Beatrice steeled herself and then strained to see what was inside—but Drake turned back at her. His face was not twisted in horror but frozen in dismay.

"I don't understand," he said. "It's empty."

Beatrice rushed over to him, splashing through the stream to get a look inside. He was right. The carriage was a heap of splintered wood and metal, but there was no bone or flesh. They had been chasing an empty cart.

"Do you think the killer jumped out?" Beatrice said, whirling around to stare at the moor as if expecting to see a figure running away on foot.

"No," Inspector Drake said gravely. "I think we have been duped."

"We were duped," Beatrice repeated. "*Why* were we duped? Someone wanted us to follow this carriage," she said, realization dawning. "Which means—"

Clearly following her train of thought, Inspector Drake turned toward Stabmort in dismay. "We must get back to the main house," he said.

Arabella—

I know that you know. Eventually the truth will come out, but in due time. It is not your decision to make— you would do well to remember that.

I look forward to seeing you at this evening's ball. I'm sure you will look stunning as usual!

Frank

CHAPTER 25

Fisticuffs

Beatrice and Drake burst through the front door of Stabmort Park, Drake limping, still half-covered in mud. They left a trail of sludge and rainwater as they ran.

Beatrice suddenly put out a hand to stop Drake.

"Wait. Listen," she hissed. He stopped moving and fell silent.

There were muffled yells deep within Stabmort Park.

"It's coming from the parlor," Beatrice whispered. She and Drake exchanged a look—and then they took off.

The noises grew louder as they approached, raised voices shooting insults back and forth. Beatrice could hear the rush of her blood pounding in her ears as she ran, her drenched gown heavy and cold against her skin. She approached the parlor doors and shoved them open, drawing in a sharp inhale.

A crackling fire dwindled in the marble fireplace, and the chandelier above still flickered, lighting the room in a soft glow that made the pastel colors look muted. The furniture was pushed back to make space for what was unfolding in the center of the room.

Mr. Grub and Captain Peña stood across from each other, their hands and voices raised. The rest of the guests encircled them, hugging the wall for safety: Arabella and Louisa huddled by the fireplace, Frank standing in front of them and Mary crouched below. Mr. Steele had his arm draped protectively across Mrs. Steele, and Miss Bolton clutched Caroline, who swooned. Daniel paced at the edge of the room as if trying to defuse the situation, his face pale. Everyone was so caught up in the unfolding scene that they did not even hear Beatrice and Drake enter.

"Everyone listen to me!" Mr. Grub yelled. In one hand he held a worn copy of *Fordyce's Additional Sermons* (the little-known addition to the edition, containing sermons considered "too dull" to be included in the main volume). "I gathered you here so we can take back our *rights*. So we can reclaim this night!"

"We all only came in here because you *threatened* us," Mrs. Steele cried, her voice shaking.

Beatrice now realized why everyone was huddled at one end of the room: In Grub's other hand, he held a pistol.

"Someone had to take charge. Isn't anyone else tired of this Inspector *what's-his-name* ordering us around?" Grub continued. He waved his pistol in the air. "And where is he? Clearly he lacks the resilience to do his job."

Beatrice looked over at Drake, but he shook his head almost imperceptibly. She could practically see his mind whirring, calculating his next move.

"My father hired him," Daniel told Grub in a firm voice. "If he has put trust in Inspector Drake, then we all must, too."

Beatrice looked at the group in front of her and noticed, with a cold trickle of dread, that Mr. Ashbrook was not in the room.

Where was he?

"For all we know, this 'Inspector Drake' is the murderer himself," Grub went on.

"Avast your tongue," Captain Peña said. He put a hand to the cutlass sheath at his waist. "He is a member of the law. You would do well to respect that. And to respect any other officers present. And to never turn your back on the ocean."

"Well, *I* am a gentleman," Mr. Grub said stiffly. "Therefore I should be exempt from any suspicion and permitted to leave."

"Why would you want to leave, unless you are the murderer trying to escape?" Mrs. Steele yelled.

"You shall not abandon ship, sir," Captain Peña insisted. "You have drawn your weapon with ladies present; I will not stand for such aggression. Your actions show your guilt." Captain Peña reached for the scabbard at his waist, but then he started. He looked up at Grub, his expression fierce. "What have you done with my cutlass?"

"Please, we can work this out!" Caroline cried. "No one else must be harmed. Find compassion within yourselves—"

"Grub is clearly the murderer," Mrs. Steele yelled. "Our own cousin, a killer!" She whirled around to her husband. "Quick, what are the rules concerning inheritances in this situation?"

"I think he would still inherit our estate," Mr. Steele said, "but I'm not sure. Does anyone know? Is anyone familiar with inheritance law?"

"We know everything there is to know about inheritance law," Daniel said. "None of us has ever worked a day in his life."

"I'm not the killer," Grub insisted. "Louisa is the one who served Mr. Croaksworth the poisoned punch. We all saw it. What do you have to say to *that*, Louisa?"

"You don't need to answer him," Mrs. Steele said. She stood in front of her daughter and Arabella, blocking both young women from Grub's view.

"You think your children can do whatever they want. Even reject a perfectly appropriate suitor," Grub told her, voice taut with disdain. "Your entire family has broken the code of etiquette that upholds our town, and now look at us. We have been thrown into chaos." He pointed the pistol at Mrs. Steele. "I will have *order!*"

Several things happened at once. Drake rushed forward, Mr. Steele stepped in front of Mrs. Steele, Frank lunged toward Louisa and pulled her back, Daniel caught Caroline Wynn as she fainted, Miss Bolton screamed, and Captain Peña sprang at Grub. Drake reached him first; he shoved him back onto the floor just as Grub's spindly finger pulled the pistol's trigger. Beatrice braced herself for the explosion of gunfire.

But instead, there was a tiny *crack,* and a little flag popped out of the pistol. It unfurled, one word printed on the side: "bang."

"My gag pistol!" Mr. Steele cried. "I thought I lost it!"

"He *stole* it," Mrs. Steele gasped.

Grub writhed on the floor, a heap of limbs and fabric. He scrambled to grab several items that had scattered from his jacket: a pair of spectacles, a glimmering ring, a crumpled ticket.

"My spectacles," Daniel said, and pulled them from Grub's reach.

"The ring!" Louisa said breathlessly.

"My—" Frank said, then fell silent.

"All mine!" Grub yelled, trying to gather the items. Drake stepped forward and grabbed the wrinkled ticket.

"Gretna Green," he said, reading the words upon the ticket.

"Beatrice? Where have *you* been?" Mrs. Steele said suddenly, finally noticing her other daughter's presence. "And why are you so *wet?* Daniel—avert your eyes," she added in a rush. "You must not see her like this."

"Inspector," Caroline said weakly, now revived from her faint, "why are *you* so *muddy?*"

"Were you two alone together?" Daniel said sharply, looking from Drake to Beatrice. "Where was your chaperone?"

Beatrice froze as everyone stared at her, and then at Miss Bolton.

"I—I thought Beatrice was resting," Miss Bolton said weakly.

"How dare you try to steal away my beloved," Grub said from the floor. He made a grunting noise as he struggled to his feet.

Daniel crossed the room and took Beatrice by the shoulders.

"Are you all right? Did Drake hurt you?" he said quietly, intensely. She had never seen him like this, and she felt both surprised and touched at his concern.

"I am fine, Daniel," she said immediately.

"I did not do anything to Beatrice," Drake cut in, his voice irritated. Daniel looked at Beatrice a moment longer, sweeping his eyes over her as if searching for any potential harm. Then he whirled around and jabbed a finger at Drake.

"If you hurt a hair on *Miss Steele's* head—"

"Daniel, he did nothing wrong," Beatrice insisted. But Daniel glared at Drake, his finger still raised in the air.

"An inspector with no honor will find himself a goner," he said warningly.

"You are the one who suggested she assist," Drake said, exasperated.

"With a chaperone!" Daniel roared.

"I will never forsake my duties again," Miss Bolton said, her eyes pooling with tears.

"And *I* will never be so hasty as to bestow trust upon a man who is no gentleman," Daniel shot back. He turned again to Beatrice. "Do you promise, Miss Steele, that you are unharmed?"

"Yes," Beatrice said. She looked from Drake to Daniel. Drake was staring at her with a strange expression that she could not decipher. Daniel held out a hand, and she felt a rush of gratitude.

In spite of everything, he was still her friend. In spite of everything, he still stood up for her in the midst of potential scandal. She took his hand.

From the corner of her eye, she saw Drake cringe.

"Inspector Drake is an honorable—" Beatrice began, turning toward Drake, but was interrupted when the back doors to the parlor suddenly opened. A lace-capped servant with a white apron stepped inside and dropped a curtsy.

"Beg pardon," she said politely, "but dinner is served."

"Blast," Frank cursed. "Did no one inform the servants?"

"Please go into the dining room," Drake said. "It is time to put an end to this. I know the identity of the murderer."

There were whispers of shock and confusion. Beatrice dropped Daniel's hand and rushed to Drake's side.

"Who is it?" she whispered, but Drake did not look at her.

"Please, everyone, move along. You will have your answers soon enough."

"Drake—" Beatrice began.

"*Miss Steele,*" Drake interrupted, his tone icy, "proceed to the dining room with the rest of the guests. I no longer require your assistance. You are a lady, and I am not a gentleman. We must not forget that. Your *friend* Daniel has made that clear."

"But—" Beatrice began, but Drake pushed past her and strode into the dining room. She was forced to follow, her body tingling with vehemence and confusion.

"Wait . . . somebody got murdered?" the servant asked as everyone pushed past her in a mad scramble.

THE ASHBROOK AUTUMNAL BALL

SUPPER MENU

To be presented at one A.M.

Cold pheasant
Boiled turnips
Raw pig tongues
Pigeons
Pig testicles
Fricandeau
Veal udder

And for dessert

Lemon and raspberry ice

CHAPTER 26

Dinner

The dining hall at Stabmort Park had blood-red wallpaper, a high ceiling, and a crystal chandelier. Tapestries hung on the walls, depicting tenets from Swampshire's code of etiquette in woven lifestyle scenes.

One scene showed a woman curtsying and a man bowing, the word "politeness" stitched above it. Another read "contentment." This showed a gentleman and lady sitting in a room, staring at each other with mild smiles upon their faces.

But it was the third tapestry that Beatrice eyed. It had always haunted her as a child, and tonight, she was acutely aware of its presence.

It was a series of scenes entitled "Beware Disorder," meant to demonstrate the dangers of straying from appropriate conduct. In the sequence, a gentleman got a job, a lady attended school, a young couple traveled the world instead of settling in Swampshire, and a group of women took in the horrifying sights of Paris. In each scene, the disorderly people ended up at the bottom of a squelch hole.

Underneath the tapestries was a long table, surrounded by high-backed wood chairs. It was set with fine china, dishes covered with silver cloches, and flickering candles set in gold candelabras. Overall, it was a fittingly somber room in which to discuss murder.

As Beatrice entered, she saw that the seat at the head of the table was already occupied. Hugh Ashbrook sat there, swathed in a blanket, fast asleep. Daniel took a seat next to Mr. Ashbrook, saying quietly to Arabella, "It must be the fainties."

"Commotion irritates his condition," Arabella whispered back. "Best to let him rest, for now."

Even amidst everything, Beatrice thought, Mr. Ashbrook had anticipated that the ball's normal supper would still take place. She looked upon the smooth brow of the peaceful patriarch, and she felt a sudden rush of empathy. After dealing with the tremendous loss of his beloved wife, he had clung even harder to his belief in order. It must have been a small comfort to him, she thought, that some things could still proceed exactly as they should.

And, she thought as Inspector Drake took a seat at the opposite end of the table, he *was* correct. Here they were, at dinner—precisely on time. She took a seat at Drake's right hand.

She wanted to be angry at him, but she found that she was only frustrated with herself. He had seen something she had not. Was it something from Grub's pockets? The ticket, the ring, Daniel's spectacles . . . It was infuriating, and discomfiting, to know that she had missed something, after she had thought herself so skilled at observation over the course of the evening. To think she used to imagine that she was helping Huxley, writing to tell him her theories, her predictions about his cases. She knew nothing—she was a fool.

Beatrice sat back, mind whirling, as the other guests filed into the remaining chairs. There was a small scuffle as Mr. Grub and Mr. Steele fought over who would sit closest to the dish of pig testicles, until Mrs. Steele hissed, "Just sit already, I want to know who the murderer is." Mr. Steele plopped into the far chair by a dish of cold pheasant, defeated.

There was none of the chatter that normally accompanied the onset of dinner; there was only a tense, suspicious silence.

A servant filled everyone's wineglasses, and Inspector Drake raised his in a toast.

"To the truth, which I have ascertained," he said, and drank from the glass.

Everyone else watched in terrified silence, too on edge to move. The candlelight glinted across their faces, their features seemingly shifting in the shadows cast. They were familiar one moment and strangers the next.

"Mr. Edmund Croaksworth visited Swampshire for the first time this evening. He arrived at the ball fashionably late, made his introductions, played a game of cards, and danced one final minuet, before dropping dead of belladonna poisoning," Drake said.

"We know all this," Mr. Steele said. "Get to the good stuff."

"Due to the severity and quick onset of the symptoms, it is most likely that Mr. Croaksworth was given a high dose of poison sometime during or shortly after the fateful card game," Drake continued. He reached into his pants pocket and withdrew the scorecard from the study. "It was a game played by Mr. Hugh Ashbrook, Miss Caroline Wynn, Mr. Croaksworth, and Frank."

"Caroline?" Miss Bolton gasped. "But a lady would never—"

"The score sheet clearly lists all of their initials," Drake interrupted, "and yet no one admits to playing in the game. Mr. Ashbrook claims he doesn't remember it." He indicated Mr. Ashbrook, who was still fast asleep. "Caroline used perfume to cover the scent of cigars, and then claimed she was resting. Captain Peña lied and said it was *he* who played cards." Drake continued.

Caroline paled. Captain Peña put a steadying hand on her shoulder. Beatrice's eyes darted around the room, taking in the reactions of each guest.

"This is no doubt because you were not betting money. It was an old tradition from Daniel and Mr. Croaksworth's school days—playing for secrets." Drake placed the ace of hearts on the table and flipped it around to display the purple iris. "Frank decided to play with a trick deck he bought in Paris. Perhaps he thought this would guarantee he would win. But an extra ace was not enough to defeat Croaksworth; Frank lost."

Next to the card, he placed the miniature of Louisa on the table.

"This is the item you bet, and it is what you lost to Edmund Croaksworth. It reveals your secret: She was not interested in Croaksworth. For Frank and Louisa Steele are engaged."

Mrs. Steele gasped. "This is not true!"

"Frank has sent love notes to every woman in town," Beatrice added. "He winks more than he blinks; Louisa knows he isn't serious." She turned toward Louisa, expecting her sister to agree.

But Louisa had turned toward Frank. Across the table, the two shared a glance. It was quick, and they both turned away almost immediately, but that brief, desperate glance was more revealing than any evidence Drake could have provided.

And he *had* found evidence, Beatrice realized with horror as Drake set two items on the table.

One was a ticket to Gretna Green. The other, an orb-shaped ring. Exactly the size of the one she had seen on Frank's finger, beneath his glove, earlier that evening. A ring Louisa had just recognized, though she had not danced with Frank that evening—how had she known of it?

"There is little other reason to visit Gretna Green than for a quick marriage," Drake said, gesturing to the ticket. "The two planned to elope."

"But Frank is from *France*," Mr. Steele said in confusion.

"And he hardly has a fortune to speak of," Mrs. Steele added. "Louisa is destined to marry a wealthy man, not a poor rake. She is looking for a man like Mr. Croaksworth, a man who—"

"Did no one think to ever ask *me* what type of man I am look-ing for?" Louisa suddenly cut in.

"You have hardly been out in society!" Mrs. Steele shot back. "You couldn't possibly know!"

"If I am old enough to wed, I am old enough to know," Louisa replied. Her voice was so assured, so articulate. It was as if the words had been brewing within her for a long time—and now they had been forced to the surface.

"Louisa," Beatrice said, and her sister turned to look at her with wide, desperate eyes. "We are only trying to protect you. Frank's promises sound sweet, but he's all talk."

"I am sitting right here," Frank said.

"I'm aware," Beatrice said dryly. "Louisa, I know it's easy to get caught up in the passion of romance—"

"No," Louisa said, shaking her head, "you don't know at all."

Beatrice swallowed and fell silent. Though it stung, Louisa was right. When it came to matters of the heart, Beatrice *didn't* know.

"Croaksworth won the miniature of Louisa off of Frank during the card game, thus discovering their secret," Drake went on.

"As interesting as it is to hear about Louisa and Frank's sala-cious personal lives, what does this have to do with the murder of Edmund?" Arabella cut in.

"You aren't astonished by these revelations," Beatrice said in re-alization, turning to Arabella. "You knew already, didn't you?"

Arabella pursed her lips, offering no rebuttal.

"What did you speak about so seriously with Mr. Croaksworth, when the two of you were dancing?" Beatrice pressed.

"He apologized for what had transpired between us, years ago," Arabella muttered. "There is no sense in hiding anything now—he proposed, but his parents separated us." She lowered her voice, shooting a glance at the sleeping Mr. Ashbrook. "I was not eager for the match at the time, to be completely truthful, so I was relieved. But my father . . ." She sighed. "He told everyone that we mutually decided not to wed, to save our family any embarrassment. I think, despite how angry he was at Mr. and Mrs. Croaksworth, he still held out hope that Edmund and I would be together someday. Edmund was the only man he thought good enough for me."

"And did Mr. Croaksworth attempt to rekindle your romance tonight," Beatrice asked, mind whirring, "since his parents were gone and could no longer protest?"

"I do not know if that was his initial intent," Arabella replied, "though my father was certain that it was. It is the only reason he permitted Edmund to cross the threshold of Stabmort Park, after offending us so deeply years ago. But then Edmund met Louisa. He asked my blessing to pursue her. His parents may have been harsh, but Edmund had a heart. I assured him that I had no feelings for him."

"And your father was fine with you giving up any chance at marrying Mr. Croaksworth?" Beatrice pressed.

Arabella's eyes flicked to Hugh Ashbrook once more. "A lady cannot simply *give up* a chance at a man like Edmund," she whispered, her voice so quiet that Beatrice had to lean forward to hear. "So I told my father that Edmund rejected me again. A simple white lie."

"Why suggest playing whist for secrets, when you and Louisa clearly had so much to hide?" Beatrice asked, her words sharp with bitterness.

"I was bored," Arabella said dourly. "So I teased her. You really can be *so* vexing, Beatrice—"

"I'm sure you can all discuss these family matters later," Drake interrupted before Beatrice could ask any further questions. "But now, there is the business of a *murder.*"

"Yes, but I am trying to determine—" Beatrice began again.

"The truth is this," Drake spoke over her. "Louisa and Frank murdered Edmund Croaksworth."

There was silence as his words settled over them like a haze, shifting the air in the room. Everything went still.

"They did no such thing," Beatrice said, her sharp voice cutting the silence like a knife.

"Of course not," Mrs. Steele agreed. "Perhaps Louisa was taken in by Frank's advances—I just should have watched her more carefully. She is too kind, too naïve—"

"He is very charming," Miss Bolton chimed in. "One cannot blame you, dear Louisa."

"Just because a person has a lover does not mean they are a killer," Arabella added.

"*I* think it makes sense," Grub said, his mouth full. He was the only one eating; his plate overflowed with pig testicles. "You are all taken in by Frank's charms; you don't see his foul nature."

"*He* is not the foul one, you barnacle," Captain Peña growled.

"I don't understand," Daniel said. "Frank is my friend." He looked at Frank in confusion. "You hardly knew Croaksworth."

"I never laid a finger on him," Frank said immediately.

"You'd better swear you didn't lay a finger on my daughter either, young man," Mrs. Steele growled.

"I am sure we have all had attachments which, for whatever reason, cannot come to fruition," Caroline Wynn broke in, her voice gentle. "Louisa knows now that she cannot be with Frank; she shall exit this engagement with grace."

"I do not think Louisa and Frank will part so easily," Drake said, and everyone turned to look at him, "for they have another secret. Louisa is avoiding drink, indicating changed tastes, and excused herself due to nausea. If my theory, based on these observations, is correct . . ." Beatrice drew in a breath.

"Louisa," she said, "are you . . . with child?"

Louisa finally met Beatrice's eyes. Her face was filled with fear, hope, and a stubborn pride—and Beatrice knew that it was true.

And it made sense, she suddenly thought: the dress that didn't fit, Louisa's glowing aura—Beatrice had been completely obtuse not to notice what was right in front of her eyes. Or perhaps she had purposefully not looked deeper.

"Why didn't you tell me?" Beatrice whispered.

Mrs. Steele fanned herself. "Louisa, say it isn't so!"

"You knave!" Mr. Steele shouted at Frank.

"Stop, all of you!" Louisa stood. "I love him. You don't understand!"

"I will not send her away!" Mrs. Steele said immediately, looking around wildly at her neighbors. "Send me away instead! It was my failure as a mother that led to this moment. Louisa must not be punished."

"It is *Frank* who should be sent away, not Louisa or you, Mother," Beatrice said, staring daggers at Frank. He cowered, his normally arrogant air gone.

"Frank claimed that Louisa spent time alone with Croaksworth, that they had met before and engaged in . . . salacious acts. She did not deny this claim, which clearly was not a rumor Frank heard, but one he meant to start," Drake said, raising his voice above the confused murmurs. "Their plan has become clear: murder Croaksworth, tell everyone the child was his, and collect the inheritance money for themselves."

Mrs. Steele swooned, Arabella and Daniel gasped, and Frank pounded his fists on the table.

"This is ridiculous!" he shouted. "I have done nothing wrong other than woo a beautiful woman."

"You would not have seen any money anyway," Drake shot back. "The Croaksworth fortune would never be allowed to pass to an illegitimate heir. Your mistake was not waiting to kill the man until *after* the wedding."

"Perhaps we thought we might get something," Frank allowed, looking desperately at Louisa, "but we didn't *murder* anyone—we merely thought to provide for our child through a few lies and risky gambles—"

"You imbecile!" Mrs. Steele shrieked at Frank. "How could you drag my daughter into *gambling*?"

"He didn't drag me into anything," Louisa said tearfully. "I would do anything for my child." She clutched her stomach protectively.

"If you think any of this is funny, you are sorely mistaken," Mr. Steele told Frank.

"Of course I don't think it's funny!" Frank insisted.

"Even worse! You have no sense of humor!" Mr. Steele threw his hands in the air in exasperation.

"My parents are artists. I have no money. How else was I to provide for my wife and our future children?" Frank said desperately.

"You didn't have to swindle Mr. Croaksworth," Beatrice said. "You put yourself—and my sister—in terrible danger. Why not just get a job?"

"A *job*?" Frank said. "How dare you!"

"Well, it doesn't matter anymore," Drake said firmly. "For the law shall determine your fates."

"No," Beatrice said, her entire body feeling as if it were on fire. "*No*. Whatever is going on between Frank and Louisa is irrelevant. You have no proof that they were involved in the murder."

The empty vial of belladonna with Louisa's name felt as if it were burning a hole through Beatrice's bodice. She pressed a hand to her chest to keep it firmly in place.

"Miss Steele," Drake said to Beatrice, looking at her with pity. "After the card game, your sister was seen giving Mr. Croaksworth punch, which obviously—considering the timeline of his death—contained poison. I have provided more than enough evidence to condemn her *and* Frank. Now is the time for you to step aside and let her face the consequences of her actions." He nodded toward Frank. "Can someone please restrain the man?"

Captain Peña dutifully stood and marched toward Frank.

"Please," Frank yelped, ducking to avoid Captain Peña's clutches, "you have this all wrong! Yes, I played cards against Edmund Croaksworth, using a trick deck to attempt to beat him. Yes, he won the miniature Louisa had given me, but he did not realize the extent of our relationship. He was not the most astute man, you understand. And yes, you are even correct that Louisa and I are expecting a child. Arabella knew! She can attest to our love; she helped us keep it secret."

"You told Arabella before you told me?" Beatrice turned toward Louisa, but her words were drowned out by Drake's.

"It all makes sense now," he said loudly. "Arabella covered up your affair, and in exchange, Louisa kept Mr. Croaksworth occupied this evening. That way, he would not focus all his attention on Arabella. She could pretend that he had rejected her and not have to explain the truth to Mr. Ashbrook."

"Naturally, Croaksworth became enamored with Louisa at first sight," Miss Bolton chimed in.

"Who wouldn't be?" Frank said, nodding. "She is the most beautiful woman I have ever known. And I have known so, so, so many women." His eyes filled with tears and adoration as he gazed upon Louisa. "But when Croaksworth perished, we panicked," he continued, his voice now growing desperate. "We had hoped that over the course of the evening, Louisa might convince him to fall for Beatrice instead, and that their relationship would allow Louisa to marry whomever she liked. Beatrice is witty, after all; she is a lovely woman with plenty of charms to captivate a man—"

"*Truly* not the time, Frank," Beatrice said.

"Noted." He swallowed hard. "With Croaksworth gone and Louisa's pregnancy advancing, the clock was ticking. I came up with an idea: Take advantage of the situation. Imply to you, Inspector Drake, that there was a possibility Louisa conceived a child with Croaksworth. Then, our baby could collect the inheritance. No one else was using it. It was a victimless crime."

"He's right," Louisa agreed. "It was a foolish plan—and Frank clearly did not consult me enough before putting it into action—but I did not know what else to do in such a situation."

"I love this woman," Frank announced. "I wish to marry her. I do not care if we are banished; banishment with the woman I love would still be heaven."

"And *my* heaven is when I am with *you*!" Louisa cried.

They struggled to kiss each other despite being kept apart, their lips brushing air. Out of all the horrific sights Beatrice had seen that night, this was one of the worst.

"That is enough!" Inspector Drake yelled, but the room had already broken out into chaos. Mrs. Steele shrieked and fainted yet again. Mr. Steele began hyperventilating, whipped out his pooting pillow, and began to breathe in and out of it.

"*Keeping calm is the only balm!*" Daniel yelled as Captain Peña wielded his empty cutlass scabbard at Frank, blocking him from bolting.

In the middle of it all, Beatrice could do nothing. It was as if she were glued to one spot, forced to watch as her entire world crumbled.

"No!" she finally shouted. Everyone stared at her. "It was someone else," she said, her words echoing in her own ears.

"It is not Caroline," Drake said in exasperation. "Let it go."

"*Me?*" Caroline whimpered.

"Not Caroline," Beatrice said, her mouth growing dry as everyone continued to stare at her. Louisa's eyes were wide as saucers, glassy in the candlelight. "Someone attacked me tonight. Louisa would never have done this. And, in spite of his mistakes, I know Frank would never hurt me, either. Not to mention that I would have smelled of his cologne had he come anywhere near me," she added.

"Someone *attacked* you?" Mrs. Steele repeated, appalled.

"I must have been growing close to the truth," Beatrice said, her mind whirring. "Why else would the murderer attempt to harm me?" She swallowed hard, feeling her sore neck throb.

As she glanced around the table, her eyes fell upon her empty champagne flute in front of her. Empty, because someone had instructed the champagne delivery to be canceled.

There *was* someone who had been particularly harsh to her that evening. Her gaze moved to Mr. Ashbrook, asleep in his armchair at the head of the table. She dropped her eyes to his hands and felt a chill run down her spine.

His fingers poked out from under his blanket, and she could see now that he wore gloves. Rough, dark gloves—such as the kind one would use for gardening.

"Someone canceled a case of champagne," Beatrice said, her blood turning to ice. "How did he know that we would have nothing to celebrate? This man also has an entire cabinet of tinctures and tonics. He knows how to heal the body; he would know how to kill one."

Arabella made a noise, but Daniel put a hand on her arm to silence her as Beatrice continued.

"Everyone knew that the Croaksworths thought the Ashbrook family beneath them. This was the reason for a broken engagement between Arabella and Mr. Croaksworth. Now we know that Arabella told her father that she had been rejected by Croaksworth a second time this evening. And if the killer thought that someone had offended his family name once again, that his own daughter had been personally insulted, rejected as a suitable wife not once but twice . . ." Her eyes flickered to Louisa. "We all know a parent would do anything for a child."

"If you are going to accuse someone, just say it," Arabella spat.

"I'm sure—she can't mean—" Daniel stuttered.

Beatrice looked at him, wishing she did not have to speak the truth—but it had to be told. "I'm sorry, Daniel. I see it now. The killer is your father. Mr. Hugh Ashbrook."

"No!" Arabella shouted, and sprang to her feet. "Father! Defend yourself!"

"He is not well," Daniel said immediately. "Not since Mother's death. He has the fainties; he is not in his right mind—"

"That is just it, Daniel," Beatrice said, "he is *not* in his right mind. This explains how he could have done something so terrible."

"Sir, speak up! Address these accusations!" Captain Peña said. He rose to his feet and reached over the table to whip the blanket off the still-sleeping Mr. Ashbrook.

As the fabric was pulled away, it became immediately clear the man was not sleeping, nor would he ever wake up.

His throat was sliced open in a clean line, blood drenching his pressed suit. In one gloved hand he held a knife, its serrated edge covered in blood, and in the other, a crumpled note. Beatrice stood and crossed over to him. With trembling hands, she pulled the note from his clutch. The writing was tidy but the letters shaky.

"'I do not deserve to have my health, or even my life, for I killed Edmund Croaksworth,'" she read. "'Forgive me.'"

CHAPTER 27

Paramours

Racked with sobs, Arabella threw herself over Mr. Ashbrook's body. Beatrice watched as the crumpled note fluttered onto the table, landing in a gravy boat. The liquid seeped into the edges, blurring the red ink of the note.

I killed Edmund Croaksworth. Forgive me.

"Hugh Ashbrook," Mrs. Steele whispered. "A murderer. And now dead. Who would have thought . . ."

"Beatrice did," Daniel said, looking from his father's body to Beatrice. "She was the only one who saw the truth."

Beatrice held Daniel's gaze. She felt none of the satisfaction she normally had when correctly predicting a killer in one of Sir Huxley's cases. How could she, when the killer was a man she had known all her life? How would Daniel and Arabella pull through this? And what, she thought, would Mr. Ashbrook's actions mean for the future of their community?

"I just don't understand . . ." Inspector Drake muttered. "How could I have been so wrong?"

"You weren't wrong about *everything*," Beatrice said. She watched as Louisa gently pried the now sobbing Arabella away from Mr. Ashbrook and pulled her into an embrace.

Mr. Grub reached across Mr. Ashbrook's body to grab a plate of rolls. Captain Peña pushed away his hands.

"Have some respect, sir. How can you eat at a time like this?"

"We are at dinner," Mr. Grub said irritably. "One cannot waste food which has already been paid for."

"Dinner is over." Mr. Steele stood, the legs of his chair screeching on the floor. "I think we have all had quite enough for one night."

Beatrice had never heard such harshness in her father's voice. The other guests seemed just as surprised by it as she was; everyone fell silent. Mr. Steele went on.

"Mr. Ashbrook was ill. His mind was addled. He thought his daughter had been disrespected, that his family name had been besmirched—and he committed a terrible atrocity." Mr. Steele shook his head. "He then tried to atone. It is tragic." He crossed over to where Mr. Ashbrook slumped in the chair, his body terribly still. Mr. Steele drew the blanket over Mr. Ashbrook, respectfully covering his face. Arabella whimpered, and Louisa tightened her embrace.

"Inspector Drake shall compose a report detailing what has occurred," Mr. Steele continued. He turned to Drake. "Can you at least handle *that*, sir?"

Inspector Drake nodded, his face ashen.

"As for Louisa and Frank," Mr. Steele said, and turned to look at his daughter. His face crumpled. "We will deal with you in the morning," he choked out. "Let us hope we find some humor and light in a new day."

"The guest rooms are made up," Daniel said, his voice hoarse.

Beatrice turned to look at him and felt her heart break for what seemed like the tenth time that evening. He was obviously stunned, his blue eyes glassy, his broad shoulders slumped in defeat. "*A man prepared*—" he began, and his voice cracked.

"*Is a man who cares,*" Beatrice completed quietly. Daniel met her eyes and gave her a grateful nod. "I can show everyone to their rooms," Beatrice continued. Daniel was trying to perform strength, but she could see how fragile he was. She would be there, now, when he needed her most.

"Thank you," Daniel said, and he turned to Arabella. He gently untangled her from Louisa, and Arabella wrapped her arms around Daniel.

"How could Father have done this?" she whimpered. "To our friend . . . to himself . . ." She broke off, tears flowing down her face. Daniel handed her a handkerchief. Tears fell from his own eyes, streaming down his cheeks.

"We shall never know," he said quietly. "Come now. You must rest." He led Arabella from the room, pausing at the door. "Thank you for everything, Beatrice," he whispered. "Your actions tonight will not be forgotten." He helped Arabella out of the room, her sniffles fading into the hallway.

Caroline swooned again, and Captain Peña slipped his arm under her.

"Come," he said, "I will take you to your room—"

"No," Caroline said weakly. "Take me to the kitchen. I must put together a batch of scones; we shall need them in the morning for strength."

"I shall assist you," Miss Bolton said immediately. "You are so thoughtful." She rushed to the door and opened it, then deferentially stood aside to allow Caroline and Captain Peña to pass through.

As Caroline stumbled out, clutching Captain Peña for support, Beatrice noticed Inspector Drake watching them. He frowned as he cast his gaze to the floor but then shook his head and looked away.

He had been wrong, and Beatrice had nearly missed the truth, as well—she had put it all together too late. She felt the heaviness and guilt of both deaths on her conscience. *I should have seen it sooner.*

"I will also compose a report about Louisa's actions," Mr. Grub said, licking his fingers. He picked up a tureen of veal udder and tucked it under his arm, then turned to Beatrice. She shuddered as he whispered, "My love, you would do well to reconsider the offer I made you. I doubt you will find anyone else willing to tether himself to your family after such a scandal." He flounced out, a trail of udder juice dribbling from the tureen and dotting the carpet as he walked.

"How dare he," Mrs. Steele hissed. She moved to follow after Grub, but Mr. Steele held her back.

"Leave him be, Susan," he said. "He has a point." He looked over at Louisa, and then at Frank, who lingered awkwardly. "This is certainly not the match we were hoping for, but we can't worry about that right now."

Mrs. Steele looked at Beatrice and then at Mr. Ashbrook's body. Beatrice could tell what her mother was thinking.

Daniel. There is still Daniel. He was the head of Stabmort Park now; his father—who had never approved of Beatrice—was gone. And with tonight's scandal marring *his* family, Beatrice might be more of an advantageous match than she had been before.

But Mr. Steele was right. Now was not the time for these considerations. Beatrice could feel the weight of exhaustion, her eyelids heavy, her limbs weak. She turned to Louisa, who stood alone now, looking small in her blood-spattered white dress.

"Louisa," she began, unsure of what she was going to say.

Louisa finally looked up at Beatrice, her face set. "Are you happy now, Beatrice?" she said.

"What?" Beatrice drew back, her sister's words like a slap. "What are you talking about?"

"That is what you have always wanted, isn't it? To know everyone's secrets." Louisa's stare was cold, her voice devoid of its usual warmth. "And what a triumph that they have revealed you as the only respectable person here."

"This is certainly not what I wanted!" she said immediately. "Especially your choice to tell Arabella everything before confiding in me, your own sister! She is rude, arrogant, vain—"

"But she doesn't judge me," Louisa interrupted. "She doesn't treat me like a baby! She *respects* me. She respects *my choices*. And she understands that we all have secrets."

"Why do you think *I* wouldn't understand?" Beatrice pressed. "Why—"

"Because I resent you!" Louisa cried. Her words rushed out, as if a dam had broken within her. "If you would have just married a wealthy gentleman—like the eldest daughter is *supposed* to— I could have been free to marry Frank in spite of the fact that he is penniless. But instead you spend all day in your turret, thinking only of yourself. Maybe I brought scandal upon our family—but it was your fault."

"I have not been thinking of myself!" Beatrice said, her face hot. How long had Louisa thought these things? How long had she kept this resentment bottled up, leaving Beatrice naïve about her sister's true feelings about her? "I've been thinking about . . . planning to . . ." she sputtered, trying to explain herself.

"Do you actually expect me to believe you are locked up there pining after a man?" Louisa continued. "If that were true, you would be engaged. Instead, you are alone. Perhaps you always will be."

Mrs. Steele drew in a sharp breath, and Mr. Steele took a step forward, looking from Louisa to Beatrice, helpless.

"At least I have my dignity," Beatrice said in a low voice. Her cheeks stung with embarrassment, with betrayal—with frustration, both at Louisa, for saying such things, and at herself, for having proven them true.

"Beatrice, no," Mr. Steele began.

Louisa laughed bitterly. "You don't have *dignity*," she said sharply. "You just only see things your way. Why do you think no man has made you an offer? You are too brazen, too headstrong. You think you're better than everyone else. But really you are an embarrassment!"

Beatrice looked to her parents, who shrank slightly but offered no rebuttal to Louisa's words. Her gaze moved to Inspector Drake, frozen in the corner of the room, watching the family dispute. Her cheeks burned as she met his eyes, and he quickly looked away.

It was true; she could see now. She had thought herself so witty, so skilled at observation—but she lacked the self-awareness to realize that everyone thought her ridiculous.

"Maybe I am brazen," she said finally, "but you are the one caught in a scandal. If anyone has embarrassed this family, it is *you*."

Mrs. Steele gasped.

"Beatrice," Frank said quietly.

Louisa stared at her sister for a moment, and then her face crumpled. "I hate you," she whispered. Then she turned and fled from the room.

Beatrice moved to follow, but Frank stepped in front of her.

"That's enough, darling."

"Don't call me that, after everything that has occurred," Beatrice said, feeling a rush of anger toward him. "And do not tell me what to do. What do you know?"

"I love her," Frank said simply. "You may not believe me, and your family may not approve, but all I care about is that we are together. Etiquette be damned." He turned and tried to follow after Louisa, but Mrs. Steele stepped in front of him.

"Oh no, you don't. Louisa will stay in *my* room tonight. And the door will be locked, to keep everyone *honest*." She stomped from the room, pushing Frank roughly down the hall.

"A bit late for that," Mr. Steele muttered, and followed after his wife.

Once more, Beatrice found herself alone with Inspector Drake. He stood at the table, watching her, his expression unreadable. Any pride she had felt at discovering the truth, when he had not, vanished. Now she felt only shame and regret.

"Go ahead," she said, swallowing a lump in her throat, "tell me how foolish I have been. Maybe you have always seen it."

"Miss Steele," Inspector Drake said, his voice surprisingly gentle, "I have never considered you foolish. We were both mistaken this evening." He shook his head. "But it does not matter now. I must write my report, as your father requested." He drew in a breath as if he were going to say something else but then seemed to think better of it. Instead he just nodded at her respectfully and then left the room.

Beatrice stood there a moment, her cheeks burning, the room painfully silent. And then there was the rustling of fabric, and Mary crawled from underneath the table.

"Mary," Beatrice said, startled, "how long have *you* been here?"

"I am always here," Mary replied, "but you all simply don't notice, as you are too busy acting in an outrageous manner."

"Yes, clearly propriety has gone out the window with the frogs—" Beatrice began, but Mary cut her off.

"I am not talking about propriety. I am talking about family. Are you really going to let all of this ruin your relationship with Louisa?"

"She thinks me embarrassing. She resents me," Beatrice began heatedly, but Mary cut her off again.

"You *are* embarrassing, Beatrice. And you *did* place the burden of securing a fortune on Louisa. And she *did* bring scandal upon this family."

"How is this helping, Mary?" Beatrice asked, exasperated.

"Louisa has always been passionate," Mary replied. "*You* have always been curious. What if these traits were strengths, not weaknesses? Louisa has found a husband, and they love each other; their bond will be far more valuable to their child than any fortune. You see things others do not, and you have shown tonight how this can be used to pursue justice."

"But I did not see Louisa for who she truly was," Beatrice said, her throat constricting.

"You would have, if you were not blinded by expectations," Mary said sagely. "Let go of what everyone is *supposed* to be, and you shall see who they truly are. Let people be who they truly are, and they shall reach their greatest potential."

"Mary," Beatrice said as she took in her youngest sister as if for the first time, "that is perhaps the wisest thing I have ever heard."

"When one lies awake in the night looking at the moon, one has many hours to ponder the mysteries of the universe," Mary said somberly. "Go to Louisa and mend things at once. Life is too short for anger to stand in the way of a relationship."

Beatrice felt her frustration melt away. Mary was right. How could Beatrice have let it come to this? Nothing could break her bond with Louisa—especially not a list of rules created by some man, years ago. She could not stand for another second to go by without reconciling with Louisa. *She must make it right.*

She clasped Mary's hand. "Thank you, Mary."

"I only hope you afford me the same understanding when you learn my true form," Mary murmured as Beatrice rushed from the room.

Dear Vivek,

My little drake. Today is your eleventh birthday. You seem so grown-up, and yet still you follow me around like a duck. You are the brightest spot of my life, and you shall never know how much I love you, my darling.

This morning you turned to me and asked, "Will my father attend my birthday celebration?"

We never speak of him. I knew not what to say. You are so inquisitive, so serious—I should have known that you would begin to ask these questions. I only wish I could give you the answers you desire.

Your father was a gentleman, or so I thought. I met him when I first arrived in London. It was so different here than in India. I missed the hot sun, the vibrancy of my home. But your father made me feel as if I could make something of this place. We were in love.

But as I always say, a single man in possession of a good fortune sometimes is actually not single. He's often a total liar. Sadly, this was the case for your father. As soon as I realized your existence, your father revealed the truth: He was already married. He already had a family. I was simply a pretty face to him. A game to play, a prize to win.

You are not ready to know all of this yet. I shall seal this letter and give it to you on your eighteenth birthday. But I shall also send a copy to your father. He will know that though he rejected you, though he is a despicable person, none of that will stop you from growing into a talented, upstanding young man.

You make me proud to be your mother.

Nitara Varma

CHAPTER 28

Reconciliation

Beatrice flew down the hallway, the words she wanted to speak echoing in her mind.

I am sorry, Louisa. I am so sorry.

Beatrice raced down a creaking staircase. She pressed her hand against the velvet wall to steady herself, her palms damp with anxious perspiration.

Louisa would not have withdrawn to a guest room with their mother, Beatrice thought. Her sister was upset, and that meant one thing: She would be in the kitchens, soothing her sorrows in sugar. Though it was ill lit in the depths of the house, she knew the number of steps on the staircase and counted them as she rushed. *Eleven, twelve, thirteen—*

She heard a sudden *thunk,* and everything went black. She had just enough time to understand that the noise had been something hard colliding with her skull before she toppled down another flight of stairs.

She landed in a crumpled heap at the bottom floor of Stabmort, head throbbing. She forced herself to push her body up, though every movement was painful, and stumbled to her feet. The realization of what had just happened washed over her as she stood.

Someone had attacked her. Again. *Absolutely ridiculous.* But this time she felt no fear, only anger.

She turned just in time to see a dark figure, covered with a riding cloak, rush down the staircase. In its hands the figure held up a silver candlestick. It glinted with a streak of red, and Beatrice put a hand to her skull. She drew it back to see a smear of blood.

Beatrice tripped forward, trying to run, but the figure threw the candlestick aside and rushed at her, gloved hand grabbing for her throat. The two of them crashed into the bath room, illuminated by the green glow of the water. Beatrice tried to reach for her assailant's face, to see the identity of her attacker, but the figure was too strong. She felt herself shoved back with great force and was suddenly submerged in water.

Beatrice tried to push to the surface, but the figure held her down. Her eyes burned from the hot spring and her vision blurred.

This is the end, she thought. *And I never got to reconcile with Louisa.*

Then, suddenly, the pressure of the hand pushing her down released. Beatrice burst through the surface of the hot spring, gasping for breath, in time to see Louisa holding the candlestick. She dropped it with a clatter and shoved the door to the bath room shut, sliding the bolt in place. She whirled around to face Beatrice, her eyes full of terror.

"I had just started on a seed cake when I heard a thunk. I came running and saw—I don't know *who* it was," she gasped, pointing to the door with a shaking hand. Beatrice could hear the sound of heavy footsteps fading into the distance as her attacker fled. "They got away," Louisa said, and dropped to her knees to help Beatrice from the spring.

Beatrice collapsed onto the edge of the bath and coughed up luminescent water, choking on the sulfurous taste. Louisa gripped her hand and pulled her to her feet, and Beatrice immediately wrapped her sister in a hug.

"I'm sorry," she cried immediately. "I was insufferable. I was so caught up in my own pursuits that I did not realize—you have grown up. You are a woman now. A woman who deserves to make her own choices."

Louisa stiffened and then hugged Beatrice back with such force that Beatrice thought her ribs might snap.

"*I'm* sorry!" she sobbed. "I don't hate you. I've never hated you. I was hurt that you have seemed so distant lately, and I lashed out. The moment I left the room I was so ashamed—you were right. I should have told you everything."

"I wish my distance hadn't made you lose your trust in me," Beatrice said. "You can come to me with anything. You know that, don't you? You don't have to go to Arabella."

"There is more to her than meets the eye too, Beatrice," Louisa said softly. "And can you blame me? I thought that if you knew what a scandal I was going to bring upon our family, you would never speak to me again."

"Louisa," Beatrice said, "I was wrong. You could never truly bring a scandal upon us. You are the best person I know."

"You still think that, even knowing that I fell for a seducer? That I am with child? That we conspired to lie in order to inherit Croaksworth's fortune?" Louisa asked, blinking down at Beatrice. "And probably broke even more rules from *The Lady's Guide* that I don't even know about?"

"Yes," Beatrice said firmly. "In any case, I wouldn't know either. I have never read volume two."

"Thank goodness," Louisa cried in relief, "neither have I." She threw her arms around Beatrice once more. "I shall not lie to you again. From now on, we will have no secrets from each other."

Beatrice drew in a shaking breath as she gently pulled back from Louisa's embrace.

"Louisa," she began, "you said we all have secrets. And mine is tearing me apart." She drew in a shaking breath. "You were right when you said that I was not in the turret pining after a man. The truth is that I have been reading articles about crime. And I have realized that I don't want to give these up. I want to be an inspector." Her words echoed in the bath room. *Inspector. Inspector.*

She was tired of hiding. If Louisa could shed the fear of judgment and shame, then she could too. It was time to admit that her crime-solving pursuits were not a fleeting fancy or secret hobby. It was more than that: This was her calling.

"You mean, you want to be like Drake?" Louisa said, knitting her brows together.

"Not like *him*," Beatrice said hotly. "*I* would not be so arrogant as to state that I had solved a case, when in truth I knew *nothing*—"

"First of all, he didn't know *nothing*," Louisa interrupted. "Second of all, I think you might be more like Drake than you realize."

Beatrice stared at her sister and let out an incredulous laugh. "When did you get so insightful?"

"Sneaking around with a lover forces one to learn subtext," Louisa said with a shrug. "But I must say . . . I think you would be a wonderful inspector."

"And you will be a wonderful mother," Beatrice said. "Frank may be incorrigible, but if anyone can keep him in line, it is you."

Louisa's eyes filled with tears, and Beatrice could feel a lump in her own throat.

"When he proposed, he took me to that lily field, the one just past town," she told Beatrice. "He had set up a game of ninepins amidst the flowers. If I won, he said, I could have whatever was in a small box in his pocket. Of course I beat him, as he knew I would—and this ring was inside." She held up her hand, on which she wore the gleaming piece of jewelry. "He said he would keep it for me until we found a way to tell everyone the truth. I know that people think Frank is all talk," she went on, "but he has fulfilled every one of his wild promises to me so far." She pressed her hand to her chest. "Even now I can hardly talk about him; I fear my heart will beat out of my chest. I fear I will explode with passion!"

"That sounds . . . uncomfortable," Beatrice said, and Louisa laughed.

"Perhaps."

"I had always thought a person should consider the right spouse a comfort," Beatrice went on.

To her surprise, Louisa shook her head. "Oh, no," she said, "for me it is quite the opposite. I feel as if I am embarking on some terrifying adventure. And yet . . ." She smiled. "It is one I am ready for."

Beatrice smiled back, but then winced in pain. She drew Caroline's handkerchief from her pocket and pressed it against her aching head to stem the bleeding. The cut was shallow, but she could feel it throbbing where she had been hit.

"Wait," she said, realization finally trickling over her like cold water. "If someone just attacked me, but Mr. Ashbrook is dead—"

"The killer is still out there," Louisa said, her face turning ashen.

Beatrice had been so focused on reconciling with Louisa, so angry at being delayed, that the truth had been slow to sink in.

"The wound on Mr. Ashbrook's throat," she said, her voice hoarse. "It was clean. But he held a serrated blade. He didn't kill himself. He was murdered—and his killer is still at large. *Inspector Drake could be in danger.*" She rushed toward the door and pressed an ear against it.

Was the killer waiting on the other side?

"You have to go to Drake!" Louisa cried, and Beatrice nodded.

"I will see this investigation to its end," she said. She took Caroline's handkerchief from her head and folded it. As she did, she saw a flash of embroidery.

It read "EC." She had assumed this stood for Edmund Croaksworth. But now, as she examined the monogram, she knew it could have been sewn by only Caroline herself. Beatrice would recognize those irritatingly perfect stitches anywhere. But why would Caroline have a handkerchief with "EC," and not "CW"?

And why, Beatrice thought with a shiver, was the "EC" of the handkerchief stitched in the same script as the engraving on Edmund Croaksworth's pocket watch?

"You mustn't go out the door, in case your attacker is waiting," Louisa said, interrupting Beatrice's thoughts. "You should take—"

"The tonic pulley," Beatrice finished excitedly. "I had almost forgotten."

She circled the pool of water and went to the far wall of the bath room, and she ran her hands along the wall. Her fingers found a small panel, which she slid to one side to reveal an opening.

Mr. Ashbrook had devised this system for servants to send down his tonics. That way, he could indulge in a health drink without interrupting his soak. As children, Beatrice and Louisa had been charmed by the tonic pulley and delighted in sending Mary up to the kitchens via the small compartment.

Now Beatrice squeezed inside.

"Wait until you know it is safe, and then lock yourself in a guest room with Mother and Father. Do not open the door for anyone," she instructed.

Over the course of the evening she had made a fool out of herself in front of everyone she knew. But she had also learned how to investigate a crime. Tidy explanations would not suffice. Inspector Drake was right—she needed evidence, she needed proof. But Mary was also right—Beatrice could not allow herself to be blinded by the façade she saw. She needed to see her friends, her family, and Caroline Wynn for who they truly were.

"Beatrice," Louisa said, her voice soft, "be careful."

"I have seen your good name besmirched, my own reputation destroyed, a young man killed, a family friend murdered in cold blood, my family terrified, and a ball completely ruined. I am furious," Beatrice said. "When I find the killer, it is *they* who should be scared of *me*."

With that, she gave the tonic pulley rope a tug and heaved herself up through the dark innards of Stabmort Park.

DIED,

> In London, of a carriage accident, Miss Nitara Varma, seamstress and mother, aged 34. An immigrant from India, Miss Varma is survived by her son, Vivek, aged 12, who goes by "Drake."
>
> NOTE.
>
> At Drake's request, an inquest has been opened to investigate the crash.
>
> "This was a terrible accident," said Chief Constable Clemens. "The wheels were not properly affixed; it is a tragedy no one saw coming."
>
> "If it was a question of wheel affixation, why were the wheels intact after the crash?" the precocious Drake asked reporters. "The evidence does not line up. If I were in charge, I would ensure that the evidence always lined up."

CHAPTER 29

Bloodshed

Beatrice raced up the stairs and to the parlor as if she were outrunning a hailstorm on an afternoon walk. She frantically turned over everything in her mind.

The dirt and honeysuckle on the carpet. Louisa's empty vial of belladonna. Caroline's handkerchief.

What did it all mean?

She picked up her pace. The family portraits of the Ashbrook ancestors blurred as she ran, their faces blending into one blond, elegant sneer.

She came to a halt outside the parlor door and grabbed the knob—but it was locked. The noise of a scuffle emanated from inside, making the hairs on Beatrice's neck stand on end.

She was right. Drake was in trouble. She only hoped she was not already too late.

She whirled around. A statue of Venus was standing, solid, serene, and bosom-forward, just across from the doors. Thinking quickly, Beatrice slid onto the ground and used her legs to push it over. It toppled and fell, its enormous Cupid's kettle drums crashing into the doors and splintering them in half. Beatrice burst inside through the hole and gasped at the sight unfolding within.

Caroline Wynn stood over Inspector Drake, holding Captain Peña's cutlass—the one that had gone missing—to the detective's throat. Drake strained against a pair of handcuffs, a beautifully embroidered handkerchief stuffed into his mouth as a gag. His eye was wide with fear, his long arms tense as he tried to break free.

Caroline no longer slumped demurely; she stood up straight, looking taller and more imposing. Her normally sweet expression was gone, and her face was now set in a sneer.

Both Drake and Caroline turned to stare at Beatrice, who was covered in splinters of wood, emerging from the giant marble bosom.

"It *was* you?" Beatrice said, gaping in stupefaction.

"Mademoiselle Beatrice," Caroline said, "you have joined just in time to witness my escape."

Her voice had shifted. It no longer sounded proper and practiced. It was rougher, deeper, and vaguely . . .

"French," Beatrice whispered. "You are *French*. Who *are* you?"

Caroline smiled more widely. "You're very perceptive—it might be inconvenient for me, but I can't help liking you for it."

Beatrice took a step forward, but Drake shook his head in warning. Beatrice gave him a nod to signify that she had things under control; she grabbed a poker from beside the fire and brandished it at Miss Wynn.

Drake looked meaningfully at Caroline's hem, and Beatrice traced his gaze. He had noticed something before, in the dining room, Beatrice thought. Now she could see exactly what he'd observed: The bottom of Caroline's gown was dark with damp. Her shoes, poking out from beneath her skirt, were not silk slippers. She had changed into leather boots. Footwear no lady would wear to a ball—unless they meant to weather a storm.

"You have been outside," Beatrice said. "But only your hem is wet. You went into the stables and set off an empty carriage, didn't you?"

"Excellent," Caroline said conversationally. "I meant to distract you and make a hasty exit. The first part of my plan worked—but I underestimated the weather. It is too fierce, even for me."

"Yet you still mean to make an escape," Beatrice surmised. "You have not changed out of your riding boots, and clearly you were on your way to the stables when Inspector Drake interrupted."

"So smart, Miss Steele. Everyone else bought my act, but *you* never would. It was always so fun to taunt you. I'll miss that," Caroline said with a tinkling laugh. Then she lunged with the cutlass, slashing Beatrice in the side. As blood bloomed on the fabric, Beatrice came alive with anger.

"You cad," she growled, "you have ruined my best gown!"

"*That* was your *best*?" Caroline said. "I'm sorry, but you really should thank me."

It was actually satisfying, Beatrice thought furiously, to have a real reason to loathe Caroline. She had never been able to explain her dislike before, but now that the lady had stabbed her, Beatrice thought her hatred much more justified.

Drake struggled to break free, to enter the fray, but the restraints held him back.

Beatrice dodged a blow from Caroline and aimed another slash of the poker. Caroline retreated and paced the room, turning her wrist around and eyeing Beatrice. Waiting to pounce.

"You are still trying to escape, even though everyone thought Hugh Ashbrook was the murderer," Beatrice said, struggling to catch her breath. "If you are the killer, you could have gotten away with it. Which leads me to think that you have some other reason that you must leave." She tore a piece of fabric from the bottom of her gown and pressed it to her bleeding side. The cut stung, but it was not deep. Caroline was not as skilled with a sword as she might have been, or else she had not truly been aiming to make a fatal blow. Beatrice had to suspect the latter, as Caroline had never been less than perfect at anything.

"You have a dark secret. You told this to Captain Peña," Beatrice said, mentally scrambling to put together the pieces. "You asked if Mr. Croaksworth had confided in Inspector Drake, and now you've tied up Drake. . . . Croaksworth knew something about you, didn't he? Something you do not want to come to light. Could it have been worse than *murder*?"

Inspector Drake finally worked the handkerchief out of his mouth and spat it angrily onto the ground.

"He recognized her from years ago, when she lived in London. He knew that she is not 'Caroline Wynn,'" he growled, his voice hoarse. "Caroline Wynn doesn't exist. This woman is Verity Swan."

"Isn't it funny how long it took you to recognize me?" Caroline asked, delighted. She tugged at her chestnut hair, and it suddenly fell free, revealing that it was merely a wig. Underneath, Caroline's curls were a slightly darker shade of chestnut. "Mr. Croaksworth was a simple man, but he never forgot a face. Though I must say I found him rather forgettable when I met him at one of his social clubs, which I used to frequent. Dare I say . . . boring, even? So much inane conversation about whether I preferred crown molding or double crown molding. No surprise—he liked both. When he greeted me this evening, I told him he was mistaken for calling me Verity, and he believed me. Still—I was concerned that he had told you the truth. With so much coming to light this evening, I knew it was time for me to leave Swampshire for good."

"Wait," Beatrice said, mind whirring. "Verity Swan . . . why do I know that name?" And then it clicked.

It was the first case she had ever read in the paper—the first case to pique her interest in crime.

DeBurbie, who was active in the social scene of London, was well-known for his collection of precious jewels, which mysteriously went missing on the day of his death. Sir Huxley and Drake disagreed about the culprit. Drake inexplicably suspected DeBurbie's beautiful lady companion, Verity Swan, but Sir Huxley revealed that the lowly butler was the true killer.

"Viscount Dudley DeBurbie's fiancée! One of the people of interest in his murder," she said with a shiver. She looked at Drake, aghast. "That was the last case you worked with Sir Huxley. The case which led to your schism. How could you not recognize her?"

"She was wearing a wig!" Drake said defensively.

"The same color as her hair!" Beatrice shot back.

"Verity had a heart-shaped mole," Drake insisted.

Both Beatrice and Drake whipped their heads around to look expectantly at Caroline, who wiped the skin of her cheek, thus removing a layer of makeup and exposing the telltale beauty mark. Drake gasped as Beatrice shook her head at him in exasperation.

"You switched necklaces," Beatrice said, looking to Caroline's long, elegant neck. "You wore emeralds earlier this evening, and now you wear a pearl. The emeralds were DeBurbie's, weren't they? But you switched when you saw Inspector Drake, fearing he would recognize them." She curled her fingers around the fire poker. "Apparently, you needn't have worried."

"I saw your hem!" Drake said furiously, straining urgently against his handcuffs. "I surmised that you set a carriage off to distract us, that you were trying to get away—even if I hadn't worked out *why*, I caught you trying to escape. I suspected you."

"But I suspected that you would suspect, which is why I did not face you unarmed. I took the cutlass for exactly a moment like this," Caroline replied. "*Les femmes ont toujours une longueur d'avance.*"

"All along, you were concealing your true identity," Beatrice spat. "Is your real name even Verity?"

Caroline shrugged. "I go by many names. Caroline, Verity, Madam Jessica, Emmeline Clément . . ."

"EC." Beatrice drew in a sharp breath. "The initials on your handkerchief. And the pocket watch. It was yours, not Mr. Croaksworth's."

"I told you that we could not make assumptions—" Drake began, but Beatrice shot him a withering look, and he broke off.

"For clarity's sake," Caroline said sweetly, "why don't you just call me Caroline?" With that, she thrust forward, slashing at Beatrice, and Beatrice ducked and kicked her in the ankle. Caroline let out a cry of pain and fell back against a grandfather clock. It teetered and then fell through the parlor window. The pane shattered, sending shards of glass flying. Caroline and Beatrice leapt away from the window to avoid the harsh rain now blowing into the room.

"You are a con artist," Beatrice spat, "preying on young gentlemen. Taking them for all they are worth. You stole DeBurbie's jewels, and then you came to Swampshire to steal from the men here."

"A lady has few ways to make money, *ma chère*," Caroline said, her French accent becoming even more annoyingly pronounced. She straightened her back and gripped the cutlass, shivering from the rain now blustering into the room through the broken window. "But if one can play pianoforte and laugh at many stupid jokes, one can get far."

"That's why you couldn't marry Captain Peña," Beatrice surmised.

"He is a good man but has no money," Caroline said. "I could not give up hopeful suitors. They are my source of income. Their gifts and favors pay for all I have."

Beatrice pressed her lips together, and Caroline smiled.

"You are impressed, aren't you?"

"Of course not," Beatrice said, but Caroline smiled wider.

"You've never been a good liar, Beatrice. You may see others for who they truly are—but the watched are also watching you."

"I don't approve of the things you have done," Beatrice said, tightening her fist around the fire poker.

"We are not so different," Caroline replied. "We live in a world that thinks women are delicate and helpless and simple. A world that assumes every woman has the same desires. It's so limiting. But *we* refuse to be bound. We have desires of our own, *n'est-ce pas?*"

"That may be true, but I am *not* like you," Beatrice said, both awed and disturbed by Caroline's words. "I'm not just going to *murder* people because I'm unhappy with how society works."

"Such a lovely sentiment," Caroline said, "but you were right before: I did not kill Edmund Croaksworth."

Beatrice suddenly lunged forward and put the fire poker to Caroline's throat. "Show me your hands," she demanded.

Caroline held up both hands, her wrists perfect and unblemished. In that moment, Beatrice knew—with sinking disappointment— that Caroline was telling the truth.

Whoever had attacked Beatrice, twice now, had to be the killer. And they would have a mark where her earring had jammed into their flesh. Caroline had no such mark.

"But your scent was in the tonic room," Beatrice murmured. "*Evening rose.*"

"Your cousin isn't the only person who likes to steal from Stabmort," Caroline said with a shrug. "Mr. Ashbrook's collection is worth a fortune."

Beatrice lowered the poker slightly, thrown off, and Caroline lunged forward and knocked it aside with her blade. The poker fell to the floor with a clatter. Caroline moved forward with the cutlass, and Beatrice, now unarmed, held her breath.

At that moment, a carriage and ponies blasted across the front yard and came to a stop outside the shattered parlor window. Captain Peña sat up in the driver's seat, clutching the reins.

"Only one man can captain a ship in *this* storm. And, *c'est vrai,* I really do love him." Caroline looked at the window and then stepped forward. Beatrice steeled herself, but to her surprise, Caroline lowered the cutlass. "You are smart, *ma chère,*" she said in a low voice, so only Beatrice could hear her. This close, Beatrice could see details in Caroline's face that she had never noted before. The lines on her forehead, carefully covered with powder. Her eyes, sharper, more astute than she'd let on. "You play by your own rules," Caroline went on. "You could make an excellent con woman." She stretched out a hand. Wind whipped her chestnut hair across her face. "Come with me. Together, we would be a force to be reckoned with. The rich gentlemen out there wouldn't stand a chance."

Beatrice stared at Caroline's outstretched palm.

"If you are going to mold yourself into some silly shape," Caroline said, "why not use it to your own advantage? Aren't you tired of having nothing? Don't you want to take something for yourself?"

"Yes," Beatrice said slowly, "but I do not want a few jewels, and gifts, and simpering praise. I want justice."

Beatrice leapt forward—not to go with Caroline, but to stop her from getting away. The woman seemed to anticipate her move and jumped for the window. She lunged toward the carriage, but Beatrice caught hold of her annoyingly delicate ankle. Caroline was stuck, halfway in the parlor, halfway to freedom.

"My love!" Captain Peña yelled to Caroline.

"Suit yourself, Beatrice," Caroline said. "We could have been great." With that she flipped her drenched hair, somehow managing to make the movement graceful as she simultaneously kicked Beatrice away. She boarded the carriage and slammed the door.

Captain Peña cracked the reins, and the horses took off. Beatrice made a move to chase after them, but she stopped at the window, panting in anger. The carriage and ponies were already a speck in the stormy distance.

Caroline Wynn was gone.

CHAPTER 30

Tricks

The parlor furniture rattled as wind rushed in through the open gash in the wall, the once-pristine pastels covered in glistening shards of glass and rainwater.

Breathing heavily, Beatrice turned to Inspector Drake on the settee.

"I can't believe I have been bested by Verity Swan a second time," he growled. He pulled against his handcuffs, the metal eating into his wrists. "She slipped through my fingers *yet again!*"

"Excuse me," Beatrice said tartly. "You could thank me for *saving your life a second time.*"

Inspector Drake scoffed as he continued to pull at his handcuffs.

"Let me. Where is the key?" Beatrice said impatiently.

Inspector Drake motioned to his pocket. "I cannot reach it," he said. Beatrice crossed over to him and knelt down. She awkwardly, slowly, snaked a hand into his pocket to withdraw the small iron key. She unlocked the handcuffs, and they fell to the floor with a clang.

Drake rubbed at his wrists where the irons had been, clearly still fuming, but then leaned back with a heavy sigh.

"Where did you learn to fence?" he asked, eyeing her.

"I read that Sir Huxley thinks an inspector must know how to fence, so I secretly taught myself from a book," Beatrice replied. "I never thought I would actually use the skill, but I must admit that it was exhilarating."

Drake leaned against the love seat, a lock of his dark hair falling into his eye. "I am a fool. I saw the water at Caroline's hem— I came down here because I suspected that something was amiss— but then she swooned. It caught me off guard. The next thing I knew, I was chained to this ridiculous settee."

"I hate to admit it," Beatrice said, sinking into a seat next to Inspector Drake, "but I rather like her now."

"*Now?* Wasn't she your best friend?" Inspector Drake asked.

"I never said that!" Beatrice said irritably. "We hardly knew each other, clearly—but now that I know she was a con woman the whole time, I have more respect for her. The fact that she managed to fool even *you* . . ."

"I am hardly infallible, Miss Steele," Drake said, and raked a hand through his dark hair in exasperation. "I think this evening has been proof enough of *that*. Perhaps I *should* just leave the crime solving to Huxley."

"The DeBurbie murder was the first crime that caught my attention," Beatrice said. "I remember when the butler was convicted."

At the same time, they both said, "I never thought he did it." They shared a small smile.

"Sir Huxley did not want to accuse Verity Swan. It would have been uncivilized, considering that he was in love with her." Drake said. "Logic went out the window. Verity suggested that the butler seemed nefarious, and Sir Huxley jumped on him as the prime suspect."

"I remember your division from Huxley because of it," Beatrice said. "I read of it in the papers."

"He kicked me out of our partnership," Drake said. "I lost access to our office—access to society—and he got everything he wanted."

"Except for Verity's hand," Beatrice said.

"Sir Huxley had plenty of women waiting in the wings," Drake scoffed. "Once he arrested the butler, he was lauded for his chivalrous crime-solving skills."

"And all the distraction allowed Verity Swan to disappear with the jewels," Beatrice added. "That was two years ago," she realized. "Just the time 'Caroline Wynn' arrived in Swampshire."

"No doubt she planned to hide out here in the middle of nowhere until public interest in the case died out," Drake said with a sigh. "Huxley got a weekly article in the paper, I got a tiny flat at the edge of town and hardly enough business to afford bread. And Caroline got away with everything."

"Well. Not everything," Beatrice said. She reached into her pocket and pulled out the emerald choker, its gemstones glittering in the candlelight.

"How did you—" Drake began.

"I took it from her pocket when she was droning on, trying to get me to join her," Beatrice said with a shrug. "I could not resist giving her a small taste of her own medicine."

Drake smiled slightly. "I should turn you in. After all, when I realized Huxley was too emotional, I vowed to never make that same mistake."

"You know, Inspector," Beatrice said gently, her fingers curling around the necklace, "you *are* allowed to experience emotions. They're not *always* bad."

"I would have disagreed, until I met you," he said, still holding her gaze.

"Your insistence on proof is not *so* wrong, though," she allowed. "After all, there was none that indicated Caroline was the murderer."

"I wish we had been able to come to these conclusions before this investigation became so bungled," Drake said, shaking his head bitterly.

"It's not the best handling of a case that I've heard of," Beatrice admitted. "But perhaps it's because we have been going about it the wrong way."

"So . . . what should we do now?" Drake asked, looking at her expectantly.

"We reconsider the evidence," she said, and tucked the necklace into her pocket.

Drake nodded slowly, leaned forward slightly closer—

And then paused.

"Is something wrong?" she asked, breathless.

He reached down toward her bosom and withdrew the vial of belladonna.

"How dare you, sir?" Beatrice said quickly, reaching for it. "And that's inconsequential! We should get back to what we were just about to—"

But Inspector Drake whipped the vial out of reach. He examined the label and then looked at Beatrice, realization dawning on his face.

"Louisa," he said in a low voice. "Louisa *did* do it, didn't she?"

"No," Beatrice said, her voice raspy. "No, she didn't. I knew you would think she did. It's why I kept this from you—"

"I trusted you," Drake interrupted, shaking his head. "Against my better judgment, based on my *emotions*, I trusted you. But you could not overcome your bias." He wrapped his fingers around the vial, shaking with frustration. "How could you do it, Beatrice? People's *lives* are at stake."

"Sir Huxley would—" Beatrice began.

"Do you want to know the truth about Sir Huxley?" Inspector Drake interrupted, jumping to his feet. "He doesn't do a damn thing! When we were partners, he was so obsessed with being a *gentleman* that he was blinded by his devotion to manners. *I* did everything in terms of finding evidence, taking statements—all the 'boring' work that Huxley did not care to do."

"But then you parted ways, as you just said," Beatrice shot back. "Huxley has been solving cases on his own. And in any case, this isn't *about* him—"

Drake laughed humorlessly. "Isn't it? 'Solving cases.' More like he publishes all his case details in the paper, so that informants will write to him and tell him who did it. All he really cares about is entertaining ladies who want to be with him, and gambling with gentlemen who want to *be* him."

"What are you talking about?" Beatrice demanded. "Huxley is no fraud. You are just bitter."

"I am bitter. That I admit," Drake said. "But I am also right. Why do you think Huxley always asks 'fans' to write to him? He's a hack."

"But . . . are those letters truly helpful to Huxley?" Beatrice asked, suddenly breathless.

"I have heard that much of his fan mail is just crazy conspiracies from batty admirers," Drake allowed. "But Huxley must occasionally receive something helpful, in order to crack so many cases."

Realization passed over Beatrice at these words.

She was one of these admirers. His most devoted reader. She had been writing to Huxley for years, giving her thoughts on cases. She'd never believed he'd actually read them. But now she thought:

Were her letters among the ones that contained crazy conspiracies, or were her insights key to solving the crimes?

"Why don't you go sit by a fire somewhere warm?" Drake interrupted her thoughts, voice dripping with condescension. "Your parents will be devastated if one of their daughters is in prison and the other catches her death of cold. Because Louisa murdered Croaksworth . . . I am firm on this."

He took a step over the parlor doors, now lying splintered on the ground.

Beatrice stayed where she was, reeling.

Then she picked up the fire poker and stepped in front of Drake's path, blocking his exit.

"What are you doing?" he growled.

"I'm sorry, Inspector," she said, astonished by her own behavior but unable to turn back now. "I must ask that you return the handcuffs and key."

He did nothing. Her palm felt damp. She could not bring herself to actually stab him, and she knew that he knew she was bluffing.

And so she dropped the poker and charged at him. Beatrice had never been as athletic as her sister, but the element of surprise was on her side: Drake was so shocked that he dropped the irons and key. She grabbed for them and pushed him into the love seat, clamping them around his wrists.

"What are you doing?" he yelped again, and she backed away, breathing heavily.

"I hate that it has to be this way," she said, and dropped the key into her bodice. Then, as he squirmed, trying in vain to break free, she reached into his pocket. She withdrew the vial of belladonna and placed it on the floor. With one satin-slippered foot, she stomped it to pieces.

"You're making a terrible mistake," Inspector Drake growled.

"No, Inspector," Beatrice said. "I am trusting my gut. I will return for you once I have proven, once and for all, that my sister did not do this—and once I have apprehended the villain who did. Because if there's one thing *I'm* firm on, it's that Louisa is innocent."

She left Inspector Drake shackled to the love seat, thunder and lightning still raging outside.

Dear Edmund,

I hope your travels are going well. I am writing to keep
you updated on my examination of your father's will.
Your father's affairs are mostly in order, and rest assured
your fortune is secure. Mr. Croaksworth senior owed no
sums of money and had carefully protected his principal
balance.

However, I have found a few documents among his
belongings which you should see. They are nothing urgent, but they might be of interest. These will be waiting
for you upon your return from Swampshire and Bath.

Sincerely,

Mr. Oliver Taylor, Esquire

CHAPTER 31

Proposals

Beatrice flew through the hallways, on edge, jumping at every shadow—and yet determined. She had always felt validated when Huxley came to the same conclusions as her in his cases, but now she realized that she was not just a like-minded fan. She had been the one helping Huxley figure out the truth all along. She did not have to hope Huxley would arrive in Swampshire and put a stop to everything. There was no doubt left in her mind: *She* would be able to catch the killer. After all, she had done it before.

She found herself at a door and pushed it open, keeping her footsteps quiet, hardly daring to breathe.

The study. This was where the poisoning had to have occurred, she was sure. Something had happened during the fateful card game that she and Drake had missed.

She had looked at it before through a clouded gaze, she knew. She had jumped to assumptions about who was at the card game, what had occurred. Now she would look again, with determinedly fresh eyes.

Beatrice stepped inside, crossed the room, and shoved aside the rug concealing the trapdoor. She pulled it open, but before she could descend the staircase into the small chamber below, a movement in the corner of the room caught her eye.

She looked up to see Mr. Grub as he stepped into the moonlight, drenched in blood.

"Help," he said weakly, and then crumpled to the ground.

Beatrice gasped and jumped to her feet. She tried to catch Grub as he collapsed, but he was sturdier than his lanky frame suggested, and she crumpled under his weight. With difficulty, she managed to shove him onto an armchair.

His head lolled to one side, one long string of drool trickling from his scaly lips.

"Cousin," Beatrice whispered urgently, shaking his shoulders. "Mr. Grub. Can you hear me?" He gave a groan of agony, indicating that he was awake—barely. "You must focus," she said intensely. "Who did this to you?"

"I—didn't—see," Mr. Grub gasped. "Hit—me—from—behind—"

She looked wildly around the study, but the room was silent. No one else was in sight. Was it the same cloaked figure who had attacked her? She looked back at Grub.

"You are bleeding badly," she whispered, and took out her handkerchief. He was covered in red, but she could not tell from whence the liquid was seeping. "I think I will have to sew up the source . . . and I apologize in advance, for I'm hopeless at stitching. . . ." She dabbed at his head, where blood matted his greasy hair. She suddenly froze.

There was a tiny bud amidst his curls, and she plucked it out.

"Honeysuckle," she whispered.

"Sweet," Mr. Grub said, "like you, my dear Beatrice."

His voice was suddenly calm, no longer panting and strangled. He took her hand, and she realized with horror that he was staring at her steadily.

"You're not injured at all," she said, trying to wrench her hand free. Mr. Grub held fast.

"Red ink," he said. "Aren't I clever?"

"What?" Beatrice asked, horrified, and Mr. Grub leaned forward a bit closer.

"I had to get your attention," he whined. "It's not easy to do this, Beatrice. You are always so distracted."

"I don't understand," she choked out. She looked around for some means of escape, but Mr. Grub held fast to her hand.

"I always knew you would be my wife," Mr. Grub panted. "It makes sense, doesn't it? We are so well matched." He used his free hand to wipe red ink and snot from his nose. "You are not afraid of death—and death follows me everywhere. You are perhaps the only woman who could stand to marry me."

"Trust me, I really could not," Beatrice said in horror, but Grub's grip on her hand grew tighter. His own hands were rough and callused.

"I heard that Edmund was coming into town, trying to woo all the women," Grub went on, "and therefore tonight would be my last night to secure you for myself. One way or another."

"Mr. Croaksworth was interested in *Louisa,* not me," Beatrice said. She was so close to the door, to freedom. But Mr. Grub blocked her path, his hand tight around hers.

"Then why did she spend all evening speaking to Edmund about *you*?" he demanded.

"She loves Frank, weren't you paying attention at dinner?" Beatrice said, mentally calculating angles at which she might strike. "That's why she was telling Croaksworth about me, thinking that perhaps she might make him fall in love. Then I could secure our family's fortune, and she could be free to marry the man she truly wanted. And," she continued, "I might also mention that Croaksworth is now dead, so he's hardly a threat."

"But what about Daniel?" Grub asked in a low voice.

Beatrice gave no reply, but instead dropped her gaze to Mr. Grub's boots. They had patches of dried mud, barely visible, as if he had attempted to wipe them off but missed a few spots.

"Mr. Grub," she said, feeling the honeysuckle from his hair still crumpled in her fist, "were you down at Adler's End?"

She recalled the beginning of the evening. A spot of mud caked into the carpet. The sprig of honeysuckle. And then she thought of the trench by the stream. A hole, like a grave, just beside a patch of honeysuckle. A shovel next to it. Grub's rough hands, callused—as if from digging.

"I know how females are," Grub said. "You want to be caught up in some dramatic affair of the heart. But it is time for you to accept my proposal."

"You dug the grave," Beatrice said, horror making her blood turn cold. "Why?"

"Everyone knows I want you," Grub said, squeezing her wrist so tight that she felt her hand go numb. "I had hoped you would change your mind, accept my offer. I even filed that legal suit to help force your hand. But if it didn't work, how could I stand for the indignity? How could I watch you with some other man, or worse—how could I watch you alone, no man able to enjoy the fruits of your loins?"

"So you thought to either marry me or kill me? As always, I am struck by your romanticism, but I can accept neither of these options." With that, Beatrice tore her hand away and leapt backward. Grub scrabbled for her, his fingers curling around the sleeve of Drake's coat. Now she was grateful for its shabbiness, for the sleeve tore off in Grub's hands. He grabbed again, but she dodged just out of his reach.

"You have always played hard to get," he whined. "Why must you torture me?"

"You would never get away with it," Beatrice said, her body trembling. "You couldn't even dig a grave deep enough to hide a body. That shallow trench would have exposed . . ." *Me,* she could not bring herself to say.

"I was only going to do it if you refused me," Mr. Grub said reasonably. He sank down on one knee and looked up at her. "You are my inheritance. And I always get my inheritance. So if I cannot have you . . . no one can."

"Is this why you murdered Mr. Croaksworth?" Beatrice pressed. She was so close now. She needed to know the truth.

"I had nothing to do with that," Mr. Grub said, his beady eyes widening. "Though it did not pain me to see him go." He rifled around in his pocket and withdrew a paper, written in the red ink.

To Beatrice's horror, she saw that it was some sort of poem.

"I wrote this for you," Mr. Grub said breathlessly, "just now, in the study. *Oh, how your eyes shine like coins, you shall be mine—like coins—*"

"What's going on in here?" a voice demanded. Beatrice and Grub turned to see Daniel standing in the study doorway, his golden hair shining, his expression horrified at the unfolding scene.

Beatrice seized the moment of distraction. She ripped the rug out from under Grub, and he stumbled. A small, furry false rat flew out from under the rug, and Grub tripped over it, shrieking. He completely lost his footing and went toppling into the open trapdoor. Daniel, quick on his feet, lunged forward and slammed the trapdoor shut. He slid the latch to lock it.

Daniel and Beatrice looked at each other for a moment, both breathing heavily, and then Beatrice collapsed into Daniel.

"He was going to kill me," she cried, and Daniel wrapped his arms around her.

"I would not have let him," he said firmly, his embrace warm and strong. "I am here now. You're safe." He cleared his throat and then pulled back to look at her. His eyes were sparkling with emotion in the low light, and Beatrice felt the air change.

"What is it?" she asked, her voice barely a whisper.

"Beatrice . . . I know the timing is not ideal. But nothing about tonight has been ideal." The candlelight glinted off his perfectly coiffed golden locks. "My father took every tonic he could, but it could not stop the inevitability of death. Through his tragic demise, I have been awakened this evening to the frailty of life . . . and the importance of telling those you love how you feel."

"Those . . . you love?" Beatrice repeated breathlessly.

"I can't risk either of us getting killed before I have the chance to say that I love you, Beatrice," Daniel said, clasping her hands with both of his now. "I think I've always loved you, even if I couldn't see it before. You are my best friend, and I want to spend the rest of my life making you happy. *Happy wife, happy life.* Excuse me," he said, breaking off to pull a pencil and notebook from his pocket. "That is an excellent original saying that I just came up with. In spite of the importance of this moment, I must write it down." He scribbled the phrase, replaced the notebook in his pocket, and then clasped her hands once more. "All this to say . . . Will you do me the honor of becoming Mrs. Daniel Ashbrook?"

Beatrice blinked up at him, speechless.

She hardly knew where to begin in her response. An inspector she had just tied up was waiting in another room, her cousin had just tried to murder her, there was still a killer on the loose, she was bleeding and wrapped in the aforementioned inspector's jacket, and in the midst of all of it, her oldest friend had just asked for her hand in marriage. It was how she had always imagined the perfect proposal.

"You would never have to worry again about your family's future," Daniel went on. "I could take care of you. We shall be quiet and comfortable, far away from crime and murder such as the one that took place this evening—*An Ashbrook-married wife shall never bear strife.*"

He was right; a life with Daniel would be comfortable and socially acceptable. Marrying him was the right thing to do. He was her perfect match.

But I want more, she thought. *I don't want to hide who I am.*

"Daniel," Beatrice said slowly, "I don't want to be far from crime and murder. I love murder. Love solving it, I mean," she added hastily.

"I see," Daniel said, his brow furrowed. "Is . . . that your reply?"

"Perhaps we should not be so hasty in letting everyone else decide what is best for us," Beatrice said softly. "The world is so much bigger than Swampshire, isn't it? Haven't we always talked about wanting to see it? Wanting to experience more intrigue, passion, poetry—" She looked down at the poem Grub had written to her. It lay abandoned in the center of the study floor, the red ink smudged across the page like a bloodstain. Red ink like the letter from Alice Croaksworth. Red ink, which Grub had stolen. Red ink that originally belonged to someone else.

She could hear Drake's voice in her mind as she stared at it. *Look with unbiased eyes. . . .*

She turned her gaze to Daniel's hand, holding her own, and she reached to push back his sleeve. There, etched into the skin of his wrist, was a long scratch.

"I don't understand," Daniel said, still staring at Beatrice, waiting. "Is that a no?"

"I know who did it," Beatrice said, looking at Daniel as if seeing him for the first time. "I know who murdered Edmund Croaksworth."

My darling SB,

I have received the gown which you created for me. I am floored by the scarlet hue. This shall be my choice for the Color of the Year, naturally—you have truly outdone yourself. Your artistry is unparalleled, but of course, you know this.

My autumnal ball takes place tonight. Edmund Croaksworth shall be in attendance. You may remember that he made me an offer, years ago, just after I returned from Paris. His parents put a stop to the marriage—they had some objections, I never really understood why—but I was relieved. He never held a candle to you. It will be agony to pretend that I am interested in him now, as I know I must, for Father's sake. Father thinks only of our family's legacy. Rest assured, though, that when I flirt, it is all just for show. You are the only person I have ever loved.

Each time I see the roses, grown from the seeds you sent me, my heart breaks. I shall fill the ballroom with them tonight and pretend that you are here with me.

Yours,

Arabella

CHAPTER 32

Revelations

The study was quiet. A fly circled an abandoned port glass on the small desk. It landed on the rim, then slipped and slid into the liquid, drowning slowly, a tiny buzz against glass.

"You attacked me," Beatrice said, her voice catching in her throat. "You tried to kill me."

"Beatrice? Are you having a touch of hysteria? Has it come for you already?" Daniel asked, his face a mask of concern.

Beatrice backed away from him, her heart pounding.

"I can't believe I didn't see it before," she said. She crossed to the desk, where a silver notebook lay. Written neatly across the cover were the words "*Advantageous Advice,* by Daniel Ashbrook."

"If one were to need loose paper, they would not find it in Stabmort Park," Beatrice said.

"*A paper with no book is a very messy look,*" Daniel recited, his voice soft.

"Yes," Beatrice said. "One would have to tear paper from a notebook, wouldn't one? And this one is always close by. After all, you are constantly adding aphorisms."

She flipped to the back of the book, where there were several pages missing, as if they had been ripped out. She held Mr. Grub's note to each of the torn edges, until she finally found the one that matched perfectly.

"Mr. Grub is always stealing things from Stabmort Park. Paper . . . ink . . ." Beatrice murmured. "And someone else must have had the same idea. Someone else tore paper from this book, to write a letter. Alice Croaksworth."

She looked up at Daniel. A sliver of moonlight illuminated half his face. He seemed, suddenly, like a stranger.

"A letter?" Daniel asked, his voice full of surprise.

"Your father said he did not play cards in the study," Beatrice continued. "He was odd, yes, but never forgetful. I think you were the one playing cards. The 'A' stood for 'Ashbrook'—just not the Ashbrook you made us believe it was. You lied."

Daniel regarded her for a moment. "I don't know what you are on about, Beatrice. If this is your way of refusing me—"

"I thought Mr. Croaksworth was your friend," Beatrice interrupted. "But now I think that you were his murderer."

Daniel held her gaze and then slowly turned away. He walked at a leisurely pace toward the fireplace, where a tiny sparkle of embers shone. He picked up a poker and began to stoke them, easing the embers back to a flame. "Edmund was my friend, once. We grew so close at school. He introduced me to Alice, in the hopes that we might form an attachment—I introduced him to Arabella for the same reason. He even made her an offer." He shook his head bitterly. "If only Arabella had married Edmund back then, all of this could have been avoided."

"She was never interested in Mr. Croaksworth," Beatrice said, thinking of the sketches along the walls of Arabella's bedroom. All signed with the same name. *Sophie Beaumont.*

"Arabella had a silly infatuation with a dressmaker from Paris," Daniel said. "A *woman*."

"Is it a silly infatuation?" Beatrice asked, shaking her head. "Arabella clearly pines for her still." She had guessed it before, and now she knew it was true. Arabella had never cared for any man.

"Maybe she does, but it doesn't matter. We couldn't afford for her to be selfish. We needed that security, especially after Mother died," Daniel said, his voice growing more desperate.

Beatrice remembered Daniel at his mother's funeral, dressed in black—his face ashen. "The consumption took your mother so quickly," she said. "None of us expected it."

"Yes, she went quickly," Daniel said, "but the money went even faster. Mother had always tried to keep a handle on his spending, but once she was gone, we realized the extent of my father's addiction. He spent our principal on tonics, creams, gels—anything to ward off his imagined illnesses. He whittled away our entire fortune."

"You're broke," Beatrice said with a shiver. *The canceled champagne.* This had not been a sign of Mr. Ashbrook's knowing that there would be nothing to toast, but an indication of the Ashbrooks' dwindling bank account. She thought of the portrait of Great-Aunt Agnes, falling from the wall. She and Miss Bolton had considered this some dark omen, but they had not seen what it truly revealed: a house rotting from the inside. Mold creeping into its foundation. Wallpaper slapped over it, to keep up appearances—but Stabmort Park was crumbling nonetheless.

"We shall soon lose the house, all of Arabella's clothes, my library, everything. And *a gentleman with no fortune is no gentleman indeed—he is nothing but a corpse, who shall rot in the weeds.*" Daniel gave a log a sharp poke, turning it over and sending sparks flying. "Back at school, when I first received the news that Mother had died and we no longer had a fortune, I thought Edmund would be sympathetic," Daniel continued. "He was, at first—he told his parents, thinking they might help us. But instead, they told him that he could no longer associate with me."

"So *that's* why the Croaksworths thought you inferior," Beatrice said, finally understanding. "And that is why they forced Edmund to break off his engagement to Arabella."

Daniel smiled, his teeth shining menacingly in the firelight. "Yes. But I got my first revenge. Two years ago, I met up with Alice in Bath. It was long after my school days, but she remembered me fondly, and we sparked up our old companionship. I can be very charming when I want to be. She fell for it, and we eloped. It was the perfect plan: I could punish the Croaksworths for belittling me and gain access to their fortune for myself."

"You and Alice were married?" Beatrice said, stunned. "I never heard of it."

"We kept it quiet," Daniel said with a shrug. "We didn't even tell Edmund. Still, it all turned out to be for nothing. Her parents cut her off the second they learned of the marriage. I had no way of reinstating our fortune."

"You could have taken a job," Beatrice said, staring at him in horror.

Daniel stopped stoking the fire. "How dare you! I would never stoop so low. The mere suggestion is disgusting!" He began to stoke the fire once more. "I did the *gentlemanly* thing. I led everyone to believe that I was still single, in the hopes of securing a wealthy wife."

"The Croaksworths knew that you and Alice were married," Beatrice pointed out.

"Yes, but they did not want anyone else to know that. Not even their son," Daniel explained. "They told everyone she was on an 'extended holiday,' to avoid any scandal. They were so proud that they would rather have lost their daughter than accept me as her husband. They took the secret with them to the grave. Thank goodness for propriety."

"But Edmund didn't fall for the 'extended holiday' lie," Beatrice shot back. "His parents may not have told him, but before you eloped, Alice sent him a letter from Bath on a page torn from your book. He and Inspector Drake were on their way to Bath to search for her, only stopping in Swampshire on their way—until he determined *you* were responsible for her disappearance. Edmund had read that letter over and over again. No doubt he knew it by heart—he must have recognized the paper the moment he saw you use it to keep score."

"So *that's* how he figured it out," Daniel said, understanding passing across his handsome features. "He became suspicious after we played cards, but I could not determine *why*. Now it makes sense." He pulled a paper from his pocket and unfolded it. "I suggested that we play for secrets, like we did in our school days. This was mine."

I am in love with Beatrice Steele, the note read.

"That's not true," Beatrice said, her chest tight, and Daniel laughed.

"The thing about playing for secrets, Beatrice, is that you are on your honor to tell the truth."

"And you have no honor," Beatrice said stiffly.

"I hadn't wanted Edmund to come to Stabmort Park in the first place, but I thought it could have all been worth it if he revealed something useful. I could use it to blackmail him and get back the money I deserved," Daniel explained. "But he insisted that he had no secrets. He was an open book. So instead, he bet a very large sum."

"Twenty thousand pounds," Beatrice recalled from the slip of paper she had seen.

"Frank and Caroline drooled over the money. I was irritated, but what could I do? I had to agree. Perhaps I might even win the money, I told myself. I bet my secret, Frank bet something wrapped in paper—I suppose that was his miniature of Louisa, which he assumed constituted a secret—and Caroline, for some reason, bet a pocket watch. She and Croaksworth had their own issue going on, it seemed; she followed us into the card room before anyone could protest. Most inappropriate for a lady."

She wasn't a lady, Beatrice now knew, and Caroline had clearly meant to stop Croaksworth from revealing anything about her during the card game. But Daniel did not need to know this; his own actions had far eclipsed anything Caroline had done.

"We all lost," Daniel went on. "I didn't realize that my false secret might reveal anything to Edmund. He was always dim back in our school days."

"Perhaps you underestimated him," Beatrice said, tense.

"Perhaps I did," Daniel said. He dropped the paper with his secret into the fire, and Beatrice watched the edges curl. "Perhaps I underestimated Alice, too—I never knew she managed to smuggle a note to her brother."

The air was tinged with the scent of smoke from the fire, and Daniel's glittering blue eyes were like a stranger's, peering through the haze at Beatrice.

"Edmund confronted me," Daniel said. "He demanded I tell him where Alice was. I didn't know how he'd guessed that I was involved—all I knew was that I could not allow him to stick around."

"Miss Bolton heard you arguing in the hall, after the game," Beatrice said, remembering.

Mr. Croaksworth sounded angry, Miss Bolton had said. *He said something like, "I cannot prove anything yet, but I will."*

If only they had listened to her warnings. She was right that the house was haunted—and Daniel was the specter.

"I put him off and told him we could discuss the matter later," Daniel said. "Isn't it lovely, the way one can use etiquette for one's own purposes? From the moment Edmund told me he would be passing through Swampshire, I crafted a plan in the event that I needed to get rid of him," Daniel said, his tone unbelievably casual for the horrid words he spoke. "And after our conversation, I could see that my plan would have to be executed. My father keeps belladonna on hand in his tonic closet. I knew this would be fatal—Arabella is always droning on about plants, so I have learned far too much about botany. I easily replaced my father's bottle with my own begonia tonic, and no one even knew it was missing."

"That's why the door was open to your father's tonic room," Beatrice said with a rush of frustration. There had been so many signs, yet she had simply not thought this possible.

"Initially I thought it fortuitous that Edmund brought a guest," Daniel continued. "I could easily pin the blame on him."

"You slipped the empty vial of poison into his pocket," Beatrice said with a shiver. She put a hand into Drake's jacket pocket and withdrew the glass container. "Inspector Drake was right . . . it *was* the murder weapon," she whispered. "You put it there in the hopes that he would be thought guilty."

"It was just my luck he proved to be an *inspector*," Daniel said in irritation. "I had to find another suspect, and quick."

"Louisa," Beatrice whispered. "How could you frame my sister?"

"*A killer leaves no hints, if he acts without a conscience,*" Daniel said with a shrug. "I saw her own vial of belladonna and realized my opportunity. I took it and left it for Drake to find in the greenhouse, along with the flower from Louisa's hair. She was distracted tonight; it was simple to take both."

"You brushed against the nettle plant when you planted the evidence," Beatrice hissed, touching her neck where a rash had broken out. "It was on your gloves, still, when you tried to . . . to *strangle* me." Her voice broke. Daniel had tried to strangle her. Daniel had tried to frame Louisa for murder. How could this be real?

"It was easy enough to convince my father that he had been the Ashbrook at the card game," Daniel continued, as if she hadn't spoken. He seemed to be enjoying himself now. "The old man would believe he had any ailment with a small suggestion. I told him that memory loss is a side effect of the fainties, and he accepted it without question—"

"Frank and Caroline knew," Beatrice interrupted. "They knew it was you at the card game; they played with you and Mr. Croaksworth."

"The three of us made a pact not to tell," Daniel said. "Caroline did not want any more attention—clearly she was hiding something. Frank was terrified about his involvement with Louisa coming to light after he had bet her miniature. Neither ever suspected *me;* I simply suggested it would be easiest to all say we were never there. They thought me deferential and polite. Coming to *their* rescue with a plan. Always there to do the right thing."

In the firelight, Daniel's golden locks framed his head like a halo. Mr. Croaksworth's last words echoed in Beatrice's ears: *The angel isn't an angel at all.*

"He tried to warn us about you," Beatrice breathed. "Mr. Croaksworth told us of your true nature, but we had no idea."

"*If a man insists on prying, this could lead to his dying,*" Daniel growled. "I did not *want* to kill Edmund; it was his own fault."

"You murdered your own father," Beatrice said in a choked voice, almost unable to stomach the thought of Daniel's slitting poor, bumbling Hugh Ashbrook's throat. "But not with the knife in his hand . . ." She shivered as she recalled the clean line across Mr. Ashbrook's neck.

"*A murder is a cinch—just use a quill if you're in a pinch,*" Daniel recited. "I should have done it sooner," he went on, unresentful. "Then perhaps I could have preserved a shred of our fortune. I tried to avoid it tonight, even still—he was family, after all—but you and Drake were circling. I could not risk the truth coming to light. I played upon what I knew of you, Beatrice. I knew if I put gardening gloves on my father's hands, you would use this to verify what you already thought was true. And that no one would ever realize that the killer all along was me."

"I did," Beatrice hissed.

"Yes," Daniel said, his voice dangerously soft. "You caught me."

"It was your bad luck that Inspector Drake showed up," Beatrice said. "Why did you even suggest that *I* aid in his investigation?" Beatrice searched Daniel's face. "You thought I would ruin it, didn't you? You thought I would make a mess of things. But you were wrong. That's why you tried to strangle me, to drown me— I was better at all of this than you expected. Even when everyone believed your father was the murderer, you knew there was still a chance I'd discover the truth."

"Why are you acting so offended, Beatrice?" Daniel asked with a smile. "Be honest: You love murder."

"I love *justice*. It's an important distinction," Beatrice growled.

"We both know the truth about people." Daniel laughed. "We both know we are better than the rest of them, despite what is in our pockets and bank accounts. Or rather, what *isn't*. We both know that we deserve more."

"Why does everyone want to tell me who I am?" Beatrice said, shaking her head. "I may want more—but not like this."

The flames in the fireplace flickered, casting an eerie glow over Daniel's face. There was no warmth in his cold, glittering eyes as he extended a hand to her.

"Marry me," he insisted. "We can assure everyone that my father was the killer. We could forge a will, say that Edmund came here to tell me that he would leave me everything. I am his best friend, after all. I can save your family, provide for you. We shall be the top of society in Swampshire. The richest, the most accomplished. Now that I am master of Stabmort Park, I can give you anything you want."

Now she saw why he had told her everything, why he had savored every word of his confession. He actually thought that Beatrice would be impressed. He actually thought that it would win her over.

"Daniel . . ." Beatrice said slowly. "What happened to Alice?"

"She was no longer useful." Daniel shrugged, flipping his hand dismissively.

Beatrice stared at Daniel's smooth hand and then at his chiseled face. She had once thought it so handsome, that she could be happy with him, but now she saw Daniel for what he was: a monster.

"I have a saying for *you*," she said. "A man who would kill another woman or man shall never win *my* hand!" She spat directly into his blue eyes.

Sputtering, Daniel wiped his face. "That was a *slant* rhyme, which isn't even a real rhyme," he snapped. His expression twisted into a look of pure hatred. "You have always been a pain, all these years. *A lady who cannot leave others alone is destined to find herself skinned to the bone.*"

"I see who you are," Beatrice said, clenching her fists to steady her hands. "And soon, everyone will know what kind of man you are."

"I think not," Daniel said, his sinister smile returning. "You think I would tell you everything and then let you go free? Since you refuse to marry me—*you shall burn in hell, so you can never tell!*" He turned and, in one swift motion, used the fire poker to push several logs into the room. They rolled along the carpet, leaving a trail of flames between Beatrice and the door. "And *that's* how you create a saying," he said smugly.

"You'll never get away with it!" Beatrice choked, holding her hands up to shield herself from the flames. "Drake and I will hunt you down!"

"Before you're both burned to a crisp, you mean?" Daniel taunted. "I think not."

"You forget that Sir Huxley is on his way. I have pointed him in the right direction before—I can do it again," Beatrice shot back.

"Oh, silly Beatrice," Daniel said, one hand on the door. "I never called Sir Huxley. There's no one coming to save you." With that he slammed the door shut, leaving Beatrice in a burst of smoke and flame.

Dear Daniel,

Merry Christmas! Enclosed, in this package, is your gift.
May it always make you think of your dear friend,

Beatrice

CHAPTER 33

Pursuit

The study quickly became clouded with dark smoke and rising flames. Beatrice tore a strip from her gown and used it to subdue a line of crackling fire, stifling a large enough patch to allow her to cross the room. She felt her way for the door, her eyes and throat burning, and rattled the door handle.

It was locked, and Beatrice knew the sturdy wood of the study door would not be as easy to break as the flimsy parlor doors. Of course Daniel had locked her inside, she thought furiously. He would not underestimate her now.

"Or would he?" Beatrice whispered breathlessly, and reached a hand into her pocket. She withdrew a small book.

Doors of the English Countryside.

Squinting to see past the smoke, she flipped furiously through the pages. And then she found it: "Chapter Seven: An Ode to English Locks (and What to Do If You Lose Your Keys!)."

No doubt Daniel had used the information to pick the lock on his father's tonic cabinet, Beatrice thought as she skimmed the instructions. He had probably found it amusing to lend it to her—had probably thought she would never suspect a thing.

She drew two hairpins from her hair and placed them in position, as the illustration in the book demonstrated. She pushed, wiggling one of the hairpins in an attempt to click the tiny pins inside the lock into just the right place.

She could feel heat behind her, flames creeping closer. Her breath caught in her throat, and tears streamed down her face from the sting of smoke. Her fingers kept slipping on the hairpins, her palms damp with perspiration. But finally, she heard a *click*—and the door swung open.

Beatrice burst into the hallway. Smoke billowed out behind her, flames creeping up the walls like vines. They ate away at the family portraits, singeing painted torsos and necks.

But Daniel was nowhere to be seen.

She felt movement behind her and whirled around—but instead of Daniel, she found herself face-to-face with Mary.

"I smelled smoke," Mary said, her nose twitching.

"The house is ablaze," Beatrice said, her voice raspy. "And Daniel is a killer."

Mary's eyes widened.

"I shall take care of him," Beatrice added, and Mary nodded.

"Leave the evacuation to me. I'll get everyone out. I'll take them on my back if I have to." She took off down the hall at an inhuman speed. Beatrice turned in the opposite direction, rushing down the hallway.

Where had Daniel gone?

When he had attacked her, he had disappeared just like this, she thought. He had vanished, a dark figure gone as if by magic.

Her eyes fell on the reflection of a huge mirror. Its gilt frame was not covered in dust, as were the rest of the portraits and mirrors hanging in the hallway. Miss Bolton had mentioned something about this earlier in the evening, Beatrice thought—and now she could see that one side of the mirror was not smooth.

It had hinges—like a door. And the door was creaking open.

Beatrice ducked just in time for Daniel to burst forth from behind the mirror. It swung open to reveal a dark, narrow tunnel leading somewhere into the depths of Stabmort Park.

The motion of Daniel's launching himself out of the tunnel sent portraits and mirrors falling from the walls. They landed in a crunch of glass and wood splinters, and Beatrice raised her hands to shield her face from debris.

"You really just can't stay where you belong, can you?" Daniel snarled as he walked across the glass, his shoes crunching pieces into the carpet. He wrapped a handkerchief around his hand, stooped over to pick up a large shard, and then lunged for her. She ducked and rolled over on the floor, her hip landing on something hard.

It was the only item left in her pocket, and she pulled it out. Daniel approached and raised the shard of glass once more—and Beatrice hit him directly in the crotch with *The Lady's Guide to Swampshire (Travel Edition)*. He doubled over, howling in pain.

"You need that more than I do," she panted, and then scrambled to her feet. The flames climbed up the walls, damask curling as it burned, but she could feel cool air coming from the tunnel behind the mirror. So she pushed herself into the depths of Stabmort Park and began to run down the narrow passageway.

It was dark, and she ran her hands along the stone walls as she raced down the tunnel. There were strange markings on the walls, like tally marks—but she could not stop to examine them. She could hear footsteps not far behind her.

Daniel was giving chase.

"*A lady who fights back shall end up with her skull cracked!*" His voice echoed in the tunnel.

Beatrice ran faster, her breath hoarse as she turned a corner.

There was a sudden beam of light and dust, and Beatrice squinted to see a door ahead burst open. Into the tunnel stepped Inspector Drake, one handcuff still on his wrist, the other around the now-detached arm of the settee.

"Mary came into the parlor and freed me from that damn settee," he choked out. "Your sister has animalistic strength—"

"The killer is Daniel!" Beatrice interrupted, rushing to him. "I looked at the evidence. I was unbiased—"

"And I knew I had to come find you, because I had"—Drake swallowed as if the words were bitter—"a *hunch*."

There was a noise behind them, and Beatrice grabbed Drake's wrist.

"Daniel is gaining. We must keep moving."

"This way," Drake said, moving to the room from whence he had come—but at that moment a heavy tapestry fell from the wall, crackling with flames, the fire blocking their path.

And so they turned, now forced to trudge deeper into Stabmort. As they took off down the tunnels, the air grew colder, the corridor damp, but there were pinpricks of light from small, ancient-looking torches along the walls.

"When you left me in the parlor, I had nothing to do but turn over the evening's events in my mind," Drake called out behind her as they ran. "I kept coming back to your confidence in Louisa. In spite of the evidence, you believed in her innocence. And so I considered everything using your methods."

They turned a corner and were confronted with a stone staircase. Beatrice looked back at Drake, and he nodded. She began to ascend, and he followed behind her. In the distance she could hear pounding footsteps.

Daniel still pursued.

"I thought about my *feelings*," Drake said, as if disgusted with himself, "and I kept coming back to Daniel."

"You believed in his innocence?" Beatrice asked, confused.

"No," Drake said, "I believed in his guilt. Or, rather, I thought that there was something off. From the moment I met him this evening, I disliked Daniel, with his manners and his gentility and his *rhyming*. Yet everyone else seemed to love him—not unlike your relationship with your *best friend*, Miss Caroline Wynn." Beatrice stumbled, and Drake steadied her, then went on as they continued to climb the narrow stairwell. "You disliked Caroline because you felt her behavior was disingenuous. I realized this was how I felt about Daniel. Or at least, his treatment of you."

"Of me?" Beatrice asked, her legs aching as she climbed, each stair seeming higher than the next.

"You and Daniel were friends, clearly, and you were the obvious choice to be his wife. Yet he had not made you an offer. Would a true friend have left a lady scrambling? He would have known about your concern for your family's future and your dire financial situation. If he cared for you, wanted a wife, and had no reason to object, why wouldn't he marry you at once? He was protective of you, concerned with your reputation, suggested that you assist me, and declared you the most upstanding woman in Swampshire. You are personable, witty, attractive. . . ." He cleared his throat. "I mean to say, there is nothing *objectionable* to your looks."

"You flatter me," Beatrice said dryly, but her cheeks felt warm.

"The point is, there was no reason for him not to make you an offer of marriage. And then I remembered something that my mother wrote once in a letter to me." Drake drew in a deep breath. "*A single man in possession of a good fortune sometimes is actually not single. He's often a total liar.*"

"Your mother was wise," Beatrice said with a bitter laugh.

"I began to consider: What could Daniel be lying about that would stop him from marrying you? First, perhaps he did not care for you. But then he could have easily married another young woman he *did* care for. Second, he might not have wanted a wife at all. But for someone so concerned with maintaining his image as a gentleman, it seemed wholly unlikely he would so blatantly disregard expectations—"

"He was already married," Beatrice interrupted. They had reached a small landing, which opened up—into yet another staircase. Drake nodded again, and Beatrice began to climb—her feet now aching. "To Alice Croaksworth."

"*I knew it*," Drake whispered. "That is to say, I wondered. . . ."

"But he disposed of her," Beatrice said, her chest tight in horror as she recalled everything Daniel had done. "He told me. She is gone."

"What if she is *not* gone?" Drake asked, his voice taut. "Miss Bolton said that this house was haunted. I could understand why—this entire evening I have had the feeling that there is another presence, watching us. I dismissed this. But what if . . ."

Beatrice came to a stop. Drake crashed into her from behind and then put his hands around her waist to steady himself.

"I beg your pardon," he said, clearing his throat. But then he saw why she had stopped.

The staircase, dark and dusty, had ended in a ceiling. There was nowhere else to go. In the distance was the sound of Daniel's footsteps getting closer.

"So what you are saying," Beatrice said, trying to catch her breath, "is that you have a *feeling* that Alice Croaksworth is still alive, and here in this house?"

"Precisely," Drake said.

So Beatrice lifted up her hands to the ceiling and pushed.

The ceiling gave way, revealing an opening into a small turret.

"Every respectable mansion has a turret," she said at Inspector Drake's astonishment. "Some just don't make good use of theirs. This one has been boarded up for years. *Why?*"

She hoisted herself into the turret, and Drake gave her a push the rest of the way up. Then he clambered inside after her. They both fell to the floor, panting, and then looked at where they had landed.

They were inside a tiny, round room with a small bed covered in a quilt, a table with a nubby candle, and a washbasin. A small window, nailed shut, let in scant moonlight. The room was covered with the same strange marks Beatrice had seen on the stone walls, and she now realized, with horror, that they were tally marks. Cowering in the corner of the room, wearing a rumpled white nightgown, a silver locket gleaming at her throat, was—

"Alice Croaksworth." Inspector Drake inhaled.

She stared at them with wide green eyes. The same green as Edmund Croaksworth's. Her hair was matted, and her skin was ghostly white, as if she had not taken a healthy turn about any gardens in quite some time. She clutched her locket, the silver glinting in the moonlight, and stood up. She coughed feebly, and then—

"*Took you long enough!*" she yelled, shaking her head. "None of you *listen!*"

The loud noises they thought were thunder, Beatrice realized. They *had* sounded as if they were coming from inside the house—and they were.

"I knew it," Drake breathed. "I was sure she was alive."

"Well, if you knew, why didn't you try to come find me? I could have died just from waiting for anybody to figure it out," Alice snapped, putting her hands on her hips.

Beatrice held out a hand to Alice, who merely looked at it with a raised eyebrow. "My name is Beatrice Steele," Beatrice told her. "This is Inspector Vivek Drake. We are here to help you. You are safe now; we will not let Daniel harm you."

"Some rescuers *you* are," Alice retorted, gesturing toward Beatrice and Drake in front of her, every finger dirty and bandaged. "I had been hoping for a dashing prince after all I've been through. You two look worse than I do."

"Beatrice," Drake said suddenly, "Miss Bolton said she saw Arabella in a window of Stabmort Park, her hands covered in blood. But it wasn't Arabella she saw, was it?"

"That was me!" Alice exclaimed. "I finally found a route out of this horrible place by punching through a mirror. The effort tore up my hands," she explained, holding up her wrapped palms, "but I made it to a window and waved to some woman in an insane hat, trying to signal for help. My effort failed—Daniel heard me pounding at the window and forced me back into this horrible place. He sealed up my escape route to ensure I could not get out that way again."

"You knew what he was planning tonight, didn't you?" Beatrice asked. "Your noises were not just telling us of your presence—they were a warning."

"Yes, but a great deal of good it did," Alice shot back. "I risked the wrath of a lunatic to try to alert someone, to try to protect my brother. But your lot can't read between the lines, can you? And unfortunately I couldn't expect Edmund to piece it together on his own; the weather here offered *far* too many opportunities to distract him."

"I'm so sorry, Alice," Beatrice choked out. "We did not save him. But we can still save you."

Suddenly, Daniel burst through the floor of the room, panting. He heaved himself to his feet. Drake stepped in front of Beatrice and Alice, his hand raised.

"Do not take another step forward. It's over, Daniel."

Daniel looked at Alice, hatred in his eyes. "You thought yourself smart, didn't you? Making noises for guests to hear . . . making your way through the tunnels in the night, trying to escape . . . But of course you never could find your way out. Everyone knows Croaksworths have no sense of direction." He laughed bitterly, then coughed. He looked down. Smoke seeped in from the stairwell below, the smell of singed French furniture filling the room with a scent like burned baguettes. "It is time for me to go," he said, and looked back up at Alice. "You should be grateful that I didn't kill you," he said. "After all, I am a gentleman. I could not kill a lady, in good conscience."

"You do *not* have a conscience," Beatrice spat. "And you are no gentleman."

"Just because I have no fortune—" Daniel began, but Beatrice interrupted.

"Being a true gentleman isn't about performing etiquette correctly or having a fortune or proper schooling. It's about treating others with respect. Being a good person. The only gentleman in this room is Inspector Vivek Drake."

Daniel laughed. "You are a fool, Beatrice. But I will not kill you. I will leave you to fend for yourself. Isn't that what you have always wanted?" He snatched the quilt off Alice's pitiful bed. With a shudder, Beatrice realized: It was the one she had sewn him for Christmas. The quilt she had taken such time with, though it had not turned out as she'd imagined; the quilt he'd claimed he had put in his bedchamber. That he'd claimed to love.

"This was too ugly to use anywhere else but this hellhole," Daniel said with a grimace, "but now I see its use." He lunged forward and shoved the tiny turret window open, grunting to force out the nails at its base. He knocked a small pail off an iron hook next to the window, and wound the edge of the quilt around the hook to secure it. "I shall leave you all with one last piece of wisdom: *A good stitch saves in a fix.*"

"Daniel, no—" Beatrice cried, but it was too late. He plunged backward out the window, gripping the quilt—

And it tore in half.

Daniel Ashbrook hurtled to the ground and landed with a sickening squelch, and the swamp mud swallowed him whole.

A good stitch *would* have saved in a fix, but a true friend of Beatrice's would have known: Beatrice could not sew to save a life. Only to end one.

CHAPTER 34

Escape

Beatrice rushed over to Alice and put a hand, softly, on her shoulder.

"You don't have to be afraid anymore," she said, "he's gone. Daniel is gone."

Alice nodded. "I see that. Do not get me wrong; I could not be happier to be free of him. But the problem remains: What do we do *now*? There is no way out!" Alice gestured wildly to the trapdoor. Smoke now billowed into the room, the smell acrid.

Beatrice turned to meet Drake's eye, hoping he would have some plan—*any* plan.

"We can't go the way we came," Drake said, voice strangled. "Everything will be in flames. But that way isn't an option, either," he said, indicating the open window. Rain and wind blustered inside, as well as tiny pellets of ice.

"When it hails it pours, as they say in Swampshire," Beatrice said quietly. Drake's mouth twitched. Beatrice took him in, her eyes prickling.

It was the end. She now knew for certain. She could see Drake thought the same thing as he turned his eye on her, his expression sober.

"You compromised evidence, concealed evidence, bested me with a fire poker, and—hang it all—taught me how to be a true inspector," Drake told her. "I am honored to have known you, Beatrice Steele."

"You flouted my town's etiquette, insulted me repeatedly, and accused my sister of murder," Beatrice said. "Thank goodness I was able to teach you, for you were hopeless without me, Vivek Drake."

His lips turned up at the corners. "Yes," he murmured, "I think I was."

"I meant what I said," Beatrice went on. "You are a true gentleman."

Drake smiled in earnest now, a sad but sweet expression softening his scarred face.

"A pity we must stop *now,* just when things were getting good," Beatrice said, feeling slightly light-headed. "My mother will be devastated when I die single."

She met Inspector Drake's eye, and her chest tightened. He looked at her with an inscrutable expression that made her feel warm in spite of the freezing rain rushing into the room.

"Well," Drake began, and took a step forward. "I do have something to ask you."

There was a sudden clatter on the roof. Drake lunged toward the window, and Beatrice edged over to see the source of the sound.

"I promised I would never leave you alone again!" a voice cried, and Beatrice gasped.

A blurry figure stood on the roof, and as it moved forward,

Beatrice could see: It was Miss Bolton, her clothing singed and rain-soaked.

"Did you know there is a tunnel which leads to this roof?" Miss Bolton said breathlessly. "I followed it, looking for you, Beatrice."

"You should not have come here," Beatrice said, incredulous. "There is no escape. It is a sheer drop."

"There is always an escape, my dear." With that, Miss Bolton held out her hand. Confused, but with no remaining reasons to protest, Beatrice took it and let Miss Bolton pull her out onto the roof. Drake followed, helping Alice out of the window.

They stood on the roof of Stabmort Park now, rain and ice tearing at their clothes and skin. The estate was just a blur of smoke and flames, the surrounding land dark and misty.

"Everything in this house was made in France; it's turning to ash in seconds. We must go now!" Miss Bolton yelled over the crack of thunder and rush of rain. She fastened a chin strap on her hat and then pulled two straps down and fastened them around her waist. "Take hold of me, and do not let go!" she instructed.

Both confused, but with no other options, Beatrice and Inspector Drake wrapped their arms around Miss Bolton's corseted waist.

Alice paused. "Well, at least I made it outside. One must celebrate even the smallest victories." She stretched her bony arms around them all.

"As I said, this piece is necessary to survive a ball," Miss Bolton told them. Before anyone could ask what in the world she was talking about, she fell backward off the roof, taking all of them with her.

For a split second they hurtled toward the ground, Alice quivering, Beatrice screaming, and Drake with his one eye firmly shut.

Then Miss Bolton pulled something within her hat, releasing a large silk parachute. It ballooned out and filled with air.

As they continued to fall, their descent slowed slightly by the chute, Beatrice caught the silver glimmer of Alice's locket once more and saw the etching upon it. It was a Scottish terrier. *Like Drake's spoon,* was the singular thought rushing through her mind as she plunged downward.

"What are you thinking, madam?" Drake yelled to Miss Bolton. "This will never support all four of us—"

But he was cut off as they slammed into the ground, collapsing into a tangled heap: Beatrice, Inspector Drake, Miss Bolton, and Alice, the ghost of Stabmort Park—all freed at last.

Dear Alice Croaksworth,

I know it has been several months since you were in Swampshire, and I'm sure you want to leave us all in your memory. I have heard you are now living in a very open-air mansion in Bath, and that you are enjoying your return to society. This news brings me much comfort.

My reason for writing is because I noticed the Scottish terrier on your silver locket. This piece of evidence—as well as the particular shade of green in your eyes, and your wealthy father—led me to develop a theory.

Since you left, I have been investigating this theory. Please find a detailed report of my findings attached, which includes drawings of a particular spoon, your locket, and the similarities of both to the Croaksworth family crest. If this is of any interest to you, there may be someone with whom you could share your fortune and, in fact, your companionship. You may not have lost your entire family yet.

Sincerely,

Beatrice Steele

Dear Mrs. Susan Steele,

I received your letter this afternoon, and I admit that I was surprised to hear from you. After Beatrice exposed Daniel Ashbrook as a murderer, thus—in your words—"ruining her engagement," and after I revealed the existence of Alice Croaksworth, thus—once again, in your words—"ensuring that the Croaksworth fortune was no longer up for grabs," I thought you did not wish to speak to me ever again.

To answer your first question, yes, I am in London and "back at the crime solving." Unfortunately, the Ashbrook murders were not widely publicized in town, as most people here have not heard of Swampshire. The newspapers incorrectly filed the article about it under their serialized fiction section. However, Sir Huxley has been slowing down in his crime-solving ability as of late, and I have become a bit of a second option for those who require investigative services. Therefore, I have found myself with a good number of new cases. I have altered my methods slightly, and I am learning to observe people in addition to evidence. This has led to increased success.

To answer your second question, I left Swampshire because I live in London and my business is here. I did not mean my exit as any insult to the town or people. Swampshire may have terrible weather, but apart from Daniel (and your cousin Grub), I actually liked all of you very much. I have no plans to return, but if you are ever in London, you shall always be welcome at my office. It is no Stabmort Park, but at least this guarantees that I am not hiding anyone in my walls. There is simply not enough space for that.

Lastly, thank you for gifting me such an interesting eye patch, tucked inside your letter. What a kind thank-you for my services, and what an unusual shade of pink you chose for its fabric. I will treasure it always . . . though I shall wear it only on special occasions. I would not want to make others jealous of its artistry.

Best wishes,

Inspector Vivek Drake

Dear BS,

My most devoted reader: I apologize that I have never written until now, but I assure you, I have always greatly enjoyed your letters detailing your theories about my cases. I may not know anything about you, or even your real name, but I feel as if we know each other thanks to our years of one-sided correspondence.

To be clear, I don't need your theories, professionally speaking, because I always solve cases with my famous method: decorum above all. I am merely saying that it's great to hear from fans.

However, I have noticed that you have stopped writing to me as of late. Perhaps you are busy. But I admit that I have missed hearing from you.

I hope that you will write soon and tell me your thoughts on my most current investigation, the Case of the London Menace. Once again, I shall certainly be able to solve this by myself, and I'm definitely NOT using your letters in order to solve all of my crimes.

I hope you will write back soon. As encouragement, I have enclosed a signed sketch of myself. I thought my hair looked rather good in it.

Hoping to receive a prompt response detailing who you think the London Menace might be, even though I certainly already know.

Sir Lawrence Huxley

EPILOGUE

Three Months Later

Frank Fàn and Louisa Steele were married on a beautiful winter morning. It was surprisingly sunny for Swampshire. There were only two short hail showers, and frost coated the ground with a hoary sparkle.

Louisa was a blushing, rotund bride, with a bouquet of pink roses grown by Arabella. Frank was a proud groom and managed to keep all his winks for his beloved.

After a simple ceremony, they returned to Marsh House for the wedding breakfast. Mrs. Steele and Beatrice had prepared hot rolls, ham and eggs, drinking chocolate, and an enormous wedding cake, which Mr. Steele had already sampled and found to be excellent. There was one thing Mr. Steele took very seriously, and that was his pudding.

Their friends arrived in clusters to join in the celebration, gathering around the table, all in good spirits and eager to put recent events in the past thanks to the union of two young lovers. Beatrice helped Louisa into the seat of honor and then scanned the crowd of guests. Captain Peña and Caroline were of course not in attendance. Everyone was crushed that Caroline could not make it, though Beatrice had insisted that Caroline was not her real name and that she was a con woman. The rest of Swampshire knew this could not be true, as Caroline had politely sent her regrets along with a lovely basket of moist scones.

But Miss Bolton was there, as well as Arabella, who wore a fetching black veil. Though Arabella had been forced to accept that Daniel Ashbrook was a murderer who kept a woman locked in their attic for years and killed their own father, she told everyone that she still would observe traditional mourning customs (after all, her admirers in Paris had sent her an entire wardrobe for the occasion, and she thought she might as well put it to use). The town council agreed that it was best not to exile Arabella for her brother's crimes, though everyone *was* put out that there would be no more balls at Stabmort, since the mansion was now ash in a field where frogs had taken up residence. The town council had also agreed not to exile Louisa for her scandal. With most of the Ashbrooks gone, they had begun to rethink their dedication to Baron Fitzwilliam Ashbrook's guides to etiquette. Miss Bolton had even proposed drafting up a list of amendments.

To Arabella's chagrin, she had been forced to move in with Miss Bolton. It was only temporary; since both Daniel, Mr. Ashbrook, and Stabmort Park were all gone, Arabella had made arrangements to move to Paris as soon as possible. But Miss Bolton would not be lonely: In addition to housing her menagerie of animals, Miss Bolton had taken Mary under her wing. After saving every attendee of the autumnal ball, Mary had proven to be the most loyal of companions (and almost equally furry). Mary now considered Miss Bolton both a mentor and—in spite of their age difference—a bosom friend.

Beatrice felt a bittersweet pang as she looked over the guests. They did not know that Beatrice herself would soon be leaving, too.

She had accepted that she would never be a proper lady, as perhaps *no one* was truly proper. Everyone wanted to tell Beatrice who she was, but the truth was that no one could determine this except Beatrice herself. And so she was going to set out from Swampshire and find her place in the world. To do this, she reasoned, she had to actually *see* the world. It had been tempting to pawn a certain emerald necklace in order to fund this adventure, but Beatrice could not bring herself to do so. She entrusted it to Drake so he could return it to DeBurbie's relations. Though she had felt a twinge of regret in parting with it, she knew it was the right thing to do.

However, Miss Bolton stepped in as a benefactor to support her journey. She gave Beatrice a purse, with the understanding that it would never be paid back, insisting it was "owed to Beatrice, the most loyal theatrical patron." Beatrice did not yet know where she would go, but for the first time, she was excited to find out what her future would entail.

For now, though, it was Louisa's day, and it would be perfect.

"Did you see the write-up of my hat parachute in the social papers last week? Several milliners have contacted me asking for the design," Miss Bolton said, holding a bit of cake up to her newest hat. It was an elaborate two-tiered contraption, with a little bed on top. In the bed sat her newest adoptee: a floppy-eared puppy. It woke up and stuck out its tongue to lap up the cake. Mary, who sat on the floor, did the same with her own slice.

"I heard of the intrigue surrounding it," Arabella said, "from Sophie Beaumont."

"The famous dressmaker?" asked Miss Bolton, impressed.

Arabella nodded and, for a brief moment, actually smiled. "Yes.

I'll be living in an apartment with her when I get to Paris," she replied. "Sophie and I will be starting a salon to discuss botany, mathematics, the importance of social reform—"

"Yes, yes, very nice, no one finds social reform more important than *I* do," Mrs. Steele interrupted, and turned to Louisa, eager to direct the conversation back to her beautiful daughter. "Louisa, my dear, how are you feeling? Would you care for more water? A bit of cake?"

"I'm fine, Mother," Louisa said, pressing a hand to her large stomach. Indeed, she was beaming, and her other hand was entwined with Frank's.

"Of course you are," Miss Bolton cut in, now petting her little dog by extending her arm very high and patting the air until she found its head. "I expect you're *all* doing well, now that you don't have to worry about securing this home any longer."

"We don't know that the child will be a boy," Frank said, "though of course if it is, he will be a true heartbreaker."

"I meant that Mr. Grub won't inherit anything," Miss Bolton continued. "Not now that . . ." she began, but then clearly decided not to bring up the events of the last ball in Swampshire on such a festive day.

Truthfully, the events of that ball were frequently discussed in Swampshire, though usually in hushed tones. Rumors flew about what had actually occurred, but what was most widely agreed upon was that Daniel Ashbrook had murdered Edmund Croaksworth and Hugh Ashbrook and then fallen to his death. Beatrice Steele had figured the whole thing out. She and Inspector Drake had escaped with Alice and Miss Bolton, the four of them unscathed, other than several broken bones from a rough landing.

(Of course, there were always those pesky gossips who would say things such as "Beatrice pushed Daniel out the window because he wouldn't marry her," but Beatrice was grateful that most people did not entertain these rumors. At least not within her ear-shot.)

What Miss Bolton was referring to was not, unfortunately, Mr. Grub's death. Though he had been left under the trapdoor of the study, Mr. Martin Grub had somehow survived, a fact that be-fuddled doctors. However, he was personally arrested by Inspector Vivek Drake for the attempted murder of Beatrice Steele. This disqualified him from his inheritance, a fact Miss Bolton had de-termined. As it turned out, she *was* quite interested in inheritance law. She had combined this interest with her theatrical skills, pen-ning a play titled *To Be or Not to Be? If You Are, You Might Be En-titled to Compensation.*

Therefore Miss Bolton had saved the Steele family from losing their estate—unless, of course, another cousin turned up to claim something, which seemed unlikely. They were not any wealthier after Louisa's marriage to Frank, but they had their home. And they had one another. Mrs. Steele had to admit that their situation was sufficient—even agreeable.

"We should discuss only happy topics today," Beatrice said, tak-ing a seat next to Louisa and fondly fixing a lock of her sister's bright red hair. Louisa looked at Beatrice in surprise.

"You don't want to discuss anything salacious? Anything violent or gripping?"

Beatrice shook her head. "Today is *your* day."

She would miss Louisa most, when she left on her upcoming journey. But Louisa had her husband and would soon have her baby. She had found purpose and happiness, and Beatrice had to do the same.

"Have you thought of a name yet?" Beatrice asked, squeezing her sister's ring-adorned hand.

"If the baby is a girl, we were thinking . . ." Louisa said, glancing at Frank, "of naming her Beatrice."

"Oh!" Beatrice said, her cheeks growing warm.

"We would call her Bee Bee for short," Frank said quickly, "to avoid any confusion."

"Drat," Miss Bolton said. "That's what I was going to name my dog."

There was a sudden commotion as Mrs. Steele cut another piece from the cake, and several firecrackers went off with a series of *pop*s. Mrs. Steele screeched, and the table broke out into a din of guests screaming and Mr. Steele chuckling jovially. Even he had forgiven Frank, after he realized that the trusting, desperate-to-impress young man was a perfectly unwitting victim for pranks.

In the chaos, Beatrice slipped out and made her way to her favorite perch in the turret. The one place she had always felt most herself.

The newspaper she had been reading just before the fateful autumnal ball was still hidden under the window seat, gathering dust. In truth, she had little appetite for these papers now. She knew Huxley was a fraud, and after experiencing crime solving for herself, she simply could not get a thrill out of secondhand investigations.

A soft knock at the door made Beatrice look up. Louisa walked into the nook, still beaming with happiness.

"Louisa," Beatrice said quickly, "you mustn't climb the stairs in your condition—"

"I'm fine," Louisa said dismissively. "I am even stronger than before, honestly. Now, you must come quick!"

"Why?" Beatrice said suspiciously.

"Remember your theory about Inspector Drake? The letter you sent to Alice Croaksworth? Well, I sent her a letter, too," Louisa said in a rush. "I told her that you were going on a trip, and perhaps . . . you'd need a ride." She pointed out the tiny turret window.

Beatrice turned to see a carriage, a long way off on the moor. Even from a distance she could see its door, glinting with a large painting of what she had learned was the Croaksworth crest, which featured a Scottish terrier.

"It's her," Beatrice said, jumping to her feet. "Alice is *here*."

She rushed downstairs and out the front door, too eager to wait for the carriage to make its way up to Marsh House. It was warm for winter, and she began to perspire and acquire mud and frost along her hem, but she was too distracted to notice as she approached the carriage door.

It swung open as she stepped forward, and Alice Croaksworth emerged.

Gone was the waif in a nightgown; she now wore a crisp velvet suit, with a top hat perched on her coiffed curls.

"Hello, Beatrice," Alice greeted her. "I trust you are doing much better than the last time we met."

"I am," Beatrice said warmly. "It is so good to see you. Did you receive my note? I didn't know—you didn't respond—"

"I don't like to spend my time writing letters," Alice said firmly. "I prefer walking in open fields, stargazing, training in hand-to-hand combat, and trying to decide what to do with my enormous fortune now that the rest of my family has died. As I have no living relatives left, the bank was forced to give the sum to me." She met Beatrice's gaze. "You gave me quite a proposal for what I might do with such riches."

"I know it's a lot to ask," Beatrice said softly. "I'm sure you want to get married, to save your money—"

"I've already been married, and you saw how *that* turned out," Alice said sharply. "No, I'm done with all that."

"I understand," Beatrice replied, "as the last two men who proposed to me both tried to kill me."

"You understand, *and* you saved my life," Alice said, clasping

Beatrice's hand. "And to top it all off, you have discovered my half brother."

"So my theory is correct?" Beatrice said. "Inspector Drake's father . . . was your father?"

"Indeed," Alice said with a sharp nod. "Inspector Drake's spoon has confirmed that he is, in fact, a Croaksworth. As did a letter, found among my late father's documents, from Drake's mother, Nitara. It seems that when she fell pregnant, my father confessed that he was already married and would have nothing to do with the child. As such, I have offered Inspector Drake—on your suggestion—a portion of my fortune to expand his investigative business in London. He should have a proper office, for starters, in the heart of the city. And, if he should desire it, Drake shall have me as a sister."

"That is excellent," Beatrice said. "It has all worked out."

"Almost," another voice said from inside the carriage.

Alice moved to allow Inspector Drake to step out, and he stood in front of Beatrice, looking just as stern and stoic as ever. Beatrice felt warmth flood through her at the sight of him.

"How is your wrist?" he asked awkwardly.

"Healed," Beatrice said. "How is your ankle?"

"Fine," Drake said. He was silent for a moment, regarding her, and then said finally, "I need a partner I can trust in this new endeavor. There are too many cases for me to take on alone. And I have determined that Sir Huxley's informant was you all along."

"Yes, I put that together long ago," Beatrice said with a little smile. "It was why I felt confident in my decision to handcuff you. You rattled my confidence in Huxley—and thus made me believe in myself."

"How . . . sentimental. That wasn't my intention," Drake said dryly, "but in any case, if you were able to solve so many of his cases without even being present at the scenes of the crimes, I can only imagine what you could do if you were actually there. With me."

Similar to how she had felt after the other proposals she had experienced, Beatrice was speechless. But this time, she felt a ripple of excitement, as opposed to dread.

"You really want me?" she asked finally, meeting his eye.

"It seems I have no choice," he said with a little shrug. "Alice insisted. She refuses to supply funding unless you and I are equal partners in the venture."

"You hardly protested," Alice snorted. "You said that Beatrice had an unusual knack for solving crimes, that you felt entirely in debt to her because she gave you a family, and that you missed her terribly in spite of how much she irritated you!"

"I don't remember saying any of that," Drake said stiffly.

"This is what you meant to ask me in the turret, isn't it?" Beatrice said, her heart suddenly beating very fast.

Drake flushed, visibly flustered. "Yes," he replied, avoiding her gaze. "That is precisely what I meant to ask."

"It would be in London, since of course there's much more crime there than in Swampshire, now that Daniel's gone," Alice said, raising her eyebrows at Drake's behavior. "I could put each of you up in proper town houses above the office. Money is no object."

"I—I don't know what to say," Beatrice said, looking from Inspector Drake to Alice.

"If she doesn't want to do it, she shouldn't do it," Drake said quickly. "In fact, it was a silly idea. I don't need any help, and certainly not from *her*."

"Is that so?" Beatrice cried. "Well, *I* don't need any help from *you*! I had independently decided to leave Swampshire, even before you showed up with this proposition."

"This will never work," Drake said, shaking his head. "You have no idea what kind of crimes you would even be in for—"

"Actually," Beatrice interrupted, withdrawing several newspaper clippings from her pocket, "I have been cataloging some recent grisly murders. I have *plenty* of theories—"

"No doubt unsupported by any kind of actual *evidence*," Drake scoffed.

"You can familiarize yourself with the cases while I get my suitcases," Beatrice continued, handing him the clippings.

"You have already packed?" Drake asked, incredulous.

Beatrice gave him a smile. "A lady is always one step ahead," she told him.

With an expression of both pain and pleasure, Drake began to follow her toward Marsh House.

As Beatrice and Drake waded through her yard, footsteps squelching in the mud, Beatrice was flooded with excitement. She felt the anticipation of all the horrible and gruesome crimes they would solve, together. Drake's boot suddenly sank into a particularly deep hole, and he let loose a slew of curse words under his breath. Beatrice held out a hand, and Drake begrudgingly clasped it. As she pulled him loose, Beatrice knew that this was just the beginning of a perfectly exasperating partnership.

THE LADY'S GUIDE TO SWAMPSHIRE, VOLUME 1

[Excerpt, pages 67–68 of 1,265]

Dress
- A lady must always dress for dinner.
- Acceptable dress fabrics include muslin and satin, with ribbons for trim. Warmth should not be considered.
- One's bosom and shoulders may be displayed, but never one's ankles, for decency's sake.
- Young ladies must dress in pale colors. Older women may wear brighter colors. The exception is the Color of the Year, which everyone must wear during the winter season.
- The Color of the Year shall be announced at the autumnal ball.

Acceptable Hobbies
- Drawing
- Music, such as the harp or pianoforte
  * Performance pieces should be melodic (never atonal) and inspire goodwill and healing in all those who hear them.
- Turns about the garden to maintain a rosy complexion
  * Natural methods of maintaining a good complexion are preferred; however, if it is a special occasion, or if one is exceedingly ugly, one may wear a bit of rouge.
  * Ladies may use swamp mud to encourage a healthy glow.
- Languages, such as French and Italian
  * One may speak French, but one must never travel to France.
- Reading
  * Acceptable reading material includes sermons, poetry, eti-

quette guides, and social columns. Ladies must not read grisly articles, scandalous novels, or anything excessively funny.

☞ Writing letters
  * Letters should be poetic in nature. A lady may not write letters to a gentleman, unless the two are engaged.
☞ Performing arithmetic
  * Ladies can perform mathematics for enjoyment but may not invent any new theorems, for this could make a man feel bad about himself because he did not think of it first.
☞ Botany
  * A lady should have extensive knowledge of herbs and flowers, and should be able to identify any tree on command.
☞ Fitness
  * The ideal Swampshirian woman has well-developed muscles and can run vigorously.
☞ Dancing
  * At a ball, ladies must not dance two dances in a row with a particular gentleman, unless the two are attached.
  * Ladies must not rescind acceptance of a dance.
☞ Nursing baby birds back to health
  * Healing is permitted, whereas harming is not; ladies are excluded from all hunting excursions and may not bear weapons.
☞ Baking
  * A lady's scones are never dry.
☞ Visiting the poor
  * Ladies may visit the poor and bring them scones.
☞ Needlework
  * Stitching should be even, pretty, and strong.

Acceptable Topics of Conversation
- The weather
- Hats

Unacceptable Topics of Conversation
- Gossip
- Theater or actors
- Personal conflicts
- Missing persons cases
- France

Proper Decorum
- Ladies must be introduced to a gentleman by a gentleman. A lady may not introduce herself.
- Ladies must follow every single rule at all times, unless they are extending charity to someone in need.
- Ladies must not be annoying or persistent.
- Ladies must not press for information.
- Ladies must not dwell on gore.
- A lady always enjoys a ball.

ACKNOWLEDGMENTS

In the words of Jane Austen, nobody minds having what is too good for them. This is exactly my feeling about how grateful I am to everyone who helped bring this murderous book to life.

First of all—thank you to *you*, dear reader!

Thank you to Jon Collier, a master of mystery who first heard this idea and encouraged me to write it. I named two of my dead bodies after you, in a sign of utmost respect. Thank you to my early readers, Andrew Watt, Dan Crockett, and Jeff King. Your notes, joke pitches, and literary expertise were invaluable. Andrew—thank you for Shakespearing the term "picto-funny." Dan—thank you for reading this even though there are no cowboys in it. Jeff—thank you for encouraging me not to marry that mysterious widower whose first wife, Rebecca, had a little too much of a grip on him, and for keeping me sane through karaoke. Thank you Kelsey Creel, Gates Curry, Lisa Henry, and Bre Vergess, for your encouragement at the most early stages.

To my Curious Hos—Belinda, Francesca, Schuyler, and Yvonne—thank you for being the best, weirdest, most talented writing group ever. I have porcelain dolls of each of you in a secret cabinet. Thank you to Andrea Hearn, my favorite Janeite, who encouraged me to drop my fake economics major and just be honest with myself that I wanted to study English.

Thank you to my manager, Daniel Vang, for believing in this project from the beginning, and to my agent, Rachel Kim, whose incredible notes made this book better than I could have ever imagined. Thank you so much to Random House for making my dream a reality, and thank you to everyone who worked to get this into the hands of readers! I am so grateful to each and every one of you. To Emma Caruso, my amazing editor, I am overjoyed that I have the chance to work with you. Your thoughtful notes and sharp wit challenged me in the best way. You are clever and well-informed—not just good company, but the best!

Thank you, Maddie Hughes, for your encouragement and notes, and for allowing me to constantly interrupt your days for advice on all things mystery and Regency. I wish I could be Elizabeth, but you truly are my Jane Bennet.

Thank you, Anthony Troli, for your notes, for coming up with my title, and for two very special bottles of champagne. And of course, thank you for letting me borrow Livy's likeness.

Thank you to my dad, Brent, who first took me to England and thus created a lifelong Anglophile. (And thank you for taking me to mime-infested France, which actually, *j'adore*.) Thank you to my sister-in-law Meredith, who could actually cure the fainties. Andy and Jesse, thank you for being the best brothers, and for giving me a piping-hot milk/melk/milks sense of humor. Can't wait to catch the next Burt Watson concert with you both.

Lastly, thank you to my mom, Pam, who never forced me to marry for money and who let me read whatever I wanted. You are my constant inspiration and role model. If I loved you less, I might be able to talk about it more.

You Are Cordially Invited to

A Most Agreeable Murder

Mystery Party & Reader's Guide

Dear Reader,

First of all, thank you so much for reading *A Most Agreeable Murder*. I hope that the story of Beatrice Steele gave you some laughs, some excitement, and a respite from weirdness by sweeping you away into . . . an even weirder world.

I wrote the majority of this book over the course of a lockdown, wanting to create an escape from stressful and unpredictable times. The mysteries of Agatha Christie and the witty novels of Jane Austen have long been my go-to comfort books. Is it bizarre that murder stories, and Regency-era women characters with little agency, are so reassuring? I think not—because at the end of Christie's novels, the killers are caught, and Austen's heroines always come out on top in the end even when the odds are stacked against them. I wanted to combine the satisfactions of these worlds into a place where I could escape. A place with humor, hailstorms, and inexplicably glowing frogs—a loving pastiche of all of my favorites. So I happily let Swampshire and its squelch holes swallow me right up.

The Regency era is a strange, short period of history that has always fascinated me. Manners were essential, marrying was often for money, and beauty rituals were deadly—belladonna really was used to dilate the pupils during this time! But this was also before the industrial revolution, before many advances in crime solving. There was no DNA evidence, and even fingerprinting was not used in England. An investigator would have to rely on astute observations, and on the ability to understand people, in order to solve a crime. Regency-era novels like *Persuasion* give us a glimpse into how women learned to interpret every look, every word, every tiny insight they observed. If they were so good at doing this in order to catch a husband, I thought, what if they turned these skills toward catching a killer? And thus, Beatrice Steele was born.

This book combines a few of my favorite things: mayhem, manners, and murder (solving it, not committing it, of course). But now that we can experience things in reality again, and not just in our minds, I want to share another thing I love: an ornate, over-the-top, costumes-required theme party. With tea, of course. I may not be English, but I am from Kentucky, so I know the beverage well. Ours just has ice and a lot more sugar (and sometimes bourbon) in it.

And so, I thank you again for reading, and please enjoy the following tips on how to party like it's 1799.

Yours, except on a full moon—

Julia Seales

APPROPRIATE
DISCUSSION TOPICS

1. *A Most Agreeable Murder* is a comedy of "manners-meets-murder" mystery. What influences or allusions did you notice in the story, and what did you think of the author's reinterpretation of them?

2. Beatrice Steele is described as "curious by nature, and therefore noticed too much, felt too much" (7). What did you think of Beatrice as a character? How does Beatrice's curiosity help her or hurt her over the course of the novel? Who are some other characters with supposed weaknesses that ultimately become strengths over the course of the novel?

3. The residents of Swampshire emphasize "decorum above all," and hold a preoccupation with image and reputation. How does this end up being harmful in the long run, and what lessons might we draw from the book in regards to our own interest in the way others view us?

4. Why do you think so many of us, like Beatrice, are fascinated by murder? Why has true crime had such an enduring hold on people's minds and imaginations?

5. What did you think of the structure of the book? How do you think the elements, such as newspaper clippings, excerpts from letters, and secret notes, play into the overall mystery of the story?

6. Who was your favorite character in the book? Why?

7. Why do you think Beatrice and Drake are at first skeptical of Miss Bolton when she reports seeing Arabella covered in blood? In what ways is Miss Bolton considered an unreliable witness, and how might her gender reinforce this?

8. What did you think of the Steele family as a whole? How does their family structure mirror or reject tropes found in books or shows set in the Regency era?

9. Beatrice and Drake debate the merits of "conjecture" vs. "evidence" over the course of the novel. How do both of these things help them find the murderer? If you had to pick one, which do you feel is more important in solving a crime?

10. How do the female characters in the story (Beatrice, Louisa, Arabella, Mary, Caroline, Miss Bolton) fulfill or resist the expectations for women, according to the Swampshire code of conduct? How does the novel explore how expectations placed on women have changed (or remained the same) compared to the Regency era in which this story is set?

11. Many Swampshirean men are quick to clarify that they are "gentlemen," whereas Drake has a "job." How does class play a role in the novel?

12. By the end of the novel, only one character was a murderer, but as Louisa points out, "we all have secrets" (236). What are the things these guests are hiding about themselves? How do these secrets influence their decisions and contribute to the mystery? What revelation most surprised you?

13. What do you think the future holds for Beatrice and Drake's "perfectly exasperating" partnership?

14. Author Julia Seales combined deep knowledge and research of the Regency period with contemporary voice and comedy. What did you think of the balance? In what ways do you think humor can shed new light on or help us reexamine well-known parts of history?

MENU

MISS BOLTON'S RYE AND SHERRY PUNCH

Ingredients for 1 serving:

1 oz. rye whiskey
1 oz. dry sherry
3 oz. lemonade
Top with club soda

Surreptitiously withdraw rye whiskey, sherry, and lemonade from your hat and combine. Pour over ice into a punch glass and top with club soda. Insist you are just drinking sherry, as a lady must, and any scent of whiskey emanating from your glass is purely due to the accuser's imagination. Garnish with a lemon peel, if desired.

MRS. STEELE'S
"MARRY ME" NO-BAKE CHEESECAKE

Ingredients:

18 Biscoff cookies
6 tablespoons butter, melted
2 teaspoons white wine
1 teaspoon salt
1 teaspoon vanilla extract
1 package cream cheese (8 oz.), softened
⅔ cup sour cream
2 cups powdered sugar
Fresh fruit of choice for topping
Six teacups

INSTRUCTIONS:

Crush 18 Biscoff cookies into a fine powder. Mix with melted butter, and then press equal portions into the bottom of six teacups to form a crust. Place teacups on top of a block of ice hewn from a river (or into a "refrigerator") while you prepare the filling.

Mix white wine, salt, vanilla, cream cheese, sour cream, and powdered sugar. Whip until creamy. Think of the combination as two people coming together: one beautiful girl in need of money, and one handsome man with more than enough for the both of them.

Dole out the cream cheese mixture onto the cooled crust, and then cool the teacups in the refrigerator until the cream cheese is set (at least one hour). This shall give you time to dress in your finest outfit and pinch your cheeks until you look rosy and eligible.

Top with fresh fruit of choice and serve. Expect a marriage proposal within an hour of a wealthy gentleman enjoying his portion.

CAROLINE'S MOIST SCONES

Ingredients:

2 cups all-purpose flour
¼ cup sugar
1 teaspoon salt
1 tablespoon cream of tartar
1 tablespoon baking powder
¼ cup cold butter, in chunks
½ cup milk
1 cup chocolate chunks

INSTRUCTIONS:

Preheat oven to 350 degrees and line a baking sheet with parchment paper.

Mix together flour, sugar, salt, cream of tartar, and baking powder. Work in the butter until crumbly and then add the milk, forming a moist paste. The moistness is, of course, key. Personally, my scones are so delicious that I do not even need any add-ins or toppings, but if you are merely average at baking, I recommend disguising poor workmanship with copious chocolate chunks. Add those now.

Form dough evenly into balls. Dough will be sticky. If you are a terrible baker and it's *too* sticky, add a little more flour. If you are Beatrice Steele and it seems too dry, add 1 or 2 more tablespoons of milk.

Place on the baking sheet and bake for 30 minutes. Remove from the oven and let cool. Serve while playing a beautiful piece on the harp, so everyone can enjoy your many talents.

PROPS/DÉCOR

- A teacup that's thrifted can kindly be gifted.
- A frog-shaped ice mold is a sight to behold. Add a water-proof light before freezing, for a glowing cocktail so pleasing.
- Edible glitter placed in a vial makes convincing fake poison for guests to revile.
- If the weather is fair but you need atmosphere, play sounds of rain and thunder for your guests to hear.
- Copious candles scented of fresh grass and mud shall distract visitors from a soup tureen of blood. (If one cannot get blood for your silver tureen, tomato soup can be used for a sight less obscene.)

RULES ON
HOW TO PLAY WHIST

Number of players: 4 (two pairs of partners). Choose your partner wisely, especially when gambling for high stakes.

The deck: A standard 52-card deck.

Card ranking: Ace (high), K, Q, J, 10, 9, 8, 7, 6, 5, 4, 3, 2

How to deal: Starting with the player on the dealer's left, give out the entire deck of cards, one at a time, face down.

The trump card: The final card dealt will be the trump card. This is placed face up, so all players see what will be trump suit for that round. Then the dealer picks up this card, and it becomes part of their hand.

Object of the game: This is a trick-taking game. Each partnership tries to score points by winning tricks, and the partnership with the most points at the end wins.

How to win a trick: The player on the dealer's left leads first, starting with any card they choose. (Note: this does not have to be the trump suit.) The turns continue in clockwise rotation. Each player *must* follow suit if possible. If a player cannot follow suit, they may play any card they choose. When all four cards are played, the trick is over, and the highest card in the trump suit wins. If no cards from the trump suit were played, the highest card of the suit led wins the trick.

Gameplay: The winner of a trick leads the next trick. Players continue until all cards have been used, at which point the round has ended. Players count up their score for that round, reshuffle, and deal new cards for the next round.

Scoring: Teams receive 1 point per trick over 6. For example, if a team wins 10 tricks total, they would receive 4 points (10 – 6 = 4). The first team to 13 points wins.

Cheating: One may keep a trick Ace up one's sleeve, but keep in mind that being caught cheating shall result in banishment to France.

Keep reading for a sneak peek at
Beatrice Steele's next adventure in
A Terribly Nasty Business!

The Neighborhood Association of Gentlemen
Sweetbriarians (NAGS) Presents:

THE LONDON SEASON

Miss Beatrice Steele and her chaperone,
Miss Helen Bolton, are invited to attend
the Season at the local assembly rooms of Sweetbriar.
Enclosed in this invitation, you will find a
map of the neighborhood, as well as
a schedule of upcoming events.
We look forward to your introduction
into London society!

Note: This invitation is for the Tulip and Carnation club
Seasons only. Invitations to the Rose are handled separately, in the
very unlikely event you receive one.
We advise young ladies not to get their hopes up.

Cheers!

CHAPTER 1

An Exit

In the northwest corner of London was a neighborhood named Sweetbriar, known for its theater, its well-kept pleasure garden, and an unfortunate infestation of flying squirrels. This is where Beatrice Steele had taken up residence with her chaperone, Miss Helen Bolton. Except for the squirrels, it was just the type of neighborhood Beatrice had always dreamed of living in—that is, when she wasn't dreaming about solving murders. But so far, her new life wasn't quite what she had imagined.

Beatrice had grown up in a small, manners-obsessed town called Swampshire, where she always feared her secret true-crime obsession would be her ruin. Either that, or her horrifically bad skills at sketching, embroidery, and most other "feminine" hobbies. But when someone dropped dead at a country ball, she had finally gotten the chance to put her skills to the test, and caught the killer alongside the haughty but perceptive Inspector Vivek Drake.

Was it unfortunate that the killer had been her childhood best friend and assumed betrothed? Of course. But things were bound to improve from there. Sure enough, Drake had shown up on her doorstep shortly after their investigation concluded, asking if she would partner with him on a new detective office in London, funded by his newfound half sister (newly found by Beatrice, a fact she would not let Drake forget). Beatrice's future was falling into place perfectly—until her mother got involved.

"If you are going to catch murderers, you must do it the proper way: accompanied by an unmarried, middle-aged woman!" Mrs. Susan Steele insisted.

She would not hear of Beatrice's going to London unchaperoned. Without proper protection, Beatrice could fall in with the wrong crowd, gamble her money away, be shamed in the tabloids, and be forced to work as an opera singer in order to pay back her debts. Beatrice could not carry a tune to save her life. The scandal would be extreme.

Luckily, the family's close friend and neighbor Miss Bolton had been more than happy to volunteer her services. After all, as an aspiring playwright, Miss Bolton had her own dreams to pursue in the city. Beatrice was grateful for the company, as well as the comfortable townhouse Miss Bolton rented for their residence.

What she was not grateful for was Mrs. Steele's grip on Miss Bolton. Beatrice quickly learned that "chaperone" was merely another word for "spy," and Mrs. Steele had not given up on the hope that her eldest daughter would make a fortuitous match. Though Beatrice had intended on spending her days solving crimes with Inspector Drake, her first few months in London had been a flurry of social activities meant to find a man. And unfortunately this man was meant to be a husband, not a murderer.

That was how Beatrice found herself at an afternoon garden party on an overly warm Tuesday in June, taking her fourth turn around the meager gardens of the Carnation Club, trying not to faint . . . from boredom. She had spent the afternoon elbow-to-elbow with eligible ladies and gentlemen. She had already sampled the lemon ice, played two rounds of croquet, and commented five times on how quickly the grass seemed to grow in this neighborhood.

"They must water the lawn often," Miss Bolton said for the sixth time. "Speaking of water . . . this punch has obviously been diluted. It's terrible."

She and Beatrice were wedged in between four other chaperones and their charges, all shuffling through the overly moist garden.

"I can fetch you a fresh glass," Beatrice suggested, but before she could escape, Miss Bolton waved a finger.

"Not necessary. I came prepared." She lifted a lid off of her hat, revealing that it was actually a very large, wearable sugar pot. She produced a spoon, shoveled a few scoops into her glass, and then replaced the hat lid.

"Perhaps we might commence our departure . . . ," Beatrice began, stifling a yawn as they began yet another turn around the Carnation's gardens, but Miss Bolton shook her head.

"In order to become a member of an assembly room, you must attend these open events, Beatrice," she said firmly. "This is how you gain the attention of a club patroness."

The social rules of Sweetbriar had been drilled into Beatrice ever since she had arrived. There were three assembly rooms in the neighborhood: the Rose, the Tulip, and the Carnation. Once a year at the beginning of the summer, each club had a series of open events to select new members. The lucky few chosen would be invited to exclusive gatherings held at the assembly rooms, which usually resulted in advantageous marriages. Public balls were crowded in London, and there was no way to know whether the men attending were viable options for husbands. But the patronesses of the social clubs—married women with an eye for matchmaking—hand-selected their members. Therefore, belonging to a club ensured that a young lady would meet just the right sort of man: handsome, genteel, and filthy rich.

"Your mother's instructions were clear," Miss Bolton reiterated. "Go to open events, become a member of a club, marry a wealthy man, and protect your family's reputation and subsequent fortune by following a strict code of ethics for the rest of your life. It's simple."

"There are so many people here that I can hardly breathe, let alone distinguish myself from the other young ladies," Beatrice said, gesturing to the crowds around them.

In Swampshire, Beatrice had felt over-scrutinized, her every move watched in a small town in which everyone knew everyone. But now it was as if someone had created a hundred Beatrices and Miss Boltons and dropped them into a garden together.

"Yes, the Carnation lets all sorts of people into their open events," Miss Bolton grumbled as they pushed their way in between two young ladies and their chaperones. "Did you see the hat on that chaperone? So dull. No excitement or hidden compartments whatsoever," she muttered as they passed a woman wearing an understated bonnet. "The Tulip at least has a dress code. The Rose is the best—no doubt the fashion there is much more intriguing—but I haven't heard anything about their open-invitation events."

"Theirs are invite-only," a chaperone next to Miss Bolton replied.

"Excuse me, this is a private conversation," Miss Bolton said, turning toward the woman. They were nearly cheek-to-cheek.

"An invite-only open invitation is a bit of a contradiction, don't you think?" Beatrice asked.

"That's the point," the chaperone's young charge replied. She was next to Beatrice, their arms touching, thanks to the bustling crowd. "They only accept the wealthiest, most elite members of society into their ranks. The best we can hope for is membership to the Tulip. And the most likely outcome is that we all settle for membership here at the Carnation. They'll take *anyone*."

"We'll see about *that*," Miss Bolton sniffed. She locked arms with Beatrice and pushed past the other chaperone and her charge, shooting them a dirty backward glance. "The nerve of those two, assuming that we aren't the wealthiest, most elite members of society."

"Well, we aren't," Beatrice said.

"Yes, but they don't *know* that," Miss Bolton said, fanning herself.

"I thought that we would leave these social games behind in Swampshire," Beatrice sighed. "Must we engage in the Season at all? Don't you ever just wish we could . . . let it all go?"

"I made your mother a promise that I would chaperone you, and I mean to keep that promise," Miss Bolton replied firmly. "The last time I shirked my duties, you nearly died. I won't make that mistake again—"

"Did you hear that Percival Nash is somewhere at this party?" Beatrice cut in, and Miss Bolton dropped her arm. Her eyes widened.

"Percival Nash? The star of the Sweet Majestic's production of *Figaro III: We Must Figaro Again*?" Miss Bolton gasped. "I just know he would be perfect as the leading man in my play *The Mists of Time*. If I could get him to read the script—"

"I thought I saw him by the fountain. You go look, and I shall fetch us more punch," Beatrice said.

Nodding distractedly, Miss Bolton took off. Beatrice ensured that the short woman and her tall sugar hat were out of sight, then turned and rushed through a thick crowd of perspiring garden party attendees.

She felt a stab of guilt as she dodged chaperones and their hopeful charges. She hated lying to Miss Bolton. And truly, Beatrice *should* have been seeking a husband, for the sake of her family.

Since Louisa had married the impoverished (though charismatic) Frank, the responsibility of securing a fortune had fallen on Beatrice's shoulders. Yes, there was still Mary, but one couldn't pin too many hopes on Beatrice's youngest sister (nor could you pin any bows to her hair, which always seemed strangely full of dirt).

But Beatrice had come to the city to seek killers, not sweethearts. So she half-heartedly attended parties, staying just long enough to make her presence known. Then, at the earliest possibility, she made a hasty departure.

She did this now as she sidestepped a sweating, chatting couple and plunged into the Carnation Club's tall hedges.

Beatrice fell out the other side only slightly worse for wear and righted herself. She had a few tears in her white muslin but was otherwise unscathed. She straightened her bonnet and turned to make her escape.

"Party that bad?"

A chipper voice made her jump, and she whirled around to see a man standing against the hedges. He had fair hair slicked back and his face was clean-shaven, revealing a strong jawline.

"I just have . . . an errand to run," Beatrice said, as if it were perfectly normal to squeeze through a bush in the midst of an event for such a reason.

"I see," the man said. He lifted a pipe to his mouth and inhaled, now looking thoughtful. "I suppose it's a clandestine errand."

"One could say that." Beatrice was not sure what this man wanted, but her spine suddenly prickled.

The street outside the Carnation Club was empty apart from her and this man. Was he up to something nefarious?

She was about to pull out her hat pin, in case she should need to jam it in his eye—a lady really couldn't take any chances—but then he blew out a puff of smoke and broke into a smile. He looked oddly familiar, but they couldn't possibly have met, Beatrice thought. She had been in London four months, but the Season had only just begun, and Beatrice had hardly spoken to any eligible men—let alone one as handsome as this.

"Your secret is safe with me," the man said, and actually winked.

"If you say so," she sniffed. The events of last autumn had also taught her: one could never trust a gentleman who was excessively charming and handsome. He might be a cold-blooded killer.

She backed away until there was enough distance between them that she was satisfied she could easily plan a counterattack. The man just watched, a look of amusement on his chiseled face.

Finally, Beatrice rounded a corner, and the street opened up to a wider passageway.

Sweetbriar was divided into four sections, and she was currently in the southeastern corner, deemed the "Carnation Quarter," due to the presence of the Carnation Club. It was the most affordable place in the neighborhood, as it bore the worst of the squirrel infestation. It was also where Inspector Drake and Beatrice had a small office, which was Beatrice's destination.

Mrs. Steele was under the impression that Beatrice did occasional "secretary work" in this office (accompanied by Miss Bolton, of course). Beatrice knew that her mother only conceded to this because she thought it might keep Beatrice's morbid interests "under control and only discussed behind closed doors." Neither Susan Steele nor Helen Bolton knew that Beatrice snuck away regularly to spend as much time as possible on her morbid interests—and she hoped to keep it that way.

The sun was beginning to set, and the heat of the day was mercifully lifting. Londoners filtered outside, sitting at café tables and hailing carriages and strolling arm-in-arm down cobblestone streets.

Beatrice pulled the edges of her bonnet out to conceal her face. A young woman shouldn't be walking alone, unchaperoned; it was the first rule of Sweetbriar. In Swampshire she never could have managed it. But here in the city, there were so many *people*. She was aware of a few judgmental glares, but they passed quickly—Beatrice melted into the crowd before anyone could correct her behavior.

She was so busy looking up at the tall buildings, taking in the crowds, that she nearly collided with a carriage careening past. An arm grabbed her and pulled her back, and she turned to see a street mime gesticulating wildly.

"Yes, yes, I'll be more careful," Beatrice said, backing away from the black-and-white performer. He began to reenact the scene, but in his version, Beatrice was crushed under the wheel of the carriage.

"Thank you for saving me," she said, a bit exasperated.

Because Sweetbriar was arranged around the Sweet Majestic, an opera theater, there were always aspiring actors and mimes hanging about in the hopes of being discovered. This was Miss Bolton's delight—and Beatrice's nightmare.

She dropped a few coins in the man's overturned hat, hoping it would put a stop to his show, and hurried across the street.

She drew in a deep breath, trying to calm herself. London was simply so different from Swampshire. It sizzled with heat and energy and . . . a whiff of murder?

No, she realized as she sidestepped a splash of liquid—someone was emptying a chamber pot out a window above.

"Squirrel incoming!" someone else yelled, and a group of well-dressed, cosmopolitan ladies in front of Beatrice ducked.

Beatrice was too slow on the uptake, and the flying rodent came out of nowhere. It smacked her in the face, and she stumbled back. A mime—a different one this time (how were they *always* there?)—caught her and righted her. He began to reenact the scene.

"I know! I lived it!" Beatrice said, practically throwing a coin at him. "I don't need to see it again, thank you very much!"

She was out of breath and flustered by the time she reached her destination: a small office with discreet gold letters on the door, spelling out "DS Investigations."

The initials made Beatrice's heart pound. Would it ever feel real to see the "S" on the sign and know it stood for "Steele"? Would she ever truly believe that she was one half of an actual detective office in London? Her life in the city was not exactly as she'd pictured it, but this, at least, felt like a dream come true.

She wrenched open the door and ducked inside, where a small room held two desks piled high with letters and notebooks. Shelves stuffed with books lined the walls, and two armchairs faced a pinstriped chaise. Golden light from the setting sun filtered inside, casting a glow over the cozy office.

As Beatrice entered, she saw a familiar, tall man with dark skin and an eye patch. He had a scowl across his scarred face, but she knew from the flash in his remaining eye that he was glad to see her. She met his stern look with a smile. For a moment she thought she saw his mouth twitch up at the corners—but then his jaw clenched, and he affected an even sterner look.

"Miss Steele," said Inspector Vivek Drake. "It's about time."

JULIA SEALES is a writer and screenwriter based in Los Angeles. She earned an MFA in screenwriting from UCLA and a BA in English from Vanderbilt University. A lifelong Anglophile with a passion for both murder mysteries and Jane Austen, Julia Seales is originally from Kentucky, where she learned about manners (and bourbon).

juliamaeseales.com
Twitter: @juliamaeseales
Instagram: @juliamaeseales

ABOUT THE TYPE

This book was set in Caslon, a typeface first designed in 1722 by William Caslon (1692–1766). Its widespread use by most English printers in the early eighteenth century soon supplanted the Dutch typefaces that had formerly prevailed. The roman is considered a "work-horse" typeface due to its pleasant, open appearance, while the italic is exceedingly decorative.